Lauren Henderson is London born and bred. She has lived in Italy and is now based in New York, where her interests include bar-hopping, cocktail-tasting and cute bar-owners. She has written seven books in the Sam Jones mystery series and with Stella Duffy has co-edited *Tart Noir*, an anthology of sex-and-crime based, girls-behaving-badly short stories, which will be published in September 2002. She also writes for the *Erotic Review*, and her short stories have appeared in various Britfic, crime and erotica anthologies.

My Lurid Past

Lauren Henderson

timewarner
paperbacks

A *Time Warner* Paperback

First published in Great Britain by Time Warner Paperbacks, 2002

A CIP catalogue record for this book is available
from the British Library.

ISBN 0 7515 3261 4

Typeset in Garamond by
Palimpsest Book Production Limited,
Polmont, Stirlingshire
Printed and bound in Great Britain
by Clays Ltd, St Ives plc

Time Warner Paperbacks
An imprint of
Time Warner Books UK
Brettenham House
Lancaster Place
London WC2E 7EN

www.TimeWarnerBooks.co.uk

My Lurid Past

Chapter One

Have you ever looked at someone in the street and wished you had their life? Just like that, without knowing anything real about them? Because it happens to me all the time.

Yesterday I saw a girl getting off the bus at Westbourne Grove: pink fleecy sweater, lime-green lacy skirt, a fake fuschia flower in her dark hair, big trendy trainers which made her thin ankles look almost spindly. Matt white skin, straight black fringe and narrow hips. Notting Hill goes to Chinatown. She didn't look at all like me. I wanted to be that girl so badly I could feel the yearning round me like an aura.

It's not that I dislike my life, or my clothes. But somehow they're never enough. Without giving up myself, I want to be the girl on the bus too. Every time I walk into a clothes store I want every nice thing on the racks, no matter if it doesn't suit me, still less if I already have an item so similar at home that nobody but me would know the difference between them. I still crave them.

At this point you may well be thinking that this must be the shallowest expression of dissatisfaction imaginable. I want the world, but how narrowly I want it, how obsessed I am with myself – mainly with how I look. Forget travel, new perspectives, new adventures; I just want to keep transforming myself until I can be, for a brief moment, anyone I want to be. But even then I run the risk of leaving the house as the girl on the bus and seeing someone else in a club whose identity I suddenly want to assume instead. Somehow, all common sense to the contrary, I think that if I finally get my appearance right then everything deeper than my skin will fall into place too.

I do know how ridiculous that is. But I keep on believing it. Wait for it, though. I am capable of being even shallower than this. I can't even stay faithful to a perfume or a jeans label. How can I, when I'm being constantly seduced by reams of advertising and product placements? No matter how well I know that the brand of jeans I wear is the best I'll ever find, I keep trying the latest thing to hit the billboards in the hope of a miracle transformation. You never know, they just might be the pair that will turn me into the model who's wearing them. And the disappointment never lasts long enough for me to realise how unrealistic my fantasies are, because there's always something else new to try, and something after that . . .

A few days ago I went into the supermarket, the big one a couple of bus stops down the road. I practically never shop at supermarkets because I just don't have the time; if I'm not eating out – which I usually do, because it's my job – I grab a sandwich at lunchtime and some frozen meal for dinner, calorie-counted and microwave-ready, perfect for the working girl in a hurry and on a perpetual diet. But last Sunday, for some reason, I got the impulse to stock up my store cupboards. I think it was residual guilt from my job. I'm a food PR. I spend my days promoting restaurants, TV shows featuring the chefs from the restaurants, and – often equally lucrative – the spin-off cookbooks from both. I had spent most of the previous week on the phone, trying to convince dubious journalists that the latest cookbook by one of my clients would transform the way they looked at food. 'Just a few simple ingredients . . . fresh reinterpretations of all those classic old recipes we used to love . . . no more than twenty minutes in the kitchen . . .' Blah, blah, blah. The usual string of tired old clichés. Of course I assured them that for me, personally (that redundant word which cretins think sounds extra-sincere), cooking my way through the wretched tome had been an almost life-changing experience. The truth was that I had barely even rifled through its glossy pages. And, contemplating the dusty, bare shelves in my kitchen cupboards that evening, I was filled with shame. Two tins of kidney beans past their sell-by dates and an opened bag of couscous, probably ditto.

I was a disgrace to my profession. Hence the trip to the supermarket. I had forgotten how intimidating they could be, and how enormous. My nemesis, surreally enough, came in the form of the tinned tomato aisle. That there could even be a whole aisle devoted to tinned tomatoes was extraordinary. I stood there, frozen with indecision. Should I go for the own-brand stuff, which was bound to be reliable if not exciting? Or the heavily advertised labels, rich in celebrity endorsements? Or the Italian ones, which would look much more authentic on my shelves? Chopped or whole? Flavoured or plain? And should I also consider the bottles of passata – but, if I went for passata, did I want it smooth or chunky? There were tomatoes with chilli, basil, cumin, garlic, onion, garlic and onion, Italian herbs, five-spice, mixed peppers, even fennel seed. I mused for a moment about the eccentric in Product Research who had thought there would really be a demand for chopped tomatoes with fennel seed.

The aisle seemed to expand before me, stretching out to either side like a computer-generated hallucination. Tomatoes to right of me, tomatoes to left of me. It was the tomato Valley of Death. Gingerly I reached out and dropped a tin of chopped tomatoes with mixed peppers into my trolley. Then one of cherry tomatoes in their own juice (as opposed, I assumed, to somebody else's), then a jar of chunky passata with garlic and onion. Then the five-spice tomatoes, and one with Italian herbs. And I needed tomato purée as well. But did I want it plain or with mixed vegetable concentrate? And maybe I should get a tube of sundried tomato purée too . . .

By the time I had finished my supermarket tour my trolley was so full I looked as if I were stocking up a nuclear shelter. I could barely get it all into my kitchen cupboards. Not really knowing what I wanted, I had bought one of practically everything. I tried to reassure myself by the reflection that the excesses of globalised capitalism offered us far too many choices. The only way to remain sane was to limit these drastically by – for instance – refusing to buy any tomatoes but chopped ones with mixed peppers, wearing any jeans but one's usual brand, and sticking to the same sexual partner as long as one could.

It made a lot of sense. But that was the irony. Ever since I had broken up with my long-term boyfriend, I had been happily working my way through large quantities of young men of most conceivable flavours, not to mention textures. Smooth, chunky, coarsely chopped . . . Just as in the supermarket, I had been collecting at least one of practically everything; and yet, throughout this happy odyssey, I had never once felt overwhelmed by choice.

Quite the contrary. Some pretty twenty-five-year-old would catch my eye in a club and I would think, 'Hmn, he looks like James – no, the one I'm thinking of wasn't called James – what was he called? Anyway, mmn, interesting: a toned-up version of what's-his-name! I wonder what that would be like?' Or, if the guy were out of my usual range: 'Oooh, look at that bleached blond hair. He's skinny, isn't he – God, those cheekbones. Haven't had anything like him before. Definitely not a natural blond. I wonder what that would be like?' It came to much the same thing in the end.

No, picking them off the shelf had never been the problem. And afterwards it was equally simple; the length of time it lasted was dictated by a basic equation: how good the sex was, multiplied by how easy it was to hang out with them when we weren't having sex, equals a time limit that could be anything from a few hours to a few months. Up till now, the maths had worked, and it had been pretty blissful. But little did I know that the supermarket incident was some sort of cosmic warning that the tectonic plates on which my life was based were beginning to shift. Earthquake alert.

In retrospect, the signs were clear enough. An uncharacteristic attempt at domesticity; the sensation of being swamped by choice, rather than relishing it; the hopelessness that overcame me when I had finally made my selection and carried it back to my lair; and, most significantly, the profound wish simply to stuff it all into a cupboard because I didn't really know what I wanted to do with it.

It wasn't very fair on Tom, though. I do feel a bit guilty about that. But after all this time of happily cruising along, how could I tell that I was about to stall so precipitately? And Tom was just the start. It was like some awful parody of that saying that you always remember the first man you have sex with. Poor Tom would certainly be burnt into my mind as the first man I—

I'm rushing ahead. I'll start at the beginning. Rolling around on a sofa at a conference with a near-stranger trying to undo my bra.

I do pick my moments for cosmic revelations.

I wasn't expecting any sofa action at all that weekend. There are rarely any good-looking men at conferences, and the few that are tend to be gay. It's pretty much an axiom of the circuit. PR women are usually better looking, but I'm so much less judgemental about other women's looks. I see their good points as well as the soft spots. I'm much harder on myself than I am on my friends, or even other women. I'm not as slim as I would like to be and I punish myself for that by thinking about it constantly. My friends don't notice those extra pounds, and my boyfriends either don't notice or don't care; men have a wonderful ability to concentrate on the good bits. It's almost as refined as a woman's ability to pick out her own bad ones.

There are plenty of thin girls at cookery conferences, contrary to what you might think. But, equally, they are not generally as popular with men as most women imagine. I know this perfectly well from long years of experience. And yet I can't stop flogging myself about that extra half-stone, probably because the issue isn't men at all. It's perfection. I'm very good at my job, and I want to be that good at everything else, all the time. That I can't is the cross to which I'm nailed. Which, incidentally, must weigh a lot more than half a stone; if I could just put it down things might even themselves out . . .

I could tell, even across the room, that the young man I was ogling wasn't gay. His blond hair was dishevelled, and though his sweater was perfectly nice it was slightly creased and too loose fitting for him to have been anything but straight, considering that the torso beneath looked in good condition. If he were gay, he would have shown it off more. Besides, he was talking to a group of people and his long arms – he was very tall – were flailing at the air with an awkwardness that any gay man would have mastered by his teenage years.

Actually, he looked oddly familiar. He must have sensed my speculative gaze: turning round, he caught my eye and waved enthusiastically. I still didn't recognise him but the gesture was, naturally enough, more than welcome.

'Hey!' he said, surging across the room to my side with the enthusiasm and clumsiness of a Labrador puppy after a sudden growth spurt. 'You're Juliet Cooper, aren't you? You probably don't remember me. We met at the opening of Samsara, you know, that bar on Charlotte Street? Three years ago? I'm Tom.'

I racked my brains to remember the conversation we might have had. Or even to place his name.

'I made you a dry martini with a twist,' he added helpfully. 'Gin, not vodka.'

Oh no. A barman.

'You have a really good memory,' I said politely.

Now I had a classic dilemma. I wasn't doing either waiters or barmen any longer. Waiters and barmen were practically always dissatisfied with their jobs, no matter how much money they were making, and I had resolved a long time ago to put the struggling artist/writer/musician phase firmly behind me. In my twenties it had been fine, but at thirty-three, with a proper job, the imbalance was too great. I was happy with my life, and making good money, factors that the struggling wannabees all too quickly started to resent.

But Tom was undeniably eager, and I was charmed by that. He looked like a big fresh hunk of meat, the kind you could sink your teeth deep into and still never reach the other side. I was still debating my no-barmen rule when he added, pushing back a large chunk of fair hair which had flopped over his forehead, 'But I'm not working at Samsara any more.'

'Oh?' I said cautiously.

'No, thank God. Enough was enough. I've got into organising events. I'm on the staff here, actually.'

'Got bored with having to remember every food PR's favourite drink?' I said, trying not to smirk. An events organiser was definitely possible.

'I broke too many bottles to be a good barman,' he said

cheerfully. 'Boyish charm can take you only so far.'

'Funny, too,' I commented appreciatively.

'As well as what?'

I looked up at him – he was unnecessarily tall – and I was tempted to give him the answer he wanted. But he looked like he would blush too easily.

'As well as making a good martini,' I said.

'I didn't think you remembered,' he said, looking hugely flattered. I had been right, he really was like a puppy – one that knows you have a treat for it and is jumping around your ankles, panting in happy expectation, its big eyes wide. And who can resist a cute puppy looking for love?

'It's coming back to me,' I said.

And it was, actually. That floppy, straw-blond fringe, those dangerously over-quick movements . . .

But just then I spotted a food critic I really needed to talk to coming out of the lift.

'I've just seen someone I need to catch up with,' I said apologetically to Tom, nodding in Jemima's direction.

'Oh yeah, sure. Well, really nice to see you again. Will you be around later? At the banquet?'

'Definitely.'

I bet that he would search me out. And if he didn't, I would make sure we bumped into each other. I found myself smiling as I headed off to talk to Jemima.

'Who was that?' she said, squinting after Tom. 'Trust you to find the good-looking ones, Juliet.'

I shrugged.

'Oh, just some ex-barman,' I said, truthfully enough.

'Oh.'

She lost interest immediately, as I had known she would. I don't mean to say that neither of us would have been interested in Tom if he'd still been a barman/waiter/whatever; but, if we'd slept with him, we'd probably be pretty drunk, and we certainly wouldn't tell anyone but our closest friends about it. That wasn't snobbery – it was career politics. Women couldn't afford to get a reputation for screwing around, and particularly not with the hired help. Very unfair. Men could shag waitresses till the cows came home and no one would blink an eye.

Even after I'd finished telling Jemima all about some posh chocolates I was promoting, I realised I was still smiling. It was Tom. His enthusiasm for seeing me had been infectious.

'You're much nicer to me now that I'm an events organiser,' Tom said much later, as we milled around the wreckage of the awards banquet. The tables were littered with what, an hour or so ago, had been enticing sources of pleasure. Now all the crème brûlée was eaten, the dessert wine drunk, the petits fours demolished, the tablecloths thoroughly stained, and cigarettes stubbed out in every available container. It looked like Attila and most of the Huns had stopped by for dinner. Smoke hung in the air, as thick as dry ice.

I picked at the remains of my crème brûlée. Hotel banquet food is never that good, even at food awards dinners, but we're all greedy, we all need some reward for having to network and make nice all day, and so by God we all stuff our faces anyway.

Tom had tracked me down with a couple of martinis – gin, with a twist – which he had taken the trouble to make himself.

'Thanks,' I said, taking one of the martinis. It wasn't an after-dinner cocktail, but his making it was a signal to me that (a) he remembered what I liked, and (b) he was eager to give it to me. The approach was as subtle as a tongue sandwich. Young men in their mid-twenties are like heat-seeking missiles, and most attempts to treat them as anything else will go badly wrong. I was more than happy with this attitude to life, which explained why I was finding it so bloody hard to give up young men in their mid-twenties.

'Mmn, not bad,' I said, sipping the martini.

'Bombay Sapphire,' he said. 'I heard you signed up Liam O'Donnell, by the way. Congratulations! I bet everyone was after him.'

I nodded, trying to sound modest. 'I'm really pleased.'

The alcohol was beginning to get to me, not to mention the four-course dinner. My brain felt like a vodka-soaked sponge. Across the room I glimpsed Gill, one of my best friends, through a cloud of smoke. She was sitting at a table talking to some people; as I watched, she reached out and took the untouched ramekin of crème brûlée from the person next to her. I couldn't hear her words from this distance but she was obviously asking him if he minded. He shook his head, pantomiming an enormous stomach with his hands. Gill dug in with gusto. There were two empty ramekins in front of her already.

Gill had never been thin, but since her marriage she had been growing steadily plumper. The extra flesh suited her, but I knew she wasn't happy about it. How could one be, in a society where women were supposed to look like boys with breasts? Gill's husband Jeremy was very reassuring: he always told her that if she put on weight it was a hazard of her job, and simply meant there was more of her to love. Which sounded wonderful, until you knew how much loving, in a practical sense, actually went on in that household.

I shuddered. I considered marriage the deathknell to all the principal sources of fun in my life. It wasn't even a distant shadow on my horizon. I was far too busy gathering my rose-buds while I might.

'Hey,' said the current rosebud, 'you've finished your martini. D'you want another?'

I was surprised, and a little shocked, to realise that I had thrown it back so quickly.

'Maybe later,' I said.

I needed a line to clear my head. I looked up at Tom, wondering what I actually wanted to do with him. He was sweet, he was keen and he had a very nice body. I certainly wanted to have a good flirt. It was my favourite hobby. Nothing like it for whiling away an evening that would otherwise be spent in an endless round of work gossip. Besides, there were hardly any good-looking men here, and I was sure the attention he was giving me hadn't gone unnoticed. I am shallow and vain. I wanted to keep him by my side. I liked the thought that a few people would be commenting on Juliet's new conquest; it made me feel more secure, specifically about the amount of crème brûlée I had eaten. I might not be the thinnest girl here, but I certainly had the most attractive, and youngest, man. And if I went to queue for the toilet someone else would try to snap him up while I was away, meaning I would have to reclaim him. Which would take effort. Not to mention showing my hand.

The words left my mouth without any conscious awareness of my having pronounced them.

'Do you want to do some coke?' I said.

We ended up in Tom's room. It was closer. And, naturally, it was a carbon copy of mine, which was four floors above in the same wing. The similarity made me feel at home immediately. I kicked off my shoes and curled up on the sofa, tapping coke out on to the glass-topped coffee table as easily as if I had done this before. Which I had, on mine, a few hours earlier.

In about thirty seconds Tom had the lights dimmed, the

TV on – he skipped quickly through the pre-ordered porn channels with an embarrassed grin – and had joined me on the sofa. His big frame weighed down the cushions so that I found myself sliding towards him. I didn't mind that. I prefer men to be larger than me. I have a rule never to date anyone whose jeans I can't fit into.

I could feel Tom's stare on the side of my head, as intent as two barrels of a shotgun trained on their target.

'Hey,' I said, tapping the table. 'Drugs.'

It was, after all, what we were allegedly here for. Proper procedures had to be observed.

'Whoo!' he said, tilting his head back and sniffing enthusiastically.

'D'you have anything to drink up here?' I asked.

I'd meant just to do some coke and go back downstairs; there were still lots of people I wanted to see. But I needed some alcohol to settle my nerves – the line had been bigger than I'd meant to do – so we had a glass of white wine each, fast, and then I was feeling tipsy and cut us a couple of smaller lines, just to maintain the balance, and by that time Tom had found an action film on the TV which was in its final spasm of violent explosion, so we had to watch the end of that. The hero was huge and practically plated in muscle. Excellent. His jeans would be much too big for me.

Still, I was unable to really kick back and let the film take me over. Tom's presence was too distracting. That tension was building up between us, that tension which needs to be either detonated or defused. And, as always, it was me holding the grenade. The men are usually eager to hand it to you, but in the end it's the woman who has to decide whether to take the pin out. I put down my glass.

'Do you want another drink?' Tom said, already half on his feet.

'No,' I said, drawing out the word, rather evilly prolonging his moment of doubt.

He looked at me, blue eyes wide as saucers, still not quite believing what was about to happen.

'Then . . . um . . . what . . .' he mumbled.

I patted the sofa cushion right next to me, smiling at him. Tom shot towards me, dangerously fast. His limbs were so long and substantial that his attempts to rearrange himself on what was not a very large sofa gave rise to a good deal of shifting of pillows, elbows and knees sticking out at crazed angles, and muffled curses. It brought back the vivid memory of a tall skinny friend trying to fit himself into the back of a Fiat Uno; he had had to fold himself up like a slide rule, his knees scraping the ceiling.

When the curses had subsided and Tom had reached a more comfortable position, I took his face in my hands and kissed him.

He was very good at it. It's odd how often people's normal behaviour doesn't necessarily reflect what they're like when they're kissing you, or having sex. Tom, who I had guessed might be clumsy, turned out to be tentative and exploratory and a very skilled tease. God, I loved this. Our hands wound in each other's hair, my tongue running round Tom's ear . . . I breathed out gently as I took his lobe in my teeth and he let out a sound of pleasure halfway between a grunt and a moan.

As I traced my tongue down his neck, feeling him shudder beneath my steadying hands, pushing his head sideways so I could get at that lovely long muscle in his shoulder, I had a moment of *déjà vu*. I was enjoying this tremendously, and as far as I was concerned Tom could do the same back to me all night and I would be deliriously happy. Still, it had just struck me how few things there really were to do, how limited the repertoire was. You kiss someone, then you bite their ears, lick their necks, raise them up so you can reach lower down, nibble with sharp teeth at their fingers . . . how many times had I done this before?

Tom pulled me firmly on to his lap and started kissing me purposefully. I melted. He was sliding the straps of my dress off my shoulders, kissing them all the way down. I tilted my head to watch what he was doing and found myself sliding my thumb into his mouth. It was so hot and wet I moaned.

'Bite it,' I said, slipping the pad over one of his canines. He bit down, gently at first, then stronger. I shivered. Our eyes met above his mouth, my hand, as if we were watching ourselves having sex. He sucked my thumb into his mouth impatiently. I pulled it back and licked off his saliva, never taking my eyes from his.

Then we grabbed at each other. Sofa cushions flew; the sofa itself rocked on its castors. I was straddling him, rubbing up and down against him, kissing him so hard he thrashed like a fish beneath me, his hands reaching round my bottom, up my back, pulling down my dress. He kissed my breasts through the lace of my bra. It was wonderful; I threw my head back and saw myself as if from a long way away, like a girl in a porno film. I never knew whether this was a good thing, because it made me feel incredibly sexy, or a bad one, because it made me feel self-conscious. Still, my groin was grinding away at Tom's with a will of its own, at that moment when the preliminaries have really kicked in and the body is fully charged and ready to go, screaming, 'Mate! Mate!' as insistently as all the fire alarms in the building going off at once, a cacophony of whooping sirens and flashing red lights.

Tom would have fucked me then and there if I'd let him, ripped off my knickers and shoved himself up inside me with a great groan of release. And then, fifteen minutes later, it would have been over and we would have been avoiding each other's gazes as I collected my clothes and he started snoring. There was a chance it might not have gone like that, of course. Call me cynical if you must. I would just love to meet a guy who didn't rush anything, who already knew that sex was so much better the more you built up to it, especially the first time, a guy who could fool around for hours without ever having to be reined in. But then, I like enthusiastic twenty-five-year-olds. I am a creature of infinite contradiction. As Gillian says when she needs to get herself out of a particularly tricky corner: 'I am Woman, I am Mystery.'

But why the hell was all this rushing through my brain right now? Why was I thinking about anything else but the immediate and, on the available evidence, really good sex that I was imminently about to have?

Tom reached up for me.

'Are you OK?' he mumbled.

I shook my head to clear it.

'Of course!' I said, hoping I sounded more sure than I felt. My dress was around my waist. Tom's shirt was gaping open over his wide, smooth chest – for such a big guy he had the tiniest, pertest little pink nipples . . . I bent my head and licked around one in an exploratory mission. Some guys loved this and some couldn't care less. Tom seemed to fit into the former category. Heat was coming off him in waves. I breathed it in. As my breasts came into contact with his stomach the warmth soaked through my bra and made them tingle, as hot as if he had been rubbing them with his hands. It was intoxicating.

'Do you like this?' I mumbled against his chest.

'Yes – yes –' he groaned. God, he was so smooth, his skin so fair. I hadn't had a blond guy in ages, I had forgotten how pale they could be . . .

Tom sat up with a start and put one hand firmly between my legs. He seemed to be getting hotter and hotter; it was like being scalded. I rubbed myself against him, kissing him as he stroked the heel of his palm against me, feeling myself go, another restraining cord snapping, tethered less and less to the ground of reason. With his other hand he ripped down one of the cups of my bra and put his mouth to my nipple. I felt like crying.

Why? Why did I feel like crying? Where had that come from?

'Tom,' I said feebly against the top of his head. His hair was soft and silky and smelt of pine needles. He was busy with my nipple, tracing his tongue round and round it till the poor thing didn't know whether it was coming or going.

'Yes?' he said, his voice muffled by me.

But I didn't know what I meant to say. It was too stupid. Something in my head had slammed on the brakes so hard that I was skidding all over the place.

He looked up from my breast. His eyes were literally glazed with lust; there was a shiny film over them like sugar icing. I realised I had stopped grinding myself into his hand.

'Is everything OK?' he said.

'Yes. But no. I mean, yes, this is great, but no, it's not OK. I mean –' I stammered myself to a halt, baffled and furious with myself.

'Is something wrong?'

'I don't KNOW!' I said angrily.

Switching into sensitive-man mode, Tom put on his best reassuring voice.

'We don't have to have sex if you don't want to,' he said, very nobly, considering the erection that was currently pushing insistently at the inside of my right thigh, nudging me like a cat which head-butts when it wants to be stroked.

'But I DO!' I insisted. I reached for him, but the gesture didn't work. My hand fell back from his shoulder limply.

'Or we could just go on doing this,' he suggested, flicking a warm thumb over my nipple.

It felt very pleasant, and yet something inside me curled back from the sensation, as if it were wrapping itself up into a ball, not wanting to be touched.

'No,' I said, more confused than ever. 'We'd go mad.'

'Fair enough.'

'So – we should stop.'

I couldn't believe this was happening to me. Still, I wasn't going to think about it now. If I did it felt as if my head would explode all over the sofa.

'OK,' he said in what was almost a whimper. I felt horribly guilty.

I eased myself reluctantly off him. My body was screaming: What are you doing? Stay! I need to FORNICATE! and I felt as guilty towards it as I did towards Tom. What had I done to both of us? Was I going mad? And yet, somehow, I was automatically readjusting my clothing, slipping the straps of my dress back over my shoulders, and finding my shoes. I had just found the second one under the sofa – I managed to extract it without bending over in any way that could have been considered provocative, as I didn't feel this would help matters much – and was doing up the ankle strap when Tom suggested:

'Why don't I walk you back to your room?'

For some maudlin, drink-sodden, guilt-stricken reason, I was touched by this.

'OK,' I said.

Just in front of the door to Tom's room was a door leading to the stairwell. It had already occurred to me that any lift we took was likely to be stuffed with drunken revellers. I wanted to keep this whole Tom thing as quiet as possible. If people were going to tease me about it, I wanted at least to have worked out in my own head what they were teasing me about. Besides, if anyone found out that I had had him in my grasp and spared him, as it were, my reputation would take a knock. I didn't want anyone to think I was going soft in my old age. Oh God, was that it? Was I getting too old to shag?

Of course, I shouldn't have accepted Tom's offer of an escort to my room. But I had jumped at it as a way of having company as long as possible. I really didn't want to be alone with my thoughts right now. Thank God it was only four floors up to my room, though the stairs weren't much fun in heels. I stuck my head into the corridor for a quick recce to see if any people I knew were staggering back to their rooms. The coast was clear, as far as I could see through the glass panel of the fire door halfway down the hall. All systems go. I scooted along to the fire door pulling Tom behind me – it was a damn obstacle course, this hotel. And those doors were so heavy you could knock yourself out on them. Lawsuits just waiting to happen.

Just as I wrested it open, I saw Henry Ridgley appear further down the corridor, from the direction of the lifts. He was placing his feet with that resolution of purpose which, combined with the uncoordinated swaying of his upper body, denoted extreme drunkenness. He paused for a moment to study the directional arrows, working out which way to take for his room. I crossed my fingers that he would turn away from us.

Then the fire door banged shut behind Tom.

The sound caught Henry's attention. He turned his head and stared blearily down the length of the corridor, towards me. I froze in my tracks. Tom stumbled into my back.

'What's up?' he said impatiently.

There was nothing for it. I proceeded along the corridor, keeping my head ducked and my gaze fixed to the diamond pattern on the carpet – red and salmon and green, how tasteful – followed closely by Tom. Henry was still fixing us with an intent though vacant stare.

At least we didn't have to pass him. My room was about halfway down that wing of the corridor. I fumbled my card key out of my bag and shoved it into the door. It whirred, flashed a red light, and spat the wretched card out again. I could have screamed.

'Shooliet? Is tha' you?'

Damn. Henry had finally identified me.

'Shooliet!' He was lumbering towards us. Everything about him sagged; his trouser knees, his stomach, his breasts, his jowls.

'Shoo won't believe what that bashtard Folcombe jusht shaid to me! Shooliet!'

I managed to get the card back into the slot. The heavens were more merciful this time. It whirred again, the light flashed green and I heard the lock disengage.

'Quick, get in!' I said to Tom, holding the door open for him. He shot me a baffled glance. I shoved him bodily through the door.

Tom's slowness might have been fatal; Henry was almost upon me. There wasn't enough time to get inside myself and close the door. My brain raced around my skull like a rocket-charged pinball, desperately trying to find a way to avoid Henry without mortally offending him. He was one of the most important food critics in Britain; if he took against me I would shortly find myself doing PR for Burger King. And besides, I actually sort of liked him.

'Shooliet!' Henry was crying petulantly. 'Wait! I need to talk to you!'

'*Ist das die Hotel fur die Autobahn?*' I said in a polite voice.
'*Meine kleine Liebchen ist bin der Wirklistshaft. Und ich sind
Fräulein Greta Hauernbahnhof.*'

I shrugged my shoulders and smiled at him tolerantly in
the kind of way that Greta Hauernbahnhof, being a nice,
courteous sprig of Teutonic womanhood, might conceivably
do if the cognac-sodden food critic of the *Sunday Herald* and
Mode had just mistaken her for someone else and shouted
incoherent English at her in a hotel corridor at two in the
morning. Maybe I should have made her a Frau, so that it
could have been Herr Hauernbahnhof shooting into her
bedroom, but you can't think of everything. Greta was obviously a bit of a party girl.

Henry looked baffled but unconvinced.

'*Es tot mir leid. Grussen Gott*,' I said, and did the shrug/polite
smile combination once more.

'But – but –' Henry stammered. 'Aren't you . . .' He fell
back, going noticeably paler. 'Oh my God,' he muttered to
himself. 'Doppelgänger! German doppelgänger! How much
cognac did I have?'

He covered his face with his hands and shrank back against
the far wall.

'*Achtung!*' I said rather helplessly.

I wished there was some way I could reassure Henry that
he wasn't going mad, but I couldn't do it without blowing
Greta's cover. I slipped inside, shut the door, locked it and
slid the bolt. I stood for a moment with my back to the door,
breathing deeply, the way women always do in films.

The corridor was eerily silent. I peeped into the spyhole.
Henry was still standing there, his hands over his face. As I
watched, he removed one then the other with extreme caution,
squinting through the fingers. He turned his head to look
from side to side, obviously nervous of the prospect of

hundreds of Juliet-lookalikes talking pig-German to him popping out of all the doors, one by one, like a Busby Berkeley musical with dream sequences by Salvador Dali.

'Are you OK?' Tom said in what to my panicked senses was nearly a shout. He was sitting on the edge of the bed, staring at me as if I had lost my mind.

I threw myself across the room and shoved my hand against his mouth.

'That was *Henry Ridgley*!' I whispered into his ear, paranoid that Henry, in his extreme state of disorientation, might be listening at the door.

'Well, I know that,' Tom said through my hand.

'He's a terrible gossip. I can't believe you don't know that. He's famous for it.'

'I haven't been doing this job very long,' he said rather stiffly.

I looked down at him. I knew exactly what was going through his mind. When you're younger – till the end of your twenties, say – you don't care about gossip half so much. You don't understand the reasons for keeping something quiet, not flaunting yourself in the bar with someone who you may never have sex with again after that evening; you think that if someone doesn't want to be seen in public with you it means that they're ashamed of you. Of course this is often the case, but not always. It takes a while to appreciate the true values of discretion.

Out in the corridor I could hear the slow heavy steps which were Henry lumbering away from the scene of his hallucination. Tom took my hand away. He looked cross, offended and on the verge of leaving.

'I'm sorry,' I said against his mouth. 'I'm just a bit paranoid about Henry.'

He humphed.

'Really. It's not you,' I assured him. 'You're gorgeous. It's me. I'm so sorry. This has never happened to me before.'

He burst out laughing.

'You sound like you're apologising for not being able to get it up,' he managed to get out between whoops of laughter.

It was funny, I could see that. But somehow the impotency comparison didn't do much for my morale. Still, Tom was completely restored to his natural good humour.

'Here,' he said, lying down on the bed. 'Come and have a hug. I'd better wait a few minutes before I go back to my room in case Henry's still wandering the corridors.'

He was so considerate. I curled up next to him in the crook of his arm. He kissed the top of my head. We hadn't turned on any lights and the room was illuminated only by a light I had carelessly left on in the bathroom. I closed my eyes. This was very restful.

My face was like raw steak. I wouldn't have believed a blond could have so much stubble on him. It felt as if he'd been going at me with a toothbrush for hours. The last conscious thought I had before passing out with exhaustion was to wonder if I had packed my extra-heavy night cream. I was going to need it.

Chapter Two

'So you never shagged him? Why? Why? I just don't get it!' Gillian demanded.

Gillian, Mel and I were sitting in my living room, drinking martinis. The Chalk Farm area was low on cocktail bars, which meant we usually stayed in when they came to visit me. Besides, there was something very sophisticated about the idea of mixing a pitcher of martinis. It gave what I liked to think was a certain F. Scott and Zelda touch to the evening. The ready-made party nibbles I was heating in the oven might be slightly less authentic, but they were very tasty all the same.

'Yeah, what's wrong with you?' Mel chimed in. She tapped her glass with the cocktail stirrer. 'More drink!' she said imperiously.

I got up and went over to the fridge.

'I don't know,' I said rather hopelessly. 'I really don't.'

'Was there something off about him?' Mel asked.

'Oh no, he was lovely,' I said. 'Maybe that was the problem.'

Mel looked confused.

'What do you mean?' she said impatiently.

I refilled our glasses and returned the pitcher to the fridge.

'I don't know,' I said again. 'Maybe he was too nice to have a meaningless shag with.'

'So?' Gill said. 'You could have seen what it led to.'

I shrugged. 'I really don't think so. It wasn't anything serious.'

'So why didn't you just shag him?' Gill sounded almost angry with me. 'God, I don't believe you. The opportunities you get, and you don't even take advantage.'

It always surprised me when those novels about single women looking for a man painted the heroine's married friends as smug and condescending, if not actually disapproving, about the heroine's unsettled lifestyle. All my settled-down friends wanted me to sleep around even more than I did. And tell them all the juicy details. It was their way of getting some vicarious action. The only disapproval I garnered was, as now, when I didn't behave like a sex-crazed trollop. Only the other day I had had an e-mail from a happily married friend asking for details of my latest flings, concluding with the plea: 'Plant a big wet one from me on the next twenty-five-year-old you snog, won't you?' Damn. I actually hadn't thought of her at all when I was kissing Tom, so that wouldn't count. It would have to be the next one.

I had been even worse when I was living with Bart. I actually introduced the cute guys I met to my single friends, hoping they'd get off with each other and I could at least find out what they were like in bed, even by proxy. There was one who used to crawl under the table at parties and howl like a wolf. I was always dying to know if he was as good a shag as he made out.

'Don't shout at the girl, Gill,' Mel said. 'You're just making her even more confused, and then she won't be able to explain anything. Jules, start from the beginning. What did he look like? Describe him in detail.'

'Well, he wasn't my usual type at all,' I said, sitting back down on the floor and arranging the scatter cushions at my back. I had put candles all around the room and dimmed the lights slightly. It was just the atmosphere for an exchange of confidences. Visits from the girls always made me go to extra trouble with the flat; their own places were so beautifully decorated that I felt myself rising by example.

'Didn't know you had a type,' Mel said. 'Oh yeah, hang on a minute, of course you do. Under thirty, well built, with a penis.'

I sneered at her and drank some more martini. Pepper vodka and vermouth. It was very consolatory.

'Go on,' Gill said. 'Ignore her. I want to know what he looked like too. I was too pissed to remember a thing that evening.' She sighed. '*Plus ça change.*'

'Ploo sa what?' Mel teased her.

I cleared my throat. 'Well, by some bizarre coincidence he did actually happen to be under thirty and in possession of a penis,' I began. 'Tall, strawberry blond, blue eyes, and yes, Mel, very well built—'

'Shit, not you at all,' she interrupted. 'Sounds like the Aryan dream.'

I giggled. 'Nah, he was too clumsy to make a good Nazi. He'd forget to put on his swastika armband, or click his heels fast enough. They'd have drummed him out of the Hitler Youth.'

'Or given him a good flogging,' Mel said lubriciously.

'Mel.'

She shrugged, as if to say that if I didn't understand there was no point explaining it to me. Stretching her legs out in front of her, she contemplated the polished toes of her stilettos.

'When you say well built . . .' she prompted.

'Like a brick shithouse. Shoulders as wide as the Forth Bridge. But not fat. Nice arse and legs.'

'In proportion?'

I smirked reminiscently.

'*Oh* yes.'

'Ha! I thought you said you didn't have sex,' Mel said, as

if she'd caught me out. 'God, you normal people are so weird. You just go: "Oh, we didn't have sex," when you mean you didn't actually fuck.'

Mel, being a dominatrix by profession and inclination, had a tendency to put a spin on the word 'normal' which made it sound more perverse than a combination of bestiality and coprophilia.

'No, we really didn't,' I assured her, stung to the quick at being accused of hypocrisy. 'I was just having a feel around down there. I wanted to know what it was like in case I thought of having sex with him another time.'

'Oh well, fair enough. I still don't get why you didn't shag him, though.'

Gill nodded in agreement.

'Why do you care so much? Why can't you just respect my choices?' I whined.

Both of them laughed so hard they had to put down their glasses in case they spilt their drinks. Sullenly, I went to check on the progress of the party snacks. My flat had been chosen for location – just up from Chalk Farm tube – rather than size; more than six people in the living-room/kitchen area and it felt like we were playing Sardines. Still, it was cosy. I had painted the walls a dark reddish-orange and filled the living room with a pair of squashy, over-stuffed magenta and burgundy sofas. Floor cushions spilt all around the little coffee table. The walls were laden with bookshelves, mostly bearing lavishly produced and designed cookbooks which I never opened.

'Five more minutes,' I announced, leaning against the fridge. 'Anyway, why should I have to shag him? Why should I have to shag anyone who takes my brief fancy? I'm not a sodding sex tap, you know. I can't just turn myself on and off at will.'

'You sound really defensive.'

'Well, maybe that's because everyone's having a go at me.'

'We're not having a go at you,' Mel said, finishing her drink and tossing back her glass so that the olive at the bottom would slide down into her open mouth. She chewed it with gusto.

'The point is, Jules,' Gill said, leaning forward for extra emphasis, 'that till recently you would just have shagged this guy, maybe gone on seeing him a few times till it wore off, probably agonised a bit about whether you should be going out with him, in your usual Jules-ish way, and then never've mentioned him again. This is not like you. That's what we're saying.'

Mel clapped her hands in applause for Gill's summary, her eyes sparkling. Mel's black shiny bob looked like a very expensive wig; it was so perfectly razor-cut, the edges of the fringe ruler-straight, the swing of it like a model in a hair advertisement. Her makeup was exquisite. As usual she was managing effortlessly to drink without blurring the outline of her glossy red lips. Mel's face always seemed painted, in the old-fashioned sense: the black eyeliner round her long dark eyes, the rouged cheekbones, the Cupid's bow mouth. From the black glossy crown of her head down her long flat body to the pointed toes of her shoes, she was wilfully not of this decade, a cross between a starlet from a 1920s film and Morticia Addams.

The oven pinged. I pulled out the trays of food and turned them out on to plates. Mel and Gill might be bullying me, but the truth was that I, too, really wanted to analyse this, and, as my oldest friends, they were by far the best people to do it with. I was just a little scared of what they might say. They knew me too well. More truth might emerge than I wanted to hear.

'OK. There are a couple of things that were sort of

swimming through my mind while it was happening,' I admitted, bringing the food over to the coffee table.

'Go on,' Gill said encouragingly, reaching for some cocktail sausages.

'Well, the first one is the name thing.'

They looked at me enquiringly.

'The more guys I meet,' I explained, 'the more they remind me of ones I've had before, you know? It's like they've started to repeat on me.'

'Like onions,' Gill said.

'Exactly. This one really made me think of Alan. I nearly called him "Alan" once, when he was biting my thumb.'

'Alan Jarvis?' Mel said. 'Shit, he's really lost his looks.'

'God, hasn't he? I mean, it wasn't that I thought this one was going to end up all depressed and fat, dating younger and younger women and moaning about it all the time. But there were similarities. And this guy – Tom – told me a story at dinner about this girl he was in love with at college who wasn't keen on him, and that made me think of Alan too. You know he has that mad thing about falling in love with unavailable women. Married Catholics, for preference.'

'Needs a good flogging.'

'Oh, Mel, you can't just say that all the time.'

'It's truer than you'd think,' she said, looking even more sibylline than usual.

'I don't know why people ever eat main courses,' Gill said through a mouthful of mini-quiche. 'I always prefer finger food.'

'Preferably hand-prepared and fed to you by your perfectly trained slave, of course,' Mel suggested.

I had perked up. To my surprise, this conversation was making me feel better instead of worse. Opening the floodgates wasn't as scary as I had thought; at least I was finding actual reasons for my unwillingness to shag Tom, rather than simply feeling inexplicably neurotic.

'And this isn't the first time it's happened,' I went on. 'You remember that guy I had the fling with in April?'

'The Greek god one?' Gill said.

I nodded. 'I kept trying to call him Ivan. That was the name of my first proper boyfriend. I would open my mouth and literally feel Ivan's name, like a bubble, on the tip of my tongue, ready to pop out.'

Mel stared at me, a filo parcel suspended in mid-air between two long, pointed, shiny purple nails.

'Did he look like Ivan?' she asked curiously.

'Superficially, a bit. Tall and dark, very handsome. But Ivan had these sloping shoulders, and he was quite self-conscious, while this one was a total stud, very cocky. In a nice way,' I added, to be fair. 'But you see what I mean?'

I ate another sausage.

'It just feels like everything's looping round on itself. Nothing's new any more. Every new guy turns out to be a variation on one of the old guys.'

'Shit, welcome to reality,' Mel said cynically. 'If you'd seen as many as I have you'd have known that years ago. There are pathetically few types of men out there.'

'But shouldn't I be enjoying that?' I speculated. 'I mean, savouring all the variations like a connoisseur?'

'God knows where you get these ideas from,' Mel muttered contemptuously through a mouthful of samosa.

'And instead I just feel like a jaded old roué.'

'Hah!' This set Mel off laughing again. 'That's a good one! Where's the portrait in the attic?'

Gill cleared her throat. 'Have you two have finished being cynical and world-weary?'

'No,' Mel and I said in unison.

Gill ignored us.

'I expect the grass is always greener,' she said wistfully. 'People always think I'm really lucky – you know, happy in my cosy nest with my loving husband. Of course I'm happy,' she added quickly, 'but I also have a lot of twinges about not being out there free to do what I want. And I look at you, Jules, and think that you'd be happier if you settled down, and occasionally I try to set you up with men – yes, I know, it's always a complete disaster, you don't need to say it – but maybe I'm just projecting because I'm jealous of you writhing around on sofas in the wee hours with gorgeous six-foot-three studs.'

She picked up a mini-quiche, contemplated it for a moment and then inserted it, whole, into her mouth.

'God, Gill, that's a grown-up bracelet,' I said, as her sleeve slid back from her wrist.

Her mouth full of quiche, she stuck out her arm so that I could examine it. The glint I had seen was diamonds set at regular intervals into a flat but heavy gold chain.

''S called a tennis bracelet,' she said through the last crumbs. 'Jeremy bought it for me in the States.'

Mel leant forward to ogle it.

'Bet that cost a fortune,' she said greedily.

Gold and diamonds weren't to her taste – Mel only ever wore silver, and her preferred stones were dark, bloody rubies. But she had a magpie's attraction to bright, shiny baubles, the more expensive the better. Mel, who had grown up poor, had been determined from an early age not to stay that way. And so far she had done pretty well for herself.

Gill shrugged.

'Yes, it's nice. Jeremy's always good at picking out presents for me,' she said, with an edge to her voice. Before reaching out for the food again, she tilted her wrist so that the bracelet slid back under her sleeve.

I sipped my drink, watching Gill eat. She was so precise; look at how she managed not to smudge her lipstick without making a parade of it. Though Gill had been born a Sloane, the only traces of her upbringing that remained were her navy-blue eye pencil and her postcode. Except when she was cooking, Gill was always in black, usually a short-sleeved shift dress and matching jacket that skimmed her curves, with dark tights to slim her legs. Sloane girls tended to be built long and lean (like their racehorses) or short and stocky (like their dogs), and Gill fell into the second category.

Gold jewellery set off her bright blond hair and pinky-white skin. Her grooming and makeup were discreet. The Sloane female's idea of makeup is often weirdly old-fashioned, if not positively clownish, as if they think that their social position sets them above any mere beauty competition. The only giveaway touch to Gill's origins was that navy liner pencil round the inner rims of her eyes – that and the matching blue mascara. You could take the girl out of Cheltenham, but you couldn't take Cheltenham out of the girl.

'So what's the second thing?' she observed, cutting into my reverie. 'You said the first reason you didn't shag him was getting his name confused with Alan's. What's the other one?'

I got up and went over to the fridge. If I was going to talk about this in detail, I needed another drink.

'I think I suddenly went off the whole casual-sex thing,' I confessed.

Mel put her hands to the sides of her head and let her mouth gape wide, pantomiming Munch's 'Scream'.

'Not the actual sex part,' I hastened to explain, refilling our glasses. I wasn't sure whether Gill should have any more martini; her voice had just got louder and her pronunciation of words more careful, two sure signs that she was getting drunk. Gill was a tricky one; she hardly showed it until she was ready to fall on her face. Over the years Mel and I had got good at heading her off just before that happened. She hadn't started telling us how much she cared about us yet, which was the final indication. I thought she was good for one more. A little one.

'I have no fucking idea what you're talking about,' Mel said, picking up her glass. Mel tended to swear more when she was drinking. And me? I flirted.

'Oh, I still wanted to have sex,' I assured them. 'But for the first time I started thinking about all the other stuff that goes with it. Go back to someone's room, shag, afterglow barely lasts five minutes, either leave then or lie in bed pretending to be asleep for two hours, finally doze off and wake up in a panic the next morning, scrabble round for your clothes, embarrassed farewells, avoidance of each other's eyes when you meet next, sex probably not that amazing because of being the first time, wondering why you did it in the first place . . .'

Mel frowned at me.

'Talk about your worst-case scenario,' she said. 'It's not always like that.'

'No, I know . . . but look, the morning after, just before he sneaked out, Tom gave me a lovely hug and said it was the best non-sex he'd ever had. I fell asleep feeling lovely. Not at all "Oh God, what have I done" in the cold light of day.'

Mel made a loud snorting noise.

'Great,' she said dryly. 'What a fucking testimonial. Why don't you get that framed and put it over your bed. Juliet Simmons, Best Non-Sex Award, 2001. All the guys'll be queueing up.'

'Look,' I said, trying to put my incoherent feelings into words. It was very frustrating, attempting to explain something I hadn't worked out myself yet. 'If you just have sex, when it's all over there's usually nowhere to go and you both just want to get away. This way, there's much more tenderness, and you get to have foreplay all night, or as long as you can bear it. I mean, how often does that happen? You know what guys are like! The only time you really get that is in the beginning, when they're so desperate for you they'll do anything you want on the slightest possibility that they might actually, finally, get to put it in you. You can string it out for ages. And, unless the sex is really fantastic, often that kind of foreplay is almost the best part. Because, unless you know each other very well and he's brilliant at making you come, after fifteen minutes he's dead to the world and taking up most of the space in the bed, and you're staring at the ceiling.'

Gill's gaze was fixed on me, her eyes glassy with drink. Mel, however, had been observing the varnish on her fingernails for the last half of my impassioned speech. After I finished, there was a pause. Had I just made a total idiot of myself? Then Mel raised her head and said, in the calm, dispassionate tones of a judge pronouncing a sentence:

'You are totally burnt out.'

'Oh *no*!' I was horrified. 'I'm *not*!'

'That made absolutely no sense at all,' she said. 'It was the most pitiful way to explain not sleeping with someone I ever heard.'

'Made no sense,' Gill chimed in over-loudly, as if she was worried we wouldn't be able to hear her over the music playing quietly in the background.

'Come on,' I protested. 'I've done a lot of thinking about this.'

'Yeah, well, it's bollocks. You're just being really negative. All casual sex isn't half that bad. A lot of it's really good. Besides, this idea of getting loads of foreplay if you don't have sex is ridiculous. You'd get loads more if they want to make sure you come before they do. I bet you didn't get that much with this bloke – Alan Two – did you?'

'He spooned me,' I said feebly.

Mel humphed.

'And the main thing that's completely fucked up about your so-called argument,' she said, 'is that the only reason not to shag 'em the first time is if you want to go on seeing them. Because if you don't want to go on seeing them you might at least do them to see what they're like. But it doesn't sound like you want to actually go out with Alan Two.'

I shook my head. I didn't know why; I just knew I didn't.

'So what's the point? You might as well have had an early night. You gave that poor bloke blue balls and didn't get off yourself. That's why I said you're burnt out.'

Mel had put into words my worst fear. My heart sank. I felt incredibly depressed. She lit a cigarette and fixed me with a glance through the rising cloud of smoke.

'Burnt out,' she said. 'Face it.'

'I am not,' I said defiantly. 'This was just a blip.'

'Is it, Jules?' Gill practically shouted in my ear. 'Is it just a blip? Because, you know, we're worried about you, me and Mel. We love you, don't we?' She put an arm around me, nodding at Mel. 'We love you very much, and we want you to be happy, don't we? We love you SO much, Jules . . .'

It was definitely time for Gill to go home.

'God,' I said, as we came back inside, 'talk about the pitcher going to the well too many times.'

'I know. I thought that minicab was going to refuse to take her.'

Mel and I had both walked Gill down to the waiting cab; when the driver rang my bell she had declared that she had changed her mind about going home and wanted to stay here with us because she loved us so much. So it had seemed sensible not only to physically put her in the cab and ensure the driver had the right address, but demonstrate to him that she had friends who would check to see that she'd arrived there. This was a basic precaution. Minicab drivers in London did not have the best reputation with lone women passengers considerably the worse for wear. Once Gill got home, Jeremy, her husband, would take over. He was used to Gill staggering home after a night out with the girls and would make sure she got to bed rather than passing out in the hallway.

Since Mel didn't need to get up in the morning for work, she was always willing to stay drinking with me till the small hours. It wouldn't have entered her mind to offer to go; she would simply assume that I would tell her if I needed to get my sleep. Mel was like a man in many ways; she was completely free of all the pseudo-polite, beating-around-the-bush etiquette that women felt compelled to use.

Normally, being as busy as I was at the agency, I would have called a cab for her too. But this conversation felt important enough for me to want to keep it going. I brought out a box of extremely posh Belgian chocolates, made by another of my clients at the agency, which I was in the process of promoting as heavily as I was able, given how hard I was concentrating on Liam's launch. Fortunately, the chocolates were so good they practically sold themselves. It was a shame Gill had missed them. I would have to give her a box the next time I saw her.

'Gill just loses it all at once,' Mel marvelled, sitting down and reaching for a white chocolate cappuccino swirl. 'God, this is good,' she muttered in parenthesis. 'You'd think after all this time she'd know when to stop.'

'She does,' I said, curling up on the sofa and rubbing my upper arms vigorously to warm them up. The night air had been cold.

'What d'you mean?' Mel lit another cigarette. 'Well, then, why did she just pull that Little Miss Shit-Faced thing? I haven't seen her that pissed for ages.'

'She *does* know when to stop,' I said. 'I think it was what we were talking about. You know, the whole sex thing. I feel a bit bad about mentioning it.'

This had been on my mind all through the conversation. I knew – so did Mel – that Gillian's marriage was much more sexless than she would have liked. Under those circumstances, it had seemed a bit tactless to talk about why I hadn't made the most of a virile young man who was there for the taking.

Mel made a snorting noise.

'You can't be that careful, Jules. I mean, what are you supposed to do, not talk about your sex life just because Gill hasn't got laid since 1995?'

'God,' I said, wincing. Mel had a way of putting into words things that you knew already, but sounded so much worse when said out loud. I unwrapped a chocolate and stuffed it into my mouth.

'If anything,' Mel continued, 'it should make her really think about what she's doing with her life. Here you are, arsing on about all the blokes beginning to repeat on you like raw onions, and there's poor Gill getting her end away once a month if she's lucky. Jeremy sleeping next to her all night and not having sex with her. It's totally unnatural. You should be grateful for all the fun you're having.'

'I know,' I pulled a face. 'It sounds really spoilt.'

I reached for one of Mel's cigarettes. I only smoked late at night, when drunk and having a serious conversation.

'I think the thing with Tom was that I couldn't be bothered

to shag someone who reminds me of someone I've already shagged, because it just feels like déjà vu,' I said. 'But if I stop wanting casual sex, where does that leave me? I'd have to have a relationship just to get laid.'

The thought unnerved me so much that I took a deep pull on the cigarette.

'And that's so much hassle,' I continued, 'and eventually you have to move in together, and then all the problems just explode. Do you remember that line in the play we saw last year? That women admit they've got baggage right from the beginning, but men deny they've got any, they say they've just got a toothbrush and a change of underwear. Then after a few months this enormous great pantechnicon arrives at your place and starts unloading huge quantities of stuff which they totally forgot to mention.'

'Are you thinking about Bart?' Mel said.

Bart was my ex-boyfriend, with whom I had lived for almost four years.

I shook my head automatically. Then, for honesty's sake, I reconsidered.

'Well, maybe a bit. But I don't want to talk about Bart. That was ages ago. I've been single longer than I was going out with Bart now. And I've been having so much fun! And now I'm not going to have any more fun ever again because I'm going to have to have a relationship with someone and we'll probably stop having sex the moment we start living under the same roof. Oh God.'

I was a little drunk. Even I could hear how maudlin that sounded.

'You had sex with Bart when you were living together,' Mel pointed out.

'I really don't want to talk about Bart,' I said. 'It's not relevant.'

I took another chocolate. One more and I would definitely stop.

'Well, at least it proves you can still keep having sex.'

'Yeah, but look at all the other problems! Now, Gill has Jeremy. He's perfect, he loves her, he looks after her, he wouldn't dream of nicking her stereo to pay his gambling debts, and yet he's barely laid a finger on her since they moved in together.'

And Gill had promptly begun to put on weight. She must have put on at least a stone and a half since she'd started living with Jeremy. Jeremy was a keen amateur cook and hearty trencherman; he and Gillian were constantly going on foreign holidays where they renewed their love bonds by eating their way through the cream of the local restaurants rather than by having sex in new interesting positions all over their hotel room.

'I thought it was when they got married that they stopped having sex,' Mel observed.

'No, couple of years before, when she moved into his place.' I was getting depressed now. I ate a mini-quiche in an effort to cheer myself up, even though I wasn't hungry. I understood Gill's temptation all too well. 'I know loads of people that's happened to. Linda, Siobhan –'

'Kevin,' Mel added.

'Really?'

'Yup.' Mel wiped her hands fastidiously on a napkin and relaxed back into the armchair. The candles on the shelf behind her flickered slightly with the movement. 'That bird of his whose name I can never remember. Actually, it happened when he proposed, not when they moved in together. He says since they got engaged she's barely even touched him. I mean, not even brushing against him in the loo, let alone having sex.'

'So what's he doing about it?'

'They're getting married in June.'

'He must be out of his mind,' I said wonderingly.

'He loves her, the silly sod. Oh, and wait for it.' Mel raised one white finger, signalling the punchline. The shiny specks in her nail varnish glittered in the lamplight like tiny jewels. 'He thinks it'll all sort itself out after marriage. Priceless, eh?'

This pretty much confirmed my whole image of marriage: a trap into which two people willingly inserted their heads, despite knowing how painful it would be. Every time I thought of marriage it was like hearing a metal door slam loudly, a prison gate closing. Only, in my imagination, the sound was the electric door of the garage of the detached suburban house where I would have to live when I got married, opening on my remote-controlled command so that I could drive in the brightly coloured people-carrier on my return from taking the children to school. Above the door would be a baseball hoop, nailed to the brickwork by my loving husband. Slowly the garage door would descend behind me, slamming to the concrete floor, automatically locking shut. I would sit in the people-carrier for a while, staring ahead of me at the white-painted garage wall, the barbecue set, the folding chairs, the thick coil of shiny green garden hose. Then I would turn on the engine, climb out and try to wedge my head into the exhaust pipe.

'You know something, Mel?' I said, finishing off the last drop of my martini.

'What?'

'Gill asked me a few months ago how I knew when someone fancied me.'

'Are you serious?'

'No, really. I didn't know what to say. I just sort of went, Well, you know. The way they look at you. And I was embarrassed because I couldn't believe she was asking.'

'Shit,' Mel said, 'that's really depressing. Do you think that's what marriage does to you? I can't imagine what kind of state I'd be in not to be able to work out when someone fancied me.'

'I know. She said she'd give anything to have a first kiss again.'

We looked at each other. I felt incredibly confused. I didn't want Gillian's low-sex, high-starch marriage. But what if Mel was right, and I really was burnt out on casual sex? What would I do now? It would be a very uncomfortable state of limbo.

'You know what the hardest thing is?' I said suddenly, out of nowhere.

'What?'

'Deciding what the hell I actually want to do. That's what messed me up with Tom. I'd always just followed a sort of routine before. But when you start to ask yourself, moment by moment, what you really want out of any given situation, it's really hard. And it's incredibly exhausting.'

It was a kind of revelation.

'That's the problem,' I said slowly, taking it in. 'I just don't know what I want. Maybe –' I reached for another cigarette – 'maybe I've never known what I wanted from a relationship. Maybe I've just gone on doing whatever came easiest, without really stopping to think where I was going or where I wanted to end up.'

I knew I was drunk; despite the extra effort I was making to articulate each word clearly, I could hear them slurring into each other as if they were melting at the edges. But in vino – or martini – veritas. It was the truest thing I'd said in years.

Chapter Three

Oxford Street at lunchtime was packed tighter with bodies than a tube train at commuter rush. And the atmosphere was just as bad. The poor tourists were wandering hopelessly; having been told that it was a shopping mecca, they were confused and disoriented by the nasty cheap shops selling badly sewn zebra-print coats, stack-heeled boots and fake designer sunglasses. Maybe if they checked their guidebooks again they would realise that they were at the armpit end of Oxford Street and head towards their goal; more likely they would mill on to the nearest bus, drive the conductor crazy and end up, even more disoriented, in Holborn.

Little I cared. I had an important lunch appointment with a new client, and I was ten minutes late. I dashed into Wardour Street, flapping my hands regretfully at a bevy of giant Dutch girls who had spotted me as a local and were desperate to know which bus would whirl them away from here.

I probably didn't need to rush. Liam was practically never on time. But that was partly the point; he was so unprofessional that, in order to compensate, I felt that it behoved me to be even more competent than usual.

Liam was a star in the making and, not inconsequentially, a real feather in my cap. I had been made a partner a couple of months ago and, perfectly aware that if he were the first person I brought in after my promotion my reputation would be made, I had hunted Liam down like a dog. He was currently top of my priority list; I was scraping around to find time for my other clients. Looking after Liam was a full-time occupation. And not just in the business sense.

Liam was young – twenty-six – and very sexy in a rough-trade sort of way, the kind of boy who made posh girls drop their knickers, as he himself would have put it. He was small and wiry and swaggering, radiating energy from every pore. When I first met him I had been reminded of a featherweight boxer eager to get into the ring, charged up, shifting constantly on the balls of his feet. He was one of those lucky people who had tremendous chemistry with the camera; in person, especially in a bad mood, he could look almost ugly. His forehead was too low, his mouth too narrow, his cheekbones too prominent. But the camera transformed his features alchemically. On screen he was effortlessly good-looking. His colouring didn't hurt either. Blue eyes, black curly hair, and a couple of little-boy freckles on his nose that would have most of the female – and a healthy proportion of the male – television audience swooning.

Liam was like an incarnation of the id. He ate like a pig at a trough, drank and drugged like a rock star, and fucked, if his stories were to be believed, like a dog on heat. It was all very wearing.

But rather fun too.

'Jules! My best girl! Come here!' he shouted as I entered the restaurant. He was sitting at the bar, doubtless chatting up the sleekly dressed girl behind it who would have been mortally offended if she had been referred to as anything so lowly as a barmaid.

Liam didn't even seem to notice that I was late. But why should he care? It had allowed him to ogle a pretty girl while ordering drinks on the agency's tab.

'Look, Jules! I got a new tattoo to show you!' he called.

Jumping down from the barstool, he turned his back to

me and bent over. For one horrified moment I thought he was going to drop his trousers. Liam had a taste for mooning. It was understandable: he was young, horny, probably polymorphously perverse, and he had a really lovely pair of buttocks. He was lean as a fillet steak; he looked as if there was nothing to him but taut stringy muscle. But his bottom, for some reason, was very pretty, round and plump and pert. He was extremely proud of it.

I tensed, seeing his hands come round his back to scrabble at his shirt-tails. Then I made myself relax. After all, if Liam dropped trou in the middle of one of the hottest restaurants of the moment, the publicity would be excellent. And they wouldn't bar me. I was a partner at the agency now. Nobody would blame me for Liam's antics, anyway. It would be like expecting me to control a chimpanzee on Viagra.

But it wasn't his bottom that Liam was flashing. It was his lower back. Just above his buttocks, in Gothic script, was the word ATTITUDE, bracketed by curlicues, in that particular bluish colour into which black ink diffuses under layers of skin.

'It looks great,' I said sincerely. I couldn't resist running my thumb over the lettering. Liam might be outrageous, but at least he was never boring. And the tattoo was undeniably sexy.

'Ooh, cold hands. I'll have to warm you up.'

He still hadn't straightened up. Liam was such an exhibitionist he made drag queens of my acquaintance look reserved and understated. His imminent media blitz had gone to his head with a vengeance. I wondered if he would settle down after a while. Probably only after a few stints in rehab.

'Y'know, I had it before,' he added conversationally.

'Before?' I said.

'Yeah, last week. Only it was still scabby and I didn't want to show it to you till it was done.'

He let down his shirt reluctantly and turned to face me.

'Juliet! Juliet's going to make me a big star!' he said, hugging me. He lifted me up – not the easiest of tasks – and swung me back and forth.

'You *are* a big star, Liam,' I said firmly. 'Just fucking try acting like one every now and then. At the moment you're behaving like a sex-starved monkey.'

Liam loved me ticking him off. It was completely accidental; I had found myself talking to him like that at our first meeting, much to my horror, until I saw how he lapped it up. Our relationship seemed to be modelled as older sister/younger brother – in a perverse kind of way. Liam definitely wanted to fuck me – only a partial compliment, as Liam wanted to fuck practically anything – and I doubted very much that he would draw the line at incest. In my comparatively brief association with Liam, I hadn't yet found anything that he *would* draw the line at.

'Must've been painful,' I said as he put me down.

'What, picking you up? Come off it. I could pick you up right now and fuck you silly. In, out, in, out –' He gave me the sauciest of winks. 'Your feet'd never touch the ground. Want to try?'

I slapped his shoulder reprovingly, trying not to imagine the scene he had just painted in too much lubricious detail. The trouble with Liam was that his sex talk was . . . pretty sexy. It was impossible for your body not to respond when Liam flirted with you. And, unlike most boasters, I had the feeling that he would actually be capable of doing what he said. This was partly why I adopted the stern-sister tone. It was a way of disciplining myself as well as him. Cf. that extra professionalism I was mentioning earlier.

'Don't be more stupid than you can help,' I said severely. 'I meant the tattoo. Right on the bone like that.'

'Never felt a thing.'

'Yeah, yeah,' I said dismissively. He was such a liar. It must have hurt like hell.

Over his shoulder I saw Lucy, the meet-and-greet girl, waiting with the menus to show us to our table. Despite her impatience, she couldn't help smiling so intimately at Liam that I wondered for a moment if she had shagged him. Charm was brutally unfair: an arbitrary gift, often corrupting the possessor, capable of masking copious unattractive qualities, and still, despite all these reservations, so irresistible.

I beamed at Liam. Bless him. He was going to make me an awful lot of money.

Our starter – scallops with crème fraîche and chilli jam – was disappointing. The jam was too sweet, and the crème fraîche overpowered the scallops.

'Like eating scones for tea, innit?' Liam said through a mouthful. 'I say, lovely lashings of whipped cream!' he added in an upper-class bray. 'Fancy a lashing, Jules?'

'God, Liam, give me a break. It's too early in the day for innuendo.'

'But you do, don'cha? Like a nice lashing? You're going to that perve thing tonight, right?'

It was the three-year anniversary of one of the fetish clubs I went to regularly with Mel. They were throwing a huge dance party; people would be flying in from all over Europe to attend it, if the last anniversaries had been anything to go by. I had cleared my diary for this afternoon – to give me enough time to go home and dress up – and tomorrow morning (which unfortunately was a work day), to allow me to recover, and I was really looking forward to it. It felt like decades since I had dressed up and gone dancing.

I should never have told Liam anything about my private

life. Unfortunately I had sensed, in the dating stages of our professional relationship, that he would relish any hints I dropped about walking on the wild side; he gave weight to that kind of thing, not wanting to feel that he was signing up with a dull old stick of a PR. Another agency who had been courting him, sensing this, had sent their motorbike-riding, dog-track frequenting, official wild-boy partner to chat him up. Bad judgement. I could tell at once that Liam wanted to go with a woman. When didn't he?

So, out drinking much too late, while I was still courting him, we had got into an infantile sexual boasting match, and I had mentioned going to fetish clubs, knowing it would impress him. And it had. Apart from the older sister factor, and what I liked to feel was my obvious competence, it might even have clinched me the deal. Liam was childishly impressed by anything he thought of as cool.

However, now that I was a partner at the agency, I needed to cut down on late nights and fooling around with unsuitable men. Women still had to be much more careful. It was very unfair. The motorbike-riding partner at that other agency was busy trying to shag his way through every barmaid and restaurant hostess in London, and no one batted an eyelid. (Apart from the married men, who were dying with jealousy.) But if I embarked too obviously on a similar path with the barmen and waiters, I would be a running joke. If I didn't eventually lose my job for bringing the agency into disrepute, my life would be a nightmare because of all the sleazy clients and contacts who would hit on me and, thinking I was easy, refuse to take 'no' for an answer.

In short, if I were too wild it would be detrimental to my career; but the worse Liam – and the motorbike-racing partner – behaved, the more positive attention he got. The double standard was very pronounced. This was one of the reasons

I had been so keen that nobody should know about my dalliance with Tom.

'Can I come along to your perve night?' Liam said hopefully, clearing his plate. Unusually for a cook, Liam always finished his food, even when it wasn't that good. He had the kind of metabolism that seemed to burn up food faster than he ate it. And he ate, as with all his appetites, voraciously.

'No, you can't,' I said firmly.

I knew better than to ask Liam not to tell anyone else about my attendance at the Rubber Ball; he would have blabbed it out immediately. He was mischievous by nature and as verbally incontinent as if he had Tourette's syndrome. Better to treat the whole subject so casually that he would think everyone knew and took it for granted; in which case, mentioning it would make him look uncool. Which, for Liam, would be worse than anything.

'What are you going to wear?'

'I'm not going to tell you,' I said primly, 'you'll just get a hard-on.'

'Got one already, just imagining you in tight PVC—'

'Liam? Shut up. We're going to talk about your career now.'

This sentence was guaranteed to make his mouth close and his eyes open. He still couldn't quite believe what was happening to him.

Liam had undergone his restaurant apprenticeship in some very good kitchens and then, unable to tolerate working for someone else a moment longer than necessary, he had left to freelance for an upmarket catering agency. He specialised in private dinner parties and very soon became a buzz-word on the circuit, his outrageous antics firmly balanced by the excellence of his cooking. (I was willing to bet that he had fucked most of the hostesses, and probably some of the hosts, for whom he had cooked.) From my long-ago stint as a waitress,

I still remembered a couple of waiters I had known, one gay, one straight, who both had the knack of insulting their customers so charmingly that they pocketed double the tips of those of us who were busy striving to be polite and efficient. It had been a useful, if depressing, lesson in life skills.

Liam had that knack in spades. He took the piss out of his clients mercilessly, and they loved it. Mind you, a quickie on the kitchen counter after the dinner guests had gone home probably didn't hurt matters either.

As his fame – or notoriety – had spread, Liam had come to the attention of an entrepreneurial TV producer with her own company, specialising in cookery series. Felicity had a well-developed eye for talent. She had already made TV stars of a series of unlikely characters; in an earlier generation she would have been in Hollywood, spotting Lana Turner sitting at a drugstore counter. Liam – who, after all, had never run a restaurant or had any professional reputation beyond a comparative handful of ecstatically happy dinner-party hosts – was, on paper, an equally implausible star. Until you met him. And until you put him in front of a camera. Though Felicity had barely needed to do that. She had an infallible instinct for a telegenic subject.

So, at this precise moment, Liam was poised on the brink of fame. The BBC series was to be launched next month, and his book, *Sorted!* – photographs of Liam taking at least equal space with those of his recipes – would be published simultaneously. We were organising a big, big party. And when I say 'we', I didn't just mean the agency. I was co-ordinating it with the in-house PR departments of the BBC and the publisher, plus the PR used by Felicity's production company. It was a massive undertaking, and I was at the apex. Not only did I have to organise everyone else's efforts, but – much more tricky – ensure that they were putting in their fair share of the budget and that no one was treading too heavily on anyone else's toes. Meanwhile, of course, I was simultaneously sorting out all the other details of Liam's publicity campaign, which also needed to be co-ordinated with all the other competing interests.

I had spent my entire professional life to date cannily avoiding a situation so fraught with pitfalls. But it had come with the territory – Liam – and he was too valuable for me to pass up. It was the biggest challenge of my career. All my competitors at the agency, not to mention Richard, our managing director and the person directly responsible for my recent promotion, were watching me very closely. It wouldn't be enough not to screw up – though that in itself would be a major achievement. No, I had to make this a raving success.

If I let myself dwell on what I had undertaken, I would already have been hospitalised for stress. Instead I was focusing on one small part of the task at a time, without yet allowing myself to take in the bigger picture. It was a technique that had worked very successfully for me so far. And right now the subject under discussion was the press Liam should be doing in the period up to the party itself.

I ran through the long list of interview requests as the waitress cleared our plates. I wanted Liam to be aware how much interest we had already secured for him, especially since I was going to recommend that he not do all of them. This was just common sense. If he appeared right now in every single newspaper and magazine that wanted to do a story on him, he would be an instant sensation and then people, oversaturated with Liam-info, would tire of him just as quickly. We wanted to build him up more gradually. After the series had started to air, we could embark on another wave of press. Having seen a couple of episodes I knew how good it was. We would have even more media attention when the series was actually running; we could afford to pace ourselves.

After reading out the list to him, I pushed it over so he could look at it. The ones I had recommended we do were picked out in highlighter. Liam barely focused on it, though. He looked stunned. I had seen this reaction before, though never on so large a scale; the reality of what was happening to him was hitting home in a succession of great juddering shocks. It had been months since they had finished shooting the series, not to mention editing the book. Liam had been sitting around, living happily off his advance, but seeing it as magic money rather than the start of what, if well managed, could be a long and prosperous career.

I grinned. It was more than pleasant to see Liam temporarily speechless. The waiter poured us some more wine. Liam had even emptied his glass without refilling it immediately, a sure indicator of his psychic disorientation. Clients of mine, whose businesses had taken off beyond their expectations – people I had managed to get a good puff in the *Sunday Times* magazine, say, and found themselves deluged with orders on Monday morning – were surprised, delighted, certainly; but to them it tended to be an added bonus to an already existing enterprise. Liam, however, had it all in front of him. Besides, he was by nature a braggart. And there is nothing more calculated to disorient a braggart than to have all his wildest boastings fulfilled in one stroke.

He dug into his chicken saltimbocca without speaking. I was pleased by the way he was reacting. There was some humanity down there, under the thick layer of bravado. Normally Liam was cockier than an entire display shelf of vibrators. It was refreshing to see him with the batteries removed.

'Oh,' I added, 'and I'm assuming this is a yes already, but how would you feel about posing naked for a women's magazine? Don't get too excited, they cover your bits,' I added before Liam could respond.

'Uh, yeah, OK. Whatever you say,' he muttered, still too dumbstruck to take it in.

I took a forkful of grilled salmon, staring dispiritedly at the large bowl of mashed potato, gleaming with butter, next to Liam's plate. If I took even a little I wouldn't be able to stop. I sighed, imagining the horror of having to pose naked for a men's magazine, even with my bits covered. Lucky Liam, whose only body fat was on his luscious buttocks. To distract myself, I reflected on the topic of mash. It was definitely this year's way to eat potato. Last year had been roast; by next year I predicted a surge of New York-style spiral chips, dusted with chilli. Or maybe the mash would hang on for longer than twelve months, triumphantly defeating all comers.

I had an unusual flash of sympathy for the people I met at parties who announced their disapproval of my job as soon as they found out what I did for a living. I knew all the arguments to counter theirs, but even I had to admit that these food fads were ridiculous at best, and obscene at worst. How many people were starving right now as I sat agonising about potato-preparation fashions, let alone my own fat and starch intake, at the most happening restaurant on Frith Street? And I didn't just mean media chicks living on cigarettes and diet frappuccinos.

Liam was recovering from his shock. He downed about half his glassful in one go and grinned at me.

'All right, Jules,' he said, finishing his chicken. 'Let's have a butcher's at that list of yours, shall we? Or, tell you what, forget that, why don't you just decide what I'm doing and tell me when to turn up for it. You know I trust you.' He looked solemn. 'And we got to talk about the party food as well. You know I want to make sure that's perfect.'

Naturally what we were serving at the launch would be

entirely made from recipes in Liam's book. It was nice to see that he was able to take that as seriously as it deserved.

'And then,' he refilled our glasses and waved the empty bottle at the waitress, 'let's get pissed. I feel a bender coming on.'

He leered at me. 'And I don't just mean in my trousers, darling.'

It was four thirty when I finally extricated myself from Liam's company and staggered out on to Frith Street. After a long and alcoholic lunch, we had, after a couple of coffees and a couple of brandies for Liam, exited, blinking, into the daylight. Liam expressed in the strongest terms his wish for more alcohol as soon as possible, so I took him to Jane's, a private members' club a mere minute's walk away, where his launch party was to be held. This was convenient, as I'd been meaning to take Liam there and show him around; and, also, it was the furthest I felt capable of going. I hated drinking at lunchtime; or rather, it was the sensation of hopeless befuddlement, allied with the strong wish to lie down somewhere comfortable and pass out, that I disliked. The drinking itself I was perfectly happy about.

The lighting in Jane's was as dim at four in the afternoon as it was at the equivalent time in the small hours of the morning. The walls were a dirty dark red, and the fires were always lit. A boisterous group of up-and-coming young actors were playing dirty-word Scrabble at the biggest table in the bar, firelight flickering over their faces as they squinted at the board. Liam wasn't a Scrabble boy, though. I took him through into the pool room, and ten minutes later I was mercifully excess to requirements. I left Liam with his new best friends, happily rummaging in his back pockets for some cash with which to bet on himself.

It seemed even brighter outside than it had been when we came out of the restaurant, probably because my hangover was now fully upon me. I hailed a cab and set off home. A brief twinge of conscience struck me about not going back to the office, but I did my best to dismiss it. Liam was very important to the agency; I had made myself positively ill in the effort to keep him amused, entertained, and generally happy with his choice of PR; I was therefore entitled to go back to my flat until my head stopped screaming. From the cab I called my assistant Lewis.

'Nothing come up, has it?' I said feebly.

'Don't you worry. Richard said he wanted to see you but when you weren't back at four I rang him and told him that you were still deep in conference with Liam.'

'Oh, Lewis, you're a treasure.'

'No prob. All I have to do is mention Liam's name and everyone shuts up, it's like a magic spell. Is he still going strong?'

'*Oh* yes.'

This was true enough, even if it gave the wrong impression. I didn't tell Lewis that I was going home. Despite his being the best assistant I had ever had, my native prudence stopped me from giving away more than was necessary. I had seen women treat their assistants as if they were their best friends, and they had always paid a price for it. Some women in business were reluctant to admit there was any kind of hierarchy. But those lower down the totem pole loathed it when their bosses pretended they were all equal, and took any revenge they could.

Folding shut my phone, I scrabbled in my bag for some headache pills. By the time I got home I had already swallowed two of them, dry. I washed away the chalky residue at the back of my throat with a glass of orange juice, took off most of my clothes and crawled into bed like a wounded animal creeping back to its lair to curl up and die.

An hour later the phone rang, trilling me out of a blissfully sound sleep. My head was still sore, but the painkillers had kicked in. I was over the worst. Blinded by my eye mask, I scrabbled for the receiver.

'Hi, Chris,' I said resignedly into the approximate area of the mouthpiece.

'Ju? Is that you? I thought it was the machine.'

'It was. I heard you leaving the message and I picked up.'

Chris was the only person for whom I would have done this in my current state of suffering. The mere sound of his voice was enough to make me drop everything else. Chris was my baby brother and my first priority. It had always been that way, ever since our father died when we were little and Mum told me that I had to look after Chris. I was seven and very serious: I thought of it as a job and threw myself into it with great dedication. Unfortunately, I was like Sisyphus rolling the stone up the hill in hell, condemned to struggle eternally but never reach the top. Chris always needed help and it was usually more than anyone could give. Still, I kept on trying. Maybe that was why I had always done so well at work. I had been trained since a very small age to be responsible. And organising press launches and countrywide publicity tours was a snap of the fingers compared to the knotty task of sorting out my brother.

'Is something wrong?' I asked.

A gusty sigh preceded the inevitable bad news.

'You know that gig I was up for?' he asked rhetorically. 'I didn't get it.'

'Oh, Chris, I'm so sorry. Was that the one in the café?'

'Yeah. I really thought I'd got it.'

'Bugger.'

'Yeah.' Another gusty sigh. 'They didn't even call me. I had to ring them. Bastards.'

I clucked my tongue sympathetically.

'I thought it went so well!' he exclaimed. 'I did these new songs I've been working on, and some Nick Drake covers.'

'New songs?' I said cautiously. 'You didn't do the ones you told me you were going to do?'

'No, I've got these new ones. Wait till you hear them, Ju, they're really good. Kind of macabre.'

My heart sank. I dragged off my eye mask and sat up, pulling a pillow behind my back as a prop.

'Sounds a bit – um –' I scrabbled for a word that wouldn't offend him – 'well, downbeat. I thought you were going to be playing something more cheerful.'

'*Cheerful*,' Chris said with scorn.

'Well, OK, not cheerful exactly –' I had to pick my vocabulary so carefully with Chris. He was hypersensitive to the way I spoke about his music. 'But, you know, upbeat. Relaxing. I mean, when people are eating, they want to feel secure . . .'

My whole face was creasing up in a grimace of frustration; I could tell by the quality of his silence that I was getting it wrong. Chris waited for me to wind down hopelessly before he spoke.

'I'm not mood music, if that's what you mean,' he responded with infinite contempt. 'They could just get some ambient CDs if they wanted to be fucking relaxed.'

'No, of course, I do see that. Sorry if I put it the wrong way, I'm just getting over a stinking hangover. Lunchtime drinking, always a big mistake.'

I had meant this as a plea for forgiveness, but obviously it too had come out wrong.

'Out lunching on the expense account?' Chris said.

Chris only had to refer to my expense account to make me feel instantly guilty. Chris and Mum had basically made feeling guilty around them my default setting. I had done well for myself in life, while Chris was still living on the dole and trying to galvanise his musical career. Mum, I knew, blamed me for this somehow. It wasn't logical, but Mum had always marched to a different drum. Whether Chris blamed me too, I didn't know. But he certainly was good at turning the guilt screw.

'Yes,' I said defiantly, ploughing ahead anyway. 'It's this new client I've just signed up. First one since I made partner, and I'm really proud of it – everyone was after him. He's a TV chef. The series starts next month, you ought to watch it. There's a book out, too.'

Then I felt like a bitch, boasting about my career triumph when Chris had just failed to get the café gig.

'Anyway,' I said deprecatingly, 'no big deal. But I had to take him out to lunch, and it was a long one.'

'Well, I'm glad your work's going well.'

'Thanks,' I said happily.

'At least someone's in the family is.'

I took a deep breath and looked at my fingernails to calm me down. They were varnished silver, for the evening's partying, and reminded me of the fun I was going to have later.

'You're the creative one, remember?' I said, boosting his ego as hard as I could. 'That's what Mum always says. I mean, it's much more prestigious. There's just not as much money in it.'

Chris didn't answer, but the silence was much less laden with tension than before. Slowly, my stomach began to unknot itself.

'I've got to see the benefits people in a couple of weeks,'

he said gloomily. 'They sent me another letter.'

'I'm sure it'll be fine,' I said firmly. 'So how's Mum? Have you spoken to her recently?'

'Yeah, I rang just now to tell her about the café thing. She was a bit upset by that, but she sounded OK generally. She said could you ring her.'

'Sure.'

We made our goodbyes and I hung up. The left side of my face had begun to throb; my eye felt as if it were swollen and protruding. I cupped my palm around it and as my fingers touched my temple I realised that it ached right up to the hairline.

It was invariably like this. I felt so responsible for Chris's bad fortune that sometimes I thought it was going to consume me. In my mind it was as if I had taken all the good luck and success in the family and left none for him. I knew that Mum thought that was what had happened and resented me for it. But what could I do? Would my failing at work make Chris succeed at his? I knew that idea was ridiculous. And still I tried to stress Chris's creativity at my own expense, or help him out professionally, even though it always went wrong. It was useless.

Bart had complained about this a lot. He said that I had no energy left over for our relationship because I put it all into worrying about my family. Actually, he had once shouted at me in the middle of an argument that I was married to Mum and Chris, and that it was time I stopped being the man of that household and started being his girlfriend instead. Bart had an inexplicable fondness for those self-help books that promise to sort out your life in three hundred pages or ten easy chapters. Typical. As long as it was me and not himself he was analysing. God forbid he should actually have picked up a book called *How To Stop Gambling In Ten Easy Steps*, though. That would have been much too close to home.

I lay down again and fumbled for my eye mask, swept by another surge of conscience. Poor Chris. My eye felt the size of a ping-pong ball; I could hardly believe the lids would close over it. Sliding the eye mask with great care over the afflicted area, I turned on to my right side and hugged a pillow for comfort. My brain was racing with ways to help Chris out; I couldn't recapture that earlier, charmed, deep sleep. Instead I lay uncomfortably for what felt like an eternity, suspended in that twitchy, dozy semi-consciousness that comes when the body wants to rest and the mind can't switch itself off, a twilight that never turns to night. I was positively grateful when the alarm went off.

Chapter Four

Clerkenwell was crawling with Rubber Ball attendees, converging on the area with a stealth and silence quite unlike the usual bright, drunken thronging would-be clubbers. Dressed in black, our shiny carapaces concealed under long dark overcoats, our heels clicked on the cobblestones like giant beetle claws. A couple across the street, dressed in dark ankle-length coats, caught my attention. The man turned his head assessingly as he heard my high heels and gave me a glance of identification. They were unmistakable: his hand resting on the back of her neck, her ducked head, were enough to declare them master and slave.

But as I rounded the corner of St John Street, the noise rose to meet me as if a volume control had just been slid up to maximum. I couldn't hear any music yet, just the heady babble of a large crowd of revellers sounding as excited as if they had just got out of prison on night release. Which for many of them was close to the truth. There was strength in numbers – as soon as perves found themselves surrounded by like-minded company, the party about to begin, they could let loose. Although the night was cold, plenty of people in the queue, unable to wait, had already taken off their outer layers and were flaunting with great enthusiasm the minimal amount they wore underneath. They might look like costumes, these arrangements of straps and chains and custom-moulded strips of vinyl; but, for the most part, they were expressions of the wearer's real self.

I passed a man wearing only black rubber briefs and the most beautiful, elaborate nipple clamps I had ever seen, like silver sunflower petals surrounding his nipples, which formed the head. I could see the edges of the petals digging in; the skin around them was already flushed.

Mel was halfway along the queue, wrapped in an ankle-length coat, the texture of which was so matt that it absorbed the light like a black hole. Her slave knelt subserviently at her feet, his rubber cape spilling out behind him on to the pavement. This was his first public appearance and apparently he was very nervous. Mel had been training him up hard and decided that tonight would be a perfect opportunity to make his come-out. It was very mild by fetish-world standards, a big dress-up party without any back rooms or torture implements. This was what I liked about the fetish scene, the opportunities it presented to behave badly and dress up outrageously in complete safety, and it shouldn't prove too frightening for a beginner.

'Hey,' I said in greeting. We didn't kiss, not wanting to spoil our careful makeup. 'I walked here from the tube and the streets are infested with people in black. It's like those horror films where swarms of dark insects eclipse the moon.'

'Or a vampire convention,' Mel suggested, looking at that moment very much like a vampire herself, or at least the popular conception of one: dark slick of hair, white face, hollowed cheeks, and the unnaturally scarlet mouth.

'I've always liked this area,' she added thoughtfully. 'Next to the meat market, very appropriate.' She gestured across the street to the arch of Smithfield market. 'We should hang up some bad slaves on the hooks every so often.'

The line moved forward and we all shuffled along. Leather coats scraped against the vinyl beneath, a soft and predatory sound, like rubbery bat wings unfolding. I felt sorry for Mel's slave, bare-kneed on cobblestones. Still, he was probably too excited to even notice his discomfort.

'This is Mistress Sophia,' Mel said to him coldly, indicating me with the black leather switch she carried tied to her wrist. 'If you're very lucky she might condescend to watch while I discipline you.'

He bobbed his head at me as nervously as a royal groupie greeting the Queen.

'Well, what are you waiting for, you stupid little worm! Greet her properly! You know I won't tolerate disrespect from you!'

Heads turned approvingly as the slave scrambled over to kiss my boots.

'Sorry, mistress,' he panted.

'And don't speak to me until I tell you to!' She kicked him in the chest with the sharp toe of her boot. 'Get behind me! I don't want to have to look at you, you disgusting failure.'

The man wearing sunflower clamps was staring at Mel in naked worship. His bad luck; she had her hands full tonight. Still, there were always other opportunities. If he could afford her.

'Love that wig,' Mel said to me, her voice returning to its normal tone.

'Thanks.'

I touched it in reflex. Long dark ringlets bouncing on my shoulders. Wigs were so miraculous: they transformed you so completely. For a few hours, this was the closest I would ever get to being somebody else. I was the exception here. For me, this was definitely a costume.

Under the pink neon sign at the entrance to the club, near-naked bodies glowed rosily. We handed our coats to the cloakroom girl. Mel's was heavily lined, and I had a zip-up fleece underneath which I checked in too. It looked ridiculous over PVC but would be vital later, when I had worked up a sweat dancing and needed to wrap up against the cold night air.

I hadn't made a huge effort in the dressing-up department. The hangover and mental exhaustion of that afternoon had left me depleted, and I had just pulled on one of my little PVC dresses, fishnets and stack-heeled shiny boots – basic fetish wear. But Mel, as always, was superb. She looked like the human equivalent of the switch she carried so negligently. Long and thin, she was clad in a black rubber halterneck sheath which flattened out her small pointed breasts till one could barely even see her nipples; the twin juts of her hipbones were considerably more prominent. The collar of the dress was fastened at her nape by an exaggeratedly huge silver buckle, apart from which her back was completely naked right down to the start of her narrow buttocks. Each vertebra stood out like a tiny knuckle, her spine as taut as a weapon. She looked striking in all senses of the word, almost inhuman. I could already see would-be slaves casting her yearning glances; two smooth, oiled boys in tiny rubber briefs were goggling at her as if they had just seen the Second Coming.

Meanwhile Mel was stripping down her own slave. When all his clothes were removed she finally refastened the rubber cape around his neck. All he wore apart from that was a cage arrangement around his penis and balls which looked potentially agonising. I looked away. Call me vanilla if you must, but there was something about seeing another set of genitals in close proximity to a lot of spiked metal that made my own close up tighter than a clenched fist.

'See?' Mel said to her slave. 'Mistress Sophia can't even bear to look at your pathetic cock. I'd make you go down the stairs on your knees if you weren't so pitifully clumsy. Up! Move!'

We did a circuit of the premises, partly to get our bearings, partly so that Mel could keep her slave moving. She said this helped to calm down high-spirited or nervous subjects who might otherwise get over-excited, both by the spectacle and the anticipation of how they would be called upon to play out their own role.

The club was filling up, but velvet curtains still covered the stage area. People were already in place around the catwalk, though, waiting for the show to start; I noticed a couple of TV crews setting up cameras. Great – that meant it should be a good show tonight. Others had already begun staging their own theatrical displays. Between the stage and the main bar was a channel seething with bodies draped over the meagre furniture in closely packed, writhing tableaus, fishnet-clad limbs spilling out, leaving only a small pathway down the centre.

Movement was by necessity slow, and I found myself paused in a traffic jam in front of a man holding a woman whose head was thrown back voluptuously while another woman bent at her feet, licking the patent heels of her stilettos. His eyes met mine; I looked back, enjoying him enjoying my voyeurism. He was dark, with a shaved head and a studded collar. Leaning forward over the body of the prone woman he was steadying, he kissed me on the mouth. It was just a brief pressure of the lips, but it was powerfully sexy; his breath was as warm against my skin as a hot breeze, his mouth full and smooth as fruit. How could Mel possibly say I was burnt out?

The logjam in front of me yielded. I moved on, smiling. Behind me I could hear Mel reprimanding her slave for crawling too slowly.

'Beat him!' a man's voice called out. 'Teach him a lesson!'

The kiss had energised me. I wanted to move. Shouting at Mel that I'd see her at the bar, I headed off in the direction of the thumping handbag house coming from the far end of the club. There was already a sizeable crowd on the dance floor; I worked myself into the centre and let rip. I loved to dance, and I was good at it. This was a discovery I had made with infinite satisfaction in my teenage years. I had never been part of the cool posses at school. I had never expected that I would be able to dance. Ever since then, it had never failed to make me happy.

Spinning round, I bumped into a slab of flesh, as solid as if it had been carved out of wood. It was a man as large as a wardrobe, wearing a black rubber singlet and black leather trousers. For a moment I thought his size was fat; then I saw his flat waist and realised that he was just built on a giant scale. His muscled frontage rose as sheer as a cliff. I looked up but he was so tall that I could hardly see his face.

'Sorry!' I mouthed.

He raised a hand to absolve my clumsiness. I couldn't be sure but I thought he was smiling. I looked around me. It was early yet, and the dance floor wasn't packed. He had been dancing closer to me than he needed to. I was very flattered. His body was amazing. I wiggled my fingers back at him flirtatiously and moved a little back to see if he would follow me. He didn't immediately, and a skinny guy with a stubbly little moustache and studded chest harness slipped in between us. I was very disappointed. Then the crowd moved and shifted with a change of song and suddenly Wardrobe Man was there in front of me again, edging Harness Moustache out of the way. It wasn't hard. His arm was practically as wide as Harness Moustache's whole body.

Just as events reached this promising turn – I was definitely feeling flirtatious tonight; I had Mel's gloomy prognosis to disprove – someone grabbed me from behind and practically goosed me. Swinging round angrily, I found myself freezing to the spot in disbelief, or as well as one can on a crowded dance floor.

'Hey, Jules! I found ya!' Liam yelled into my face.

He was wearing black leather trousers, and from the waist up he was naked. Around his neck was a big gold chain, which was wrong – gold like that was more gangsta than fetish style. But he had compensated for that mistake by lining his eyes with black pencil. This was striking, though more naughty-little-boy-playing-with-his-mother's-makeup than the decadent, *Cabaret*-influenced effect I bet he had been aiming for.

'Liam,' I said furiously. 'What are you doing here?'

'Having fun! It's great! I'm really glad you told me about it!'

He ground his hips against me.

'Fancy a dance, then?'

This was one moment at which I didn't find Liam remotely attractive. I was livid. His presence was enough to ruin my entire evening. How could I possibly go wild with my newest client lapping it all up and telling everyone in London about it tomorrow?

'No, I don't,' I snapped. 'I need a drink.'

I marched off the dance floor. I couldn't help throwing a glance of regret over my shoulder at Wardrobe Man. I couldn't tell for sure, but I thought I caught his eye, up there eight feet off the ground, and it seemed to me that he looked regret-ful too. Unfortunately I also saw that Liam was following right behind me. Great. I wouldn't be able to get rid of him for the whole night, and Wardrobe Man would think he was my boyfriend.

I got myself a gin and tonic and a bottle of water. Despite having crashed my evening out, Liam didn't offer to pay. It wasn't so much that he was used to the agency's always pick-ing up the tab – he had managed so far in life to get along on so much charm that others were prepared to buy most of his drinks for him. Liam liked older women, partly for their experience and partly for their deeper wallets. I had seen him get off with girls his own age, but right now he seemed more drawn to sugar mummies.

Well, tonight I was off-duty. I wasn't going to subsidise his enormous drinking habit and I didn't have to talk to him if I didn't want to. Sulking, I withdrew to a pillar at the back of the bar and leant back against it. Its paint was already sweaty against my bare shoulders from the heat of the crowds. I consoled myself with gin.

'Jules! There you are!' Liam clinked his beer bottle with my glass. 'I lost ya for a moment!'

His curls were defined with sweat, his blue eyes shiny.

'How did you know where this was?' I said crossly. 'I didn't tell you.'

He winked at me.

'Asked the lads in my local record shop,' he said. 'They've always got tons of flyers up.'

God, the fetish scene was getting so mainstream nowadays.

The crowd around the bar parted like the Red Sea to let Mel, slave in tow, walk through. She was talking to a friend of hers I recognised from previous nights out. Mel had been a regular on the fetish scene for years, way before it became so popular. As a result, she had a great deal of status. I loved coming out with her because I could bask in her reflected glory. The mere phrase 'Friend of Mel's' was enough to open a lot of doors.

'Heya,' she said to me, bringing her slave to a halt. 'Back so soon?'

Then she took in Liam. Mel didn't know who he was, but she could tell from my demeanour that all was not well with me. Her eyebrows went up.

'Who are you?' she said to him.

Liam was openly goggling at her. His eyes were stretched

as wide as they could go. The only difference between him and a cartoon character under hypnosis was the lack of crazy spirals spinning round and round the irises and the exclamation marks popping out of the top of his head. He couldn't get a word out.

'Mel, this is Liam O'Connell, my new client,' I said between my teeth. 'He just showed up here unexpectedly.'

I had told Mel enough about Liam already for her to realise the situation.

'Oh, *really*,' she said, openly sizing him up.

She took a sip of her drink. The slave shifted slightly at her ankles and she kicked out at him absently with one foot. Then she shrugged.

'I expect you deserve a little reward,' she said.

She dipped her fingers in the drink. They were loaded with rings, and the fingernails had been specially done for tonight, painted in black and silver with tiny symbols on the tip of each one. She let her hand fall by her side, and waited. The slave didn't move.

'Good,' she said. 'All right, you may drink.'

Eagerly he licked her fingers clean, looking pathetically grateful. He was mid-forties, with receding hair and a flabby paunch. It was hard to form more of an idea of him than that, even when I saw his face; he had subsumed himself so completely in his slave identity that his features seemed blurred, almost anonymous, as if he had blotted his individuality by sheer negative force of will.

Liam was enthralled. He had just about recovered his powers of speech, too.

'So,' he said, in an attempt at his usual cocky, flirtatious manner. It came off more as a parody, however. 'You come here often, then?'

Mel just looked at him. Her stare was like a form of

superpower with susceptible men. She didn't smile, or move her features in any way. She just stared at them.

'Expect that means yes,' he said feebly.

This was very promising. Maybe Liam would be so fascinated by Mel that he would trail after her like a dog all evening and leave me alone. That wouldn't exactly be fair to Mel, though.

'I was going to check out the show,' she said to me, ignoring Liam in a way that only made him keener to get her attention. 'Want to come along?'

'Sure.'

She looked down at her slave.

'I wonder if this deserves to come too,' she said. 'Perhaps I should simply tie it up here. We don't want it getting overexcited.'

'It' whimpered pitifully at the idea of being abandoned. This was precisely the reaction Mel had meant to elicit.

'Pathetic creature,' she said contemptuously, switching his bottom. I looked away. It wasn't the sight of the slave getting the punishment he craved that bothered me; it was his white, saggy, hairy bottom, barely covered by a leather thong. Ick. At least Mel didn't have to lie when she repeatedly told him how disgusting he was.

The TV crews I had noticed before were now jammed at the end of the catwalk among a phalanx of photographers. Bouncers from the club were ensuring that only the show, and the immediate spectators, got filmed. Any audience members who didn't want their faces on – I squinted at the camera logos – Dutch and German cable TV, just had to stay back in the crowd. Or zip up their masks.

Thrash metal blared out, and a series of impossibly tall models, clad only in huge metallic pieces of body jewellery and plenty of glitter, leaped down the catwalk, making animalistic gestures and snarling. A black guy in a tight corset and a beige rubber G-string, his hair a wild explosion of dreadlocks, danced among them, his arms upraised, holding a riding crop above his head, singing along with the music and pulling crazy faces. Beside me a flurry of movement sent me off-balance. I clutched at my drink as my neighbour steadied me. Cursing, I looked round to see who had pushed me and realised that it was Liam, thrusting his way through the crowd. He got hold of the edge of the catwalk and pulled himself up on to the stage.

The crowd went wild. Half of them were yelling: 'Get off!' and the other half were applauding madly. Liam, revelling in the attention, threw his arms wide and started gyrating his hips like a perverted Elvis impersonator. Then, playing to the cameras, he turned round, stuck his bottom in the air and started to spank himself. The girl beside me screamed her appreciation. The guy with the riding crop was dancing even more frenziedly, competing with Liam's antics. One of the models pranced over to Liam. In her five-inch heels and towering hairdo, she was at least a foot taller than he was. She grabbed hold of the waistband of his leather trousers and mimed pulling them down for the benefit of the audience. They loved it. Liam's hands were busy at his crotch. I knew exactly what was coming. I could barely watch. Sure enough, the trousers loosened and started falling down his legs. Underneath he was wearing boxers. The crowd booed their disappointment.

The model, mugging for the audience, spanked Liam once hard on the bottom and started to pull down the boxers. His arse crack had only just come into view when a pair of bouncers erupted from behind the curtain and grabbed hold of him under the arms. Much taller than Liam, they swung him right off the ground, his trousers dangling at his ankles. Defiantly, Liam wiggled his bottom for all he was worth as they carried him off-stage to the mingled cheers and boos of the crowd.

Mel tapped me on the shoulder.

'That's him gone for the evening!' she yelled in my ear.

I took in her expression. She looked very smug.

'Did you do that?' I shouted back in disbelief.

Mel's lips curved in a bright red shiny V.

'Told him I bet he could do better than that bloke in the corset!' she yelled back. 'He didn't exactly need much encouragement, he was up there before I finished saying it!'

A combination of Liam's natural exhibitionism and his wish to impress Mel – no wonder it hadn't taken much.

'I owe you big time!' I shouted in her ear.

'Forget it! Piece of piss!' she yelled back.

I was free. Exhilaration swept through me. I felt so light I could have jumped up and danced on the stage too.

I turned and forged my way back through the orgy pit. It was lit all in red, and I expect to a less accustomed eye might have seemed like a pit of hell. But it took only a few moments to appreciate the oddly formal yet explicit way the participants were fondling each other, clear demarcation lines in each group of what each would permit. The atmosphere could not have been happier; a good aura permeated the room like the red glow backlighting the action. It was a fetishists' love-in.

I got my beer and stood drinking it, watching the red-lit mass of writhing bodies before me. This was a perfect moment. I felt as if we were all sharing a huge, wonderful secret. Inside these walls the most raucous and crazy scenes could unfold, everyone celebrating a Bacchanal without the need to rip any ritual victims to pieces: and then we would all put on our coats and slink off into the night again, anonymous and solitary as before. My feet were twitching to the beat I could hear pounding through the corridors from the dance floor, like the fallout from a constant series of explosions. I hadn't danced enough.

The dance floor was hot and slippery and intoxicating. In

its centre a boy on a podium gyrated madly, his face running with perspiration, his expression ecstatic. His outfit, an all-in-one singlet and cycling shorts, like a 1920s male swimsuit, looked as tight as a sausage skin. Every so often he would lift one leg slightly and the sweat accumulated underneath the rubber would run out down his thigh, a hot salty stream tinted white by the talcum powder he had applied to help him pull on the suit. I was there only a couple of minutes before someone found me, as I had hoped. Wardrobe Guy appeared, moving in front of me in a way that left no room for doubt as to what his intentions were, smiling as if we had arranged to meet right here and he was happy that I had kept my promise.

I kept dancing automatically, sneaking glances up at him through my eyelashes. He was actually very good looking, and his body was pretty godlike, if you liked muscles, which I did. He knew I was checking him out, and he moved in closer, dancing so his hips were right up against me, smiling down at me with that same easy, unaffected smile that earlier I had taken to signal lack of interest. And it happened, the click that happens when someone is that close to you, and you know at once if you like it or not; I found myself smiling back, and letting him dance with me, and a few seconds later his arm was around my waist and we were sliding against each other. The music rose higher, louder, blocking out anything but him, his rubber singlet, the smooth golden chest underneath.

It was intoxicating, but a little overwhelming, as if I were falling into him, losing myself. I pulled back, reluctantly; but I needed to catch my breath. He looked down at me quizzically.

'You're too tall for me!' I shouted up at him, wanting to inject some humour into the situation.

He laughed and said something I didn't catch. We kept dancing, and after a few moments he held out his hand to me, nodding his head towards the far wall. My hand was in his before I knew it, and it felt so good, so big and warm, that I found myself following him, through the packed masses on the dance floor, over to a concrete block against the wall. God, the width and solidity of his back, the black rubber tight around it, his golden shoulders rising above the singlet like twin mountain ridges . . . He sat down on the block, legs wide, and guided me gently towards him. I stood looking down at his handsome face, brown ruffled hair, eyes gleaming with excitement, the well-defined caps of muscle on his shoulders. Wow. I bent down and kissed him, a low slow touch of my lips against his, like a screen kiss from an old film. Then I straightened up again and surveyed the effect.

His expression mirrored mine, or at least how I felt I must look. Smug, with that ridiculously self-satisfied smugness that sweeps over two people who have just confirmed their mutual attraction; we were glowing with anticipation, unable to stop smiling, unable to keep our hands off one another. He pulled me towards him and kissed me, his arms wrapping round my back, one huge hand on my shoulder, so warm I leant into it like a cat wanting to be stroked, bracing myself so I didn't lose my balance. I wound my hands in his hair and worked my tongue into his mouth and gave myself up completely to what we were doing. Nothing else but this, nothing to think about, completely safe in this place from any consequences, a man I had met ten minutes ago whose name I didn't even know; nothing could be more liberating.

Time dissolved, slowed to nothing, speeded up like a clock whose mechanism is loose and whose hands spin crazily round and round the dial. I had no idea how much later it was when, needing to take our hands and mouths temporarily away from each other's to avoid complete insanity setting in, we went to get a beer – his back, shouldering a way through the crowd, was solid as flesh over a carved oak statue – and leant against a pillar, kissing, passing mouthfuls of cold beer to each other, licking the spills off one another's chins. I was dimly aware of something happening in the area of my lower back but paid no attention till he looked over my shoulder and tapped me, signalling me to turn round.

Mel had been poking me in the back with her switch.

'Don't know why I bothered!' she said, laughing. 'I should just have left you. I'm off.' She took in my new acquaintance with that swift up-and-down glance that could strip a man bare in a quarter of a second. Leaning towards me, half-yelling in my ear, she said: 'What is it, Shag A Giant week? Didn't you say the one last week was six-three?'

'Bye, Mel,' I said firmly. 'Have a nice life.'

Her slave, sitting back on his heels, looked utterly exhausted and deliriously happy.

'Time to go home,' she said, nodding towards him. 'You're staying, yeah?'

Pieter – that was his name; he was Dutch; these were practically the only pieces of factual information we had exchanged, beyond the locations of our upper-body erogenous zones – caught that. He took my hand in his, enveloping it as completely as if it were a child's.

'You're staying?' he said anxiously.

I smiled at him. His expression of concern dissolved immediately. So did Mel; she might not have existed for me. I didn't even see her go. Pieter was pulling me towards him insistently, and I let myself follow.

'Yeah,' I said against his mouth, which smelt of fresh beer. 'I'm staying.'

Chapter Five

'Jesus,' Lewis said respectfully. 'You look like death.'

'Shit,' I said, instantly depressed at my failure to pass for human. 'Could you get me some—'

'Cappuccino with a double shot of espresso? Right on it. You want a pain au chocolat too?'

'I will have your babies if you want me to, Lewis. When I said it before I was joking. But now I really mean it.'

I fumbled in my purse for some money. He waved his hand dismissively as he reached for his jacket.

'Give it to me later. When your hands stop shaking.'

'Oh God.'

My office was behind Lewis's; it was small, poky and eccentrically shaped, but it had a window over Brewer Street. Hidden from view by the open door, I checked myself out in the mirror, and sighed. There hadn't been much I could do with the raw material. Four hours sleep was just not enough. I had used all the weapons in my beauty arsenal, but even the heaviest guns hadn't helped much. First thing this morning I had looked as though I had soaked my face overnight in bleach before rubbing kohl into the circles under my eyes.

I was a badly done patchwork. The lightening cream under my eyes was the worst offender. It was supposed to reflect the light and conceal the dark circles beneath, and was performing this task so successfully that the rest of my face looked like old cooked veal by comparison.

I sighed again, took off my coat, hung it on the peg, sat

down at my desk and turned on the computer, opening my endless list of Things To Do For Liam's Launch. All this activity was so exhausting that I could do nothing but stare blankly at the busy screen until Lewis returned with my coffee and pastry.

'Hypnotised by the screensaver?' he said.

'What?' I roused myself. 'Uhh. Coffee.' I popped the plastic lid.

'You went to the Italian place, right?'

'*Certamente.*'

'Good boy. Get one for yourself?'

'Yup.'

He sat down opposite me and sipped at his own.

'Aah, God, this is good,' I said through a mouthful of chocolate and buttery pastry. 'Italian cappuccino. Fuck those American chains and their grande super-lattes with extra foam.'

'I like you in a poloneck,' Lewis said appreciatively. He was always noticing what people wore; this tendency, when I first met him, had led me to speculate that he might be gay. He was always well groomed, well dressed – in clothes that actually fit him – polite, charming and attentive. One could see why my doubts had arisen. 'You should wear polonecks more often,' he added. 'They make your neck look really long.'

I spluttered into my coffee. I had had to wear my poloneck because my neck was liberally adorned with red sucky marks. A turtleneck would have done for the bruises, which started lower down – Pieter simply hadn't known his own strength – but the lovebites had required emergency measures.

'Something I said?' Lewis asked, his eyebrows raising, or rather pivoting. His brows were two thick straight lines and when he asked a question, they hinged upwards from the outer corners like Tower Bridge opening to let a boat through.

'No, no,' I lied. 'Just a little delicate this morning.'

My phone rang. In my debilitated state it sounded as loud as a car alarm.

'Want me to get that?' Lewis asked, reaching for the receiver as I nodded gratefully.

'Hello, Juliet Cooper's office,' he said politely. 'Yes, she is – let me just check if she's still in a meeting –'

He clicked the Hold button.

'Melanie from PVC Incorporated, want to take it?' he asked.

'Yeah. Thanks. Can you shut my door and tell everyone not to disturb me?'

'No prob.'

'You're a bright shining star, Lewis.'

'Twinkle twinkle,' he said, closing the door behind him. I picked up the phone.

'Mel?'

'So what happened with the Incredible Hunk?'

'Oh –' I sipped at my cappuccino foam, feeling it cling lovingly to my upper lip – 'it was really nice.'

'God, you sound gooey.'

'Well, it was,' I said defensively. 'He was so sweet. We ended up going back to his hotel room – he's Dutch, he was here on business, left this morning.'

'Did you shag him?'

Shit, shit, shit. I had been hoping that Mel wouldn't ask.

'We fooled around for hours and hours,' I said airily. 'It was fabulous. Did you have fun? I thought the show was great, didn't you?'

Mel ignored this pathetic attempt to distract her.

'Don't tell me you didn't shag this one either!' she said in utter disapproval.

My shoulders slumped.

'I knew you were going to give me a hard time about that,' I wheedled. 'But—'

'More than you let that poor bastard give you.'

I couldn't help giggling at this, despite my embarrassment. Brief three-dimensional snaps of memory flashed through my mind, like a kind of photograph that hadn't yet been invented; us in a metal-walled toilet cubicle at the club, squatting down on the black tiled floor, me cutting lines of coke on the toilet cover while he lifted my hair to kiss the back of my neck, his large body filling the tiny cubicle; me straddling his leather-covered knee, laughing, saying: 'Don't pull my wig off!' and the look of amazement on his face as he realised; watching the stage show, his hand over my PVC-covered breast, stroking it hard as I ground myself back against him; on his hotel room bed, lying on top of him, kissing him, him groaning into my mouth: 'The sound our clothes make together, it's so sexy,' just as I pulled him up so I could drag off his rubber vest, roll it up his big smooth chest and feel his skin against mine . . .

'It was lovely,' I said dreamily. I licked the foam off my upper lip. The mere action of licking reminded me so vividly of him that my groin twitched convulsively in reflex. 'He was called Pieter. A financial controller from Amsterdam. Freaky or what?'

Mel sighed, long and deeply.

'You going to see him again?'

'He asked for my phone number, so I gave it to him. I mean, why not? He'll probably be over in London for work again.'

I started giggling again. 'You should have seen me on the Euston Road this morning, coming out of the hotel. I looked so fucking smug everyone was staring at me – you know, what's she got to look so pleased about at eight in the morning, when we're all off to work? And then I noticed this guy staring at my coat pocket, sort of mesmerised with revulsion, and I realised that half my wig was sticking out. God knows what he must have thought.'

'Fuck,' Mel suggested, 'that girl's pubes are completely out of control?'

We laughed, and I hoped Mel would leave the subject there. Of course she didn't. I should have known better.

'I can't believe you did this again, Jules,' she said, her tone serious. I quailed. Mel serious was very scary indeed. 'You have a real block developing here.'

'Oh, come on,' I protested as lightly as I could manage. 'Two swallows don't make a summer.'

'You swallowed?'

'No, I meant –'

'Oh, right.'

'Look, could we try to see it not so much as a *block* but . . .' I scrabbled for the right word, 'a little pause?'

'Hmph. Frankly, I think that you like this one because he's from fucking Holland and you'll never have to think about whether you actually want to have a relationship with him.'

'Oh, *Mel.*'

There was a pause as this sank in.

'You know, I had a fake tattoo on my ankle last week,' I said finally, 'and Richard asked if it was real. And I said: "Don't be silly, Richard, of course it isn't. I can't even commit to a tattoo." And everyone laughed. I mean, I meant it as a joke. But then I realised that actually, it wasn't.'

Another silence fell.

'Oh, I had a great idea this morning,' I said, not just to change the subject. 'I thought I'd ask Gill to supervise the cooking for Liam's launch. We can't get in one of our normal caterers because all the food we're serving's from his book and they won't cook other people's recipes. Gill could organise that really well though, it's just up her street. I can hire the premises for her and she can get in whatever staff she wants. Don't you think that's a great idea?'

'Yeah, brilliant. But—'

'Oh, and thanks for seeing Liam off last night,' I said, still talking fast to avoid the subject of my commitment-phobia.

'No problem. It was my night for sorting people out, anyway. Some stupid cow got drunk and her slave went completely berserk. You know I hate that. Nothing worse than a mistress who can't control her slave.'

'Oh dear.' I felt sorry for the mistress. No doubt she had been on the receiving end of a strict lecture from Mel.

'Well, I'll let you get back to work. But I'll see you soon,' she said ominously. 'We need to talk properly.'

Oh God. I really was in trouble.

I put off ringing Gill till the next day. I knew that if I talked to her about catering for the party I would get on to the subject of last night, and I wasn't up to talking about my new weird problem to any more close friends. Instead I spent the rest of the day sorting out Liam's media commitments and the evening lying in bed, eating a comfort meal of microwaved risotto with grated Cheddar melting succulently on top (yes, that's exactly the kind of thing food PRs eat on their rare evenings in), while replaying selected highlights of my night with Pieter. I had a whole series of fantasies for future encounters, should he ever get in touch with me, but as these progressed I had to admit that Mel might have had a point. All of my projected scenarios involved him and me meeting in foreign countries where we would meet at midnight in dark cocktail bars, attend fetish clubs, and have sex in a variety of implausible locations. None of my fantasies took place in daylight, nor were they remotely romantic: no country-hotel weekends, no intimate dinners, no letting him anywhere near my flat and certainly no long conversations where we lay in one another's arms and told each other about our childhoods.

It was when I remembered having told Pieter in the club that my name was Sophia that I realised how right Mel had been. Talk about fear of intimacy. I finished the one glass of wine I had allowed myself and put on a porn film to distract myself from my psychological shortcomings.

The phone rang at about ten-thirty. I had turned off the light only a few minutes before and was already dropping off to sleep, further lubricious fantasies of Pieter lulling my tired muscles. Or rather, bits of Pieter. It was as if I had spent our time together concentrating on individual parts of him with such attention that they were more vivid to me than him in his entirety. I could picture perfectly his chest, tanned golden, with those tiny flat rosy-pink nipples, like studs set into his skin; his forearms, smooth and solid, his fingers, his chin . . .

I picked up the phone half convinced that it was him ringing to ask me to pack all my PVC items of clothing and meet him in a hotel in Paris next weekend. Just because I hadn't been able to have sex with him last night didn't mean I wouldn't manage it on a second date. Well, OK, call it a second meeting.

'Hello?' I said hopefully.

'Juliet,' my mother purred softly. My temples tightened as if she had put a vice around them. I knew this tone of voice: forgiving, saintly, it indicated that though I had recently committed various sins of omission towards her, she had already pardoned me out of the goodness of her heart. It would still be necessary, however, for her to rehash my iniquities for my benefit, showing me where I had gone wrong. We might not be Catholic, but Mum had the Mother Superior act down to a fine art.

'Hi, Mum,' I said warily.

'I told your brother to ask you to ring me,' she said gently, 'but perhaps he forgot.'

My heart sank. I heard it fall.

'No, he didn't,' I said, sighing. 'I've just been really busy.'

Already she had elicited an admission of guilt and a weak excuse. My mother's technique was superb.

'Oh, I see. Yes, Chris did say he caught you at a bad time.'

If Chris had told Mum I was in bed with an afternoon hangover when he rang, he was dead meat.

'Such a shame Chris didn't get that job in the restaurant,' she went on. 'He was so optimistic about it. I thought it was as good as settled.'

Instant depression and a whacking load of guilt. This always happened when Mum talked to me about Chris. She would dump his latest problem on to my shoulders and expect me to come up with a solution. And when I couldn't, as was often the case, I was the one she blamed for the failure.

'I know,' I said tentatively. 'Me too. I think he might have played some of his more gloomy songs, though. I was a bit worried when he told me. I mean, it's a café, not a club. I think they probably wanted something more relaxing.'

I turned on the bedside light and sat up against the headboard. I was fully awake now, and it was a mistake to be too relaxed when talking to my mother; all my senses needed to be on full alert.

'I'm sure your brother knows what he's doing, Juliet,' Mum reprimanded me. 'He must be the best judge of his own music.'

And every time I did offer some suggestion, if it wasn't what Mum wanted to hear I got snubbed for it. I should just have taken the hitback womanfully and let it go; but tonight the familiar old pattern made me resentful, and I persisted.

'Still, even if he'd got that job,' I pointed out, 'the money wouldn't have been that much. I mean, he'd have eaten free a couple of nights a week, but that's about it. He needs to think bigger.'

'What do you suggest he does?' my mother said with awful sarcasm. 'I expect you want him to take a job writing Muzak for McDonald's?'

I writhed.

'It wasn't Muzak, it was jingles,' I said wearily.

A couple of years ago I had met through work a man who ran a very successful jingle-writing company – musical tag-lines for ads – and pitched Chris to him. Chris could write catchy tunes, when he wanted to – though usually he didn't. Still, I had thought that it might be a way for him to subsidise his real songwriting, and the jingle guy, as a favour to me, had told me that he'd listen to a tape Chris put together and had even said that Chris could ring him to get an idea of what was required. It had seemed a good idea to me, or at least one not so paltry as to be dismissed out of hand. Particularly as I had had to flirt madly with the guy to get him to agree.

Unfortunately, both Mum and Chris had reacted as if my sole intent in making the contact had been to humiliate Chris. Chris had forgotten all about it by now but Mum had used it ever since as a stick to beat me with.

'I still can't believe you wanted your brother to write *jingles*,' Mum said contemptuously.

'It wasn't as bad as it sounded, Mum,' I muttered defensively for the umpteenth time. 'I just thought it might be a way for him to earn really good money, working part-time. Chris writes tunes so easily, I thought he could just dash a few off . . . What's so bad about that?'

'If you can't see for yourself . . .' my mother sighed.

'There's nothing wrong with supporting yourself financially

till you get a break. Salman Rushdie wrote advertising copy before he became a novelist,' I pointed out. This was a piece of information I had read recently and stored for the next time this topic came up.

Mum merely sniffed and refused to answer, her usual practice when her interlocutor made a good point. I ground my teeth in frustration.

'So how have you been?' I said finally, feeling driven to it.

'I was wondering when you'd ask.' She sighed yet again. 'So busy. I've hardly had a moment to myself. I had the Holmeses and the Davises and Jean Withers over to dinner on Saturday. The *work*, Juliet. You have no idea how hard it is entertaining people.'

'I do work in PR, Mum.' I tried not to make this too sarcastic, but I might as well not have bothered. She ignored it completely.

'I was on my feet from eight in the morning to seven in the evening, at the stove. It did my legs no good at all. I was in terrible pain the next day.'

Mum suffered from varicose veins. They were one of her pet complaints, or excuses.

'And then the washing-up! I was at the sink till one in the morning!'

I took the receiver away from my mouth and stared at it in disbelief before replacing it, saying: 'But, Mum, you have a dishwasher.'

'I can't put Grandma's dishes through the dishwasher, Juliet! Don't be so ridiculous!'

'I'm not being ridiculous,' I said stiffly, 'and don't be dismissive. I didn't know you were using Grandma's plates – I mean, why? It's just the Holmeses and—'

'I'll be the judge of that, thank you,' Mum snapped.

'I was just thinking of your legs,' I said crossly. None of

Mum's ailments ever prevented her from doing something she really wanted to do; but then of course she could complain about the pain retrospectively. Either way she won. If one could call it winning.

'Well, don't,' she said coldly. 'The amount of sympathy I get from you I can do without.'

'So what did you cook?' I said, trying to mollify her.

'Oh, vegetable terrine, with different layers, beef en croute with those layered potatoes in cream, green beans, stuffed roasted tomatoes – I must have done five main courses – then cinnamon meringues with strawberries and syllabub. Then of course I had to make coffee. I was totally exhausted by the time they finally went.'

'I'm not surprised. Sounds like you made a banquet.'

'Oh, I had to. Had to,' she repeated. 'I owed the Davises a dinner, and Jean is always very hospitable. I didn't have a choice.'

I should just have kept my mouth shut. Sometimes I managed it; more often I didn't. Chris, if he had been listening to the conversation, would have told me I had brought it completely on myself.

'Oh, Mum,' I said fatally, unable to bear this catalogue of woe and helplessness, 'there's always a choice.'

I asked for it, and I got it. Mum exploded.

'What do you know about choices?' she said bitingly. 'You with your nice flat and your nice job? You lead an entirely selfish life, Juliet, you think of no one but yourself. You certainly don't care about your poor brother in his council flat, trying so hard to make a career with some artistic worth, struggling to make ends meet!'

No matter how strapped for cash he was, Chris always seemed to have enough money for dope. I didn't bring this up, however.

'And you've always been contradictory and aggressive. You've done nothing this whole conversation but pick at me. Well, I'm tired, it's late, and I don't need this. I didn't call you on my own money to be contradicted! I wanted a nice relaxing talk with my daughter, and look what I got!'

I knew what was coming.

'Don't hang up on me, Mum!' I said angrily, a second before the line clicked off.

I held the receiver to my chest, taking a series of deep breaths. Mum had a marked tendency to hang up if the conversation wasn't going the way she liked it. That line about calling me on her own money was vintage; I had heard it a thousand times, and it always preceded the receiver being slammed down. Still, it was my own fault; I'd provoked her. Why couldn't I just let things go? Why did her wild exaggerations and complaints about her perfectly nice life annoy me so much? That last rant had been indistinguishable from all the others with which she had favoured me over the years; but it never became so familiar that I could tune it out, relegate it to the category of interference on the line. My heart was pounding and I wanted to cry.

Miserably I put the phone on the hook, turned out the light again and slid back down my pillows. All happy thoughts of Pieter blotted out. I felt terrible. And Mum, having purged her bile, would probably now be making a cup of tea, congratulating herself on having told me what was what, and settling down for the night with the clearest of consciences. It was very unfair.

Chapter Six

I had a rule never to ring my mother back after she had hung up on me, at least until enough time had passed so that I wouldn't feel I was crawling back to lick the hand that had hit me. Still, I felt her presence in the ether the next day, hovering over me, noticing the grubby surround of the sink as I brushed my teeth, clicking her tongue in disapproval at the waste as I clumsily snagged a pair of tights and had to break open a new pack, drawing in her breath with shock at the extravagant price I was prepared to pay for my morning cappuccino and brioche. (The diet went only so far. I mean, what was I supposed to eat for breakfast?) The first thing I did when I got into work was to ring my cleaning lady – I was still haunted by the state of the sink – and arrange for her to come in that week. That was another mark against me for extravagance; my mother wouldn't have dreamt of paying someone else to clean her own house. Women who did came well below pond scum on her disapproval rating.

Being a boy, Chris, of course, got the full package: clean-up of his room and the communal areas of his house once a fortnight, plus complete door-to-door laundry service, with optional meals-on-wheels. He didn't even bother to tidy up before she came, just sat in the kitchen with a cup of tea while she bustled around, criticising his girlfriend's housekeeping skills. Though he did help her carry upstairs the pile of clean, ironed sheets.

My teeth were grinding again. Sometimes I thought my

mother had implanted a series of switches in my head when I was a baby. And she had the control panel.

I managed to distract myself to some degree at work. The morning was taken up by our weekly planning meeting, and my summary of Liam's upcoming interviews and the plans for the launch party went so well that Richard took me out to lunch. This was a signal mark of favour, but I felt I had deserved it. Not wanting to seem as if I were neglecting all my other clients in favour of Liam, I had managed to get several editorial plugs for the Belgian chocolates. Richard even told me with great bonhomie to remember that now I was a partner I mustn't hesitate to give fuller rein to my expense account.

'That's what it's there for, darling,' he said. 'Entertaining. We want you out there charming all London into using our superb services, don't we? Well, don't be shy about it. Go forth and multiply your receipts.'

This was music to my ears. I had been worried I was already racking up my card too much. It's a woman's problem; in my experience, men assume they're entitled to exploit their expense accounts to the full, and the more confident they are, the less anyone challenges them on it. Whereas women, with a lesser sense of entitlement, are more nervous and apologetic about spending company money, and as a result people come down on them much harder. I made a note to take my card for granted in future. Lewis had been a tower of strength on the chocolate front. I would have to take him out for some expensive cocktails to thank him for his help.

Early evening was a launch for a range of flavoured jello shots at a bar in Berkeley Square. We had the account, and the drill was that as many of us as possible should turn up for any agency launch. As had been anticipated, the product drew the crowds much more successfully than our previous event, a British Beef promotion at which making conversation with the British Beef people had been harder going than a rutted cart track in Wales halfway through a blizzard. As a newly fledged partner I had felt duty-bound to attend. I had spent three nightmare hours nodding my head in feigned fascination as a British Beef bigwig rabbited on about the loneliness and isolation of the average British Beef farmer. By the end of the evening I would have asked for nothing better than to be set down in some nice isolated farmhouse miles from anywhere with a shotgun by the door to discourage rambling red-faced old bores from coming anywhere near me.

'Wow,' Lewis said, holding a small plastic cup of bison vodka and cranberry jelly over his mouth. He squeezed the bottom with one deft pinch of his fingers, allowing just enough air up the sides to loosen the jello. It slid out of the cup, its shape as perfect as a well-made sandcastle, and plopped neatly into his mouth.

'I can't do it that well,' I complained, trying with mine (pepper vodka and Bloody Mary mix tomato jelly). I held it above my open mouth for half a minute, attempting to imitate Lewis's pinching gesture. During that time I ran the full gamut of embarrassment from A to Z, while the jelly stayed firmly in its cup, wobbling at me with what looked suspiciously like a smirk.

'Fuck it,' I said finally, conceding defeat, and popped the little spoon off the lid of the cup. 'Mmn, this is nice. Kind of odd, but nice.'

Lewis took another jello shot from the tray that the regulation eyebrow-pierced, goateed, black-clad waiter was carrying round. In New York, waiting staff were supposed to look like Identikits from a model factory; in London, however, the preferred look was counter-culture, as if we wanted them to keep us up to date by demonstrating the absolute latest in facial tufts.

'What's this one?' Lewis – who would have been much sought-after as a waiter in New York – asked the young musician/actor/whatever.

'Lemon vodka, citrus jelly,' said the m/a/w lugubriously.

'Ooh, that sounds good. I'll have one too.' I reached for one. 'Is that candied peel at the bottom?'

The waiter stared at me morosely and moved on without answering.

'God,' Lewis said, 'he was like the gloomy butler in a bad horror film. You know, the one who leads you to your room and won't answer any of your questions about what that strange rattling noise is behind the fireplace.'

'Juliet? Juliet! There you are.'

Richard swooped down on me. Swoop was exactly the right verb. Richard was tall and bony, with wide, knobbed shoulders hunched up to his ears in an effort to disguise his height. His balding head, sunk between these outcroppings, and the habit he had of darting it from side to side, completed his resemblance to a bird of prey. He always wore polonecks; these clung unflatteringly to his vertebrae, which were as prominent as Adam's apples. Many people in PR did impressions of Richard, and a couple of them could imitate him with such accuracy it brought tears to the eyes.

'Someone I want you to meet,' Richard was saying. He nodded politely at Lewis as he swept me over to a couple of men in suits. They had to be the clients.

'Klaus, Johan, this is Juliet Cooper, our newest partner and a rising star in the agency. Juliet, Klaus Senn, the MD of Eis Vodka. And this is Johan Groothuizen, his deputy.'

We all shook hands. Richard beamed at us as benevolently as was possible for a man with a strong resemblance to a vulture, and strode off to network with someone else.

'These shots are absolutely delicious,' I said, spooning up

the last of my citrus jelly. Flatter the client: first rule of PR. 'I'm sure they'll do really well.'

'Thank you!' said Klaus Senn, smiling and adjusting his tie. 'Well, Richard has done a wonderful job,' he continued. 'We are very pleased.'

'The ads look great,' I said sincerely. 'Shooting them out like bullets – very clever. Just a shame you couldn't package them like bullets too.'

'It was not practical,' said Johan. 'Unfortunately. That would have looked very striking indeed.'

Klaus sounded unmistakably German, which was understandable, since Eis was a German company. But Johan's accent was, for some reason, eerily familiar.

'Are you Dutch, by any chance?' I said curiously.

'Yes!' He looked very pleased that I had got it right. 'Yes, I am from Amsterdam. How did you know?'

'Oh –' I hoped I wasn't blushing – 'I met a guy, uh, someone, in a club a couple of nights ago and his accent was just like yours.' I waved my hand in a vague gesture. 'Also he was very tall. Like you. Are all Dutch guys so, um, big?'

It was lucky none of my colleagues had heard that one. I wasn't even drunk, not on three jello shots. It was the memory of Pieter still gooing up my synapses, causing idiotic things to come out of my mouth whenever the conversation skewed round to any reference to him. Let a week pass, and it would all be over; until then I was doomed to make a fool of myself.

Johan, however, seemed positively flattered. And Klaus Senn was laughing.

'You have tall men in England, no?' he said. 'Richard is very tall.'

'Yes, but not, um, big.' I was digging myself into such a hole here. 'You know. Wide.'

I made another gesture, this one flapping and rather desperate, as if I were semaphoring a non-existent friend to come and rescue me. Johan intercepted my hand and removed the empty plastic cup, summoning a waiter and depositing it in his tray.

'Have you tried the blueberry shot?' he said. 'It's very good.'

Without waiting for my answer, he took one off the tray and handed it to me.

'Thanks,' I said feebly.

'It's true,' he said amiably, 'we are very big in Holland. But, you know, we appreciate the differences when we come abroad. Your hair, for instance. Nobody in Holland has hair this colour.'

'Oh.' I touched my hair automatically. 'I don't have hair this colour either, actually.'

'It is dyed?' said Klaus.

'Afraid so.' I made a self-deprecating face.

'Still, it is very pretty,' he said kindly.

'Thank you.'

The one advantage to having mousy hair was that it could be dyed practically any colour one wanted. At the moment it was a dark red which my colourist had poetically compared to falling oak leaves. Autumn was upon us, and the colour had seemed very appropriate.

I dug into the blueberry jello, feeling that my conversational skills were so poor this evening that I could only redeem myself by appreciating their product. Naturally I would have complimented it even if it had tasted of fish oil and rancid cheese, but fortunately I didn't have to feign appreciation.

'This is delicious,' I said fervently. 'I think it's my favourite so far.'

They both beamed at me. Klaus fiddled briefly with his tie again. Since it hadn't needed any adjustment, and in fact looked exactly the same after as before, I assumed that this was his usual technique for dealing with praise.

'Have you tried the vodkas straight?' Klaus enquired. 'They are really excellent. The blueberry one is particularly good.'

'And they are not too sweet, like most flavoured vodkas,' Johan chimed in seriously. 'We went through many, many testings before we approved them.'

'I know,' I said, finishing my shot with a deft twist of the spoon. 'Some of the other ones taste like you're drinking perfume.'

This observation was a roaring success. Klaus even clapped his hands in pleasure.

'This is exactly what we said to ourselves! Exactly! Like drinking perfume!'

'Who's drinking perfume?' Richard said, descending on us again. 'Mind you, a lot of the stuff nowadays smells like you could drink it, doesn't it? All that vanilla they put in perfumes nowadays. Remember those massage bars who wanted us to take their account, Juliet? Looked like soap, smelt like cake, went very odd after it'd been on for ten minutes.'

He surveyed the room.

'This is all going very well, isn't it?' he commented cheerfully.

'Very well,' Klaus agreed just as happily, toying with the end of his tie. I wondered what he used as a substitute when he was naked. Well, ties were supposed to represent the phallus, weren't they?

'We were just regretting that it is you who manages our account, weren't we, Johan?' he was saying jocularly. 'Why did we not meet Juliet first? We could have had a pretty girl – excuse me, woman –' he corrected himself, nodding politely in my direction – 'to come to all our meetings. *Nicht war*, Johan?'

'Absolutely,' Johan said with unmistakable significance. And he looked me straight in the eye.

I was a little taken aback. Not by Klaus's heavy-handed compliment, which was pretty much par for the course, but Johan's interest. I didn't usually get chatted up by straight-looking businessmen in suits. Still, Pieter probably looked just as respectable as Johan in his work clothes. An image of the latter dressed in a rubber vest and leather trousers flashed before my eyes. It was not at all unpleasant.

'She'd have done a very nice job for you,' Richard said, patting me on the shoulder. Luckily I was wearing heels; he was so much taller than me that otherwise his hand would have landed on the top of my head. Richard was liable to this sort of physical contact with the female members of the agency, unusually for a man in these times of sexual-harassment suits. But nobody was going to sue. It was an open secret that Richard was gay.

Meanwhile, I was readjusting my idea of Johan. In *Atlas Shrugged*, the heroine says that while most people feel much better about themselves when they realise that someone else finds them attractive, she's the opposite – her estimation of the other person rises sharply when she knows that they're after her. I had always thought this a damn fine philosophy. I was much more interested in Johan now I thought that he had the good taste to fancy me.

I gave Johan a more detailed survey. He had a good body, as far as I could see under the grey suit; a nice face, not hand-some, but with a good deal of decision about it; grey eyes, a little pouchy, but with a direct stare which boded very well; fair hair, which might thin later but looked reasonably plenti-ful for now. One would have to get his clothes off, really, or at least see him in a t-shirt and jeans. No wonder men preferred suits, no matter how much they complained about them: look at all the flaws they were capable of hiding.

From the bar I could see Lewis signalling. He was talking to a young soap actress who had been invited to lend some glamour to the launch and had turned up dressed to the nines. She looked more than happy in Lewis's company. I couldn't blame her. Besides his undoubted good looks, Lewis was so skilled at making himself pleasant to women I suspected him of having taken a How To Be A Gigolo correspondence course. I speculated as to what Lewis would be like in bed. Maybe a little too confident. Young men as handsome as Lewis often have the kind of confidence that comes from having had lots of one-night stands, rather than long-term experience, which is the only real way to learn. Still, I bet he'd be sure enough of himself to listen when you told him what you liked, which was always a big plus point.

The actress was throwing back her head and laughing in a way that signalled to me that Lewis was probably on to a reasonably sure bet. Lucky boy. She was by no means the only tabloid celebrity present; a healthy sprinkling of them were scattered through the crowd, together with enough up-and-coming arty types to add credibility value to Eis Shots. No wonder Richard was looking so content.

'Lewis is waving at us,' I pointed out. 'I think that means the photographer's setting up the shots.'

Great. He was holding the actress's arm. We could get her into the photos too.

'Not jello shots! Photo shots!' Klaus bellowed happily.

'Very good, Klaus, very good,' Richard said perfunctorily. 'Klaus, Johan, can I shepherd you over to the bar?'

Klaus beamed at me as he went; Johan removed the second empty shot cup from my hand.

'I will dispose of this for you,' he said, giving me another direct stare before Richard guided him off.

That left matters in no doubt whatsoever. There are a myriad unmistakable signs that a man is interested in you: insisting on paying for your dinner is the most obvious, but there are many, many others, and one of them is a hyper-attentiveness to the most trivial tasks he can perform for you. I decided that I might very well be attracted to Johan.

Three men in just over a week. I was on a roll.

'Oh, that's just what Laura always says,' Gillian observed. (Laura was the assistant helping Gillian on her new book.) 'She says that as soon as you've got one, the others sense it and flock around. They smell the other men in the air.'

'Urh, sounds like I've got a series of dogs pissing on my leg,' I said, helping myself to meatballs.

'So that's why you always wear those boots,' Gillian said.

'Oh, it's just my work uniform.'

Little sweater, slit skirt, knee-high boots: it took me everywhere.

'I don't know how you wear those heels the whole time,' Gillian commented.

'Of course you don't,' I said, 'you're taller than me. Anyway, if they're on boots, it's much easier. They just feel like an extension of your leg. The way I should have been if God had been thoughtful enough to give me a few extra inches.'

'I love hearing women talk,' Jeremy said cheerfully. 'I just sit here and keep my mouth shut and learn all your secrets. Other men are wildly jealous of my arcane knowledge.'

'Anything you're curious about, you just have to ask,' I offered.

Jeremy and Gillian had been together ever since I had made friends with Gillian; they had met at college and been together pretty much ever since. Having always known Jeremy so safely, as Gillian's settled boyfriend, we had struck up one of those easy friendships which is only possible when at least one of the participants is happily installed in a serious relationship, with no latent sexual attraction to throw a spanner in the works. I imagined Jeremy as a sort of older brother, and certainly he treated me the way I thought he would a younger sister, teasing me about my exploits from the comfortable security of his marriage to Gillian. The three of us, stuffed with Gillian's excellent cooking and lubricated by Jeremy's equally good wines, had often talked about the most personal of matters late into the night; I couldn't conceive of being able to discuss the quality or quantity of the female orgasm, for instance, with anyone else's husband without feeling horrendously self-conscious. But Jeremy felt like part of the family. Or – almost – another girlfriend.

Perhaps that was why, for all his companionship, Gillian and he had such infrequent sex.

'This is really good, Gill,' he said, digging into a minia-ture meat pie.

'I like the meatballs best so far,' I contributed.

Gillian sighed. 'You guys are supposed to be helping me improve them, not just fill your faces. Could I have some constructive suggestions?'

Gillian's latest commission was a collection of mince recipes for a major supermarket chain which published its own series of cookbooks, sold in small-size, hardback editions at the check-outs. It was the third she had done for them. Though the work wasn't massively prestigious it was very well paid, and the books were published under her own name. She had spent the day working on recipes with Laura, and I had been invited round for dinner, post-Eis Shots, to eat up the results. I loved it when Gill was working on a cookbook. The last one had been

Mexican, which had been horribly fattening but irresistible.

'Those ones look a bit funny,' I said, prodding the tartlets. Gillian had made them using mince instead of the pastry surround, pressing it into oiled muffin tins and baking them with a quiche filling of leek and blue cheese.

'They look bloody weird,' Jeremy poured some more wine. 'But give 'em a try anyway. They taste fantastic.'

'OK.'

I helped myself to one and looked at it dubiously. 'What do I do, eat it all in one bite?'

'The custard's set,' Gillian said impatiently. 'You can just cut into it, it won't run.'

'Right.' I cut it in half and popped one into my mouth. 'Mmn, that's delicious,' I said in surprise. 'The mince goes really crispy.'

Gill beamed with pleasure.

'You'll just have to shoot them really carefully,' I warned. 'Make them look incredibly appetising. Or no one will actually cook them.'

'I know,' Gillian said. 'Still, the brief was to be inventive. They want some unusual stuff as well as – you know, boring old meatballs.'

'These meatballs are definitely not boring,' I said, eating yet another.

'So where were you this evening?' Jeremy asked me. 'Yet another launch party?'

'Eis Shots,' I said. 'It was a good one.'

'What are ice shots?' Gillian said. She wasn't eating much, I noticed, just pushing the food round her plate lackadaisically. It wasn't like her. Still, maybe she had overdosed on mince during the day.

'Eis,' I corrected. 'Like the vodka. They're little vodka jelly cups.'

'How revolting,' Jeremy said.

'It's more a clubbing thing,' I informed him.

'Jelly and drugs,' Gill observed dryly. 'A good combination, right?'

'And also they don't have that much alcohol content,' I explained. 'They're quite small. Which means that often bars can keep on serving them even if they've got an early alcohol licence. No, it was a good launch. You always know something's going to take off when the whole agency turns out for it.'

'How's your gorgeous assistant?' Gill asked.

'Lewis? Oh, fine. Very efficient, very cute and a total slut. He's working his way through all the girls at the agency. I think he thinks I don't know, bless him.'

I leant back in my chair, my stomach pleasantly full, looking around the big kitchen. Gillian and Jeremy had a beautiful house, and the kitchen was its heart; painted a pale, glossy yellow, with a terracotta floor, full of hanging plants and gleaming copper saucepans, every faded burn mark and scratch on the polished old wooden table bearing witness to the work it had seen, it was exactly what a kitchen should be. Beyond, shaded in darkness, was the conservatory, a faint glow of moonlight tumbling through the glass and falling gently through the herbs which were ranked in pots along the wide sill: rosemary, sage, thyme, basil, chives . . . We sat in a pool of light, contemplating the beautiful serving plates piled with food we would never manage to finish. It was like a tableau of contentment. I drew a long deep breath of satisfaction and sipped some wine.

'God, this is nice,' I said happily.

'I'll drink to that!' Jeremy clinked glasses with me. 'To the cook!' he added.

We toasted Gillian, who smiled at us. She looked a little

wan, though, after her day spent slapping piles of mince into shape. At this moment all the pleasures of solid coupledom flooded in on me. Not just the material advantages, the lovely house one could afford on two incomes, especially if, like Gillian, one had married a banker; but the warmth, the cosiness, the mutual support, these moments by candlelight when friends came round and clinked glasses to your settled happiness. An end to running.

In parallel, I suddenly felt ashamed of what my mother called my selfish life. Like a repentant sinner at the confessional, overcome with guilt, I saw my flings with Tom and Pieter as shallow and sordid in comparison with what Gillian and Jeremy had built for themselves. As gorged with food as a foie gras goose, my senses lulled by the wine, sex seemed very far away and trivial to boot. This was what mattered, this happy companionship, not a series of meaningless flings with unsuitable but tight-buttocked young men.

'I think you should introduce me to some bankers, Jeremy,' I said, eliding the last two words a little under the influence of his excellent Californian cabernet. 'Maybe it's time I settled down.'

Jeremy's jaw dropped, his rather plump mouth forming an O which echoed perfectly the shape of his round, rubicund face.

'Are you serious, Juliet?'

'Oh, I dunno.' I drank some more wine. 'It's just seeing what you guys have made here, all this domestic contentment – maybe I need to get a bit serious, stop fooling around –'

Gillian was shaking her head emphatically. 'You can't force yourself not to have fun!' she said with great feeling.

'Well, if she feels it's time . . .' Jeremy said judiciously. 'Most of my colleagues are atrocious, though, Juliet. I mean, I could scarcely see what you would have in common.'

'You never know.'

I smirked, thinking of Pieter, who, after all, was a financial controller – God knew what that was, the phrase made me think of the Fat Controller from Thomas the Tank Engine; but one had to assume that it was a perfectly settled, respectable profession. And then there was Johan, who definitely had possibilities. I wondered whether he would ring me.

'You can't just make yourself marry a man in a suit,' Gillian insisted. 'I mean, that would be such a disaster! You'd wake up after the wedding and think, God, what have I done –'

'Whoah, whoah,' I said, brought down to earth with a bump. 'Who said anything about marriage?' I raised my hands in a defensive gesture, as if warding off evil spirits. 'I was just, you know, speculating about dating different kinds of men.'

'Dipping your toe in the water,' Jeremy added helpfully.

'Exactly.'

I smiled at him in thanks. He reached for the wine bottle. Jeremy and I shared the solidarity of being fully fledged lushes. Together we tacitly encouraged each other to drink rather more than we should. I knew Gillian didn't approve, and now it struck me that drink certainly wouldn't help with any libido problems Jeremy might suffer from. Feeling guilty, I waved the bottle away when my glass was only half full.

'Do we have any pudding, Gill?' he said optimistically.

'Mince pies,' I said, and roared with as much laughter as if this had been the height of wit. Jeremy chuckled too, bless him.

'We've got some chocolates in the larder,' she said. 'I didn't make anything special.'

Jeremy hauled himself to his feet and started clearing the plates into their state-of-the-art dishwasher. I eyed it wistfully.

Yet another highly expensive consumer gadget that could only be afforded by a two-income household. And of course, Gill and Jeremy didn't have kids. That liberated an enormous tranche of spending money.

I caught Gillian's eye and grinned at her. She sketched a smile back, but it was no more than that. Something was wrong.

'Everything OK?' I said, under cover of the clatter which was Jeremy stacking plates. 'Are you tired? Do you want me to push off?'

'No, stay,' she mouthed. She reached out and pressed my hand briefly. 'I want you to. It's early yet.'

The Venetian stained-glass kitchen clock said that it was eleven thirty. I winced. It was all right for Gill, who didn't have to be at work by nine thirty. Inventing new ways with mince scarcely required the alarm to be set for the crack of dawn.

Jeremy was producing boxes of chocolates from the larder with the childish enthusiasm of a little boy who has just been given Magic Tricks For Beginners as a Christmas present.

'Ooh, peppermint creams.' I reached for them. 'There's something about the mint that cuts through all the rich food you've just had. Kind of freshens the palate.'

'That's the worst excuse for eating chocolate I've ever heard,' Gillian said dryly, unwrapping a cherry truffle.

'Shall I put some coffee on?' I suggested. If Gillian wanted me to stay, I needed some kind of stimulant. And by now I knew where everything in their kitchen was kept.

'No, I'll do it. I quite fancy some too.'

She stood up, smoothing down her dress. 'Jerry,' she said briskly, 'Jules and I want to have a bit of a girls' talk, and you should be in bed by now anyway, shouldn't you?'

Jeremy's pink, happy face crumpled in disappointment. He

looked as baffled at his dismissal as I was. That was one reason Jeremy was so lovable. He was utterly without guile; every emotion he was feeling was clearly legible on his face. Without a word he shifted his bulk out from under the overhang of the table and heaved himself to a standing position.

'Well, I'll be saying goodnight, then,' he said, his voice subdued. ''Night, Juliet.'

I jumped up, as well as I could with all that food comfortably breaking itself down in my digestive tract, and came round the table to kiss him on one plump cheek.

'See you soon,' I said, squeezing his shoulder in what was supposed to be a gesture of solidarity.

He turned and left the room, his shoulders slumped, looking inconsolable. I raised my eyebrows at Gillian, frowning, pantomiming incomprehension. She shook her head at me impatiently and poured boiling water into the cafetière. Not until it was on the table, with cups, saucers, milk and sugar all carefully arranged between us, the kitchen door shut, did she sit down, look me in the eye, and say:

'Jules, this is really hard for me, OK? I'm just going to spill it all out and get it over with.'

I was so self-obsessed that by now I was completely convinced that I had done something so awful that Gillian could no longer be my friend. Or she was going to read me a terrible lecture about my selfish lifestyle. My heart was pounding in fear.

'What?' I blurted out.

'It's so difficult –'

Gillian pushed her cup away impatiently and propped both her elbows on the table, head sunk between them. I waited, too panic-struck to utter a word.

Her hands were cupped over her face. When she finally spoke, the words were muffled by flesh and what sounded like incipient tears. But I still heard them clearly enough.

'It's Jeremy, Jules. I can't do it any longer.' She sniffled. 'I'm leaving him. I want a divorce.'

Chapter Seven

I was not a good friend to Gillian. A good friend would have let her talk everything through, giving her plenty of space to express her feelings. In this kind of situation one should serve as a sounding-board, offering opinions only when they are explicitly sought.

I did the opposite. I whined and protested and tried to talk her out of it.

My reaction was undeniably selfish. It seemed to me that only bad consequences could spring from a breakup (I refused to say divorce). Gill would lose her lovely home, to which I so enjoyed being invited. She would be single and miserable, requiring me to be a rock of strength, not my strong point. I would never see Jeremy – of whom I now realised that I was very fond indeed – again, as ours was the kind of friendship that functions only in a triangle, feeling awkward and self-conscious as soon as the mediating party is removed from the equation. Besides, even if I did meet up with him, I knew exactly how it would be; all he would want to do would be to ramble on endlessly about Gillian, sobbing helplessly and pleading with me to intervene.

'Have you tried to talk to him about it?' I said hopelessly.

I felt stupid as soon as I said it. Caught in a cliché. The time-honoured phrase that one always trots out, head tilted to the side, expression studiedly serious, like a bad actor playing a therapist. And I knew perfectly well that it wasn't good advice. Every time I had tried to talk through problems with Bart we had ended up letting even more worms out of cans than had been wriggling around before.

'It's so humiliating,' Gill said, tracing patterns with her fingers on the wooden table. 'You try saying to your husband: "Why aren't we having sex, don't you find me attractive any more?" He made me feel so pushy and demanding. I just got stuff like, "All couples settle down and stop having so much sex after a while, it's perfectly normal, don't make such a big deal out of it." And occasionally he would do it, but that was even worse in a way.'

'Like he was forcing himself?'

Gillian nodded. 'Or, you know, performing a sort of duty. It was obvious he didn't want to. It was so perfunctory. Once I went to the bathroom afterwards, turned on the taps and just cried and cried.'

'Oh, Gill, that's awful.' I reached across the table and took her hand. She squeezed mine back but withdrew hers almost immediately. She was not in the mood to be comforted, that was too passive; she had by no means finished spilling out confidences.

'So he started getting me presents,' she continued. 'And taking me on more and more expensive holidays.' She looked up eagerly. All these details had been pent-up for so long that no matter how unpleasant they were, she was experiencing a real release in talking about them. 'At first I thought the holidays were a good sign, like he wanted to get away from the house, out of old patterns. I mean, people usually have more sex on holiday, right?'

'Oh yeah. Even if we were in a bit of a rut at home, Bart and me used to fuck like rabbits when we went away,' I agreed.

'There you go!' she said almost triumphantly. 'That's been the thing with Jeremy, you see. I've stopped trusting my own instincts. Or my experience. I let myself be persuaded by him, because it was easier, in a way. But at the same time I knew it wasn't normal. I mean, of course you think about sex more when you're abroad, and it's lovely and warm, and it's just the two of you. I got so horny in the Canaries . . .'

She trailed off. I waited for her to continue, but she stayed silent for a long time, and when she finally did speak it was to ask something quite unexpected.

'How's Bart doing? Have you heard from him?'

'Not for ages,' I mumbled reluctantly.

How I wished I hadn't mentioned Bart. As soon as I did my friends took it as a signal that they could ask about him without upsetting me. And they never could.

My ex-boyfriend was the most lovable person imaginable, so warm and easy-going that everyone relaxed around him. He was like a human Jacuzzi. When we had been together, I had naturally taken great pride in how endearing he was; all my friends loved him, and their boyfriends were constantly ringing up to ask if Bart could go out to play. Football, go-karting, or just lying round the house smoking spliffs and watching crap TV: Bart was the ideal companion. He projected the sweetness of a child uncorrupted by the world. Even Jeremy had loved him, and the two of them had nothing in common.

I had once told Bart that he was like Just William grown-up – if one could use the term 'grown-up' anywhere near Bart or William. The psychologists generally use Peter Pan as the archetype of the adult male who is refusing to let his mental age catch up with his physical one: but that had never made sense to me. Peter Pan was too naff, too prissy. My friends' boyfriends would have rather been seen dead than go to football with Peter. Whereas to Bart and William adulthood meant even more fun games to be played. Sex, beer, spliff, blackjack, poker, five-card stud . . .

While I was with Bart I had basked in his popularity, feeling that I had drawn a very high number in the eligible-man stakes. The downside was that when I had finally realised that if I didn't break up with him I would go insane, hardly anyone was at all supportive. It was like my current attitude to Gillian.

'Was it really that bad?' they would murmur hopefully. 'Couldn't you try talking to him about it?'

'Bart's a COMPULSIVE GAMBLER and a TOTAL LIAR who owes me LOTS OF MONEY,' I would sob miserably. 'I can't go back. I was going mad trying to work out what was true and what wasn't. He pawned my stereo for gambling money.'

Staying with Bart was impossible. But leaving him felt as if I were ripping out some vital part of me, like performing a caesarian on a mini-Bart, tiny, naked and covered in blood, pleading with me to be allowed back in. I hurt all the time. And instead of telling me to dump the lying, gambling-addicted bastard, all my friends could say in small, sad, we-love-Bart-so-much voices, was: 'But he loves you so much . . . I'm sure you could sort it out with a bit of counselling . . . you can get counselling for everything nowadays, can't you?'

I took a deep breath. I needed to stop thinking about Bart; it never failed to plunge me into depression.

'I'm sorry, Jules,' Gill said. 'I shouldn't have asked.'

She had the wistful, remembering-Bart look in her eyes, and that nostalgic-about-Bart tilt to her head. I recognised them both. Still, they didn't last more than a moment before her own problems swept in to overwhelm her and she sank her head in her hands again, rubbing her eye sockets with the tips of her fingers. Gratefully I stepped back off the edge of the abyss that opened up every time Bart's name was mentioned, took another, hopefully calming, breath, and looked at her. As she raised her hands, a heavy gold bracelet slid down her wrist and caught on her bare forearm.

'The tennis bracelet,' I said, indicating it. 'Was that one of the presents you were talking about?'

Gill lifted her head and grimaced, more at the bracelet than at me.

'It must have been really pricey,' she said, twisting it round so the diamonds caught the light. 'And you know the trouble? I like it a lot. I like everything Jeremy's got me in the last few years, all his guilt gifts.' She signalled the last two words in inverted commas. 'He knows exactly what to buy me; he's got really good taste. I mean, I almost wanted just to leave them in the boxes, to make a point, but that seemed crazy. I wear this all the time, actually.'

'It's kind of ironic, isn't it?' I refilled my coffee cup. Clearly this was going to be a long night. 'I mean, usually men are supposed to give women presents so they can have sex with them. And here's Jeremy, um, doing the opposite.'

Luckily Gill saw the funny side.

'It's ridiculous, isn't it?' She didn't actually manage to laugh, but she made a humphing noise of appreciation, and almost smiled.

'At first I thought he had a girlfriend somewhere,' she said. 'You know, it's the classic thing; cheat on your wife but buy her lots of luxury goods to keep her quiet.'

'No way!' I exclaimed. The thought of Jeremy having an affair was for some reason very difficult for me to digest. 'I mean, I just don't see that. He's so devoted to you.'

'I know. It didn't make sense when I thought about it. But you wouldn't believe how much goes through your head in this kind of situation. I must have read hundreds of women's magazines, all those wretched articles about keeping your sex life alive and how to spot if your husband's cheating and Five

Women Tell How They Put Their Marriages Together Again Better Than Before. God, the amount of crap that's out there.'

She let out a gusty sigh.

'You feel so isolated,' she said. 'It's supposed to be the other way round, isn't it? No one talks about men who don't want to have sex with their wives. Or if they do, they just tell you to ask your husband about his secret fantasies, or buy some red crotchless knickers. Jesus, if it were only that easy. Believe me, I've tried everything.'

'Women's magazine articles are completely pointless,' I observed. 'At best you take out of them only what you want to hear. And at worst they make you clinically depressed.'

'I thought I was going mad at one point,' Gillian said, her tone deliberately matter of fact.

She pushed back her hair with both hands. The tennis bracelet glinted on her forearm, the diamonds flashing multi-coloured under the table light, echoing the gold-set diamonds of her earrings, the white-gold streaks in her beautifully cut blond hair. It seemed impossible that someone so perfectly groomed, so together, should be stuck in the middle of such a messy situation. I had the idiotic, childish idea that one progressed in life from one stage of increasing maturity to another, and that Gill, being way ahead of me on almost all fronts, would, at the least, effortlessly remain at the level she had so far attained. The concept of her slipping back into the chaos that was my personal life, not to mention my wardrobe, was inconceivable. I looked around once more at the lovely kitchen, symbol up till now of everything that was right in Gill and Jeremy's marriage. It didn't need a woman's magazine. I felt clinically depressed without one.

'I cannot go the rest of my life without having sex,' Gill announced as formally as if she were the official spokeswoman at a White House press conference.

'Well, no, of course not,' I mumbled, wishing cravenly that she could. 'But I thought . . . um, I thought . . . I mean, you've hinted you know, about, um, flings you've had in the past –'

And the way she had mentioned the Canaries, it sounded as if something had happened there. Why don't you just keep on doing that? I wanted to say. Jeremy would probably turn a blind eye. He wouldn't be happy about it, but he must realise you've got to get it somewhere.

Gill looked at me, her mouth open, like a goldfish cruising up on a lump of fish food. She closed it and opened it again, increasing the resemblance.

'What?' I said warily, pretty sure I didn't want to hear this.

'That's the problem,' she said, tentatively, but with the increasing speed that made it clear I had touched on a subject she had been longing to talk about. 'I mean, I wasn't going to tell you, but since you've brought it up –' Her skin glowed, her eyes sparkled. She looked suddenly bright, alive, like a lamp that has had its old, failing light bulb substituted with a new one of much higher wattage.

'Oh my God,' I said, my heart sinking still further. Problems with Jeremy were not irrevocable; discontented spouses often talked wildly about separation or divorce, letting off steam rather than expressing truly serious intentions. There were still options: marriage counselling, a sex therapist, lacing Jeremy's bedtime cocoa with enough Viagra to make a bromide-dosed elephant shove 'Let's Get It On' on the stereo and tear off his wife's underwear with his trunk. But if Gill was saying what I thought she was, then all bets were off. Jeremy was dead meat.

'You're having an affair, aren't you?' I said reluctantly.

Now she lit up like a Christmas tree. She beamed and nodded and wrung her hands together in a gesture of combined guilt and excitement. My eyes fell to the tennis bracelet, shining glossily on her pale wrist. No wonder she had such mixed feelings about it. I hadn't picked up on half of them.

My reactions were equally mixed, and none of them did me much credit. I was (a) relieved (I wouldn't have to be a tower of strength to Gill after all, as she would be too swept up by her new affair); (b) worried (what if the guy turned out to be a broken reed? Suppose he had seen the affair as just a happy fling with a safely married woman and promptly made his excuses as soon as Gill announced that she was leaving Jeremy? Then my tower-of-strength requirements would be doubled. And I was so busy at work right now, I didn't even have time for myself, let alone anyone else. What a selfish bitch you are, Juliet); and (c), surprisingly, jealous (if it worked out, then how unfair it was that Gill had so easily managed to pop from one man to another, with no dating angst or personal commitment problems. Selfish selfish yet again, Juliet, I can't believe that you're actually envying poor Gillian right now. You really are a totally egocentric cow).

I spent the entire ride home in the minicab energetically despising myself. I was so exhausted when I got home that I didn't even get properly undressed, just crawled into bed in my bra, knickers and tights. I do this sometimes when I'm feeling insecure, and this was definitely one of those times. Gillian's news had unsettled me completely. Everything in life seemed frighteningly ephemeral. I was very depressed. Besides, it was four in the morning. I felt like the apocalypse was taking place in my head.

The next couple of weeks at work were dominated by preparations for Liam's launch party. Preview tapes had already been sent to selected journalists, and so far the feedback had been excellent. Still, I was definitely not resting on my laurels. After Liam was safely launched into the world – cheering crowds, ribbon cut, bottles of champagne smashed over his bows – I would resume the social life that I had put on hold, go away for the weekend, take the time to work out why exactly I was picking up gorgeous young men and then refusing to have sex with them. I didn't quite promise myself that I would also stop smoking, lose that final half-stone and set up my own world-class PR agency with branches in New York and Miami, but I wasn't far off. It was as if I thought that after the successful launch of the first client I had brought to the agency as a partner, everything in my life would magically fall into place, like the long corridor of doors swinging open one by one as Ingrid Bergman kisses Gregory Peck for the first time in *Spellbound*. I knew I was attaching too much weight to Liam's career possibilities. Still, better there than on my hips.

Every night Gillian and I talked on the phone, which consumed all my remaining emotional resources. The day after our dinner, she had told Jeremy that he had to move out; unfortunately, she had omitted to mention that she was seeing someone else. I thought this was not only a terrible mistake, but also unfair to Jeremy. He wasn't a fool; he would sense perfectly well that there was more to the story than Gill was telling. Her line was that the breakup had been caused by a problem that she had tried and failed for years to bring to Jeremy's attention, and to bring into the narrative the question of a new lover would only distract Jeremy from seeing the central issue.

I understood this perfectly well. When I had broken up with Bart there had been another guy, though a completely meaningless one, and Bart had fastened on his existence with the tenacity of a bulldog on crack. He completely discounted the fact that we had been fighting with increasing animosity for the whole of the previous year. Bart had been sleeping on the sofa so often that he resented my sitting on what he considered his bed. His solution was to go out and have a meaningless fling with some poor girl to whom he promised eternal love, only to dump her within a month. He told me all about it with a beaming smile; now we were even and could get back together. Bart's childlike nature was both his greatest attraction and his worst enemy.

Still, I had told Bart about the affair. The longer Gill kept Jeremy in the dark, the worse it would be when he finally found out.

And the more all her friends would have to lie to him in the meantime.

Jeremy had rung me up, at work and then at home when he couldn't get through to me in the office any longer because I made Lewis screen my calls. It was too upsetting to talk to him at work, and besides I could never get him off the phone. He pleaded with me as if I were the Oracle of Delphi who for reasons of her own was wilfully refusing him the answer to his problem. But there was nothing useful I could say. He never mentioned sex at all. Instead he dredged up hundreds of little incidents, analysing each in compulsive detail for the key to their breakup. It was like watching someone playing Blind Man's Buff, stumbling round the room, a thick scarf tied over their eyes, their hands stretched out in front of them, hearing the other people darting out of their way but unable ever to connect with them. I found it horribly painful. I would have hated it if he had confided in me about his and Gill's sex life, or lack thereof; but the fact that neither of us mentioned the central issue felt ridiculous, as if we were sitting in a room with a giraffe whose presence we were determinedly ignoring by discussing the weather instead.

Our talks always ended the same way. I would plead exhaustion; Jeremy would apologise and then return to his monologue; this theme would be repeated with increasing insistence on my part for the next ten minutes, until finally I managed to put down the phone.

After the fifth conversation of this sort I rang Gill.

'You have to tell him about Philip,' I said, almost without preamble. I was so worn out by all the beating around the bush with Jeremy I had run out of the usual social conventions. 'He keeps asking me if I know what went wrong and I just can't do it any more.'

'Then don't talk to him,' Gill said callously.

'Gill! I really care about Jeremy! And he's so unhappy!'

But Gill was at that stage where she had to demonise Jeremy so she could deal with the fact that she had left him for someone else.

'He's got friends of his own to talk to,' she said curtly. 'I don't see why he's bothering mine.'

'He's in a lot of pain,' I pointed out with equal directness. 'And he knows there's more going on than you've told him.'

'But that's not the point.'

'Gill,' I said, irritated into brutality, 'it's part of the bloody point. You're fucking with his mind. It's like dragging someone out of the theatre at the interval and telling them that's all there is of the play, even though they can see everyone else queuing up for ice-cream. People go nuts when someone leaves them, but they go extra nuts if they sense that they're being lied to.'

'Nuts and ice-cream,' Gill said pertly. 'All we need's a banana and we've got a sundae.'

'Fuck off. Come down from your sex cloud for two seconds and do the right thing with Jeremy.'

There was a long pause.

'I can't, Jules,' she said finally, sounding human for the first time in the conversation. 'I'm too scared. He'll just go to pieces and then I will too. It'll rip me apart.'

'He'll have to find out sooner or later,' I said more gently.

'Maybe it'd be better if it came from someone else,' she suggested. 'Then it would, you know, be more in stages.'

'You're not suggesting –'

'No, no!' she said hurriedly a second before I exploded. 'I was just, you know, saying it generally.'

I sighed.

'I was going to ring you tonight anyway,' she said, brightening up. 'I wanted to ask you over here to meet Philip.'

From Jeremy's unhappiness to an invitation to meet its cause in a matter of moments. I wasn't impressed by the idea of meeting Gill's new boyfriend at the house out of which she had just thrown her husband. A house, let me add, which had been bought mainly with the latter's money. Maybe it was unfair of me to see it in those terms. But Gill was in love, and trying hard not to feel guilty about it, so she was about as morally sensitive as Henry Kissinger. The selfishness of lovers is a theme usually ignored, and on the rare occasions it is mentioned it is always justified by the force of passion.

I had been almost as guilty as Gill in my time. I knew what it felt like to be the wheel grinding flour into dust; I knew the violent efforts you make to ignore the pain you're causing. Still, I wasn't going to meet Philip in Jeremy's house. What if Jeremy found out? And he would; people always do.

What a little Puritan I was being. Next I would start telling Gill that her marriage vows were sacred, to go back to Jeremy, and sublimate her sex drive in good works.

'I'd really like to go out,' I said, thinking quickly. 'I've been in every night for almost a week, I'm working so hard. Why don't I take you both out for a meal?'

'Oh, I was so looking forward to cooking you both dinner . . .' Gill pleaded.

I kept my mouth shut. This was always hard for me, but I was learning through observation that sometimes it was the best technique for getting one's way. I bit my lip and breathed slowly and waited for Gill to realise that I wasn't prepared to enter into negotiations.

'Philip loves it when I cook for him,' she said at last in a wistful tone that indicated that she had given in.

'Doesn't everyone?' I said rather curtly. At the moment everything Philip did was being proclaimed as the *ne plus ultra*, from his silk socks (from Sulka, I had the instinct that Philip might be a shade pretentious) to his lovely thick hair, and I was wearying fast of hearing about his manifest virtues.

Gill sighed, indicating that she was finding it hard to relinquish the little fantasy picture of me and Philip sharing a joke, as the gossip magazines say, in the warm golden light of the kitchen while she set a series of delicious dishes on her – or Jeremy's – dining table. I found it baffling, to say the least, that she could not only invite me to recreate a scene that had only a week ago been played out with a completely different actor but do so without any consciousness of what she was asking. Clearly she wanted to create as domestic a situation as possible in order to emphasise the stability of her affair with Philip.

Still, I was adamant. Gill wanted me to be best friends with Philip right now; but years ago she had wanted me to be best friends with Jeremy, and I had obliged. Now I was supposed to pretend that poor Jeremy had never existed. It was too much. When I referred a moment ago to the selfishness of lovers, I didn't just mean the way they treated their exes.

Chapter Eight

'So where're you meeting the scarlet woman and her paramour?' Mel said, rolling the words around her tongue with considerable relish.

'My local Thai. Just down the road.'

'That's convenient.'

'Hollow laugh. Gill suggested it. Work it out.'

'Gill?' Mel sounded incredulous. Gill hated leaving her cosy corner of Fulham to brave the wilds of North London. 'Oh hang on, I get it . . . Gill wants to come to Chalk Farm because it's safe, right? One hundred per cent guaranteed that you won't bump into Jeremy.'

'Got it in one. Jeremy can't ever have been to Chalk Farm in his life. Probably thinks it's a riding stables in Hertfordshire.'

'I don't know why you didn't just go round to hers,' Mel said callously. 'Food's just as good and it's a lot cheaper – all you have to pay for's a bottle of wine and a cab home.'

'And there. I can't get to Fulham by tube, the time I finish work these days. I'd get there much too late.'

Mel hooted. 'Hark at madam!'

'Nah, you're the madam,' I said to distract her. 'I'm just Mistress Sophia, or whatever the name is this week.'

It didn't work. Mel was well off on the scent.

'"I can't get to Fulham by tube!"' she quoted. 'Far cry from the old days, eh, Jules? Charging around London to crappy temping jobs? We must have known the whole fucking tube map by heart.'

'Not just the tube map.' I corrected. 'I still know every shortcut in Soho, Covent Garden, Holborn, the City – two bloody years, a new job every week. That's a lot of reading the A to Z.'

Mel and I had met working as temporary secretaries in a law firm in High Holborn. Naturally, being Mel, she had done half the work I did, as our bosses were too intimidated by her to request that she do more than the absolute minimum of her job description. Naturally, too, I resented this bitterly and for the first two days refused to exchange a word with her. Then I happened to be standing by her desk as one of the partners, a particularly annoying woman, walked past. I said 'Stupid cow' under my breath, and Mel, without even raising her eyes from the magazine she was reading, said, quite unoffended, 'Do you mind.' She turned a page and added casually: ''S'not my fault they're giving you all the data entry.'

'No, no,' I said, horrified, 'I didn't mean you, I meant her.' I gestured to the partner, who was just entering her office.

'Hah!' Mel looked up from the magazine, her eyes gleaming. 'She don't even come near me. You want to know why? 'Cos she knows I saw her at a party last month having a butt plug shoved up her arse by some pig-ugly bloke.'

I stood, gaping.

'She was wearing a mask, but I'd recognise that saggy bum anywhere,' Mel said triumphantly. 'Here we go.' She flicked a meaningful glance over at the partner's office. 'She's watching us through the glass. Want to bet she don't give you any more grief from now on?'

After a first meeting like that, it was impossible for us not to establish a friendship. It wasn't so much the illicit glamour of Mel's louche social life that attracted me, as her insouciant reaction to being apparently insulted by a total stranger.

'No more shopping together at crappy street markets!' Mel was saying now, off on a surge of nostalgia. 'Now you're all Harvey Nicks and Joseph trousers –'

'Which cost about a tenth of all that made-to-order rubber gear you've got,' I said pointedly. 'I know the price of that stuff. That new corset alone must have set you back half a grand.'

'Business expense, sweetie,' Mel purred. 'Shame it's not deductible, eh?'

'Talking of which, I can probably write off tonight's dinner as business,' I said, cheering up. 'In fact of course I can.'

'*You* won't be paying,' Mel said, her voice even more worldly wise than usual. 'He'll insist on it. He's in property, isn't he? He'll flash his platinum Amex and puff up his chest and grab the bill from the waiter. Want to bet?'

'Mel Danson, ladies and gentlemen. Cynical But Right.'

'My motto, innit?'

Mel's accent had poshed-up, as she called it, since the day we had met; the dominatrix who had trained her had insisted that she lose a bit of the Cockney for professional purposes. Still, she enjoyed slipping back into it for dramatic effect.

'Wish you were coming too, babe,' I said regretfully.

'You're joking. I'm much too scary. Gill'd never inflict both of us on him at once.'

She was quite right.

'I just feel I need some moral support,' I said wistfully. 'I liked Jeremy. Oh God, I'm talking about him as if he were dead. Which is exactly what Gill wants.'

'Why do you care?' Mel really didn't understand.

'Well, you liked him too, didn't you?' I tried to use the present tense, but it wouldn't come out.

'Sure. So what?'

'Doesn't it feel a bit like betraying him – you know, charging along to meet the new Mr Gill?'

Mel blew into the mouthpiece. 'I don't remember you promising till death us do part,' she said. 'Why the fuck do you care? Is it 'cos they were married?'

'Dunno. No. They just seemed like a really nice couple. I liked knowing it was out there.'

'Even if you'd run a mile from having to do it yourself,' Mel said cruelly.

'I went out with Bart for nearly four years,' I protested.

'Come on, Jules. Bart's not exactly the kind of guy you marry and settle down with. He just lasted longer than your other dumb blonds.'

I drew in my breath involuntarily. No one had put it quite that clearly before. She was quite right. It was the truth. I recognised it for a moment, before my brain shied away and focused on what I was going to wear that evening instead. I wasn't up to dealing with that kind of revelation yet.

I showered and changed for my rendezvous with the scarlet woman and her paramour. Occasionally, at those blissful moments when I had something new I really wanted to wear and, being on the lower end of my weight spectrum, could fit into it easily, getting dressed to go out was a positive pleasure. Much more often, however, it was a forty-minute trek through my wardrobe, resulting in a heap of clothes piled on the bed and a hand mirror propped on the desk so I could see what I looked like from behind. Tonight was no exception. I had read somewhere that most people wore twenty per cent of their clothes eighty per cent of the time, and it had struck me as one of the profoundest truths ever expressed. Unless I were feeling particularly upbeat and slender, I fell back inevitably on the skirts that could be relied on to minimise the bulges and the sweaters that skimmed ditto. It was always shaming to survey the amount of coats and bags and shoes I possessed. They were completely unnecessary and yet I couldn't stop buying them.

I had always wanted to be the kind of person who had a signature look, like the girl at university who had a seventies red suede jacket which she wore with everything. My scattergun approach to dressing was just another expression of my inability to commit myself to one thing – or person – and stick with it. Mel was the opposite of me in this respect; her looks now were a distillation of what they were when we had met, as if she had become her own essence. All the elements had been there already: the razor-cut bob, the pointed nails, the high heels. She had spent the intervening period honing herself to a perfection of which I was jealous. In those ten years I had learnt better what suited me, what to do with my hair, but I still felt batted back and forth by whichever winds of fashion were prevaling at the time. I worried that, unlike Mel, I lacked an inner core of certainty.

Most of my existential crises were over clothes. Either I was irredeemably shallow or the victim of an increasingly consumer-oriented global capitalist conspiracy. Obviously, I preferred the latter hypothesis.

Gill and Philip were already in the restaurant when I arrived, sitting side by side in a Vietnamese-looking slatted wooden booth and squirming their bodies into each other in a way that suggested that either they were about to have sex, or the wood was infested with ants which were busy crawling around their underwear. I wondered if my presence were really required.

'Jules!'

Gill broke into a huge smile when she saw me hovering at

the end of the table. Recovering her hands from wherever they had been, she pulled me towards her to be kissed.

'Phil,' she said, 'this is Juliet, one of my oldest friends.'

It looked as if Gill had recently had smile-enhancing plastic surgery. She was beaming like Julie Andrews in *The Sound Of Music*. Contrarily enough, it made me increasingly cranky.

I slid into the booth opposite them and Philip immediately called over the waiter to ask what I would like to drink. Score two points in his favour. Gill was now hugging on to his arm with both hands and smiling up at him as if she were an old-school Presidential candidate's wife. I knew that she was in the first flush of love and sex, not to mention divorce proceedings, but her enthusiasm still felt a little forced, as if she were throwing herself bodily at Philip in the assumption that the harder she hit him the better she would stick.

'So!' she said brightly. 'What have you been up to?'

'Oh, you know. Organising Liam. It's a full-time job. He's being so argumentative at the moment. He only does it to annoy because he knows it teases. But it's still irritating.'

'And he's really nervous too,' Gill pointed out.

'Oh, you picked that up?'

Gill having agreed to take on the catering for the party, I had given her Liam's phone number so that they could discuss any adaptations that needed to be made to his recipes for serving on a large scale. It had gone very well, according to Liam, anyway, who had been vastly reassured by Gill's obvious competence. I hadn't had a chance yet to ask Gill for her perspective.

She was nodding. 'Lots of bluster, of course,' she said cheerfully. 'But I could tell he was a bit overwhelmed by the whole thing. He's a charmer, though, isn't he? Is he as good looking as his photo on the book jacket?'

'Not really,' I said. 'He's very photogenic. But everyone falls for him anyway.'

'Everyone?' said Gill, raising her eyebrows at me.

'Come off it, Gill. He's my client. And he's a twenty-six-year-old brat with an advanced case of satyriasis.'

'Oh well, you'll just have to fall back on your gorgeous assistant, then.'

Gill always mentioned Lewis. She definitely had a crush on him.

Philip didn't ask what we were talking about. Either Gill had already filled him in on my current work preoccupations, or he was politely letting us catch up, or he had tuned out of what he considered girls' babble. I inclined towards the final explanation, probably unfairly. Minus four points.

After we had ordered, however, he started to question me politely about my work. It was classic cocktail-party conversation, done by rote, the kind where you are momentarily washed up by the tide of people on to a small promontory next to another person, and common decency requires that you make small-talk for an obligatory ten minutes or so before diving back into the sea to circulate once more. As soon as Philip began I knew exactly how our dialogue would run; I could have closed my eyes and blocked my ears and just thrown out the correct responses at regular intervals. There are always a series of questions that people trot out from social convention, one answer leading inexorably to the next. And the people who ask them are invariably the ones who aren't really interested in you, but simply feel they have to keep the wheels of conversation turning. The awful thing was that I could criticise Philip for this as much as I liked, but I knew that in about ten minutes it would be me putting the same kind of 'So! Tell me all about yourself!' questions to him, and I would see by the over-polite expression in his eyes that he, too, had gone through this routine a hundred thousand times before.

Gill didn't seem to notice how formal Philip and I were being with each other, how little we had clicked. Her gaze was flickering from one to the other of us, checking up on how much Philip liked me and – to a lesser extent, frankly – how much I liked Philip. But mostly she looked at him, smiling when he smiled, smiling wider when he laughed – which wasn't very often. He didn't seem to find me very amusing. I found myself making the comments that were usually guaranteed to crack a smile at the least, and Philip would listen to them straight-faced as a little silence fell into the space which I had obligingly left for his laugh.

Meanwhile Gill gazed at his profile as adoringly as a heroine on the cover of a romance novel. All she needed was a wind machine and an off-the-shoulder dress that had been Superglued halfway down her bosom. I had often noticed how the convention on these covers was for the heroine to stare worshipfully at the hero, while he looked directly at the reader, fixing her with a masterful gaze to indicate that he much preferred early twenty-first century career women to swooning Victorian bimbos.

I had definitely taken against Philip. His point score was in the low minus twenties by now and I was blaming him for everything. Technically, it wasn't his fault that my Tom Yum Koong soup was hotter than the flames of hell – it felt as if tiny devils were rubbing chillies into the lining of my nose. But if Philip hadn't been present, I would have had the relief of cursing and blowing my nose and complaining that the soup, which had a two-star chilli rating, should tonight have carried five, plus a Health and Safety warning and a skull-and-crossbones symbol. Instead, being too cool to show weakness in front of a man who didn't laugh at my jokes, I was forced to suffer in silence, sniffing surreptitiously every now and then and dabbing at my runny nose with my napkin when he wasn't looking.

'So! What do you think?' Gill said enthusiastically once our starters had mercifully been removed and Philip had gone to the toilet. Maybe his soup had been as hot as mine, and he too was sneezing away in the gents'. The thought cheered me a little.

'My soup was so hot!' I said, playing feebly for time. 'All my sinuses are burnt out. I'm not going to be able to use my nose for days.'

Gill did not, as I had hoped she would, make some crack about my recreational drug use that would have distracted us until Philip returned. Instead she said impatiently: 'No, Philip! What do you think? Isn't he lovely?'

'He seems really nice,' I said sycophantically. 'It's not much time to get to know someone, though, Gill. Twenty minutes partially distracted by Tom Yum Koong scorching its way down your digestive tract.'

She looked disappointed. I tried a little harder.

'I'm looking forward to getting to know him better,' I lied womanfully. I was unable to forget how easy it had been to get along with Jeremy from the moment I had met him. We had taken the piss out of Gill, as friend and boyfriend do in order to bond, and argued about films, and generally behaved like humans rather than dinner-party robots.

But Gill didn't seem to realise that I was, at best, prevaricating. She gave me a lovely smile, the first real, non-Julie Andrews one I had seen from her this evening.

'I'm so happy,' she announced unnecessarily.

'That's great.'

I drank some more beer.

'So what about that guy you met at the conference?' she asked.

'Who?' I said blankly.

'You know!' Gill looked shocked. 'Tom!'

'Oh, him.'

I finished my beer and signalled the waiter for another. Clearly Gill was in that stage of amatorial bliss where she wanted everyone else to be as happily matched as she was. It doesn't last that long, but is very exhausting for all concerned; the friend in love rushes round trying to set you up with men who she would have known perfectly well you wouldn't have touched with a bargepole if it weren't for the fact that she was wearing rose-tinted glasses two inches thick.

'It was just a thing, Gill,' I said, since she was clearly waiting for an answer. 'A been-and-gone thing.'

'And that other one?' Gill was trying her best.

'The fetish club Dutchman? He hasn't rung me yet. Which is rather disappointing, because he was hotter than Tom Yum Koong soup. Oh, lovely, thanks.'

This last was for the waiter. I downed half my new beer in one go. The stress of this evening needed amortising in one way or another, and this was the only method immediately available.

'Out of sight, out of mind,' Gill said, with more disapproval than I would usually have tolerated from her – and, to be fair, more than she would usually have shown. I made allowances.

'It's important to distinguish between serious stuff and playing around,' I said, shrugging. 'I'm just being honest. And, you know, if it's not serious, one man does tend to wipe out the last one. Actually,' I added, 'that works even if it's serious. Men are like Band-Aids. If one rips himself off, slap another one on quick. At the very worst it'll be a good distraction.'

It occurred to me that, unless Jeremy had undergone a radical change since Gill had left him, this was one technique for dealing with her absence that was not available to him. Poor Jeremy. I drank still more beer, sensing that Gill was about to lecture me some more. It always fascinated me what wildly different stages people passed through as they went from one relationship to another; we would swear blind that we have our feet on the ground, are sure of our own opinions, and yet a lover can make us waver all over the place like a drunk trying to walk the line. When Gill was with Jeremy she had vastly enjoyed all of my amatorial adventures. Now she was less securely bolted-down, and consequently wanted the world around her to be more stable.

Fortunately Philip came back from the toilet just in time to save me from further censure. I noticed that his nostrils looked a little redder than they had been when he left, as if he had been blowing them hard, and I smirked in satisfaction. I am horribly petty and competitive.

I studied Philip, trying to work out what his attraction was for Gill. He was less Sloaney than Jeremy, and Gill for that matter; more aspirational middle class, like me. Maybe that was one of the reasons he liked Gill. Philip had all the signs of a man who was busy climbing his way up the social ladder. I couldn't judge exactly which rung he had reached. I didn't know how to read the signs that well. I knew some Sloane girls who could assess a man's income and social position by his shoes and his watch. They were the piranhas of the dating scene, those girls; they would strip a man down to the bone quite ruthlessly, moving on as soon as the meat had run out. For a man who had his own property company, Philip wasn't too flash. The aftershave and watch and hair gel and tie were all more subdued than one might expect. Gill would tone him down a few notches further if they stayed together, though.

We had got back on to the subject of Liam by the time

the main courses arrived. It was probably inevitable. Liam was such good material.

'What's the series called?' Philip was asking as the waiter put my roast duck curry down in front of me.

'*Liam at Large*,' I said, as the delicious scent of coconut milk rose before me. 'It's a round-the-country thing, every week a different city. Liam's really good at getting on with new people. They respond to him very well – he's got loads of chirpy charm. There's this one episode where he practically gets off with this woman who runs a B&B where he's doing breakfasts. By the end of it they're doing a double-act like something out of a Carry On film. It's hilarious.'

'I must look out for it,' Philip said politely.

I forked up a piece of duck from the aromatic curry and stared at it in dismay. It had been roasted, sure enough, and cut into slices, but, disastrously, the fat had been left on. Each slice was edged with a wide border of white lard, and what was usually the crispy dark rim of skin was now soggy with coconut-milk curry. Even if I hadn't been dieting, the curry was already rich enough, and adding several cubic centimetres of duck fat would be a stomach-turning experience.

I could just imagine the scene that Liam would throw, the way he would call over the waiter to point out this fact, and probably go into the kitchen to explain it to the cook as well. I had been with him at an Italian pizzeria one lunchtime when, having asked for chilli on our pizzas, they had come with whole chillies dotted across the surface like miniature grenades. Liam had charged over to the counter where the pizza guy was working and engaged in a long emotional shouting match with him about the idiocy of throwing a handful of whole chillis on to a pizza when it was the work of a moment to deseed them. Or throw on some Tabasco if you're feeling lazy, Liam had yelled. The entire encounter had been

operatic in its intensity and, naturally enough, in the end
Liam had made firm friends with the pizza guy and the owner
of the restaurant, neither of whom, miraculously, had seemed
to mind the atrocious cod-Italian in which he had been shouting. That was Liam: able to get away with throwing up his
hands and roaring: 'Mamma mia! You Italians know notheeng!
My mamma, she is ashamed to put thees on the table in her
ristorante!' without being fed through the prosciutto slicer.

Philip was looking at me expectantly. Clearly it was my
turn to speak. I dredged something up.

'It's called *Liam at Large* – the series – because Liam larges
it up a lot, you know?' I explained. 'He's got enough personality for about four people.'

I was now hacking away at my initial duck piece with an
annoyingly blunt knife which wouldn't slice away the fat so
much as rip it into lumps. It was a clumsy business, by which
I was rather embarrassed. I didn't want to look fat-obsessed
in front of Philip. Come to think of it, Philip was having a
distinctly inhibiting effect on me. It wasn't a good sign.
Besides, I had just noticed that the vegetables at the bottom
of the curry were all large chunks of peeled aubergine. I don't
mind aubergine in small quantities, when it's grated or pureed,
but this was way too much. And I just didn't think aubergines
went with duck. They were too greasy – and God knew this
curry didn't need any more fat. The main course, which had
been my big treat, was very disappointing. I was in a sulk.
The evening felt irreparably ruined.

'Juliet! Gill! Man I don't know!' boomed a familiar voice
from halfway across the restaurant. 'Fancy seeing you here, as
they say in the soap operas!'

Henry Ridgley rolled up to our booth, his sudden appearance as welcome this evening as it had been unfortunate a
few weeks ago in that hotel corridor.

'That is, assuming it is Juliet, and not Fräulein Helga Doppelgänger!' he said cheerfully. 'How nice to see you all!'

I seemed to remember that Fräulein Doppelgänger had actually been called Greta. Still, it was scarcely for me to correct him.

'Hi, Henry!' I said with great enthusiasm.

I didn't have to pretend ignorance of the Fräulein Doppelgänger incident. Henry had cornered me the next morning and related the entire story to me in the hopes that I too had spotted a pidgin-German-speaking me-lookalike roaming hotel corridors. I had pleaded total ignorance and left Henry in the bar drowning his sorrows. That wasn't my responsibility. Any excuse would do for Henry.

Philip, I noticed, was staring at Henry, appalled. Henry's shirt collar was frayed and his tie stained with what was probably red wine – though it could have been many, many other liquids. Beef bouillon; fruit coulis; or a drop of blood from where he had all too obviously nicked himself shaving that morning. I was surprised he wasn't a mass of shaving cuts. What had once been his jawline was so layered over with sagging dewlaps of flesh that it would be easier to work a razor in and out of a bulldog's jowls.

Henry's shirt was faded pink with a dirty white collar. His cardigan was yellow, his jacket old greenish tweed and his trousers brown corduroy, gone at the knees, with enough creases to make a contour map of the Highlands blush by comparison. He looked like a remittance man from an old landed family which had finally cut him off for good.

The manager and half the staff of the restaurant were hovering expectantly behind Henry. Philip, not realising who Henry was, probably thought they were going to throw him out. I knew better. Henry's appearance, while taking shabby chic to depths previously unplumbed, was distinctive in the extreme. The manager was probably about to dash back into the kitchen and insist that fatted calves be roasted immediately for one of the most important food critics in London. I just hoped for the sake of Henry's arteries that they didn't serve it in a coconut-milk curry with fried aubergines.

'Mr Henry is friend, yes? He sit with you?' said the manager encouragingly. 'Mr Henry love Thai House, right, Mr Henry?'

Gill and I exchanged a glance. Gill's was definitely panicky. So much for anonymity in Camden Town. But we didn't have any choice. Henry, beaming happily, was already saying, 'Oh, absolutely! We're great friends!' to the manager.

'Great!' I said brightly, sliding over to make room for Henry in the booth. The slats of the bench creaked under Henry's weight as he heaved himself in.

'Mr Henry's pillows, quick!' snapped the manager at one of the waiters, who scurried off and returned in a few seconds with a pile of velvet pillows, which Henry, with much puffing and heaving, distributed behind and below his person. The whole process took a couple of minutes; Henry, rather admirably, was in no hurry when it came to his comfort.

It was an ill wind. I was actually grateful for Henry's presence; it would definitely liven up the evening. He was undeniably entertaining – unless he was roaring drunk at one of your launches. And though he was an old soak, he was an impressively important old soak. Look at the treatment he was getting here. Philip, as was only natural, had perked up every time famous clients of the agency's had been mentioned. I doubted he would mind having dinner, even accidentally, with a minor celebrity. Henry's writing for the *Sunday Times* and *Mode* made all the difference in how one perceived him; without his columns, Henry would have been a ghastly food-stained alkie; with them, he was a charming English eccentric. And so amusing!

I suddenly wondered whether anyone had thought to offer Henry his own television series. If we could edit out all the libellous bits, it would be a riot.

I made a note to ask Henry if he had an agent.

Chapter Nine

'Henry,' I said a few hours later, 'do you have an agent?'

'What?' He downed a glass of brandy. 'Foul stuff,' he said reflexively, as he almost always did. 'Where's that bottle I brought you in, Neil?'

'You finished that months ago, Henry,' said the bartender laconically.

'Did I? Lying bastard. Lying Irish bastard. You drank it, didn't you? Bloody waste, you couldn't tell the difference between Armagnac and Juliet's piss. Anyone ever drunk your piss, Juliet?'

I exchanged a glance with the unflappable bartender. It was clear that he knew Henry at least as well as I did. One of the tricks to managing Henry was never to let him embarrass you; in that respect he was eerily similar to Mel. Besides, I rather liked no-holds barred, gladiatorial banter contests. They were strangely liberating. Especially after I had had to make Miss Manners-approved conversation with Philip most of the evening.

'I wouldn't recommend it tonight,' I said frankly. 'I've had so much curry it's probably vindaloo strength.'

As I had expected, this was more detail than Henry wanted to hear. Besides, he liked to be the disgusting one. If you managed to out-gross him, he would leave the arena. And so it proved. He waved his empty glass at the bartender instead.

'Neil, more of this disgusting rotgut, eh? And whatever Juliet's on.'

'Another Grand Marnier?' Neil asked me.

'Yeah, go on.'

I didn't usually drink Grand Marnier, but somehow it felt like that kind of evening. Grand Marnier would probably not have been too happy that I associated their product with a late night at a lock-in at a spit-and-sawdust pub in a Camden back street which trendiness had not reached and never would. But it was cosy, and there was a fire going, and the saloon bar (one could tell how old-fashioned the Spit and Whistle was by the fact that it had still maintained the distinction) had saggingly upholstered bar stools which were extraordinarily comfortable. Doubtless because they had been tenderised over the years by the heavy bottoms of generations of immigrant builders.

This was Henry's local. I had been astounded to hear that he lived in Camden; I would have put him down as Battersea or South Ken. But apparently he owned a house in Camden Square. I was very jealous.

'Been coming in here for thirty years,' he had said, or rather bellowed, while banging on the locked door of the pub with his fist and shouting: 'Neil! Open up, man, and be quick about it!'

The door was shaking and the engraved glass rattling in its frame by the time I heard someone undoing the lock.

'Don't know why they don't just give you a key,' I said as Neil let us in. 'It'd be a lot easier on the woodwork.'

'You must be bloody joking,' Neil said, sliding the bolts shut behind us. 'He'd be in here at all hours. D'you know how much of our stock he'd get through if he didn't have to pay for it?'

Neil, whose age it was impossible to determine, was a tiny little leprechaun with a heavily wrinkled, bright-eyed face. Certainly he showed no signs of decrepitude; he was positively sprightly. I imagined him wrestling the beer kegs into place himself. He had that kind of small wiry build that is often freakishly strong.

The saloon bar had a comfortable sprinkling of late-night clients. Looking round, I realised that I was the youngest one present. There were few women, and all of them were cautionary tales. It wasn't that the men were in any better condition; their faces resembled aging Easter Island statues too. Only they weren't daubed unnervingly with eyeshadow and smudgy coral lipstick.

Neil obviously favoured serious drinkers only. Or perhaps hardened would be a better description. These weren't lads drinking seven pints in a couple of hours and then going out to puke in the gutter, nor career girls who thought they were cool because they could sink five vodka and slimline tonics with the help of some coke in the toilets. No faux-alcoholism here: the Spit and Whistle's clientele was the real thing. Death by cirrhosis or lung cancer positively guaranteed.

It was a place where I would always look good by comparison.

'I like it here,' I announced to Henry and, by extension, to Neil.

'We're not so big on the Camden trendies,' the latter said rather shortly as he wiped some glasses. 'But since you're a friend of Henry's . . .'

'Well, that put me in my place,' I said *sotto voce* to the latter.

'Look around you, dear!' Henry said. 'Neil knows exactly who he wants in the old Spit! Made me promise never to write about it when he found out what I did.'

'There's only two people get let in after the doors are locked,' Neil said in a more friendly tone.

I drooped in disappointment. I had just been thinking how

convenient – not to mention cool – it would be to have a local lock-in which one could enter at will. So much cheaper than membership of a private drinking club. And much less competition. Bring a date here and you would look like a supermodel by comparison.

'Who's the other one?' I asked.

'Alex, down the end there.' Neil nodded to a man at the far end of the bar, drinking from a big white mug. 'He's my other professional.'

Alex, hearing his name mentioned, turned a little towards us and raised his mug amicably. He showed no signs, however, of wanting to come over and talk to us, but returned to sipping placidly at the contents of the mug while he contemplated the grubby display of bottles behind the bar. He didn't seem to have favoured me with a glance any longer than the one he had accorded to Henry. My interest was piqued.

Fortunately, Henry was the perfect human ice-breaker.

'What're you drinking, man?' he roared at Alex.

'Coffee,' Alex said tranquilly.

'Coffee? Coffee!' Henry swivelled to fix Neil with an outraged glare. 'You let him in here so he can drink your appalling coffee! At least I sodding drink you dry!'

'Sometimes he puts a tot of whisky in it,' Neil said.

Henry huffed and puffed as if trying to blow the house down.

'Disgraceful behaviour. What was I saying in the restaurant, Juliet? Young men of today – no stamina. Outrageous.'

Henry was referring to Philip, who he had taken against immediately. But it had been Philip's refusal to order an after-dinner drink that had really galled Henry. I pulled a deprecating face at Alex, but he looked quite unruffled. It was too dark in here for me to see him with perfect accuracy, but as far as I could make out, he was nice looking, with rather beaten-up features which would have been positively ugly if he had been a girl (unfair). On a man, however, they were solid and reliable. If you were casting him in a film (I played this game a lot) he would have been the local gas-station owner in the small town who had loved the heroine faithfully since high school and whom she married in the last reel, having been betrayed by the handsome cheating travelling salesman who had turned out to have a wife in every town. He was quite tall, with a stocky build. I would definitely be able to fit into his jeans. His hair was dark; thick and shaggily cut, and his face, while with no pretensions to handsomeness, was pleasant; it might even be the kind that grew on you.

'It's not Neil's usual coffee,' he said, after I had just begun to think that he wasn't intending to speak to us further. 'I keep a supply here and Neil saves it for me.'

This set Henry off again.

'Or *does* he?' he shouted, pounding the bar with his fist. 'Or *does* he? I refer you to the recently mentioned episode of the Armagnac, my friend!'

'Wouldn't drink his muck,' said Neil with a sniff. 'Nicaraguan rubbish. I like a nice cup of instant myself.'

'Nicaraguan?' I said to Alex.

He grinned. 'Not quite. That stuff's pretty nasty. But it's a Fair Trade brand. That's why Neil gets worked up about it.'

'Left-wing nonsense,' Neil muttered, going out behind the bar to attend to some customers.

I hated it when men were more politically correct than me. Alex was probably a vegetarian too.

'Where do you get the coffee?' I asked, for some reason. I think I must have wanted to charm him. When a man doesn't seem particularly interested in me – even in a lock-in at a pub so sordid that the only other females present could have modelled for gargoyles – I go into flirting overdrive. Sad but true.

'Oh, just the health food shop on Parkway,' he said casually.

'Another local!' Henry said enthusiastically.

'Of course he's a local, Henry,' I pointed out. 'He wouldn't be a regular if he wasn't.'

Alex had returned to sipping his coffee and staring at the bottles again. I narrowed my eyes.

'Is there any more coffee?' I asked, thinking that actually, despite using it as a ploy to keep him talking, this might not be a bad idea. What with all the beer at the restaurant, and the third Grand Marnier I was shortly to consume, coffee was exactly what I needed.

'There might be some in the pot,' he said. 'Ask Neil.'

'Would you mind?'

'No, no. If I have any more I won't sleep.'

Neil eventually produced a few coldish drops of coffee, which I drank with every appearance of enjoyment.

'Funny bumping into you in that Thai place,' Henry said to me, for the first time since we had entered the pub lowering his voice to something approaching a normal tone. 'I go in there at least once a week. Cleans me right out.'

I grimaced. 'Thanks for the information.'

'My dear Juliet, when a man has to eat out as often as I do, believe me, a good swilling out of the bowels is absolutely crucial.'

'You could try stewed prunes,' I suggested.

Henry lurched forward on his stool to squint at me in an effort to see if I was joking.

'Difficult to get the dose right with prunes,' he confided. 'Doesn't take much to get the system dangerously over-excited.'

'*God*,' I said in repulsion. I had been about to propose colonic irrigation but was not prepared to risk Henry's comments on the subject.

'Can we get another Grand Marnier?' I asked Neil. 'And whatever Henry's having?'

'Cooking brandy,' Henry bellowed.

'D'you want a whisky?' I said to Alex. 'Since I finished your coffee, it seems only polite.'

'No thanks, I'm fine,' he said pleasantly.

He looked about to add something else, but at that moment Henry said in my ear: 'So! Gill broken up with her husband, then? Can't say I'm surprised. Always seemed a very dull stick.'

I swung round on my stool.

'Henry,' I warned, 'discretion, please.'

Gill had been nervous enough about Henry's known gossiping tendencies to stage an elaborate smokescreen which had involved the cover story that she was thinking of investing in property and had taken Philip out to dinner to pick his brains. This would have been plausible if not for the absence of Jeremy (without whom she would certainly not make business decisions involving large sums of money; what otherwise would be the point of being married to a successful banker?) and Gill's over-bright tone, which would have aroused suspicion in a corpse. She had then proceeded to order separate taxis for her and Philip, and gone through a little scene where she shook his hand goodnight and thanked him so much for his help. The whole thing had been about as plausible as the plot of a West End farce. All it had lacked to complete the resemblance was Philip's trousers falling down repeatedly in front of a passing vicar.

I was rather relieved that Henry hadn't been fooled; at least now I had someone with whom to discuss the situation. When he had suggested a nightcap I had accepted at once. I needed to debrief.

'So this is the new man?' Henry was saying. 'Didn't think much of him either. Another dull stick. And a bit poncey.'

'What do you mean by poncey?' I said warily.

'You know,' he said impatiently. 'Pretentious.'

By this Henry presumably meant that Philip's jacket and trousers were clean, pressed and matching, that his chin was freshly shaved and his tie unspotted. Henry took the traditional Englishman's deep-rooted suspicion of well-groomed men to self-parodical extremes.

'Gill's a very attractive woman,' he pronounced as magisterially as if he were sitting in a large leather armchair in a gentleman's club, smoking an after-dinner pipe. Any minute now he would call her a charming filly. 'She could do much better than that.'

By any standards, I reflected, most people would consider that Gill, in making a smooth transition from a very nice banker to a perfectly pleasant property developer, was doing very well for herself. Mel had been right about Philip; he had insisted on paying the bill. Apart from Henry's. He wouldn't have baulked at it – how could he? – but Henry apparently had a tab. Knowing Henry, he had probably negotiated a hefty discount in return for good publicity but was embarrassed to have the arrangement generally known. He had simply said bluffly: 'Settle up next time, eh?' and waved his hand at the manager dismissively.

'Try not to spread it around, Henry,' I pleaded. 'It's only just happened and Jeremy's in a terrible state.'

I was hoping that an appeal to masculine solidarity might do the trick, and indeed, on hearing these words, Henry's large, heavy head lifted and fell ponderously in a series of slow, contemplative nods. He made a little gesture with his hand on the bar counter, like a hanging judge reluctantly pushing away the black cap.

'Poor sod,' he was intoning. 'I remember how I felt when Jenny left me. Or rather,' he corrected himself, 'I don't. All a blur.'

'Cognac?'

'Anything I had in the house. Then whatever rotgut Neil could provide. Knocked myself out for months.'

He chuckled.

'You should have read my copy. Wasn't a restaurant I didn't savage. And completely incoherent, apparently. The subs stopped ringing me up to ask what the hell I'd meant because I just cursed them till they went away again. They made it all up, in the end. Might even have done a better job than me,' he added, seemingly struck by this thought for the first time.

I sipped my Grand Marnier, firmly resolving to leave when it was finished. It wasn't that late; we had left the restaurant at eleven. I checked my watch. Twelve twenty. No problem. As long as I didn't let Henry draw me into a marathon drinking session, I would be in bed by one.

'Just going to drain the old snake,' Henry muttered. His clamber down from the bar stool was terrifying. The stool wobbled and produced an increasingly alarming series of creaks. Just when it looked as if Henry was safely on terra firma, the overhang of his buttocks caught on the seat, destablising him almost fatally. But, with a grunt and a curse and an expert backwards jab with the flat of his hand, he unwedged his bottom, managing by some miracle not to pull the stool over on top of him, and lumbered away to the toilets.

The Spit and Whistle seemed eerily quiet in his absence. Most of the other customers weren't talking, beyond the occasional 'Same again, Neil.' I drank some more Grand Marnier and listened to my own breathing. It was almost like a yoga meditation.

Quite a few moments went by before I realised that Alex was talking to me.

'I'm sorry?' I said, turning on my stool.

'I've seen Henry in here for the last ten years or so,' he said. 'First time he's ever come in with a girl.'

'Well, I hope it won't be the last,' I said, addressing this comment pointedly to Neil. 'I like it here.'

Suddenly, realisation dawned on me. Alex – and Neil, for all I knew – thought that I was Henry's girlfriend. A bit of PR fluff who he was wining and dining through all the most exclusive haunts in Camden. Mmn, very plausible. I pondered for a moment on how to dispel this illusion. Even if I hadn't thought Alex quite attractive, in a low-key, only-man-with-a-pulse-in-a-dark-pub-past-midnight kind of way, I objected on principle to being thought of as the type of girl who dated down.

'Henry's an old friend,' I said casually. 'Or business acquaintance, really. We bumped into each other tonight at that Thai on Chalk Farm Road.'

'Yeah, Henry's always in there,' Neil said, nodding pontifically. 'Says it—'

'Yes,' I interrupted. 'He told me.'

My digestive system was feeling a little delicate; duck fat and aubergine grease. The last thing my stomach needed was for me to speculate on exactly what was passing through Henry at that precise moment.

'Do you work round here?' I said to Alex. I was specialising in banal conversational openings this evening. I blamed this entirely on Philip.

'Yes, my studio's in a side street by the canal. This is on my way home. Direct line.'

I was going to ask it. I could feel it popping out despite all the efforts I was making to restrain myself.

'So what do you do?'

I cringed. But it was said.

'I'm an architect.'

'Oh, right!' I said in the I-can-identify tone of voice people use when their interlocutor reveals himself to be someone with a respectable, even artistic-leaning job. I prayed that I wouldn't say next: 'An architect! Must be really interesting!' Anything but that. I was getting close, however. Only Henry's return from the gents' saved me from committing further fatuities. My conversational skills were dangerously low; I needed to recharge their batteries. Time to go home.

'I'm off,' I said to Henry, finishing my Grand Marnier. 'I have to be up earlyish tomorrow.'

'Nonsense!' Henry protested. He hoisted himself on to the stool in a practised manoeuvre, using both its rung and the bar rail for leverage. Getting up was obviously much easier than getting down.

'I need to polish off that bottle of rotgut so Neil has to buy something better for me tomorrow night,' he explained.

I had no idea if he was joking.

'Well, I need to get some sleep,' I said firmly. 'I've got a busy day tomorrow. Got to be up bright and early.'

God, listen to me. I was spouting more clichés than a sports commentator.

''Spect I should walk you home,' Henry said, obviously torn between the impulse to be what Bertie Wooster would have called a *preux chevalier*, and the rougher, more manly task of staying here to finish off the cooking brandy.

'I'll be fine, Henry. It's just five minutes' walk. I do it all the time. But thanks,' I added, throwing a sop to chivalry.

There was no need to discourage him. I didn't think for a

moment that Henry wanted to walk me home in order to invite himself up for a coffee. He had a reputation for randiness, but it wasn't indiscriminate. Like most men, he might well not refuse me were I to take off all my clothes and beg him to make me his, but he had no specific intentions towards me. Otherwise I would never have come out drinking with him.

'Which way are you going?' Alex said to me, putting down his mug.

'Just behind Chalk Farm station.'

'I can walk you back, if you like. I live on Prince of Wales Road.'

'Oh, thanks,' I said, rather surprised.

'Do we know this man?' Henry bellowed unexpectedly as I slid off my stool and started to put on my coat. 'Are we sure this is a good idea?'

'*Henry,*' I said in a tone of admonishment. It didn't work. Henry, for some reason known only to himself, was off on some sort of protective-uncle track.

'Complete stranger appears from nowhere and offers to walk you home – bloody suspicious, if you ask me!'

'But I'm not,' I pointed out. 'Asking you, that is.'

'Alex's been coming in here for years and never raped anyone. As far as I know,' Neil offered, passing us with a handful of glasses.

Alex and I met each other's eyes and tried very hard not to laugh. Bizarrely enough, Henry actually seemed reassured by Neil's testimony.

'Well, if Neil says you're OK, I expect it's all right,' he said generously.

'He didn't actually say that –' I started, but found Alex's hand on my elbow, propelling me towards the door, which Neil was already unlocking.

'Are you mad!' he muttered. 'Do you want to start it all up again?'

'As far as I know,' I quoted as the door shut behind us, doubling up with giggles. I must have been at that shade of tipsy where all the funny ratings are turned up a few notches.

'Very reassuring, wasn't it?' Alex agreed with a wide, appreciative smile. I liked the way his eyes crinkled at the corners. 'Almost like saying nothing was ever proved.'

We emerged from the side street on to Chalk Farm Road.

'Oh look,' I said as we passed a boarded-up restaurant on a corner. 'The Site Of Doom claims another victim.'

Alex knew exactly what I meant.

'Guess what?' he said. 'All these years I've lived around here and I've never gone in there. Must have been seventeen restaurants on that spot and I've never eaten in one of them.'

'Of course not. It's the Site Of Doom. You must have sensed the vibes.'

I wrapped my scarf around my neck, but it was mainly to have something to do with my hands; it was mild for a late November night. Alex's hands were shoved deep into his pockets in a way that explained why his trousers sagged slightly from the waist. It must be an old habit of his.

'So how do you know Henry?' he said as we crossed the road.

'I'm a partner in a PR agency,' I said boastfully. I still got a huge thrill out of the word 'partner', and I was afraid I had put too much emphasis on it. 'We specialise in food PR. I bump into Henry all the time at, uh, conferences.'

The memory of the last time I had done exactly that came flooding back in widescreen Technicolor with Dolby stereo. I stumbled on a paving stone, telling myself that I must under no circumstances invite Alex up to my flat to do some coke. I knew how easily persuaded men were under those conditions.

'I'm always amazed by how well he writes,' Alex observed. 'Considering how much he drinks, I mean. I'll read some particularly pithy review of his, and then see him in the Spit the next night falling off his stool blind drunk.'

'I can't believe you just said particularly pithy,' I said, by some miracle managing to pronounce it more or less correctly.

'I've got fewer Grand Marniers running through my system,' he observed with a touch of sarcasm.

My head snapped up. Bastard. How dare he? No one had asked him to walk me home. And I hadn't meant to needle him with that comment; I had sincerely been impressed.

'How come you see Henry in there all the time but he had no idea you were a regular?' I said in retaliation. 'You can't be very memorable.'

'Oh, I'm a peaceful soul,' he said, seeming quite unoffended. 'And you can scarcely miss Henry. Neil's very proud of him. Reads all his articles. Besides,' he added, 'Henry only really notices you if you're a brandy bottle.'

Since this was exactly what I had been thinking myself, I couldn't help laughing in agreement. It came out as more of a snort, which I heard with great embarrassment.

'You don't really seem like a pub person,' I said feebly. I just wanted to say something, anything, so the snort didn't hang in the air between us.

'I'm not,' he said equably. 'I just work late sometimes. By the time I've finished, everyone's gone home. I like to wind down for half an hour or so with a few live bodies around me.'

I must have been as half-cut as he was implying to have been annoyed by this reply. For some reason it bugged me that he had given an eminently sensible, sober reply to my fatuous remark. I felt that I was making a fool of myself. We turned into the entrance to my block of flats, and I said, trying to sound as dignified as possible: 'Well, this is me. Thanks for walking me back. I hope it didn't take you too much out of your way.'

'Oh, it was no trouble,' he said. 'Any time.'

There was a slight pause.

'Well, see you around,' he said, pulling his hand out of his trouser pocket to sketch a sort of wave at me.

I was expecting him to ask for my phone number, or at least ask if he'd be seeing me in the pub again. Why else, after all, would he have offered to walk me home? I waited, leaving a polite pause, for him to get to the point. But he didn't, and the silence drew out embarrassingly until I finally said, 'Yeah, OK. Good night, then.'

There was another pause.

'Well, good night,' he said, sketching another little wave, and turned away. I was left standing there, watching him go, his leather jacket tight over his wide shoulders, pulled equally snugly over his hips by the fact that he had just shoved both hands into the pockets. He didn't treat his clothes well. It would have been endearing if I hadn't been so cross.

What had just gone on here? Had he meant to ask me for my number and then been so bored by my moronic attempts at conversation that he had abandoned the whole idea? He looked as if he were walking perfectly casually, but was that in fact a camouflaged attempt not to break into a run? And why the hell did I care anyway? Did I have to have the entire male population of London at my feet before I could be content? Clearly I wasn't on as much of a roll as I thought, but who cared about one scruffy architect in corduroys, for God's sake? I must be drunker than I thought; sometimes it made me insecure. Alex was probably just a nicely brought-up, chivalrous person who hadn't liked the thought of a woman walking home alone at midnight. A woman he didn't find remotely attractive. Hah! I bet he'd change his mind if he saw me in my PVC frock.

This was all very silly, and I was very tired. I determined to go to bed and console myself with fantasies of Pieter. And Tom. Why not? At least in my fantasies I could have them both. Simultaneously, if I wanted. The mere idea cheered me up tremendously.

Chapter Ten

'Ju? It's me.'

I felt as if I had just been dropped down a very dark well. I was craven enough to wish that I had got Lewis to filter all my calls, and then was horribly guilty because I had had this reaction to a phone call from my own brother. I was a bad, bad sister.

'Hi, Chris!' I said, and I could hear that my voice was as bright as if I had just met him at a party and he had told me he was a birdwatching actuary.

'Is this not a good time?' he asked.

'No, it's fine. Just a busy day, that's all.'

'Yeah. Me too.'

'Oh?' I said nervously. There was an ominous quality to Chris's voice. What had just happened that was going to be left to me to sort out?

'I had my appointment with the benefits people this morning.'

Chris spoke as if this were a one-off event of tremendous significance; in fact he was always having interviews with the benefits people. I made a sympathetic noise and waited for the latest litany of complaints.

'They want me to do a re-training course.'

'Oh.'

I stared at my desk. Propped against my keyboard was a card Lewis had bought me at lunchtime in the film and poster shop across the street. It was a black and white photograph of four young men in white singlets and chinos, doing one-armed handstands on a table set for a meal; plates, glasses, cutlery, coffee cups all laid out on an immaculately white tablecloth. In their free hands each of them held a forkful of food or a glass of wine which they were raising to their mouths. Their thick dark hair fell forwards into their eyes; the muscles of their tanned backs and arms, revealed by the cutaway armholes of the singlets, were such a perfect contrast of round swellings and declivities that every time I looked at them I could picture exactly what they would feel like beneath my palm. Two of them even wore braces, which accentuated the width of their shoulders and the narrow flat waists over which their legs curved for balance, their buttocks tight. They looked as if they could stay that way for ever, the entire weight of their gymnasts' bodies balanced on one strong hand. The caption read: Los Angeles Athletic Club, 1930. They were lost and gone.

I stroked the photograph with the ball of my thumb, as if to calm myself down, as I said to Chris, 'What kind of course?'

'Oh, for fuck's sake!' His anger exploded down the phone line. 'Don't you get it? I can't do a fucking course! They last for weeks and I have to be there every day! I can't tie up my time like that!'

It always sounded offensively reactionary to suggest that the state, which had provided Chris with a flat, an income and subsidised rent for years, might eventually want him at least to make a gesture towards acknowledgement of this generosity. So I didn't.

'I told them that!' he was saying triumphantly. 'I was like, I'm a musician! I can't do that sort of thing! I mean, I've got to be available for gigs. Something could come up at any moment.'

'No, I see that,' I said carefully. 'I mean, um, I see your

point, obviously. But it's not really what they want to hear, is it?'

'Fucking bastards! They said this is it. They're going to cut me off this time.'

'Oh no.'

'If I don't do the course.'

'Oh, *Chris.* I'm so sorry.'

Hard on the heels of this automatic response came the realisation that actually I wasn't sorry at all. I was panicked. Without even the paltry income from his dole cheque, Chris would become wholly my responsibility. Or at least that was how I perceived it. If the state wasn't going to look after Chris any longer, I would have to. It didn't even occur to me to wonder why this was the case; it simply was, had always been, till death did us part. Chris was my responsibility, for better or worse. If he messed up, I had to sort it out; and if I didn't, I had to answer to my mother. I shuddered at the prospect.

'What kind of course is it?' I said again, playing for time.

'Computer skills. They made me do an aptitude test,' he said sulkily, like a child complaining about being forced to eat his vegetables. 'And they said I came out pretty high.'

'You were always really good at maths. And there's a lot of money in computing,' I said tentatively. 'I know this guy who basically trained himself how to program from a manual. He's been doing it for years now. The last time I met him for a drink he had a wodge of cash on him as thick as my thumb.'

Chris snorted. 'That's not exactly the point, is it?'

'It'd be nice to have some money for a change, though, wouldn't it?' Sensing by the quality of the silence that he was about to make another dismissive comment, I changed tack. 'Think of all the recording equipment you could buy!'

Chris was still silent, but I could tell that this had struck home. I pressed home my advantage.

'I mean, what happens if you refuse to do the course? They really cut you off?'

'Said so, didn't I?' he muttered. 'Don't go on about it.'

If I encouraged him too strongly to go on the computing course, he would refuse to do it on principle. I chose my words with extreme care.

'But if you give it a go, they'll keep paying you the dole?'

'Jobseeker's Allowance,' he corrected gloomily. 'Yeah, I s'pose. They'll try to find me a job at the end, though. Using my newly acquired skills,' he added in an uncanny imitation of the patronising voice so often employed by people at the job centre.

'They're always trying to find you jobs, Chris. I mean, that's nothing new. You can handle that. And the next time they give you grief you can always point out that you actually did a course of theirs.'

'Yeah. I 'spose so.'

From Chris, in these circumstances, that was a full-bodied cry of assent. My body sagged in relief. Too soon.

'Would you have a look at all these forms they've sent me?' he said. 'You know I can't cope with that stuff.'

'What kind of forms? Stuff to fill out? I would have thought you could do those in your sleep by now.'

Relief had made me careless.

'Well, if you can't be bothered . . .' His voice tailed off.

I had the terrible vision of Chris not returning the forms, failing to show up for his course, being summarily cut off the dole and falling heavily on my shoulders for support – financial, emotional, the works.

'Shall I come round tonight after work?' I suggested, anxious to ward this off.

'That'd be great, Ju.' He sounded very relieved. 'Thanks a million.'

'No problem. Shall I give you a ring when I'm leaving the office?'

'Nah, don't bother. Drop in to the pub first and if I'm not there I'll be at home.'

'Fine.'

I put down the receiver. Putting things down: that felt good. I rested my forearms on the desk and laid my head on them in an effort to see if that would help still further. It did, fractionally. At least with my face in the crook of my arm it was dark. I tried to clear my mind for what I needed to get done that day but all I could see were forms, a whole pile of official forms, pale blue and green with narrow white rectangles to indicate where the writing was supposed to go, and the one on top of the pile had a big stamp running diagonally across it which said in bright red ink: 'Benefits Denied'. I shuddered.

The office door opened.

'Juliet?'

It was Lewis, bringing me a cappuccino. I raised my head and gazed at him blearily.

'All getting on top of you?' he said cheerfully. 'Anything I can do to help?'

If Lewis had been my boyfriend I would have been deeply suspicious of him nearly all the time. His good spirits; his sensitivity to my moods and, having correctly diagnosed the latter, his ability to say just the right thing to lift my gloom; not to mention his habit of bringing me little spontaneous presents, like the postcard, or a bunch of flowers, or a coffee from the Italian deli; all the clearest of warning signs.

And if he had been my boyfriend I would have been right to be suspicious. I knew that Lewis was tomcatting his way through London's entire young female population. Still, as long as he didn't mess things up by sleeping with clients, I couldn't care less. The other danger of course would be to sleep with him myself, but despite his extreme handsomeness, which frankly verged on absurdity – the boy had a six-pack like a cartoon hero's – I wasn't tempted. Even without being my assistant, he was safe from me. Lewis must have more notches on his belt than Don Giovanni. The thought of being Miss One Thousand and Four held little temptation.

In short, with Lewis I had the benefit of all of his good qualities and none of the bad. Contemplation of this fact caused me to sit up straight and take a more positive view of the world.

'My brother just rang,' I said, unsnapping the lid off the paper cup.

'Oh?' Lewis sipped his own coffee.

'He's about to have his benefits cut off if he doesn't go on some re-training course.'

Lewis shrugged. 'He's a musician, right?' he said. 'So what? Do the course, keep signing on, big deal.'

'Mmn,' I said through my foam moustache.

'How long's he been signing on?'

'Oh, about eight years, more or less.'

'Jesus.'

'And he wangled himself a council flat. Bought the keys off some people at the housing department, you know how that works.'

'Fucking hell.' Lewis's eyebrows had pulled together into one thick line. 'I really disapprove of that kind of thing. I mean, here am I paying a fortune in rent and going to work every day. No offence, but I'm subsidising wasters like your brother. Well, you are too.'

This touched me on the raw. I jumped slightly, slopping the coffee, though fortunately only on some unimportant papers.

'And you know what really pisses me off?' Lewis went on,

leaning back in the clients' chair and stretching his feet up to prop them on the corner of my desk. His shoes barely rested on the edge, conveying sociability without being over-familiar. This was nicely judged, as were all Lewis's actions. He was a sort of Jeeves of the outer office.

Without waiting for the prompt, he continued: 'Whenever you talk about this kind of stuff, people always assume you're a raging Conservative. I mean, obviously we take it for granted that some people have more disadvantages or whatever. But I know all these middle-class kids dossing around all day and then complaining when someone at the job centre dares to try to make them take a job, or whining about what a bore it is to get up and sign on every other Wednesday morning – it really pisses me off.'

'Yes,' I sighed. 'I know plenty of people like that. Or I did in my twenties. In the last few years they seem to have faded away. I wonder where they've gone?'

'Out of London. It's too expensive if you're not working. Drifted away up North where the rent's cheaper and there's more unemployment, so people just take it for granted that you're signing on instead of hassling you all the time about this clerking position that's just come up at Barclays in Sydenham.'

'I don't think I've ever heard you express yourself so strongly about anything, Lewis,' I said, fascinated. 'Except football, of course.'

He made a dismissive gesture, as if to say that this went without saying.

'Succinct,' I said, 'cutting, crisp as a freshly washed iceberg lettuce.'

'I may blush. So what's going to happen with your brother?'

I drank some more coffee.

'Damned if I know.'

*   *   *

Chris wasn't among the smattering of listless drinkers at his local, but I spotted his girlfriend Sissy in the far corner. Her eyes were double-glazed and her shoulders sagged, probably from the weight of the heavy sweaters she was wearing. She was very thin, and the woolly layers made her look strangely disproportioned; her wrists and neck stuck out oddly from the thick itchy jumpers, as skinny and white as spring onions. Sissy was rolling up a cigarette. After breathing and sleeping, this was her main activity in life. Someday, I hoped, it would interfere critically with the former.

'Sissy?' I said.

God, what a stupid name. There was a girl who worked in fashion PR who had self-baptised herself Baby, and this annoyed me almost as much as Sissy did. Not quite, though. She wasn't my brother's girlfriend.

'Yeah?' Sissy said.

She looked up. The hair that had been hanging over her face parted slightly in long, greasy, indeterminately coloured strands. Her skin looked like wax, pale, off-white and clammy to the touch. I wanted to pick her up, carry her to the nearest launderette and shove her into a washing machine, boots and all. She would fit; those drums were big and there wasn't much of her. I could always break any bones that were sticking out. Crack them with my thumbs, like celery.

'Oh, hi, Juliet,' she said, with her usual lack of affect. 'You looking for Chris?'

'Yeah. He at home?'

'Yeah. You heard about this course they're making him do?'

'Uh, yeah.'

'Bastards. Computer course,' she sneered. 'Can you believe it? Just 'cos they've got shit jobs they want everyone to be as boring as they are.'

I simply shrugged instead and turned to go. Sissy's head

bent once more to her Rizla paper and Golden Virginia, one lank lock of hair falling into the open packet of tobacco, her hands hardly visible beneath the long cuffs of her enormous sweater. A Little Match-Girl for the twenty-first century: grown up, signing on and using her wares instead to light her constant stream of roll-ups.

Chris lived on the third floor of the tower block looming just behind the pub. I usually took the stairs. Pressing the button to call the lifts was like being dropped into a horror film; you never knew what was going to be behind the doors, and sometimes the anticipation could be even more terrifying than the reality. A woman with two kids was coming down the stairs as I started up and I stopped to let them all pass.

'Don't fancy the lifts either?' she said to me. 'Can't say I blame you.'

Her little girls looked like miniature versions of herself; big gold earrings almost as large as their tiny white ears, hair pulled tightly back into high ponytails, bomber jackets over skintight printed leggings. All they needed were their mother's high heels. You could probably buy those for children nowadays too. I'd seen four-year-olds on the beach in miniature leopard-skin bikinis, probably manufactured by children in the Far East not much bigger than themselves who earned twopence a day. From child labour to child porn in one easy step.

'Ju!'

Chris threw open the door almost as soon as I had pressed the buzzer. He must have been waiting for me. I felt better at once.

'How's it going?' he went on. 'Did you see Sissy at the pub?'

'Yeah.'

Chris gazed at me expectantly. I knew he was hoping for

a positive comment about Sissy – how well she looked, what a nice talk we had had. But I couldn't bring myself to lie. It wasn't even out of principle. I had trotted out lame compliments so often in the past that I simply couldn't do it any more. I covered the moment of disappointment by walking through into his front room and saying briskly, 'So, where are these forms, then?'

'Hang on a minute! Are you in a hurry?'

Chris shut the front door and came through behind me, a hangdog expression on his face.

'I mean, do you have somewhere you've got to be? I was thinking maybe we could kick back, have a drink, get something to eat . . .'

'Oh, that's really nice,' I said, hearing my voice soften. 'It's been ages since we've done that.'

'Yeah. Well, I just thought . . . Mum brought round a load of food yesterday, I could heat that up . . .'

It was a better offer than his or Sissy's cooking. Somehow everything they made came out pale brown and matted, with a consistency as stringy as Sissy's sweaters.

'Nice of her,' I said between gritted teeth. I was the career woman in the family, the child who actually went out to work, didn't have time to cook and, when eating at home, lived on ready-made meals. Yet Chris and Sissy, who could easily have dedicated hours each day to the preparation of delicious and economical meals, were the ones who reaped the produce of Mum's kitchen. Admittedly, Mum cooked only the kind of fat-laden food I avoided like the plague. But I still thought I should have been on the baking list. I wondered whether the cry of 'It's not fair!' ever really faded with adulthood.

'Have you spoken to her recently?' Chris said. 'She was pretty snippy when I mentioned you.'

'I had a hang-up a while ago. Haven't heard from her since.'

'She said it was over ten days,' Chris said, a shade of disapproval creeping into his voice. 'You should ring her, Ju.'

'Why?' I said crossly. 'She hung up on me!'

'Yeah, I know, but . . .' His voice tailed off sheepishly. Chris was the appeaser in the family.

I shrugged. 'She should ring me,' I said, hearing how pettishly the words came out.

'Ju, it's Mum, OK? She doesn't work that way! She's sitting there telling herself that you made her hang up on you because you were being so annoying. She thinks she's completely in the right.'

'I know, I know,' I moaned. 'But why should I ring back someone who's hung up on me? Did we ever stop to think about that one?'

Chris looked blank.

'But what's the alternative? Not ringing her back? What would happen then?'

'I dunno. I'm just sick of the way things are, that's all.'

He shrugged, as if to say What did I expect? Nothing would ever change, and went into the kitchen.

I sat down on the armchair and stared at the pot plants on the windowsill. The flat was musty and stale, an essence which was even more concentrated on Sissy and Chris. I had smelt it when I hugged him; even the marrow of his bones must have the same odour by now. It wasn't dirt. It was a kind of absence of cleanliness, lingering like sadness or depression, the dank, fusty smell of people who did the minimum necessary to get by. Even our mother's cleaning efforts could do little to dent the overwhelming sense of stuffiness that clung to the walls and the furniture like spores of mould.

Nothing in the room seemed related to anything else. It was like a job-lot at a bottom-range auction house: a table, a couple of armchairs, the video and TV stand, the manky old carpet had all been here when Chris and Sissy had moved in, too beaten up and ugly for the previous tenants to bother taking them. Neither Chris nor Sissy had touched the place since then. Having chairs to sit on was all they cared about; it was immaterial what the chairs actually looked like. The only traces of personality in the flat were Sissy's unspeakably horrendous ecstasy-art posters and Chris's guitar and amp collection, which took up a good quarter of the living room. Even these were dusty and looked uncared for. I could see that Mum had been in a hurry, or simply dispirited, on her last visit. Normally Chris's guitars would have been the first targets for the duster.

Chris tossed me a beer. I peeled open the tab and drank deeply, castigating myself for all the critical thoughts that assailed me as soon as I saw Chris or came round to his home. Lewis had nailed the sensation: like a rabid old Tory, slavering angrily about work-shy loafers who lived in cesspits of their own making.

'Thanks,' I said gratefully wiping my mouth. 'This is just what I needed.'

'Hard day at the office?'

I looked at him warily out of the corner of my eye, but he seemed entirely sincere; he wasn't about to launch into a tirade about the banality of my work.

'Yeah, very,' I said cautiously. 'Lots of organising. It's always my least favourite bit.'

'Rather you than me,' Chris said, letting out a long breath. 'It'd do my head in.'

I tapped my forehead. 'Exhibit A. One done-in head. So what food did Mum leave you?'

'Lots of lasagne. And a chicken casserole. And a whole cheesecake.'

'Wow. You did really well.'

'And all microwaveable, bless her little heart.'

'You microwave everything, Chris,' I said disapprovingly. 'You're probably dense with radiation by now.'

'Oh yeah, like you cook fresh organic veggies every day.'

'I go to delis where they do that for me. And yeah, I know, I can afford it,' I said, heading him off at the pass.

'I wasn't going to say that, actually, Ju,' he said defensively. 'I'm not a bastard to you all the time. I've just been really down recently about the music.'

I pulled a face. 'It was bad luck about the café gig.'

He shrugged. 'I'm going through a really bad patch. First that, now this benefits thing.' He opened another can of beer. 'The weird thing is that I actually feel better, sort of,' he continued. 'Like the worst has happened, and now I've got to deal with it. You know, I've been expecting a showdown with the dole office for so long now, it's actually a relief that it's all out in the open.'

'You do look good,' I said, noticing this with surprise. 'Relaxed.'

'Yeah, well, that's why.'

He stretched his legs out in front of him. Chris was not much taller than me, but his thinness made his legs look impossibly long from this angle, like an optical illusion. Chris had Dad's metabolism; the more he ate the thinner he seemed to get. We had the same grey eyes, the same pale skin and, freakishly, exactly the same three faint brown freckles on the bridge of our noses. There the resemblance ended. Chris's bones were more pronounced, his cheekbones higher, and his hair was dark and stuck up at weird angles, like a broken geometry design. I watched my own eyes in his face narrow as he thought over what he was telling me, and felt the family tie pull me as strongly as if the umbilical cord was still buried deep in my bellybutton.

'I'm almost grateful in a way,' he said. 'Stupid, isn't it?'

He gestured to the table.

'That's all the info about the course. I thought you might want to have a look at it.'

'And the forms?'

Chris frowned impatiently. 'I've done all those. That was easy. I don't know why you keep going on about the sodding forms.'

'You asked me to help you with them!' I said indignantly.

'No, I didn't. I don't think I did. Did I? Anyway, I've done them.' He waved to a pile of forms stacked on the windowsill. 'I just thought you might be interested in the course stuff.'

Head averted, he shoved them over to me as if he couldn't have been less interested in my opinion. Suddenly I understood. I had been very dense. This hadn't been about the forms at all. The computer course had, despite his denials, sparked some interest in Chris. It was like a miracle.

Well, he would have all the encouragement from me that he needed. Humbly, I picked up the leaflets and started reading them with as much attention as if they had been the menu and wine list from London's latest hot new restaurant. They might have been the menu and wine list from Czechoslovakia's latest hot new restaurant for all I knew; I could barely understand one word in a hundred.

But Chris did. That was the point. I was full of respect; it was a side of him I had never seen before. It was so exciting I had to refrain from ooh-ing and aah-ing over the programming specifications from sheer elation that my brother was actually on course to get a proper job. I didn't want him to think I had taken leave of my senses.

Chapter Eleven

I was nearly home when a sudden impulse swept over me, and I followed it without a moment's hesitation. Pleasantly relaxed from the beer and spliff, I was floating in a slightly blurred, benevolent haze. My only moment of really clear thinking was when I checked my watch. Quarter past eleven. Perfect.

'Keep going round the station,' I said to the minicab driver. 'Past Marine Ices.'

'I thought you said bottom of Adelaide Road!' he objected.

'Well, I've changed my mind, OK?'

Despite being liberally lined with restaurants and bars, Chalk Farm Road is never really lively. No one lounges outside a café on Chalk Farm Road watching the world go by. It lacks the Continental touch. Its gloomy appearance this time of night, plus the autumn chill, sobered me up like a dash of cold water, and the quiet in the little side street added the final touch. As I pushed open the door of the Spit and Whistle, I was wondering whether coming here had really been the stroke of genius it had seemed in the cab.

'We're closed,' Neil said automatically, without turning to look at who I was. Two great glass sculptures sprouted from his hands, formed from masses of pint glasses, stale beer dribbling prettily down their sides. He crossed to the bar and set them down in front of the sink.

'I was just seeing if Henry was here,' I said.

He shot a glance at me.

'Oh, it's you. Henry's friend. He's not here. Not yet, anyway.'

I gazed round the bar. The clientele looked just the same as the other night. The Spit and Whistle attracted such a specific set of customers that their type remained constant.

'You want a drink?' Neil offered.

'Yeah, I'll have a quick one.'

'Grand Marnier?'

'Why not?'

This, after all, was what I had been hoping for, wasn't it? Somewhere to pop into after closing time for a nightcap before heading home, where the barman knew your name (well, if I reminded him of it), your troubles (I thought I would skip that one) and what your preferences were in night-caps.

I eked out my drink as long as I could, but without the years of practice that had made the clients in Chris's local such experts, not to mention the lack of any distractions – no one came in at all, rather to my disappointment – I wasn't a great success.

I left some money on the bar for Neil.

'It's fine,' I said, waving him away as he came over from the far wall where he had been fiddling with the electric fire.

'No, you'll be wanting your change,' he said firmly.

'But I . . .' My voice tailed off. Under Neil's gimlet eyes – or rather, above his gimlet eyes, as in my heels I was taller than him – I didn't have the nerve to say that the rest was for him. God, I was getting everything wrong this evening. I must ask Henry about the rules of the place.

'Here you go,' he said, pushing a neat pile of change back to me with one very definite finger.

Reluctantly I pocketed it.

'I'll get the door for you,' he said, fiddling with the bolts and locks like an eccentric old butler in a Hammer Horror film.

There should have been a lightning crash as he opened the heavy door, or a steed rearing wildly, its hooves coming within inches of Neil's upturned face. Instead there was only a man, his hand upraised as if just about to knock, his expression momentarily frozen in surprise.

'Neil!' he said. 'Perfect timing! How did you know—'

He broke off in mid-sentence, catching sight of me behind Neil. Pleased that I had had this effect on Alex, I emerged into the street.

'I just popped in for a nightcap,' I explained.

'Working your way through Neil's bottle of Grand Marnier?' he suggested.

'Exactly,' I said as firmly as Neil refusing a tip. 'I thought I'd see if Henry was in, too, but he wasn't. So I'm going.'

Too much explaining, Juliet. Be cool. And if you can't, then for God's sake just shut up.

'Oh, no Henry?' Alex sounded disappointed. 'We've actually been talking since that night you came in, you know. Him and me. It obviously needed you to break the ice.'

'Glad to have been of service.'

And now I sounded like a pert parlourmaid in an Edwardian TV drama. I loathed myself.

'Are you coming in or what?' Neil said irritably to Alex. 'I'm freezing my bollocks off here!'

'Oh, come on, Neil, it's not that cold,' he said easily.

'Don't let me keep you from your coffee,' I said, trying for relaxed and unconcerned. I was determined not to give him any encouragement. If he wanted to see me again, after practically calling me an alcoholic the last time we met and then not getting my number, he was going to have to ask nicely.

'No, it's fine,' he said, sketching that wave with his gloved hand.

'Oh, OK. See you round.'

I turned to walk away, my teeth grinding. The effort to keep my voice light had to be compensated somewhere else. Promptly, however, I heard a few quick steps, and Alex appeared at my side.

'I meant I'll see you home,' he explained. 'When I said it was fine. I can always come back here later, it's only a few steps away.'

'Oh. OK,' I said again. It seemed a fairly innocuous remark: not pert, not drunken, and relatively light. Maybe I should stick to it for the rest of the walk.

'So how long have you lived around here?' he said, matching his step companionably to mine.

'About eight years. I bought an ex-council flat really cheap. I could barely afford it at the time, but now it's great. Apart from anything else I save a fortune on cabs, it's so close to the centre.'

Maybe 'Oh, OK' wouldn't have been an appropriate answer, but I hadn't needed to babble on that much.

'And before that?'

'Oh, flatshares all over the place. My mum lives in Princebury, it's where I grew up. But I got out of there as fast as I could.'

'I bet.'

Princebury was one of those hyper-respectable suburbs of which the only thing that could be said in their favour was that they were served by a tube line. Naturally, I had been very grateful for this when I was growing up, but it had still not been enough to keep me there any longer than absolutely necessary.

I stared down at my boots. Popping in and out of my range

of vision, they flicked the hem of my coat with every step. It was almost hypnotic.

'And your dad?' Alex was asking.

'Sorry?'

'Your dad? You said you grew up with your mother.'

'Oh, right. He died when I was seven.'

Alex didn't, mercifully, say that he was sorry. I always hate people apologising for an event with which they had absolutely nothing to do. When it particularly irritates me I tend to snap back: 'Why? It wasn't your fault.' Instead he just clicked his tongue sympathetically and left a little pause.

'And you?' I said. 'How long have you lived round here?'

'Oh, all my life, more or less. North London born and bred. Whoops!'

The sound of a motorbike in the distance had suddenly turned into the thing itself, racing down Adelaide Road and then, the tyres scorching and wailing, executing a screaming hairpin turn into Eton College Road, which we were just crossing. Alex caught my arm to pull me back. His touch made me jump; he kept hold of me, but his grip slackened, and as the rattle and roar of the bike faded into the distance we were marooned in one of those awful moments of mutual discomfort.

'I'm sorry,' he was stammering, 'I didn't mean to grab you – I just thought the bike was going to hit you – I didn't want to be all chauvinistic and protective – it was just an instinct –'

'No, that's fine, my reflexes are terrible, I mean, if I had good ones I'd probably have grabbed you –'

'I mean, just because you're a woman –' he continued hastily. 'I would have done the same if it had been a male friend –'

'Would you?' I said curiously.

There was a long pause as he thought about it.

'I don't know,' he admitted. 'Probably not.'

We both burst out laughing. The atmosphere relaxed instantly. Metaphorically speaking, lava lamps switched on all around us and lounge music started playing in the background.

'Safe to cross the road now?' I said.

'Have you checked left, right and left again?'

'Yup.'

'All right, but remember to be extra careful when you don't have an adult with you.'

We crossed the road and turned into the entrance to my block of flats.

'I was so curious when I walked you back here last week,' Alex said. 'You know what it's like, you pass a building a million times and never know anyone who lives there. I've always thought it looked nice.'

'For an ex-council block?'

'No,' he said, unembarrassed by my teasing. 'Generally. Nice red brick, biggish windows and not too many storeys. It's a rare example of forward-thinking council housing for its period.'

'I always wonder why council flats have their landings on the outside of the building,' I observed as we walked across the parking lot to the far entrance. 'Private flats: landings inside. Council flats: wind, rain, and cold outside staircases. It's like some primitive class system.'

'I ought to know, oughtn't I? Being an architect. But I don't. Perhaps it was meant to promote sociability between block dwellers. Le Corbusier and all that. The blocks of flats as little towns in themselves. Though this isn't big enough to be a town. More a little village.'

'Well, it does unite us in a way,' I admitted. 'We all moan

about it when we pass each other on the stairs.'

'There you go!' He grinned at me.

We had halted in front of the entrance door, and I was fiddling with my keys. The blindingly bright light above the door illuminated us in what I felt – and had had occasion to feel before – was a particularly unhelpful way.

'I'd ask you in for coffee, but I have to get up really early tomorrow morning,' I lied.

'No problem.'

'Will you go back to Neil's?'

He shook his head. 'Probably go home at this point.' He shuffled his feet. 'Neil likes you, you know,' he said unexpectedly. 'He was asking Henry about you the other night.'

'Really?' I was ridiculously flattered. 'D'you think he'd let me in to a lock-in?'

'You'd have to put in some drinking hours first.'

'Is that what you did?'

'No, actually,' he said smugly.

'Unfair,' I complained.

'What happened is that he was letting some people out as I came past. Must have been around midnight.'

'You work really late,' I commented.

'I know. Always have. And London's not a good city for that,' he said ruefully. 'Anyway, I was walking past, and as they went out I just said to Neil, "Don't suppose there's any chance of a coffee?" And he was so surprised he let me in.'

'That's a nice story.'

'Isn't it?' he agreed.

We stood looking at each other for a moment. Or rather, he was looking at me; I was no longer engrossed by the tips of my boots, but had concentrated my attention instead on the windows to the left of his head. They were actually fascinating, seen from this angle.

'So maybe we could get together sometime,' he suggested eventually. 'Have a drink or something.'

There was another pause.

'I'll give you my card,' I said, rummaging in my bag.

He patted his pockets. 'I don't have any on me,' he said, taking mine.

Good, I thought. Now you'll have to ring me. Or you won't. Which will be fine, too. I mean, I really don't care one way or the other.

'Well, good night,' I mumbled, putting the keys in the door.

'Good night,' he said. 'I'll ring you.'

He waited to make sure I had the door open before walking away. I trudged up the cold concrete stairs wondering why I didn't feel more pleased about the encounter. He had wanted to ask for my number, after all. I should be flattered. This proved, if nothing else, that I was definitely on a roll. And yet the predominant emotion I was feeling was nervousness. Why was I nervous? Tom hadn't made me nervous. Pieter hadn't made me nervous. Mind you, there hadn't actually been time to feel anything beyond simple lust with either of them. Maybe that was the problem.

It was the preliminaries I hated, the gradual dating ritual, things stringing out, time passing, tension building, will-he-call-me-or-should-I-call-him, all the inevitable uncertainties. I wasn't good at uncertainty right now. To be honest, I had never been good at uncertainty. I had always preferred the 'Get your coat, love, you've pulled' strategy. It was easier for women. If you didn't want to faff around getting to know each other, you didn't have to.

But now I was under this gypsy curse; I could pull them but I couldn't actually do much with them once I had them. God, it really was like some awful joke. Perhaps that was the point of Alex; I was supposed to be learning how to date properly again after years of just grabbing some attractive man and falling on to the nearest yielding surface. Well, I didn't like it. It was slow and tortuous and full of waiting time, and it made me feel profoundly insecure. I determined to shag Alex on the first date, just to prove to myself that I could.

Though of course he might not ring me. Which would make things much easier all round.

Chapter Twelve

'You're going through some kind of change,' Mel said gnomically.

'Oh, shut up,' I said pettishly. 'You sound like a bad astrologer telling me I'm menopausal.'

'No, I'm serious!'

Talking to Mel was incredibly liberating. I could be as rude as I liked. With most women, telling them to shut up would have been an international incident.

'Look at your recent pattern,' Mel was saying. 'What's it telling us?'

She stared at me quizzically, waiting for the answer. Mel was dressed today as casually as she ever got; tight jeans – blue denim was the only colour she ever wore, apart from red or purple – a black poloneck, black stack-heeled boots and a black leather jacket, on to the collar of which her hair fell, dark and glossy. In describing Mel it was very difficult not to woefully overuse the adjective 'black'. She looked like an elegant raven. In jeans.

'I didn't even know I had a recent pattern,' I said helplessly.

Mel paused for a moment to light up a cigarette. We were walking along the Westbourne Grove stretch of the canal, heading for her favourite fetish shop, where she had an appointment to try on a new custom-made corset. I loved going to these shops with her. Mel was like royalty on the S&M circuit, having posed for one of the very first covers of the most popular magazine, back in the days when the scene was much more underground. Hanging out with her always made me feel like a celebrity by association. Mel propped her bony arse against the fence bordering the canal walk and stuck her feet out in front of her, cupping her hand around her lighter. I contemplated the pointed tips of her boots. These might not have been in fashion for years, but enough Goth shops existed in London to keep her in pointy shoes, not to mention PVC bondage leggings, for the rest of her life.

'Jules,' she said, with an air of quiet reproof. She inhaled deeply and hoisted her bottom off the fence. We strolled onwards. 'Those two guys. The one at the conference and the one at the club. You didn't shag either of them. Totally unlike the Jules we know and love, who frankly can be a bit of a slapper sometimes. And,' she added pointedly, 'you didn't hunt them down like dogs afterwards so you could shag 'em later, either. The old Jules would have been too curious to find out what they were like in bed not to give it a go.'

'God,' I said, nearly but not quite struck dumb. 'That's so true.'

'Point one. Point two: you meet a nice bloke and behave like a startled rabbit who's just seen a fox and – I dunno, what do rabbits do? Don't see many of 'em round this neck of the woods.'

'I think they freeze. Like in headlights.'

'OK, you freeze. I'm just saying,' Mel continued inexorably, 'why didn't you ask this Alex bloke up for a couple of lines of coke? Or even a coffee, if you were feeling bourgeois? Since you obviously fancy him.'

'I'm not really sure that I do fancy him,' I said feebly.

'Oh, come on. You wouldn't be giving me this grief for someone you didn't even fancy.'

This was undeniable.

'Well, OK, there's something,' I admitted. 'There's definitely a sort of . . . something. It's just not so – immediate. I dunno. You know, mostly it's really obvious – you look at a bloke and go, "Mmn, have him stripped and washed and brought to my tent".'

'For a good flogging.'

'Mel, *please.*'

Mel plucked a switch from an overhanging tree and whipped it through the cold air. It hissed wickedly. Though without following through with a final thwack, the sound hung in the air, oddly unfinished.

'But with this one . . . I dunno,' I said. 'This is going to sound ridiculous, so don't take the piss, OK? I sort of feel that . . . well, I respect him.'

Mel doubled over as if she had cramps, clinging on to the fence for support.

'You're overdoing it,' I said coldly.

But she was laughing so hard I doubted that she even heard me.

'I've never heard anything so fucking funny in all my life!' she gasped.

A couple of lads, kicking a football around desultorily on the field of mud in the small park adjoining the canal walk, looked over, attracted by Mel's gusty laughter.

'Oi, gels! Share the joke, eh!' one of them called.

Mel straightened up slowly and turned to look at them. Whatever they had been going to shout next died on their lips; after a moment of silence, they ducked their heads and went straight back to kicking the ball. This was only one of the many advantages there were to Mel's having gone over to the dark side.

'*Respect,*' she said to me derisorily. 'What d'you mean by that?'

'Oh, you know . . .' My body was curling over on itself as if it too had cramps. Only these were from unadulterated embarrassment. 'I don't just want to shag him the first night, it'd feel wrong.'

'What, you want to *get to know him*?'

It was impossible to describe the sheer amount of incredulity which Mel packed into the last four words.

'We can talk to each other,' I said sullenly. 'You know, just banter, but it felt really easy.'

'Don't you talk to 'em all?'

We turned off the canal and on to the main road.

'Well, yeah, but it's more sex talk.' I perked up, thinking of the marathon night with Tom. 'That guy I met at the conference – Tom –'

'The PR one with the big willy?'

'Yes, thanks, Mel. Anyway, he started asking me about myself, you know those questions –'

Mel looked blank. I corrected myself.

'No, stupid me, of course you don't, you're too busy checking out how they respond to basic commands.'

We crossed the road and ducked down the little alley that led to the fetish shop.

'"Do you have any brothers and sisters?"' I explained. '"What's your star sign?" "What kind of music do you like?" Getting-to-know-you questions. And as soon as he started, I said I was tired and had to go to sleep. I mean, *really*.' I shivered. 'Nice men. They want to *get to know you*. They want you to *open your heart to them*. It's just like all those men who complain that women fall in love with them and then want to change them.'

'You what?' Mel said blankly.

'Well, why pick on me? Why do they try to get me to confide in them? Why do they think I was rat-arsed and probably doing coke when they met me? Precisely to avoid having any inner thoughts more profound than "Oh fuck, pissed again," as I stagger home and root around in the medicine cabinet for the headache pills.'

Mel snuffled with laughter as she pushed the button for the shop door and announced herself. An excited voice buzzed incomprehensibly through the intercom, and the door popped open. The anteroom was plastered with posters, mostly of Goth bands: the Cult, the Cure, Sisters of Mercy, Depeche Mode and Death in Vegas. The rest were of people bending over suggestively or lying in baths, wearing rubber bodysuits and masks that looked like miniature PVC snorkels.

'Mel!' A beaming girl with a strong American accent pushed her way through the rails of black rubber garments to give Mel a hug. 'How's it going? We've got your corset in back if you want to try it on.'

I've never understood why someone would wear pleated rubber knee-length skirts; it would seem to contradict all the principles of fetishwear. This girl was on the large side, so maybe she thought it gave her more of a waist. Her hair was a giant mass of coloured dreadlocks in shades of red and yellow, and her face was so pierced, not with rings but those spikes designed to look as if they go straight through the lip or nose, that I found myself worrying that, like Slartibartfast in *The Hitchhiker's Guide to the Galaxy*, she would stab herself constantly by accident. What jumped out at you first and foremost were the hair and the piercings, behind which you squinted to make out the rest of her face, as if she were some mutant without the full complement of features. I itched to pull out some eyeliner and mascara and get to work on her.

'Hi, Chynna,' Mel said, recoiling slightly from the girl's unbridled enthusiasm. Mel was not demonstrative by nature. 'Why don't you bring out the corset, and I'll see if there's anything else I fancy trying on.'

'Sure thing!' Chynna said, bustling away. This was the perfect verb to describe her retreat; the skirt made her bum look as big as the Watford Gap. A lesson to all of us with bottoms: never, never wear pleats.

'No ... no ... no ... maybe?' Mel muttered, rifling through one of the racks. My fingers lingered lovingly on a pervy maid's uniform in shiny black PVC with a neckline so deep you could probably see the wearer's knickers down it. Presuming she was wearing any.

'That'd suit you,' Mel said.

'Yeah, but when would I wear it? That's a sex game costume, not something you wear out to a club.'

'Well, buy it anyway. Once you've got 'em, you wear 'em, that's what I always find.'

'No, I'm on a budget right now. I spent a fortune on my winter coat.' I sighed and let the dress fall.

'So what were we saying?' Mel asked.

'Me and my not-wanting-to-talk-to-blokes syndrome.'

'You know, for a non-scene person, you're about as twisted as they come,' Mel said respectfully.

'Well, I'm over thirty now, and I've told guys about my family and my life and my job a million times,' I said wearily. 'I'm so bored with the subject now I reach for the bottle of gin as soon as it comes up. And I don't want to find out all about them, either. I don't even much care about their names. I just ask to be polite. And because it's easier afterwards. Quicker than saying: "Oh, that one at the fetish club with the chest like a steamer trunk".'

'Did he ever get in touch, by the way?' Mel perked up.

'No,' I said glumly.

'I haven't seen him on the scene. I mean, he hasn't come back without getting in touch with you.'

'Oh well.'

I observed a moment of silence in grief for Pieter, crossing over to another clothes rail.

'And besides,' I added, 'when I was with Bart, I had to get to know all of his family, as well. And he met Mum and Chris – he was great at handling Mum, and he and Chris got on like a house on fire. They'd smoke spliff and play endless computer games in the pub. I dunno, that felt really good, you know? He was part of the family. I don't want to get to know someone and have that all happen again and then fall apart.'

Mel clicked her tongue sympathetically. For her this was the emotional-support equivalent of a big tearful hug. That was why I confided so much in Mel; she never overreacted and smothered me in empathy. When I was confiding important stuff, I wanted a bit of distance. Mum was directly responsible for this; when I was younger, and hadn't yet learnt what a mistake it was to confide in her, she had appropriated my emotional distress with greedy eagerness and then immediately pointed out all the ways in which her life was much harder than mine. It meant I didn't let down my guard that easily. Which, at least, had been good for me in business.

I shook my head to clear it.

'How do you walk in this?' I said more lightly, picking up an ankle-length rubber skirt in dull silver, one long narrow tube without any visible slits, and holding it against me.

Mel glanced over at it.

'You don't,' she said. 'They carry you.'

'Oh.' I hung it back up. 'Anyway, that's what I have friends for. To talk to. All these Mr Carings and Sharings need to realise that I have enough friends, I don't need any more! If I'm feeling depressed and want to talk it out, I'll ring you. Or Gill. What they need to do is get me hammered on cocktails, rent a couple of Arnold Schwarzenegger films and then shag my brains out. I mean, that's what they're there for.'

'Yeah, Jules,' Mel drawled, 'that all sounds great, feminist manifesto for the new millennium, etc., etc. But this entire rant's because you just met a bloke you like talking to. So what does that say?'

I fiddled crossly with a pair of shoes whose heels were practically as tall as I was.

'Well, maybe that's what I mean about respect,' I mumbled.

Mel looked utterly baffled.

'Go on,' she said.

'It's not that I don't respect the guys I shag. I just –'

'Think they're cheap and easy.'

'Maybe a bit,' I confessed. 'Maybe I want someone to hold out a little longer. Not just jump on me straight away. Make me wait for it a bit. I see what men mean now about liking a bit of a chase.'

'You are such a mess!' Mel said cheerfully. 'You are so fucking confused you don't know which end is up! No wonder you're not shagging anyone right now, you wouldn't even know to tell them where to put it! Oh, thanks,' she said to Chynna, taking the corset from her. 'Look.'

She held it up. I oohed and aahed in appreciation. It was made of pale gunmetal rubber, with a silvery blue sheen, cut deep at the front and tied with a purple cord at the back. It was also so tiny I couldn't see how even Mel, with her slender back, could fit into it. I said as much.

'It's the only way to give me some tits,' Mel sighed. 'Hoick everything up so it looks as if I've got something there.'

'Do you want to try it on?' Chynna said, hovering as excitedly as if Mel were a socialite oil baron's wife at a Paris couture boutique.

'Yeah, s'pose I'd better. You going to try anything on, Jules?'

'No, I'm being good.'

Just at that moment I caught sight of another pair of shoes, with a heel still improbably high, but conceivably wearable. The straps were entirely made out of open zippers, which curled over the toes and round the back of the ankle to fasten with a concealed buckle a little up the calf. They were so beautiful they took my breath away. Surreptitiously, I turned one over to look at the price. No, absolutely not. I couldn't afford them.

Mel entered a cubicle, keeping the curtain half-open. Through the gap I could see her stripping off her sweater and bra and dusting herself with the talc provided in all the changing rooms so that customers could try on rubber items without getting stuck to them.

'So what do you want, Jules?' she said a little impatiently.

'Actually, I just want all of this out of my head,' I said, thinking it over. 'It's like I just opened a huge can of worms and they're all wriggling round in there.'

'Ooh, yuck. Like maggots. I saw this horror film the other week—'

'Please, Mel, not right now.'

Mel eased the open corset over her head. I was about to help her pull it tight, but Chynna, like an alien handmaiden from Planet Perv, was right in there dragging on the laces as Mel braced herself against the cubicle wall.

'Nice and tight,' Mel instructed, unable to stop the tone of command that immediately entered her voice.

'God, Mel, that looks wonderful,' I said, as she emerged and I could see her fully.

Chynna was almost overcome by Mel in the corset.

'You look fantastic,' she breathed worshipfully. 'You're so *thin.*'

'Tea and fags diet,' Mel said complacently.

'Oh, and that's another thing about nice men,' I said, my

voice rising as I remembered another offence. 'They love you just the way you are, no matter how fat. No, darling, your bum looks fine in that, you don't need to go on a diet. LIARS. It's the guys who tell you that your skirt makes you look like you're pregnant with octuplets who are doing you the real favour.' I sighed. 'I put on half a stone when I was living with Bart. More, now I think about it. He ate like a pig. Bread, cheese, chips with mayonnaise. I tell you, when you finally leave a nice man because he's bored you to death trying to have in-depth conversations about the state of your relationship, he's made damn sure that you're too fat for anyone else.'

'Chubby-chasers,' Mel suggested. 'Did you know there's a website that's nothing but naked fat girls bouncing up and down on balloons?'

'God.'

'Hey, you know what?' Chynna entered the conversation tentatively. We both looked at her, a little taken aback. 'Something else about nice men? They're scruffy.'

'Yeah, that's true,' I agreed, thinking of Alex's battered corduroys. 'They think you should love them just the way they are, too, so they don't hit the gym or do sit-ups every morning, they don't have six-packs like relief maps, and they never wear aftershave.'

'So true,' Chynna sighed. Mel, who could not be expected to see this kind of thing personally, shrugged and returned to her own preoccupations.

'It's great,' she said, contemplating herself in the mirror. The corset did manage to give her a little cleavage; her pale, slightly freckled skin rose slightly from the tight neckline, which finished barely above her nipples. The silvery blue rubber was the perfect colour for her, lending a gently rosy glow to her skin by contrast and bringing out the blue of her eyes.

'Your friend Liam'd like me in this, eh?' she said naughtily. 'All I need's a matching whip and he'd be creaming himself.'

I giggled at the thought.

'He's not my friend,' I corrected. 'He's my Problem Client.'

A sudden idea struck me.

'Why don't you come along to the launch, Mel?' I said with rising excitement. 'Go on, it'd be fun! My first client launch – I'd really like you to be there.'

'And if Liam gets out of line I can flog him back into shape for you,' Mel said perceptively.

'That too. You're about the only person who could do it.'

'OK. Yeah, I'd like to. I never see you in work mode. Be a laugh. Jules being all grown up and important.'

'Cool!' I was very glad that I had thought of asking Mel. This launch was something of a milestone for me, and Gill would be there, catering. I liked the idea of having my best friends there, to witness what would hopefully be my professional triumph.

Chynna, meanwhile, hadn't taken her eyes off Mel.

'You look perfect,' Chynna said humbly. She looked as if she were struggling hard not to prostrate herself before Mel and kiss her shoes.

Which reminded me.

'Um, Chynna?' I said. 'While Mel's trying on those other things?' I held up the zipper shoe. 'I wonder if you've got these in a size six?'

'They have nice lives, though,' Mel pointed out, as we left the shop, anonymous paper bags dangling from our hands with our goodies inside. I hadn't been able to resist the shoes. I was going to wear them for Liam's launch, though, so that made them a work expense. Not actually deductible, of course, but still . . .

'Who do?' I said, still racked with guilt at the amount I had spent on my shoes.

Mel clucked her tongue impatiently. 'Nice men! Even if they are scruffy! I mean, they do all that stuff you like, Jules. Foreign films and concerts and art exhibitions.'

'I have friends to do that stuff with.'

'I never realised you were so . . . compartmentalised, Jules,' Mel remarked.

'It's really relaxing,' I assured her.

'Or it was. Now you're breaking down,' Mel said ghoulishly. 'Your commitment phobia's beginning to bite.'

'Could you try to say something supportive?' I snapped.

'OK,' she said equably. 'Shag this bloke. Get him up to yours and do your usual coke-and-soft-music number. Not that you usually bother with the soft music, right?'

'How is that supportive, exactly, Mel?'

'Well, things'll come to a head then, won't they? You'll find out what you really want. I thought that was the point.'

'You're so ruthless,' I complained. 'Gill would tell me to get to know him first and see whether I think our lifestyles are compatible, if he treats waiters well and if he looks after stray animals and his aging mum.'

She shrugged. 'Yeah. Which is why you come to me when you need a bit of straight talking. Look, I've got to get back.'

Fishing for her car keys, she consulted her watch. 'I mean, I wanted him in a bit of pain, but it's been an hour and a half and if I leave it any longer he'll go into spasm. Fancy coming back to mine for a cup of tea? I'll just loosen up the shackles a bit while you put the kettle on.'

Mel lived on the ground floor of a suitably Gothic Victorian house. Naturally, she owned the basement too, though it was used for professional purposes only. Contrary to what I had expected the first time I had been invited round, the upper floor was bright and very welcoming. Mel had said that since she worked in a dungeon, she refused to live in one as well.

She unlocked the door to the basement and went down the steps. As soon as the door opened I heard muffled whimpering. Mel wouldn't like that. She was big on speaking only when you were spoken to.

I went into Mel's beautiful orange kitchen. It looked fresh out of the showroom, every surface gleaming. The latest cleaning slave must have been round recently. As I filled the kettle, it occurred to me that Mel, as usual, had been very unfair to me. I was scarcely the only person round here who compartmentalised her life.

I had already mentioned him in the fetish shop, and it had been bearable. Maybe that had been a try-out for something more serious. I don't know; I didn't analyse my impulse. But as I was setting the teapot down on the table I heard myself say, quite unexpectedly:

'Bart actually rang me a couple of days ago. Did I tell you?'

I had made an effort to keep my voice neutral, but it didn't fool her for a moment. Mel looked as shocked as she was capable of being. And of course I hadn't told her; that was completely disingenuous.

'Jules!' Mel cut through all my crap like a laser. 'Of course you didn't bloody tell me! Why didn't you ring me straight away?'

'Oh, I dunno. Thought I could manage on my own.' My nose was prickling. 'I knew if I rang you I'd just start crying and I didn't want to waste any tears on that stupid bastard . . . I didn't even mean to tell you now, it just popped out, I wasn't expecting it at all . . .'

I collapsed into the nearest chair and burst into sobs. Talking about Bart always had this effect on me. I could manage a few grunted words, a quick reference to him, as long as

I immediately changed the subject; but anything more than that and the waterworks turned themselves on. It was an automatic reaction which took me over entirely. I kept trying to sit up and wipe my eyes, to indicate to myself that enough was enough and it was time to stop crying, but the tap was on and the tears wouldn't stop until I had run dry. Mel didn't come over and hug me, as Gill would have done, for which I was very grateful. Physical sympathy would have made it even worse.

'How long's it been?' she asked, when I was drained enough to be able to sit up straighter and drink some tea, replenishing my bodily fluids. She had put a box of tissues on the table in front of me, just like a therapist, and her voice, too, was understanding but detached enough to reassure me that it was safe to talk to her.

'Since I heard from Bart?' I said, my throat thick with tears. 'Oh, God, must be a year.'

I sniffed, blew my nose, and sniffed again. I was beginning to get a headache. I always did when I had a crying jag.

'What did he want?' Mel said matter of factly.

'To know if I still had his record player . . .'

Oh, God, I was off again. I was sobbing in hiccups this time; there weren't any tears left to come out but my body wanted to cry all the same. It was like the dry heaves after a vomiting session.

'His record player,' Mel said in disbelief.

'I know,' I choked out. 'Can you imagine? I haven't heard from him for a year and he rings up about his sodding record player.'

'Actually I was thinking what does he need that for?' Mel said, ever practical. 'I mean, who plays records now? He doesn't DJ, does he?'

'He's got all these old records and he wanted to play them,'

I explained more clearly. My chest had stopped spasming.

'Why doesn't he just buy them on CD?' Mel pulled a face. 'Stupid of me. He probably hasn't got a penny, has he?'

'I didn't ask. But he didn't tell me how well things were going, so probably not.'

That had always been the way with Bart: either he was in the money, after a big win, or, more often, cleaned out and charming me into paying his half of the rent that month.

'How did he sound?'

I took a deep breath.

'Not too good.'

'Still gambling?'

I sniffed. 'I asked him that.'

'Oh, you know how things are,' Bart had said casually. 'Nothing too heavy. I've sorted myself out.'

'But you're still betting?'

'Here and there,' he said impatiently, knowing what was coming next. 'And don't go on about what that counsellor said that you dragged me to see, OK? I can take it or leave it.'

'I did not *drag* you, Bart,' I said, indignant. 'You went by yourself when I kicked you out.'

'Yeah, and it was a big mistake asking you along.'

'Because I actually remember what he said. God, I even went to that bloody support group he suggested. I've never had a more depressing evening in my life.'

'I told you not to go,' Bart said defensively. 'I said it would be a bunch of miserable bags banging on about how awful their boyfriends were.'

I giggled. 'So true.'

'I mean, you'd already got rid of me!' Bart was laughing too. 'What did you need the group for! I should have gone in there at the end and made a speech about being a total fuck-up! "Juliet's done the right thing by dumping me and all you lot should follow her example and dump your wankers too!" And then we could've gone out and got pissed,' Bart added comfortably.

'*Bart*,' I said, cross again. 'We were scarcely getting on that well at the time.'

'We got pissed a lot.'

'Separately. And then we cried down the phone at each other.'

'I cried down the phone,' Bart corrected. 'You just kept spouting counselling-speak about how I had to give up for myself and not for you.'

'Well, I was right.'

'Didn't help much at the time. I cried for a month. I'd wake up and the pillow would be soaking.'

'Oh, *Bart*.'

If he had said this as a plea for pity, it would have been tacky. But the relative cheerfulness with which he recounted it tugged at my heartstrings. Bart had never used emotional blackmail. Except when he was trying to borrow money. I reminded myself of this to avoid getting too maudlin about his positive qualities.

Still, it was hard not to feel sentimental. Bart and I had had two wonderful years; the next one was so-so, and the last pretty much the pit of hell. The memory of our good times, however, combined with the way we were able to joke about the bad ones to form a powerful nostalgic pull at the mere mention of his name. In many ways he had been wonderful. Bart had always been completely supportive of my career, was great with Mum and was always ready to declare stoutly that I had no cellulite at all. This wasn't good boyfriend politics; he really thought I didn't. (It had dawned on me recently that maybe no one had ever explained to Bart what cellulite actually was.)

'How's your mum?' he was saying. 'Still up to her old tricks?'

'*Oh* yes. I heard this thing on the radio the other day that really made me think of her,' I said. 'Rule One: I am always right. Rule Two: if I'm wrong, see Rule One.'

Bart thought this was hilarious.

'Just try to worry less about what she thinks,' he advised, when he had stopped laughing.

'That's easy for you to say,' I snapped. 'You've never had to deal with this kind of thing, because you've never done anything your parents approve of.'

'Except go out with you.'

'Aaaah,' I cooed extravagantly, to pretend I wasn't touched by this.

'But yeah, seriously, I trained them up from an early age not to expect anything from me. Now if I manage to cross the road without getting run over they're pathetically grateful. And you know, Jules, I don't talk about them all the time either.'

'What do you mean?' I said blankly.

'Well, we always ended up talking about your mum, or your being worried about Chris, didn't we? I mean, how much time did you really have when we were together to talk about us?'

It wasn't the first time Bart had said something like that. He had brought it up when we went to see the counsellor, but he had been saying it off and on for years before. It always made me furious. How could he blame me for not putting enough effort into the relationship when our real problem was that he was off blowing the rent money at an Edgware Road casino? And yet, thinking about it now that enough time had passed, I found myself wondering if he might have a point after all.

'And look at us now!' Bart was saying. 'We're just banging

on about your mum yet again! I mean, I know she's a night-mare, but she shouldn't be the centre of your life. I used to think that everything you did, you were sort of imagining your mum's reaction to it.'

I couldn't say anything. He was right.

'And you were always worrying about her and Chris. I mean, people have to sort out their own lives, it's not your fault if Chris is a fuck-up and your mum's round there every two minutes doing his washing. You think you're responsible for everything that goes on with them.'

'God,' I snapped, caught on the raw, 'it's always easier to criticise me than to sort yourself out, isn't it?'

I knew this wasn't fair; Bart wasn't criticising me. But I had to lash out somehow.

'That's bollocks!' he said, angry now too. 'I was trying to help!'

'Yeah? Well, maybe you should look in a mirror! I mean, you're still gambling!'

'What the hell does that have to do with anything?'

'Everything! You're not going to Gamblers Anonymous, are you?'

Bart hated the idea of GA. I knew he wouldn't be going to meetings. I could read Bart like a book. The problem was that it cut both ways.

'Look, Jules, we're not going out any more, so you can stop doing the concerned-girlfriend act, OK? That's my business! I didn't ring you for a lecture—'

'No, you rang to give me one!'

'Oh, it's useless talking to you, I should have known better—'

'Yes, you bloody should!'

We slammed down the phone simultaneously. I was breath-ing hard. Getting angry had at least helped to distract me from Bart's perceptive comments. Still, I found myself walking into the bedroom and fishing out the photo of him I kept in my bottom drawer, under the winter sweaters. I hadn't wanted to throw it out, but nor did it seem a good idea to have it perpetually on show, as if I were clinging to the past. I had taken it during a weekend break in Devon, when Bart was in the money. He went through the *Good Pub Guide* and picked out one that had rooms to rent – and, just as importantly, the symbol that meant they had excellent homebrew. Sure enough, in the photo he was sitting at a table in the pub garden, holding up a pint with a look of bliss on his face. Shaggy blond hair falling over his forehead, blue eyes squinting because of the sun on his face. Bart wasn't handsome; considered on an individual basis, his features were all good, but they didn't go well together. It was as if his face had been constructed at the end of a long day of creation with all the pieces left over from everyone else. Even with my obsession with male beauty, this hadn't mattered a bit to me. I propped the photo on the dresser, and, staring at it, another 'Aaaaaaah' slipped out.

I didn't cry. I never did when I was actually talking to Bart nowadays; if I felt it coming on he would laugh me out of it at once. And immediately afterwards I was much too confused and disoriented by the conversation to have a reaction as simple and straightforward as a crying jag. I wandered the flat for the rest of the evening, chainsmoking till I felt sick. Which at least distracted me from my confusion.

Chapter Thirteen

I rang Gill that evening, but she was out. She always seemed to be out these days. I assumed she was holing up at Philip's where Jeremy couldn't reach her. It occurred to me to wonder if she had changed the locks. If not, there would be nothing to stop Jeremy moving back in and changing them himself, unlikely though it would seem. But once divorce lawyers came into the picture – especially the kind that Jeremy could afford to hire, top-of-the-range, turbo-powered types who crunched tarantulas for breakfast – all bets were off. I wondered whether I should warn Gill. The prospect was stomach-sinkingly depressing. From relatively happy marriage to paranoia in the space of a couple of weeks. Nothing was safe.

Gill was still out on Sunday morning. I left another message. Finally she rang me that night – back, I assumed, from a weekend of passion at Philip's. She sounded tired, which was more than understandable. I was too; I just hadn't been shagging a property developer for forty-eight hours straight.

'How's it going?' I said.

'God. Another week of work looming up. My editor's hounding me for this book and I've still got loads to do.'

I had forgotten all about *Mince: The Final Frontier.*

'That must be the last thing you feel like doing,' I said sympathetically. 'I mean, in between getting a divorce and having an affair, no one really thinks: "You know what would really take my mind off all of this trauma? Buying a nice wodge of pork mince and messing around with it for the rest of the afternoon".'

This coaxed a laugh from Gill.

'I think it might help, though, strange as it sounds,' she observed. 'Well, practically anything would.'

'Have you heard from Jeremy?'

'I got a letter.' She let out a long breath. 'He won't get a lawyer. Or he hasn't yet. He still thinks we can get back together.'

'Gill, you really have to tell him about Philip.'

'You liked Philip, didn't you?' she said.

'You know I did,' I said, my forehead creasing up, eyebrows raising into a wince. We had had this conversation already. I had, if not exactly lied, softened the truth to keep her happy. To make me keep repeating the same clichés was above and beyond the call of friendship.

But Gill was desperate for a fix of reassurance. It was a bad drug to get hooked on. You thought you could take it or leave it at first: and then the more you got the more you wanted, till you were a reassurance junkie, ringing up your friends at all hours of the day and night with the same sodding questions you had asked a million times before. And the worst part was that the pleasure dulled with repetition. Your friends' weary voices trotting out the same comforting phrases, finishing with a plaintive plea of 'Feeling better? Can I go to bed now?' were never as satisfying as they had been in the first flush of enthusiasm.

Gill was silent.

'What's the matter?' I said dutifully.

'Oh, nothing. Well, everything.'

'Sure. I mean, obviously.' That hadn't come out as understanding as I had hoped, but Gill did not object. She sighed instead.

'You know I'm always here,' I said. 'You can always ring me.'

'I'm going to have to see Jeremy, aren't I?' she said dully.

'To tell him about Philip? Yes.'

There was no shirking that one.

'I'm dreading it,' she said plaintively. 'I can't face telling him in the house – where we lived together . . .' Her voice tailed off.

I couldn't blame her. My rule for difficult emotional situations – i.e., dumping people – was never to do it in your own place, and if possible not in theirs. A nice quiet pub, from which you could make your exit unencumbered by freshly minted exes throwing themselves against the door and sobbing at you not to go, was ideal. Still, my experience was very low-level compared to Gill's. Suggesting that she take Jeremy to the pub to tell him that she had broken up their ten-year marriage because she was head-over-heels about another man could have been done only by a person as calloused as a verruca.

'Maybe you could go round to his?' I proposed. 'Where's he living, by the way?'

'He's rented a flat in the Barbican.'

I could never understand the attraction of the Barbican. The idea of spending a lot of money to live in what were essentially souped-up tower blocks (albeit with their landings on the inside) baffled me. However, a girl who lived at the Barbican had told me that it was right next to the biggest Marks & Spencer in Europe, which obviously tipped the scales considerably in its favour. Jeremy was probably living entirely off M&S ready meals for one.

'Close to work,' I said, dredging up the only other benefit that came to mind.

'He says there are some nice bars round there. But mainly

for young singles who work in the City. He feels a bit out of place in them.'

The tenderness with which Gill pronounced these words stirred a faint glimmer of hope for Jeremy inside my breast. I wondered if Gill's continued need for assurances of Philip's likeability meant that she were having doubts about him. If so, this might be the perfect moment for Jeremy's rehabilitation.

'Go and see him,' I urged more strongly. Perhaps if she saw Jeremy in the pitiful surroundings of a spartan bachelor flat in a New Brutalist tower block, the kitchen floor scattered forlornly with empty Marks & Spencer microwaveable food cartons, her heart would melt towards him. It was certainly worth a try.

'I'm going to have to,' she said dolefully. 'It'll be awful, won't it?'

'Well, it might make you miserable seeing Jeremy all alone,' I said, plucking at her heartstrings with the consummate skill of a world-class cellist.

'Oh . . .'

There was a bubbling gulp, as if she had just managed to catch back a sob. I smiled smugly to myself.

'Sooner the better,' I said briskly. 'And you can always ring me as soon as you get back.'

'Thanks, Jules,' she said in heartfelt tones. 'You're a real friend.'

Yeah, I thought. To Jeremy.

Alex hadn't rung last week (too soon), or over the weekend (my card only had my work number on it). Thus I'd spent the last few days in comparative security. Now, however, with Monday, the anxiety began. It's one of my worst character traits: as soon as I give my number to someone I become immediately paranoid that he won't ring me. When and if he does, the power reverts to me. I can luxuriate in it for a little while before I have to ring him back and lose the advantage once again. It's like an eternal relay race, where you have to pass the baton back and forth without knowing whether, after your exhausting run, the other person will be there to take it.

I never know how long the gaps should be. If someone doesn't ring you for a week, does that mean you're pretty low on his priority list – below 'Pick up dry-cleaning' and 'Fix leaky washer on tap'? Because there are other explanations: he might be deliberately playing it cool, or just frenetically busy at work. And if he rings you within a few days, should you leave it longer before ringing back, to establish dominance? My New York friends are utterly ruthless about this kind of thing; they have whole lists of rules about when to return calls and one's general availability. However, I've stopped taking their advice too seriously since it's dawned on me that their relationships are flourishing no better than the ones this side of the Atlantic.

Alex had taken my number on Thursday, and I was hoping for a call by Tuesday afternoon. I had made careful computations: Monday might seem too keen, and so might Tuesday morning. The afternoon, however, expressed interest without desperation. Wednesday would be on the late side; nearly a week without ringing. I was of the firm belief that if someone liked you the call came within five days. Seven at the outside. Of course, I was using my dating calculator rather than Alex's. Men can have a very different sense of time in these circumstances.

The result of my equation (interest expressed + work number × given out late Thursday evening = Tuesday afternoon) should have meant that on Monday I would be carefree and relaxed, able to dedicate myself completely to my work without jumping every time the phone rang. Unfortunately, this wasn't the first good hypothesis that fell to pieces as soon as I tested it out. I was in the office before Lewis and the first thing I did, even before taking my coat off, was to check my answering machine, and then his, just in case any calls had been diverted to the latter by accident. It was absurd, I knew. No one rang before quarter to ten on a Monday morning to ask for a date unless they were so socially deficient that one would never have deigned to give them one's number in the first place.

Luckily, fate had planned a more than adequate distraction for me that Monday. A mere half-hour later, Richard stuck his head through the open door to my office. This was not a descriptive convention: I meant it literally. Richard's head jutted so far forward from his hunched shoulders that he was perfectly capable, without even straining, of sticking his head into someone's office while leaving the rest of his body outside the doorframe.

'Juliet!' he said enthusiastically. 'You look very nice. Good! Any meetings on today?'

'Nothing scheduled.'

'Good! Thought you might be dressed up to take a client to lunch. But you're not. Good! OK, get your coat. I'm going off to do a presentation for the latest campaign at Eis Vodka and I'm taking you with me. You got on well with them at the launch, didn't you?'

I perked up immediately.

'Give me ten minutes,' I said, 'and I'll meet you in the lobby.'

'Can you make it five?'

'I could tell you that, but I'd be lying.'

Richard nodded understandingly. This was painful to

watch. A disembodied bobbing head in my office was almost more than I could take before lunchtime. Fortunately he withdrew, calling, 'Good! Good!' as he went.

I reached immediately for my makeup bag and headed for the toilets. This kind of invitation was par for the course with Richard. He was given to picking up people in a last-minute way and carrying them off to meetings on accounts for which they weren't directly responsible. It looked impulsive, but was carefully planned. That way he ensured that the agency's employees took a higher-than-usual interest in all our business, not just their own part of it. And it gave him the opportunity to assess first-hand how well they thought on their feet. Richard, who never sat down unless he absolutely had to, was naturally prejudiced towards thinking on one's feet.

In the toilets I pinned up my hair – it was fine to wear it loose in the office but for meetings it was very distracting – and touched up my makeup. I was wearing my black cashmere twinset and my favourite dark green skirt: knee-length, with a slit up the side. With my hair up, my lipstick perfect and the addition of a beaded choker which I kept in my makeup bag for emergencies, I thoroughly approved of myself. Efficient but trendy, sexy but discreet. My hair colour was amazing. My colourist had been absolutely right about this dark red. It was gorgeous. And, as she had so correctly pointed out, with russet hair I could wear black from head to toe if I wanted without ever looking drab.

'Juliet! Lovely! You look very smart!' Richard exclaimed as I emerged into the lobby ten minutes later.

'Do you think the coat works?' I said hopefully, buttoning it up.

It was a purple mohair mix. In the privacy of my own home, not to mention in the cubicle of the department store, I loved it, but I was still nervous of taking it out into the world. When you're used to wearing black or brown coats in winter, dark plum seems almost as daring as chartreuse. 'I bought it on sale, so you can say if it looks like a fuzzy blanket.'

This was disingenuous of me – even though the coat had been on sale it had still cost so much that I had heart palpitations whenever I thought of the credit card slip. Still, I wanted the truth from Richard. He had excellent taste.

'No, it's fine.' Richard considered me thoughtfully. 'Nice contrast with your new hair.'

I breathed again. God, it was great having a gay boss.

'Good! Good! Very nice to meet you again! Good!'

Richard was beaming (inasmuch as a man who resembles a bald eagle crossed with a vulture can be said to beam). The meeting had gone very well. There are some blissfully smooth periods with client accounts where the agency and the client are almost as one. The agency embodies the client's wishes and expands on them in ways the client had never dreamt, and the client, in return, encourages the agency on to still-greater feats of achievement. We call this a honeymoon stage, as it usually happens, if it does so at all, near the beginning of an account. This was definitely a honeymoon. Eis Vodka and Sykes Collins Associates were, metaphorically speaking, wandering along a sandy beach, the sun in their hair, waves lapping at their feet, holding hands and whispering sweet nothings to each other, stopping every now and then to lie down on the sand and consummate their love.

The meeting had broken up, and its participants were filing out of the room in little departmental groups. Richard shook hands with all of them, so formally that he reminded me of the Queen at a Buckingham Palace garden party.

There had been only two other women in the room, but I took this deficit almost for granted by now. The two who had been allowed in were marketing and publicity, naturally enough, and I had caught them both looking enviously at my necklace and the slit in my skirt. The atmosphere at Eis Vodka, as with so many companies, was much more conventional than one would expect from its product line. It wasn't simply that everyone wore suits; more specifically that the suits were grey, buttoned-up, and worn with shirts and ties underneath. It might have been a meeting of very well-renumerated photocopier salesmen.

I stood beside Richard – hands clasped behind me, Prince Philip to his Queen Elizabeth – assessing them all. Johan was definitely the best looking of the photocopier salesmen. I had been eyeing him up during the meeting, and had decided that yes, I definitely did find him attractive. His build clinched it. I prefer my men to be constructed along the lines of the statues of discus throwers in the British Museum. Something you can really get a hold of. Forget your scrawny male model types with no bottoms who, like a rope standing on end in a conjuring trick, seem to have kept growing upwards without ever bothering to widen out.

(Whenever I found myself near Pimlico I always tried to pop into the Tate for a look at Sir Frederick Leighton's extremely large bronze statue of an athlete wrestling with a python. It wasn't very good, considered purely as art: the athlete looked bored, nor was the python giving of its best. They had obviously been posing all day and were dying for, respectively, a cup of tea and a mouse. Still, the model's physique never failed to have an uplifting effect on my psyche. Leighton had given himself full rein. One would have sworn that the pec deck, not to mention the calf riser, were in existence in 1877. Victorian muscle queens must have been queuing out into the street when it was first exhibited.)

Johan was approaching from south south-west, keeping a

steady, even stride, having cleared the corner of the table. He and Klaus were the only two Eismen left. Klaus had engaged Richard in enthusiastic conversation, and was practically drawing figures of eight in the air with his tie, such was his joy at the publicity triumph and expected sales success of Eis Shots. This left the field clear for me and Johan. Though I wanted to hear what Richard and Klaus were discussing, my flirting instincts were at that moment paramount. Besides, I could always catch up in the cab on the way back to the office.

I turned slightly away from the happy pair, just enough to indicate that Johan would be able to talk to me without including them, if he so wished. And he did.

'It's nice to see you!' he said, smiling down at me. 'When Richard said he would bring someone, I hoped it would be you.'

'I think it was because we had already met. At the launch,' I said demurely. 'He seemed to think we got on well.'

'Richard is very – uh –' He clicked his fingers in the air, as if summoning a djinn to bring him the exact word he was searching for. It worked. 'Perceptive,' he finished.

I smiled. I was concluding that Johan, apart from being large, might be nicely toned under that suit. Which was important too. The way he moved and stood suggested someone not unfamiliar with the inside of a gym.

'So, can we expect you at future meetings?'

'That depends on Richard,' I said, pulling a little deprecating moue. It was no more than the truth. 'I'd like to come, but it's really him running the account.' Deciding that this, together with the moue, made me sound like a pathetic fluffball, I added, 'I'm very busy with my own accounts right now.'

Johan folded his arms over his wide chest and fixed me with that intent grey stare I remembered vividly from the launch.

'Too busy to have lunch with me this week?' he asked.

I blinked, having been expecting another five minutes of preliminaries before we got down to business. Still, I admired his attitude. And his shoulders.

'That should be fine,' I said even more demurely. The rules of the game, however, did not permit me to arrange a time with him then and there. 'But I need to check my diary first. Why don't you ring me and we'll fix something up?'

I fished out my cardholder and gave him a card.

'I give you one too,' he said, his near-perfect English slipping fractionally in what I hoped was the excitement of the moment. 'Just in case.'

This was exactly what I had hoped for as soon as Richard had announced he was bringing me along: an opportunity to meet Johan again and size him up. As it were. And, of course, for Johan to decide whether he had merely been enjoying significant eye contact with me at the launch or actually wanted to ask me out. Well, we seemed to have settled those tricky points to our mutual satisfaction. I slipped his card into my wallet and smiled up at him. Eye contact is such a drab little phrase; it completely fails to convey the moment when your eyes meet and he's staring at you so hard that it feels as if he's drilling straight down your optical cables and deep into the inside of your body. I felt the impact right under my ribcage. God, I loved these moments. I almost lived for them.

Basking in appreciation like a cat in the sun, I turned to Richard. He and Klaus were clasping hands, two of Klaus's over one of Richard's, the whole structure pumping up and down like an oil derrick in full flow.

I surveyed them with satisfaction. Clearly the meeting had been a raving success for all of us.

Chapter Fourteen

Seen in a negative light, Johan's having taken my number now meant that I had two phone calls to wait for and therefore should be twice as tense. Fortunately, however, this was not how the dating mechanism functioned. As I had said to Gill, when comparing men rather unfelicitously to sticking-plasters, one man's interest will help considerably in calming down your natural anxieties about another. It's all very well for friends to say reassuringly that there are plenty of fish in the sea, but quite another for a large salmon, as it were, to jump temptingly into your lap, flapping its tail excitedly. It cannot fail to raise your spirits. Even if you prefer sea bass.

Working out dating theories with a group of friends in a bar (where else?), some years ago, I had recommended that any of us who had just met someone they liked (Object A), and with whom some contact had been made – number taken, some form of rendezvous arranged – should immediately start chatting up another person (Object B). Even if it wasn't intended to go anywhere, the flirtation with Object B would provide welcome diversion from all the attendant worries about how matters were proceeding with Object A, and would also, hopefully, stop one being too preoccupied with the horror of calculating all those phone-call equations. At least when you had Object B ringing you up as well, your focus on Object A's timing was much less likely to spiral inexorably into crazed obsession.

And I was even better placed than this. Johan was not just a distraction, a straw grasped at in the wind. I actually found him attractive, as attractive as Alex. Actually, on consideration, even more so. With Johan the contact had been immediate, an instant awareness that we were both interested in each other. Alex was a one-off for me, a sort of dark horse who had sneaked up on my blind side and whom I still wasn't a hundred per cent sure about. I wanted him to ring me as much out of pride as because I was dying to see him again.

The sheer unlikelihood of having two men I wanted after me at the same time was enough to make me dizzy. Not only was I having my cake and eating it, but I wasn't putting on any weight, either. Extraordinary. I checked my horoscope in one of the glossy magazines we always kept in the office to see if what it predicted for the week ahead was the astrological equivalent of a firework display with a nine-gun salute.

'While you realise the importance of the dramatic changes that are influencing matters ranging from your income to your ego,' it opened, 'that doesn't mean you've been enjoying them.'

Bollocks. I rolled it up and chucked it away with a deft flick of the wrist.

'Out of date?' Lewis said as the magazine landed in his wastepaper basket.

'Ridiculous horoscope.'

He clicked his tongue understandingly without taking his eyes from the computer screen.

'As my friend Gordon once shouted at a party,' I continued, '"What's that got to do with my neural connections?"'

'It's a modern superstition, isn't it?' Lewis observed. 'Like touching wood.'

'Or not having sex on the first date.'

For the first time Lewis removed his stare from the computer screen to train it on me. He looked as horrified as if I had just announced that I had recently been born again and asked him if he had ever thought about accepting the Lord Jesus into his life. I could see why. If girls stopped having sex with Lewis on the first date it would take him twice as long to get through all the ones he wanted.

'That's not a superstition,' he said, so shocked he was barely able to get the words out. 'That's just – just –'

'Prudish?'

'*Medieval*,' he finished.

Typical. I spent the day waiting for a phone call from one of two men, and guess who rang me? A third one. My brother. He was panicking at the idea of breaking the news about his computer course to Mum.

'She's going to do her nut,' he moaned. 'I know she is.'

This obstacle had never occurred to me. Reflecting on it now, however, I had to agree with him. Mum had invested a huge amount – quite literally, with all the handouts she gave him – in the idea of Chris being a musician. And Chris obviously saw this course not as six weeks he was being forced to kill before he could get back to drawing the dole and writing mournful songs about splintered hearts in the early twenty-first century, but as a whole new and exciting life direction. He wouldn't have been so worried about telling Mum if he weren't taking the course seriously.

'Yeah,' I said gloomily. 'She'll be furious, you're right.'

'So you'll come to dinner with us? To help me break the news to her? Please, Jules, please. I can't face her on my own.'

This appeal, as always, couldn't fail. Chris and I had learnt early on to band together against Mum's wrath wherever possible. The fact that we were older now, no longer dependent on her, made no difference. It wouldn't have occurred to me to point out that there was nothing Mum could actually do to Chris. The emotional blackmail would be bad enough. Certainly, if Chris finally managed to get a job and hold it for longer than a couple of days, he would be earning enough for Mum's occasional handout not to be missed. However, she would throw all the past gifts in his face, doing her best to bury him in guilt until he agreed to do what she wanted simply to avoid being suffocated.

I didn't have a choice, though.

'OK,' I said even more dourly. 'I'll be there.'

I couldn't say no. Mum made Chris and me feel guilty, and Chris, being my little brother, knew how to make me feel guilty. I, on the other hand, seemed to have absolutely no effect on either of them. Unfair again. I needed a cat – if only to kick. Cats don't do guilt.

The phone rang again. Could it be Mum? Had Chris already spoken to her to tell her that I would be coming along too? Did she suspect something and want to interrogate me? It was perfectly possible. In trepidation, I picked up the receiver as delicately as if it were made of bone china.

'Hello?' I said cautiously.

'Juliet? Hi, it's Alex.'

'Oh,' I said in such surprise that I nearly blurted out: 'But you weren't supposed to ring me till tomorrow afternoon!'

'You sound a bit taken aback,' he said.

'I didn't know you had my home number,' I said, recovering.

'Got it out of the book. You don't mind, do you?'

'Oh, no. No, no problem.'

Great, Juliet, start to stutter. That's always a sure-fire winner with the men.

'So how was your weekend?' he asked. He sounded unflustered, but as if he didn't have all the time in the world to chat. I was jealous. This was exactly the effect I wanted to produce, and he had got to it first. Well, being the one who had made the call, he had had plenty of time to practise beforehand.

'Oh, good,' I said, aiming for airy. 'Quiet. I got a lot of work done.'

'I saw Henry in the Spit the other night,' Alex said. 'We talked about you.'

'It's all true,' I said, positively breezy by now. This is the only line to take when people tell you they have been discussing you.

'Oh, good,' Alex said, amused. 'I was hoping it was.'

A little pause fell, signalling that there had been enough chit-chat; it was time for the invitation direct. If we bantered any longer it would go stale.

Alex broke the silence.

'So, do you want to go out for dinner one of these nights?' he said.

Hah! His first slip. 'One of these nights', what an embarrassing phrase. I hoped he was kicking himself.

'Oh.' I tried to sound surprised, without overdoing it. 'Yeah, sure. Why not?'

'Try not to sound so enthusiastic,' he suggested. 'I'm feeling really flattered.'

I found myself grinning. I must have overdone the cool. I liked that he had called me on it, though, rather than letting it pass.

'When are you free?' he said.

'Um . . .' I checked my diary. 'Friday would be good.'

Asked out on Monday, the earliest one could admit to being free was Friday. And it was the weekend, too. I wouldn't have to worry about getting up the next morning.

'OK. Why don't I ring you at work Friday and we'll decide where to go? Somewhere local, right?'

'Oh yes. Great. Lovely.'

I wondered whether I had over-compensated. Had I sounded gushing?

'So we'll talk on Friday,' I confirmed in a more business-like tone.

'Great. Looking forward to it.'

I put down the phone and immediately began an analysis of the conversation. Generally it had gone well; he had asked me out to dinner directly, instead of just throwing out a vague suggestion that we get together some time and forcing the two of us to stumble around the obstacle course for another ten minutes before finally sorting out a date. I wished we had fixed the time and place now, though. I was always insecure about this kind of thing. Now I had to wait for him to ring me on Friday. My conscious, reasoning mind told me that of course he would. It was my subconscious that didn't trust anything till it was nailed in place. I blamed this on Mum. She was such a fantasist; she made up stories all the time to put herself in a better light. I had learnt in childhood only to believe what she told me she had done when I saw the proof in black and white.

Maybe I should get my dates to fax me handwritten guarantees that they would be at a specific restaurant on the evening in question. I toyed with the idea of ringing Alex back to demand confirmation and it made me laugh aloud. At least Mum hadn't managed to destroy my sense of humour.

I had spoken too soon. If my sense of humour had been fully functioning, surely I would have been able to appreciate the comic possibilities – or at least the subtle ironies – in the situation that unfolded the very next evening. After all, it should have been a richly dramatic situation: Mother Desperately Tries To Persuade Son Not To Get A Proper Job And Finally Stop Signing On. I hadn't realised just how important it was to Mum that Chris be a musician. She didn't even care that much if he were successful or not. Because as long as he was struggling professionally, she would be able to treat him like a child.

'At least one of my children was doing something creative!' she complained. 'I had some hopes for you, Juliet, when you did that Media Studies degree. I thought you might go into television. Of course, I have no hopes for you now,' she added cuttingly. 'I gave them up when you started in public relations.'

She pronounced these last two words with as much loathing as if I were doing PR for the biological weapons branch of the arms industry.

'Great, Mum. Glad to know you have no hopes for me,' I said, drinking more beer and feeling horrendously guilty about not being a young British artist or a literacy teacher in a sink school in Hackney. I always drank a lot when out to dinner with my mother.

'Ju's doing really well, Mum,' Chris chipped in. 'She's been made partner.'

Chris might give me a hard time about my expense account when we were alone, but it was rare that, faced with Mum, we didn't bond together. I shot him a glance full of gratitude. Suddenly it popped into my head that I should invite him to the launch. If Mel and Gill were going to be there, Chris should be too. I felt warm, comforted, at the idea of having a small posse of people who really cared about me there. I made a mental note to mention it to Chris, and get Lewis to send him an official invite too. He'd like that.

'I know that Juliet's a partner,' Mum said crossly. 'You sound as if you had to remind me.'

'Well, I know you're pleased about it, because I heard you on the phone boasting about her to Mrs Holmes. You were saying how great it is that Ju's been made partner this young.'

It was Mum's turn to shoot him a look now, in which gratitude played a considerably lesser part. I masked my smile by lifting the beer bottle to my mouth once more. It was only in cases of extreme emergency that one of us dared to confront Mum with the truth, or documented actions of hers that did not tally with the version she was attempting to put across.

This was a minor infraction, but it still created considerable tension which needed to be allayed. Chris, as familiar as I with the subtle workings of Mum's mind, promptly moved on.

'Which is funny,' he said, 'because Ju's such an old crock. I mean, thirty-three! Wrinkle city.'

'Oi, watch it,' I retorted. 'I've had a really good thirty-three so far. You wait and see if you can say the same.'

The spotlight was off Mum, the strain relieved. Chris and I relaxed. The waiter, as if sensing that it was now safe to approach the table, came to clear away the starters. Mum told him tartly that the onion bhajis had been cold, thus letting off steam which otherwise would have scorched one of us. Thank God for scapegoats.

We had come to Chris's local Indian rather than the café, the latter now being out of bounds since its brutal rejection of Chris as singer-in-residence. Cue plenty of complaints from Mum about how hard Indian food was on her stomach. Still, she was putting it away readily enough, indigestible and cold though it might be. If later she suffered from bloating or wind she would duly inform me of it; and should I point out that she had eaten plenty she would tell me that she had done so not to spoil the evening by picking at her food. My stomach was curling up again. That was the trouble with Mum and me; I anticipated all her responses, predicting them far down the line, as if to protect myself. Forewarned is forearmed. But it never worked. It just made me paranoid instead, as if I were trying to climb inside her head and work it out once and for all.

'Two more Tiger beers, please,' I said to the waiter, who Mum had now reduced to a hunched, defensive posture. I smiled at him reassuringly. It seemed to help a little.

'I'm just off to the loo,' Chris announced a shade too loudly. Both of us became self-conscious in Mum's presence; we knew that she was assessing us constantly. He caught my eye as he pushed back the table, and I knew what his glance meant. This was the moment for me to sell Mum on his computer course. Why he thought I would be successful, goodness knew; my standing with her right now seemed little higher than the waiter's. Still, I had promised to try.

I pushed my pawn out tentatively two squares.

'Chris seems really happy about doing this course,' I began.

In retrospect this hadn't been the best opening. Mum took comments on one's sibling's state of mind as a challenge, unless she agreed with them.

'*Happy?*' she said scornfully. 'He seems *resigned*, Juliet, that's all.'

Now I had the choice of disagreeing with her or giving in.

'Oh, I don't know,' I said carefully. 'I had the impression he was rather looking forward to it.'

Mum sniffed.

'What would you know?' she said.

'I talk to Chris a lot,' I said defensively. 'He even asked me round to tell me about it.'

'I hope you tried to talk him out of it.'

I had an extremely cunning thought.

'Actually, it's Sissy who's been doing that,' I said demurely. 'She's really against his doing the course.'

This was a stroke of genius. And it was even true. I knew

that Sissy and Chris had been fighting ever since he had decided to do the computer course. Sissy was perfectly happy for Chris to be on the dole as long as he was a musician; on her scale of values a computer programmer, even a gainfully employed one, ranked as a considerably less glamorous profession for a boyfriend. And now, if Mum persisted in trying to wean Chris away from the course, she would be lining up on Sissy's side. Mum hated Sissy. She would probably have hated any girlfriend of Chris's, but Sissy was pretty much the Antichrist as far as Mum was concerned.

There was a long pause, every second of which I relished. My chess analogy had been wrong. This was more like a fencing match. I had just scored a hit, and Mum was staggering back from it.

The tactic she eventually chose was to ignore the whole topic. Mum was clever; she knew when she was on weak ground. And she also preferred to mention Sissy's name as little as possible. It was part of her overall strategy for Pretending Sissy Did Not Exist.

'Well, if you're so close to Chris at the moment,' she began, 'I know he listens to you –'

This was a big concession.

'– so why don't you try to persuade him that he's making the wrong decision?'

She was staring at me so hard I couldn't look away. Her eyes were intent. I felt myself wilting.

'You could do that better than anyone!' she continued eagerly. 'You must know lots of successful musicians – didn't they have to struggle for ages? I mean, it isn't usually overnight success, is it? Tell Chris that if he just keeps plugging away at it, he'll get there.'

Great. Chris on one side, Mum on the other, and me as piggy in the middle. Jules, could you tell Mum about me breaking that window . . . Juliet, tell your brother to put that down now and come to the table . . . Ever since I could remember they had been sending messages to each other through me. Maybe Bart's comment about me feeling over-responsible for both of them had been spot on.

Our main courses had arrived. I dug into the paratha, putting it away so fast that soon I would be piggy in a literal sense as well. I needed some kind of comfort and this evening I certainly wasn't going to get it anywhere else. Mum watched with disapproval. She was very diet conscious where I was concerned.

'It's only a six-week course, Mum,' I said, finishing a flaky mouthful and wiping my buttery hands on the napkin. 'And it'll get the dole people off his back for a long time. Why not just let him do it? I mean, why's such a fuss being made about it?'

I thought this was a good tactic. Minimise the significance of the course. Let Mum get used to things by instalments.

'It's the slippery slope,' Mum said darkly, helping herself to tandoori chicken.

'God,' I said. Momentarily overcome by mental exhaustion, I forgot to choose my words carefully and blurted out what I was actually thinking. Which was a fatal mistake with Mum. 'Why does this whole family take Chris so seriously that as soon as he decides to start a course it's like he's going to be a programmer straight away? I mean, every little decision of his seems so important to everyone! No one ever worried like this about me!'

'I didn't need to,' Mum said coldly. 'I knew you'd be fine.'

'Oh, great. Thanks for the support,' I snapped.

We glared at each other. This was the moment that Chris chose to stage his return from the toilet; he had been in there so long he must have gone through an entire packet of Golden

Virginia. Sliding back his chair, he said cheerfully: 'So! How's everything going?' before he had had time to absorb the toxicity of the atmosphere. When it finally seeped in, he muttered something about being hungry and tucked into the nearest dish without even looking to see what it contained. We all ate in silence for a while; or rather, Chris and I did, heads down, expressions determined, as if finishing our dinner would somehow make her approve of us again. Meanwhile Mum was toying with her food, sighing and pushing her fork round the plate in a way designed to demonstrate her discontent. When she signalled to the waiter for another glass of water, Chris took the opportunity to catch my eye reproachfully. I had let him down. Dinner was a disaster. And, even though I knew it wasn't logical, I felt responsible.

I paid, of course. I always did. Mum took it for granted and Chris muttered a brief 'Thanks'. Maybe once he became a computer programmer he could take us all out to dinner for a change. And assume the responsibility for Mum's moods. I could persuade him to tell Mum to be nicer to me, hide in the toilet while he made the effort, and then throw him reproachful glances when he inevitably failed. This scenario should have cheered me up; but somehow it didn't. The weight of the world was on my shoulders. Or rather, Mum and Chris. I felt as if I were carrying them on a yoke, one on either side, and even now I had left them my shoulders were aching and hunched over with the strain. Chris unloaded all his problems on to me; Mum made me responsible for the delicate balance of her moods; and not only did they dump everything on me but they then expected me to sort things out, unpick all the dropped stitches, tidy them up and hand them back with a smile on my face. This had been going on ever since I could remember, and I was sick of it. Literally. I hurt with it. My back was sore and my stomach bloated with all the food I had stuffed down to keep my mouth too busy to contradict Mum.

I massaged my shoulders one-handed. It hardly helped at all. I had a surge of longing for Bart. If he had been at dinner tonight, he would have kept Mum in a good mood. He had a trick of taking her not too seriously, which she loved from him (though she would have blown Chris and me apart at point-blank range for even attempting it). And now I could have whined him into giving me a massage. Then we would probably have had sex; but it wasn't the sex I was missing right now, it was the tenderness. I felt the tears pricking at my eyes.

In a desperate effort to stop myself breaking down in sobs in the minicab, I had the idea of directing it to the Spit and Whistle: but that was out of bounds now. My complicated rule system dictated that now Alex had rung me, I should stay out of the pub until our date on Friday. Otherwise I might seem too keen to see him, and as if my social life were not so throbbing with activity that I had nothing better to do than drop into eccentric pubs off Chalk Farm Road at all hours. Besides, it was only ten o'clock. According to what he had told me, he wouldn't have finished work yet.

Loneliness washed over me. Chris and Mum together were a lethal combination for me. I could just about manage one, but the two of them fell on me as heavy as a rock. How ironic that it should be my family that made me feel so isolated, a tiny solitary person going back to her empty flat with aching shoulders and no one to massage them for her. Just the sound of the front door closing behind me, its lock snapping shut, echoing in the hallway, just one coat being taken off and hung on the peg, no welcoming voice calling out from the living room . . . I tried to tell myself that if I had still been with

Bart he might just as likely have been at the dog track losing our holiday money, but right at this moment I would have settled even for that.

This was awful. I had to do something to distract myself. Opening a can of borlotti beans, I ate them without pleasure or even satisfaction, standing at the kitchen counter, forking them straight into my mouth without even bothering to rinse off the thick foamy liquid that dripped off their slippery sides. Evenings with Mum often had this effect on me. I felt drained, as if she had sucked a vital substance out of me, which needed replacing urgently. Eating the beans was a chore to be got over as fast as possible. When I had finished them I felt sick to my stomach, and scarcely comforted; but at least I had done something to redress the balance, fill myself up again. I just hoped I would be able to sleep.

Chapter Fifteen

The next day I was angry with myself about the beans. I could feel them in my stomach all morning, heavy as lead, slowing me down, a physical reminder of how miserable I had been last night. Maybe that was what I had wanted; a kind of token to indicate my unhappiness, a sign that something with my family needed to change. I pushed the whole thought aside, telling myself that Mum and Chris were done for the while; I had fulfilled my responsibilities for at least a fortnight and could go back to being me. Even if they were hovering in abeyance, I could still try not to think about them. I was good at that.

And, after all, I was doing pretty well on almost all other fronts. I had a date with Alex for Friday, and if I could just keep off the borlotti beans and the croissants till then I would fit without too much difficulty into my new trousers. And then Johan rang and asked me to lunch on Thursday, which was even better. I felt positively invigorated. There's a fizz that runs through your whole body when someone attractive asks you out; I buzzed around the office all day, moving so fast that I was sure I had burnt off those wretched beans by leaving time. Still on Cloud Nine, I rang Gill to see how she was doing, and hopefully fix up a time to see each other. It felt like years since we'd met.

The machine picked up. It was still Gill's voice on the outgoing message, which probably meant that, despite my lurid imaginings, Jeremy hadn't repossessed the house. Yet.

Which had to be good news. He probably wouldn't, now that he was settled in a bachelor flat in the Barbican. Poor Jeremy.

'Gill? It's me, Jules,' I said breezily. 'How's it going? You're probably out buying huge quantities of mince or shagging your brains out in Philip's love pad. Anyway, call me when you can, I've got lots of gossip and men stuff to catch you up on—'

The answerphone clicked off and I heard the static of a phone line. Gill must be there and have just managed to pick up the phone. Probably wiping the raw mince off her hands before handling the receiver.

'Gill!' I said cheerfully. 'Hi!'

There was a long silence. I heard heavy, slow breathing, and for a crazy moment thought I had a crossed line with a phone pervert.

'Gill?' I said doubtfully.

'Jules,' a voice, loaded with misery and despair, finally said. My heart sank to the bottom of my stomach. My breath caught, and I couldn't say a word. Well, I had already said more than enough. It was Jeremy.

Another terrible pause ensued. I was desperately trying to think of a way to get myself – and Gill – out of the awful hole I had dug. Unfortunately, nothing came to mind. There was no way I could pretend that I had been joking. I had mentioned Philip by name; you're not that specific if you're teasing a friend about some mythical lover. And even if I had been inventing something to tease Gill with, it would have been in awful taste, considering that she had left her much-loved husband only a couple of weeks ago. I opened my lips and found to my horror that all that was issuing was a hopeless stream of 'Aaaaaaaaaah,' as if I were an academic steepling my fingers together and pondering some abtruse new theory on which I were about to pronounce judgement. Alas, no flash of intellectual brilliance followed, which made the 'Aaaaaaaaaah' sound exactly like the moan for help it actually was.

'Juliet?' Jeremy said. He sounded as if he were speaking from the bottom of his own tomb. 'Did I hear right – what you just said?'

'AAAAAAAAAAAAAAH,' I said, much louder this time. I was scrabbling desperately for a grip on the slippery slopes of this conversation, and failing hopelessly. I could feel myself sliding down them with increasing speed, the abyss yawning below.

Through the open door of my office I saw that Lewis had swivelled in his seat and was staring at me, perturbed. I wiggled round the desk and kicked the door shut, making a helpless expression at him to indicate that I shouldn't be disturbed.

'Juliet? You have to tell me . . . you were always a friend, and even now that Gill . . . that Gill . . .' Jeremy's voice caught, and I could hear him stifling a heavy sob. 'Is Gill – is she seeing someone?'

'OHHHHHHHHHHHHHH . . .'

Well, at least it was a different vowel. I writhed in pity for Jeremy, and guilt at having dropped Gill in it.

Feebly I said, 'I can't tell you that, Jeremy, you know I can't.'

'But I heard your message.'

I barely recognised Jeremy's voice. He was obviously trying very hard to hold back the tears.

'Can you tell me,' he said hopelessly, 'can you tell me that she's not seeing someone else?'

'AAAAAAAAAAAH!' screamed the inside of my head.

'Uh . . .' I tried pathetically to stall him, playing for time. 'Well, I shouldn't really say anything at all . . .'

'But you're not denying it.'

Jeremy made this a statement. It hung between us, down the fizz of the phone line, waiting for me to make it all go away. I gripped the receiver tightly, desperately hoping that some words would magically pop out of my mouth and smooth everything over, cancel out the horror of the last few minutes. But I couldn't. I couldn't deny it. Somehow I felt that I owed it to Jeremy, in the name of all the cosy, confidential conversations we had had – he was right, we had been friends – not to lie to him outright. And that was what I would have had to do.

Besides, he wouldn't have believed me anyway. As soon as he hung up he would play back the answering machine with that damning stupid message of mine. How could I have been such an idiot?

'That's all right, Juliet,' Jeremy said, after an eternity had passed. 'I don't want to make you say any more. But I can't believe you take this so lightly.' He choked. 'My marriage is in ruins – you know how happy Gill and I were – and now she's off with another man –' He could barely get the words out by now. 'And you're talking about it on the machine as if she were just having another of the completely meaningless flings that you've been going in for ever since you broke up with Bart! I would have thought that you of all people would know how painful this is for me! I can't believe you would just – joke about it like that – Oh *God* –'

Jeremy's voice was breaking into pieces. He put down the phone, doubtless a split-second before a wrenching crying session. I wanted to kill myself. But there was something I had to do first, before I surrendered to that luxury. Frantically I searched through the heap of papers on my desk, looking for my address book, which had Gill's mobile number in it. And yes, of course, I should have rung her on the mobile, I should never have taken the risk of leaving a message on the machine at her home, on the off-chance that Jeremy might be stopping in to pick up some more of his handmade shoes and posh suits. But she hated the mobile and hardly ever switched it on, and besides I had her home phone number programmed in to my office phone and it had just been easier to press the speed dial key – Oh God, what a disaster . . .

I had to get to Gill before Jeremy could. The mobile rang but to my craven relief her message service picked up.

'Gill,' I said, quaking in my boots. 'It's Jules. Ring me ASAP. It's really serious. I'm sorry – I'm so, so sorry – but I let something slip – I left a message for you on your machine at home and Jeremy was there and heard it and I said something about Philip – Oh God I'm so sorry – anyway, he knows, or suspects, so I wanted to warn you – I'm SO, SO, SORRY! Ring me?'

I added these last two words in a very small voice. I was terrified of what Gill would say to me. The tiny thought flitted through my head for a moment that if she had taken my advice and changed the locks, Jeremy wouldn't have been able to get in, and this whole sitation would have been avoided. I decided not to try this line of defence out on her, though, for fear of getting my head bitten off. But it didn't stop me making pathetic excuses for myself. This was really Gill's fault, because she hadn't told Jeremy herself – and, after all, when had she been planning to do that? The last I had heard she was going round to his flat to break the news about Philip. Clearly she had bottled it and now that the news had slipped out, as it was bound to have done sooner or later, I was the one in the frame, just because Gill hadn't had enough courage to do it herself . . .

I felt as if my head was going to explode. Nastily, selfishly, I found myself momentarily angry at both Gill and Jeremy for ruining my happy two-date high with their shambles of

a marriage breakdown. The truth was that I was deeply embarrassed by what Jeremy had said about my lightness of tone
on the phone message. I *had* sounded ridiculously carefree
about Philip, as if he were just Gill's latest shag, rather than
the reason for her marriage breakup. But I hadn't quite known
what to say. How do you sound in that kind of situation?
Your friend's in ecstasy because she's finally having sex after
years of near abstinence, and even though you still care about
her husband – and know that she does too – you are, after
all, supposed to be on her side. Which means being happy
for her. Certainly I didn't know how Gill had managed all
these years without getting laid. I would have imploded. And
the role of a friend, after all, is not to be the annoying little
super-ego moral voice in your head.

Still, my message had been wrong. I knew that. It had
sounded wrong and shallow to me even as I was leaving it,
and it was only because of my own dating triumph that I had
been that careless. And now I had trapped myself in that
moment forever.

I tried to tell myself that Jeremy would recover sooner than
one thought. Men usually did recover quicker than women.
They mourned harder, but after a certain point they simply
shut themselves off and went after someone new. Women
tended to spread their grieving out, and often it never quite
vanished; look at the strong thread of nostalgia I still had for
Bart. I doubted he indulged in the kind of reminiscences that
I did. He had probably slammed that door shut and would
never open it again.

I threw myself into work for the rest of the day and managed
partially to divert myself from the imminent horror that would
be Gill's phone call. Waiting for a potential date to call was as
nothing to this. By the time I left, to go to drinks with a client,
it still hadn't come. I stayed later than I should have, and drank

more ditto, to ward off the message that would doubtless be waiting for me at home; but when I staggered in half-cut there was no light flashing on the machine. I tried Gill again, both at home and on the mobile, but there was no answer. And there was no answer the next morning. At this point it occurred to me to wonder whether she had heard my warning message and was hiding from Jeremy. Well, I was doing my best. At least I had lunch with Johan looming that day, and my anxieties about what to wear were a useful distraction.

If I had known in advance what would happen at lunch it would have occupied my thoughts completely. Maybe it was as well, though, that I had no idea. It might have sent me completely over the edge.

Johan had booked a table at L'Orange for lunch. I had only been there occasionally. We didn't tend to entertain at that kind of full-on, well-known but rather conventional restaurant; our clients usually preferred to be taken to more cutting-edge places, or little half-secrets tucked away in Soho back streets, packed with media people but known to few outsiders. Johan's choice befitted him, his job, and his suit; it was smart and very expensive and equally grown up. I dressed up for the restaurant as much as for him.

It could not have been less cosy. The chairs made you sit poker-straight and the lighting put everyone on show, which was nearly the whole point of the exercise. The dining room was built on several levels, which had the effect of creating a series of little stages, like the stepped glass display stands in a jeweller's window. Light reflected off the smooth shiny floors, the metal chairs, the polished chrome railings that ran around each raised area; the ceiling was a whole suspended mass of white light, great chunks of illuminated glass hanging precariously above our heads like an over-evolved chandelier.

All the customers were as smart as they could possibly be given that fashionable understatement was currently the rage. I had put my hair up and donned my better pieces of jewellery – which was to say ones that had not been bought at chain stores on Oxford Street – and it had been the right decision.

Johan was already there, of course. He rose to greet me and I was again taken aback by his sheer size. Like Pieter, he made me feel small and fragile and delicate. Don't misunderstand me; I had no wish to be a Victorian heroine. But a man large enough to make my waist appear by comparison – well, as if I had a waistline – was irresistible.

In the cab I had been a little concerned about what Johan and I would do for conversation. I so rarely went out on this kind of date that I was rather dreading all the talking it would involve. Bart and I had met at a party, both of us half-drunk, on the dance floor; we had kissed after we had been dancing for an hour and hadn't exchanged more than a couple of words. This was my preferred plan of attack. Picking men up in clubs or parties, going to their hotel room to do drugs: one could see exactly why these time-honoured methods, with the inevitable variation, had stood the test of centuries. The more you talked, the harder it was to make the first move. And also, the more you talked, the more you got to know them and the less you felt like doing filthy things with them. Or maybe that was just me.

'The oysters are very good here,' Johan said, indicating the menu that lay in front of me. 'If you like oysters.'

'I'm making myself,' I said.

'Making yourself?'

'I think I ought to.'

He looked puzzled.

'Why?' he asked.

'Oh,' I said flippantly, 'because they're so sophisticated.'

He burst out laughing. 'But you are already sophisticated, Juliet! You don't need oysters!'

'Oh, am I?' I preened. My hand suddenly felt incomplete without a long cigarette holder and an elbow-length satin glove. 'Well, then, I'll let myself off the oysters. If I don't need them.'

Johan shook his head, his expression mock serious.

'No, you do not need the oysters. You could eat a –' he scrabbled around – 'a hamburger and you would still be chic.'

'I'm blushing,' I said to hide how much I was relishing this.

'That would not be sophisticated,' Johan pointed out, tongue in cheek.

I burst out laughing. We were off to a good start.

Johan gauged perfectly the tone of the lunch. Having invited me, he naturally ordered the wine and did most of the talking to the waiter, but he managed this quite naturally, without making me feel like a kept woman. The Dutch were notoriously advanced on the sexual politics front. I was keeping a wary eye out for any tendencies to assume that, since he was paying for lunch, he considered he had the right to take me a little for granted during the couple of hours that we were in our little bubble together. But if anything he was deferential, as if he wanted to make it clear that this was by no means the case.

And he was undeniably handsome, albeit in a more conventional way than I usually preferred. Often, when I had made a date with someone I had met only briefly, I worried that I would turn up, catch sight of him, and think: Oh dear God, what have I done? But I had met Johan twice now, the second time in broad daylight, and I had needed only the initial glance of him as he unfolded his large body and loomed up behind the table to assure me that everything in that direction was absolutely fine. Out on a date with a very attractive man in as sharp a suit as could be cut for someone of his Viking dimensions, for lunch at a very smart restaurant, drinking a damn fine Chablis – I was maturing, despite myself. I never did this kind of thing. I was growing up. And looking over the narrow tabletop to catch Johan's bright eyes, observing the width of his shoulders, I didn't feel too bad about it. He might not be a twenty-five-year-old with a flawless torso and a bottom so pert that you could ski-jump off its slope; but I still fancied him. I sipped some more wine and savoured the moment.

'How is your mousse?' Johan was asking.

'Delicious. You want to try some?'

'No, it's fine.'

'Do you not like salmon? Or do you object to eating off someone else's plate?'

'That is not someone else's plate,' Johan corrected, smiling at me, 'it is your plate. There is a big difference.'

'Well, then –' I was sounding coquettish, but it was just coming out that way; there was nothing I could do about it – 'do you mind eating off my plate?'

'Not at all,' Johan assured me. 'No, it is just that I do not think the salmon will go well with my duck.'

'Foodie,' I teased. I thought this attitude a shade pompous; none of the cooks I knew ever objected to trying one taste after the other. One could always take a bit of bread to cleanse the palate if one were really fastidious. Still, I couldn't dislike someone who took food seriously.

Johan's eyes were gleaming at me.

'You think I am fussy,' he accused.

I laughed. 'A little bit.'

'And now I should give in and eat your mousse to prove that I am not fussy, yes?'

Somehow the way Johan said 'eat your mousse' was rather arousing. My inner thighs twitched together. I held his gaze determinedly, knowing that if I dropped my eyes I would look coy.

'No,' I said firmly. 'You've had your chance. I'm going to finish it myself.'

And I scooped up the last bite and ate it with my eyes still fixed on his, hoping I didn't look ridiculous. Fortunately the mousse needed minimal chewing, which was why I had risked the manoeuvre.

'You have a little left . . . there . . .' Johan put out a finger practically as big as my forearm and touched the side of my mouth so slightly that it brushed against the imperceptible, feathery down of my cheek. If someone else had made that gesture, it would have tickled; but when it comes to a man you find attractive your senses interpret even the slightest contact quite differently. I jumped. Johan smiled. I put my finger to my mouth and licked off the mousse. Johan stopped smiling and looked very serious instead. It was probably a good thing that the waiter came to clear our plates at that precise moment. Something needed to break the tension.

I remembered what Gill, or rather her assistant, had said about men flocking to you because they sense the interest of other men. It was probably true enough; but the other side of the equation was that, if more than one man is interested in you, your own libido takes a powerful upward shift. I could feel that assurance radiating out of me. Come to think of it, Johan was very confident too. We were sparking happily off each other.

Halfway through our main courses, deep in a lively discussion about London restaurants in general and the difficulty of getting really good sushi in particular, I looked up and noticed a couple who were being seated at a table on the level above ours. They were next to the railing, only a few tables away and a good four feet higher than us, so I could see them perfectly clearly. The man had his hand on the woman's bottom. Not to steer her, as men do sometimes. Usually in that manoeuvre the hand went, for some arcane male reason, at the base of the spine. No, it was simply resting on her bottom for the pure pleasure of it, and when they separated to take their seats he gave it a little slap of farewell.

I said 'man', but that might have been slightly misleading. The woman was Felicity Layton, the producer of Liam's series. And the overgrown man-child who was now pushing back his chair and straddling it, leering cheerfully at her, his elbows propped on the table, was yet another grown-up Just William. It was Liam himself.

Why was I so surprised? I knew that Liam's sex drive was turbo-charged enough to make a Formula One racing car feel inadequate by comparison. If there were no human females – alive or otherwise – around, and he had a raging stiffie beating at his button fly, Liam would have shagged a dead rabbit. Still, the Liam-and-Felicity pairing was so unlikely, I gawped at them like an idiot, trying to imagine it.

Then I wished I hadn't.

'What is so interesting?' Johan said. 'Or are you just bored with me?'

I grinned at him. 'Very.'

He looked a little taken aback. I hastened to correct him.

'My main client just came in with the producer of his series.'

Johan raised his eyebrows.

'If it was just that, you would have waved at them,' he said acutely. 'But you were looking very surprised.'

'Well –' I lowered my voice, though God knew why. 'He

had his hand on her bottom. I mean, really on her bottom.'

Johan's eyebrows went up again.

'Which ones are they?'

'You'll work it out,' I said. 'On the level above us.'

Johan had to turn his head about 45 degrees to see Felicity and Liam's table. But, as I had predicted, he spotted them at once.

'He is rubbing her knee,' he observed.

Liam was indeed leaning forward, his hand outstretched enough under the table to caress Felicity's stockinged knee. Being a modern, forward-thinking restaurant, L'Orange did not provide those floor-length tablecloths that allow total discretion – or indiscretion – for amorously inclined customers. The cloth barely skimmed the corners of the metal table. Felicity and Liam had no privacy whatsoever. I was sure that for Liam this was a bonus. And Felicity looked much too involved in what he was doing to care about a minor detail like the fact that half London could see her new star trying to get his hand up between her legs.

'They are an odd couple,' Johan observed.

Either the Dutch were good at understatement or the contemplation of Liam and Felicity had left Johan struggling for the *mot juste*. I cleared my throat.

'Um, I don't think they're really a couple,' I clarified. 'I think they're just –'

'– Having sex?'

'Um, yes.'

The Dutch were so direct about this kind of thing. In Britain we have a long list of euphemisms: Ugandan discussions, getting his leg over, having a fling. I remembered a friend of mine telling me how she had met an attractive young man one night in a coffee shop in Amsterdam and after a few hours talking had invited him back to the place she was staying for coffee. The young man had replied: 'Some coffee, yes. And then I think some sex?'

She was so charmed by this unaccustomed frankness that she had skipped the coffee stage entirely.

I looked back at Felicity and Liam. The latter was dressed, as usual, in his hanging-with-the-homeboys crossed with gay body-conscious style: huge trousers which hung off his narrow hips and even managed to flatten the lovely twin curves of his buttocks, combined with a tight t-shirt splattered with logos. He had rolled up the sleeves to show off as many of his tattoos as possible. Felicity, meanwhile . . .

Felicity was always a mystery to me. She was a very successful producer; she could do cutting-edge programmes with the best of them, or at least as cutting-edge as one could expect from a food programme. She was famous for her indefatigable attendance at the round of media clubs and parties which most of us dropped in and out of according to our energy levels. And yet despite all this socialising she still dressed as if she had been living on a remote Scottish island for the last twenty years without access to any fashion magazines whatsoever. It wouldn't have needed *Vogue*; even *Woman's Own* would have been perfectly capable of informing Felicity that it had been a long, long time since batwing sweaters, tapered trousers or the calf-length, gathered skirt she was wearing today had been current. Where did she get them from? I always wondered this when I saw women wearing new, but bizarrely outdated clothes. Was there a whole chain of shops, or catalogues, which had somehow passed me by, specialising in anti-fashion? The shoes – brown courts which looked oddly femme at the bottom of Felicity's sturdy legs – were more explicable. I had always known there were sensible shoe shops out there. I just hadn't gone searching for them.

'Oh my God,' I said as I glanced again at the ill-matched pair.

Johan, sensing from my voice that matters had moved on a few stages, looked round again. His fork clattered to his plate. Felicity was leaning back in her chair slightly, which must have been uncomfortable. Any distress to her spine, however, would be outweighed by her enjoyment of her current occupation; she had lifted one stockinged foot into Liam's lap and was busily engaged in massaging him with her toes. Liam was talking, and from the concentrated expression on his face I bet that he was giving her instructions on how to proceed.

'They are having fun,' Johan observed.

'They are, aren't they?'

I cleared my throat again. Felicity was really giving the foot action everything she had, her toes curling into Liam's crotch, her leg moving back and forward with a regular rhythmic motion that was undeniably sexy. I had a sudden urge to slip off my shoe and do the same to Johan. Liam had hold of Felicity's foot now with both hands, and as he worked it against him his eyes closed involuntarily, a blissful expression on his face. Felicity looked like a cat with her whiskers thick with cream. She leant back even further, giving her leg more space to manoeuvre, propping her hands on each side of her chair for support.

The above-and-below shots of the table were so incongruous it was hard for me to assimilate what was happening. Felicity, with her badly cut shag of grey-streaked hair and face as windbeaten as if she had spent most of her life cattle-farming on the Yorkshire moors, had always reminded me of a particularly bloody-minded teacher I had had for German. It seemed almost sacrilegious to watch her giving Liam some hot foot action. Still, that observation suddenly made a lot of sense. I bet they played teacher and student all the time.

I had never seen anyone carry footsie to this extreme, let alone in the middle of a crowded restaurant. They were practically having sex. I wondered if the people on their level realised what was going on or whether it was just us lucky ones below who had a full view of their advanced state of foreplay. And now I was getting worried for purely professional reasons. Felicity was the last person in the world Liam ought to be fooling around with. It would be a publicity disaster if the word got out that she had commissioned his series only because she was sleeping with him.

'I bet everyone here thinks he's her toyboy,' I said gloomily, pushing my plate away from me. The thought had made me lose my appetite, a clear indication of how seriously I was taking this development.

'Isn't he?' Johan asked.

'No,' I said. 'I can't really imagine Liam having sex with Felicity just to get ahead. Besides, he wouldn't need to. I mean, he'd do it with her anyway.'

'Really?' Johan was baffled. 'Does he have the Oedipus complex?'

I decided not to share my teacher-and-very-naughty-pupil theory with Johan. I felt that the conversation was more than suggestive enough already.

'No,' I explained. 'It's just that Liam would, hmmn, do it with anyone.'

I also decided not to favour Johan with the dead rabbit hypothesis.

'He is young,' Johan said, shrugging. 'When you are a young man you have no taste. Now I am older I am –' he smiled at me – 'much more fussy. So you see, you were right. I am fussy.'

We smiled at each other. But we couldn't hold it. As if

compelled by a force beyond our control, we swivelled our heads again to watch the Liam and Felicity live sex show. It was definitely increasing the sexual tension between Johan and me, like watching explicit sex scenes in a film on your first date. Felicity and Liam, well beyond that early stage of tentative, fleeting contact, were really giving it their all by now. Felicity had managed to lift both her feet into his lap and was executing some complicated, double-pull stroking technique with her soles which, from Liam's agonised expression, seemed to be hitting the spot. I couldn't even look at Johan. Felicity's legs slid back and forth; Liam, no longer directing proceedings, clutched the sides of the table, his head ducked in a vain attempt to hide his advanced state of sexual excitement; and I was so worked up by now all I wanted to do was drag Johan into the ladies' toilets, shove him up against the wall and rip off his trousers.

Fortunately for everyone else's self-control, Liam lost his. Pushing back his chair, he jumped up and practically tore down the stairs in our direction, taking them two at a time. Now I realised the advantages to baggy trousers which had previously eluded me. If I hadn't known what he was, as it were, up to, I wouldn't have been able to tell through the sheer volume of heavy fabric bunched up over the affected area. Out of sheer malice I waved to him, sticking my hand out so obviously that he had no choice but to stop.

'Jules!' he said, more distracted than I had ever seen him. 'Hey! Catch you later, yeah! I'm just, ah, going to the gents'.'

'You're in a tearing hurry,' I observed.

'Yeah, well, when you gotta go you gotta go –'

Liam shot off as if jet-propelled. I exchanged a brief glance of amusement with Johan, but it was hard to look him in the face, hard even to duck my head and concentrate on my food when I knew perfectly well that both of us had the strong mental image of an over-excited Liam dashing into the men's toilets and jacking himself off.

I just hoped he would have the decency to go into a cubicle first.

'That was a very . . . enjoyable lunch,' Johan said as we put on our coats. I sensed that he hadn't been making a significant pause so much as simply searching for a word which would convey as much of the experience as our overstimulated brains could contain.

I giggled.

'Not as enjoyable as Felicity and Liam's, though,' I said, slinging my bag over my shoulder.

'Ah well, we can work on that, no?' Johan said, straight-faced. 'Now they have shown us what to do.'

I wished I hadn't drunk three glasses of wine. I was sure I'd have had a snappy comeback if I were sober.

He bent to kiss me.

'In Holland,' he said, 'we do it four times.'

'Kissing, you mean?' I said, riposting better late than never.

'Ah – hmn –' Johan cleared his throat. It was my turn to strike him silent. He kissed my cheeks, back and forth, back and forth, so much taller than me that it made me think of a great dinosaur head ducking down, blotting out the sky. I definitely shouldn't have had that last glass of wine.

'So, I'll see you at the launch?' I said.

'But that is two weeks away.'

'Just about.'

'Well, I think we should meet before then, don't you?' Johan said, with the air of a man suggesting something which he already knows is a *fait accompli*. 'Maybe we could have dinner next time?'

This was good. This was very good.

'I'll see if I can get Liam and Felicity to entertain us again,' I suggested lightly, playing it cool.

Johan raised his eyebrows. 'What a good idea.'

'I'll call you to set a date for dinner,' I said as we exited the restaurant. Outside it was cold, a sharp wind whipping down the street, and I wrapped my coat closer around me, shivering. Johan, standing close to me, was big enough to act as a windbreak, for which I was very grateful. Directly in front of the door were our waiting taxis, parked one behind the other, half-up on the pavement, engines ticking away, in defiance of at least seventeen Westminster Council bye-laws.

'Good,' Johan said. 'I have enjoyed this very much.'

He picked up my hand and brought it to his lips.

'Is that something you do in Holland?' I said pertly.

'Only with women we can't wait to have interesting meals with again,' he said, pressing my hand significantly.

'I'll call you soon.'

'Good.'

He opened the door of my taxi for me, closing it only when he had looked in to see that I was settled. Through the window he raised his hand to me, smiling in a way which left no doubt that he definitely wanted to have an affair with me. Mind you, that had been clarified already when he had made a point of paying the bill with his personal credit card rather than putting it on account.

'Back to the account address, miss?' called the driver.

'Yes.'

The two taxis pulled away almost in unison, like a carefully choreographed moment from a heist film. I relaxed back against the seat, allowing myself this brief cab ride to give in to the tipsiness that had been threatening for the last hour. Suggesting I be the one to call was an excellent tactic. It meant that Johan, until at least the end of our next date, was a stress-free zone; no worrying about if and when he would ring me. Floating in a Chablis-induced haze I watched Johan's head, visible through the back window of the taxi in front of me. He was so tall I could even see his shoulders.

As his cab pulled away down a side street, I found myself devoutly hoping he was built to scale. That, I reflected, was one of the advantages of playing footsie. You could check the goods out before you fully committed yourself to a purchase.

Chapter Sixteen

'Jules, it's me.'

Friday evening as I walked in from work: finally Gill had left me a message. I sank down to the arm of the sofa, still in my coat and boots, and listened, picking at my cuticles nervously. At least she had called me 'Jules', which I took as a sign of friendship.

'I got your messages, I just wasn't answering the phone. I wanted to work things out first.' A long, gusty sigh. 'I don't know what to say, really. I wouldn't even have rung you, but you just kept ringing.'

What was I supposed to do? Hide out and pretend it hadn't happened?

'I suppose Jeremy had to know about Philip sometime – well, of course he had to know. God. It's been awful. Thank God at least you warned me. He just keeps leaving these terrible sobbing messages. I've been scared to go back to the house in case he's waiting in ambush. I don't know what to do. I mean, I know I have to meet up with him, but I'm dreading it. Anyway, I just wanted to say, don't ring me for the moment. I really need to be alone and get my head together.'

Humph. What was this about being alone? She was staying at Philip's!

'So yeah, I'll be in touch. I was furious with you, but it's sort of passed. I'm really, really tired now, that's my main emotion, utter and complete exhaustion . . . But I will call you, OK? Give me some time, though. I'm still a bit raw about Jeremy finding out like that.' Another sigh. 'I'll be in touch. Bye.'

I rang Mel immediately and was extremely annoyed to find that Ms I-Vant-To-Be-Alone had already filled Mel in on everything that had happened.

'I wish she'd just *talk* to me!' I wailed, conveniently forgetting the nervousness with which I had anticipated Gill's call.

'Oh, give her a bit of time,' Mel said. 'I mean, you weren't exactly a genius leaving that message. She's still pissed off, and I can't really blame her.'

I hadn't been expecting unconditional support from Mel, but I found this unnecessarily brutal.

'God, thanks for the sympathy!' I snapped.

'Oh, come on, Jules. She's got a right to be cross.'

This annoyed me so much that I practically hung up on her. I fumed around the flat for a good twenty minutes before I remembered with horror that I had rushed back from work to get ready for my date with Alex, and now the careful timetable – shower, wash hair, touch up nails – that I had planned was completely thrown off schedule. It was a scramble to get myself looking halfway decent, and I arrived out of breath and flustered in the pub where we had arranged to meet.

Not a good start. And then it was compounded by something else. He was sitting at the bar, his profile towards me, and I had a sudden rush of panic. He looked so real. Which sounded ridiculous, but no other word came to mind. He was wearing a battered old leather jacket and corduroy trousers and if he had been a girl his hair – brown, with a slight curl to it – would have been subjected to a whole battery of styling products to get it to follow some consistent policy. As it was each strand, ruggedly individualist, seemed hellbent on doing something different from its neighbours. A greater contrast with the tailored Johan could not have been imagined. Why should this scruffball make me nervous when Johan's perfect suit hadn't?

I needed a drink, for many and various reasons.

'Hey,' I said, strolling up to the bar.

'Hey, yourself,' he said with enthusiasm.

I was dressed smarter than he was, but that didn't matter. Men never objected to that.

'Can I get you a drink?' he said, hooking a stool for me with his foot.

I actually wanted a double vodka and tonic, but I was too embarrassed to ask for it. I settled for a single, wondering why I was so thirsty for alcohol tonight.

'How was your day?' he said.

I took a deep breath and pushed the Gill-and-Mel trauma to the back of my mind and tried to close the door on it. You didn't talk about your problems with your friends on a first date; that could put someone off for life.

'Good, actually,' I said breezily. 'One of the trendiest women's glossies interviewed a client of mine a while ago and the article just came out today. It looks amazing.'

'So we're celebrating!'

We clinked glasses.

'Tell me about your client,' he said. 'What's he do?'

'He's a cook.'

Liam was always good conversation material. This should get us comfortably through the first tricky quarter of an hour. But as I embarked on the familiar Liam stories, the series of anecdotes I was used to trotting out for entertainment purposes, I felt them changing. It wasn't simply the normal routine with built-in pauses for laughs at Liam's more out-rageous antics. Alex sounded genuinely interested: in Liam,

in me, in our relationship, such as it was. He asked questions
that made me think more deeply about Liam than I had ever
done before, about his violent need for exhibitionism and
attention. (The photos accompanying the article showed Liam
naked, clutching a bunch of courgettes to his crotch and leering happily at the camera. He looked like the dirtiest fuck
one could possibly imagine. I had been over the moon when
I saw them.)

'He sounds so driven,' Alex observed.

'Is that a bad thing?' I was almost defensive. I had been so
busy thinking of Liam as a client that I hadn't taken a lot of
time to go beyond that, and there was no reason why I should
have done. Alex's concentration on him as a person made me
feel, however, as if I had neglected Liam in some way.

'Not exactly. And I can see from your point of view that
it's perfect. I mean, he's really good copy, right? The more
outrageous he is, the better.'

'Absolutely.'

'It's just – I dunno, all the screwing around sounds almost
compulsive.'

I giggled. 'It's totally compulsive. He's on heat twenty-four
hours a day.'

Then I caught his expression.

'What? You think that's a bad thing?'

'No, of course not. I was just wondering what he does
when he's by himself.'

I looked blank. 'I think Liam's by himself as little as possible. He plays computer games every spare moment he gets.'

'Overstimulated,' Alex diagnosed, finishing his pint.

I thought about this.

'I never really saw him that way before,' I confessed.

'Well, why should you?' He grinned at me.

'I don't know. It just makes me feel I should have been

looking after him more. I mean, he's very young still. Maybe I should have tried to slow things down.'

'From the sound of him he wouldn't have let you.'

'No, that's true enough.'

He burst out laughing. 'You look so worried! I didn't mean you to take it so seriously.'

'It's just –' I caught sight of myself in the mirror behind the bar. I looked utterly perplexed. 'I don't know, it was just so true. Liam *is* totally overstimulated. And it's just going to get worse.'

'Nothing you can do about it. And it makes your job much easier, doesn't it? Perfect for him being a TV star.'

'Yeah, absolutely . . .' I said absently. 'But now you've said it, I feel bad. I have a bit of an older-sister thing with Liam. I mean, I want him to get through the media blitz whole, and not just because he's my cash cow.'

Oh dear. Alex had triggered my over-developed sense of responsibility. I really hoped I didn't end up taking Liam's antics too much to heart. If, as well as my mother and Chris, I thought I had to keep Liam happy too, it would be such a burden I might as well be tied into a weighted sack and thrown in the Bosphorus to drown.

'I might just have a talk with him about all this,' I said, frowning. 'Get him to slow down a bit.'

A vivid picture of the previous day's lunch with Johan flooded back to me.

'Oh God,' I said. 'Who am I kidding?'

Alex looked intrigued.

'Let's go and have dinner and you can tell me all about the latest atrocity you just remembered,' he suggested.

We went to a little Italian restaurant, round the corner from the pub, ten minutes' walk from each of our flats. I had never been into it, but Alex had assured me it was excellent, and it was. I tended to favour hipper places, ones that nodded, at least, to the latest design trends; I had always avoided this one because everything about it proclaimed it resolutely traditional. Winds of change might sweep past, lemongrass or avocado or tangeli fruit might be this year's must-have ingredient, but this kind of place kept its head down and weathered the storms of fashion, dishing out good Italian food to its content local customers. It was the Trattoria That Time Forgot.

As I sat down it occurred to me that Alex and I had been talking in the pub as if we had known each other for ages. It didn't quite feel as if we were on a date, more as if he were a friend – a friendship struck up through the internet, maybe, and only now meeting in person, settling in to how it felt to finally meet face to face … This was ridiculous. I concentrated on the menu. Carpaccio and veal scaloppine. That was easy.

'This must seem a little basic to you,' Alex said as the waiter removed the menus.

'What do you mean?'

'Oh, you must be used to more designer restaurants, right? Bet you don't come to your local trattoria that often.'

'On the rare occasions that I'm in for the evening,' I said frankly, 'my local trattoria's the ready-meal section of the local supermarket. I have an entire collection of books by food writers I know, which are all about cooking yourself a good dinner in thirty minutes, and I always feel guilty about heading for the M&S pre-baked potato instead.'

'That seems an odd thing to feel guilty about,' Alex commented as the waiter filled our glasses.

I had meant it light-heartedly, but his observation went home just as the one about Liam had. I stared at him. His eyes were hazel and slightly slanted; he had a big, square face with unexpectedly high cheekbones, as if there were some

Tartar blood in the family, way back. Despite the solidity of his face, which could easily have looked impassive, every line of it was smiling at me, not just the eyes and mouth. If he had been handsome I would have been more on my guard; or I would have been thinking about seduction. But his relative plainness set me at ease. That, and the fact that he had the most friendly, open smile I had ever seen.

'I do feel guilty about a lot of things, I suppose,' I found myself saying. 'Especially to do with my house. I mean, my home. And my family. It's my mother. She's brilliant at making me feel guilty.'

Alex nodded as if he understood.

'I'm sorry,' I said, drinking half my glass of wine in one gulp. 'That was a bit personal.'

'No, no, not at all,' he said so easily that it was clear he meant it. 'I'd much rather talk about what people really feel than, I dunno, what's wrong with the latest Hollywood blockbuster.'

'Though that can be fun too!' I said brightly.

'Of course.' He smiled. 'Does your mum make you feel guilty about stuff you do now? Or is it past sins? Mine's very big on the latter.'

I heard myself exhale, slowly and deeply, in what was almost a sigh of release. I hardly ever talked to anyone about this, and Alex was making it seem like the simplest thing in the world.

'I can't really imagine your mum giving you a hard time,' I admitted. 'You seem so grown up.'

I hadn't asked Alex his age, but he must have been a few years older than me. The odd grey hair glinted even in the muted light of the restaurant, and there was a fan of lines around each eye. Still, the heaviness of his bone structure made him seem almost ageless.

'Grown up!' He laughed. 'You sound like a teenager!'

I reflected gloomily that as far as emotional maturity went, I probably was. I didn't say this to Alex, however. Despite the amount that I was confiding in him, I still preserved some basic defences.

Not enough, though. The subject of guilt led me on, inexorably, to my current situation with Gill, and to my great surprise I found myself confiding in him, despite my earlier resolution about not burdening men with your horrors on the first date.

Alex didn't launch into waves of sympathy for me, or make any of the comments I was half expecting. Instead, he listened thoughtfully to the story, and then, when I had finished, said rather gently, 'You know, what you haven't taken into account is that your friend had to tell her boyfriend [I had made Jeremy Gill's boyfriend, in a vague attempt to protect their identities] that she was seeing someone else, and hadn't got up the nerve to do it yet. So what you've done is to break the news for her and save her that awful moment when she had to look into his eyes and watch him collapse. I think that when the dust has settled a bit you might find that she's almost grateful to you for sparing her that. Even if it didn't happen in the best way imaginable.'

I stared at him, flabbergasted. This had never occurred to me.

He shrugged his shoulders. It was a slow, almost massive movement.

'Just a thought,' he said.

'That's so comforting! Thank you!'

I really felt as if a load had been lifted from me. He was perfectly right.

'*De nada,*' he said, smiling. 'Oh look, our starters. At last, I'm starving.'

I was glad to tuck into my plate and let what he had just said settle. It was so sensible. I realised that I hadn't looked before for that kind of practical comfort from men. Bart would have sympathised with me, told me Mel had been a cow and Gill had gone over the top, and got me drunk. Which would have soothed my ego, but not dissolved the worry. Alex had just done that with a few sentences. It was almost miraculous.

The food was very nice. From the virtuous protein heights of my scaloppine I leant over to pick at Alex's roast potatoes, a procedure which, by the time our main course had arrived, seemed perfectly natural. We talked about my mother and Chris, about his parents – unamicably divorced – and his sister. But the conversation took so many twists and turns, as one or other of us would throw in something that had just occurred to us, taking each subject momentarily off-course, that often it felt like being on a roller-coaster: holding on for dear life, carried along almost too fast, but still feeling the exhilaration of speed, the wind in one's hair.

By comparison with this, lunch with Johan had been a kind of fantasy date. Handsome man, smart restaurant, all the right trappings: but I had been playing a version of myself, a kind of variation on reality, like a role-playing situation. Alex, however, left me no social pretence to hide behind. With him I was myself. Poor man. It was a wonder he didn't get hopelessly drunk.

I was the one who did that. Being myself – maybe being that open with a man – wasn't easy; I needed a lot of alcohol to help me cope. And, disastrously, I remembered that I had nearly a gram of coke in my wallet which I hadn't touched for ages. It was exactly the balance I needed to stop me passing out from the drink. I nipped off to the toilets a couple of times during dinner, returning bright-eyed, energetic and, metaphorically speaking, bushy-tailed. Both times I came back from the toilet, Alex turned in his seat to watch me. It was something which, out of pride, I would never have done; I made a point of seeming absorbed in my own thoughts, attempting to look almost surprised when the man I was having dinner or drinks with returned, as if to imply that I had been so happy by myself that I had nearly forgotten his presence. But Alex swivelled in his chair and smiled at me happily as I crossed the restaurant, expressing a straightforward pleasure in my company that was warming but made me nervous too. So I had to drink more, which meant I had to go to the toilet again . . . It was a vicious circle.

'This restaurant would be perfect for Liam and Felicity,' I said after my second visit, sliding back into my chair again. I had just been telling him about their antics at lunch. It was scarcely indiscreet of me; versions of the story had already appeared in two upmarket newspaper gossip columns. Oh God. I was really going to have to think fast about how to deal with that.

'Fewer journalists to talk about it?' Alex suggested.

'No. Long tablecloths.'

They were pink and nearly floor-length, with square white ones set crossways on top, which would be changed after each set of customers. Old-fashioned but strangely reassuring. Rather like Alex's corduroy trousers, which normally I would have brutally mocked.

'Lots of room for manoeuvre, too,' he said appreciatively, sizing up the dimensions of the table. 'Get your feet into the other person's lap without even moving back your chair.' He shot a teasing glance at me. 'Want to try?'

'Take me too long to get my boots off,' I quipped with a little nervous laugh that annoyed the fuck out of me. For the umpteenth time, I reached for the bottle. What was wrong with me? Usually I could out-embarrass most people in the sexual banter stakes.

'Will it be a problem?' Alex said, and for one awful second I thought he was really asking me to put my feet in his lap. My hand jerked and I spilt some wine on the tablecloth. Not enough to have the waiter running over with a cloth, but quite sufficient to make me feel a jittery fool.

'The gossip about him and the producer, I mean,' he continued, dabbing at the wine stain matter of factly with his napkin.

'Oh!' I relaxed. 'Well, yes, it might be. I'm not completely of the all-publicity-is-good school of thought. I mean, if it had happened after the series went out, assuming it was a success, it'd just be a storm in a teacup. But this isn't great. If people don't like the series they'll chalk it up to Felicity giving her current shag a big push-up – as it were. And even if they're fans, they can sneer about it. Liam's so young, it could easily look as if there was some casting-couch stuff going on. That's exactly what the gossip columns were suggesting.'

'And was there?'

I shook my head. 'Felicity's not an idiot. She wouldn't mess up a thriving career just to get Liam into bed. I'm sure she fancied him when she proposed the series, but that's crucial, in a way. It's a test of whether the viewers are going to find him attractive too.'

'So he's a heartthrob in the making?' Alex suggested.

'Heart-breaker, more like.'

'Hmmn. Maybe he hasn't got one of his own to break,' Alex commented. 'Or, more likely, his heart's as big as a house and he probably screws around so frantically because he's terrified of losing it if he stops for a few seconds.'

'You're very acute,' I said almost with dislike. A bottle and a half of good Chianti had put me frighteningly in touch with my own feelings.

'Oh, it's always easier to analyse other people,' he said lightly.

'Is it?' I wondered. 'You make me feel I'm not very good at it.'

'I think you've got a pretty good capacity for making judgements,' Alex said. 'You wouldn't be in the job you're doing if you hadn't.'

'Yes, but that's – no, I don't want any dessert, thank you –' I said to the waiter – 'that's different. I mean, that's much more sizing up people for what I can get out of them, what they'll do for me, or for my clients. It's not actually knowing what makes them tick.'

'Comparatively superficial?'

I spread my hands. 'It is PR.'

'I'll have the zabaglione,' Alex said to the waiter.

'It's for two, sir,' the latter said.

'I always have it, though,' Alex said. 'I'll just eat what I can manage.'

'Oh, bring a spoon for me too,' I said, light drunkenness weakening my willpower.

Zabaglione, I thought. If he always ate that no wonder he was a little – not overweight, but a comfortable armchair rather than the kind of linear chairs, design stripped down to the bare steel, of L'Orange. Certainly he couldn't boast the buff, toned, hard-pectoraled body of Lewis or one of the men doing handstands on my postcard. Tom hadn't been toned, but at twenty-five it didn't matter, they were so smooth and young and eager. And Bart had had one of those bodies that remain unfairly muscled and taut no matter how much abuse they take.

I thought of engaging with Alex's body – the body of a

man who was nearly forty and not a gym rat, slightly padded over the muscles, and I shivered in a blend of attraction and what was almost revulsion. A real body, not a fantasy-boyfriend clone. Even to imagine it was too much – again, it was too much reality. I kept coming back to that word, as if it were a shackle on my ankle. It made me aware of all the defects of my own figure. When I was with someone who was physically beautiful I felt more so myself, as if the fact that he wanted to have sex with me conferred on me a higher status. With a less-than-perfect man it would just be our two flawed bodies together: no escape from the cellulite, the little bellies, the love handles, the parts we carefully disguised from the world. Maybe I just wanted to live in a glossy magazine, discarding anything that didn't look like a perfume ad. But then what was I doing here with Alex at all?

'But you like it. Your job, I mean,' Alex added when he saw my confused expression. 'Sorry, I just skipped back a bit in the conversation.'

'We've been doing that all evening.'

'I know, we've been careering madly over the speed bumps . . . Anyway, your job.'

'I love it. But a lot of that is because I like my clients, or what they make. I'm not hawking crappy sugar-filled soft drinks – well, I only did that once – or trying to persuade the public that crisps really are nutritious. Well, not much.'

He was grinning. 'I like those little interpolations. Your honesty's popping out.'

'It's a very rare occurrence,' I said flippantly, 'make the most of it.'

I realised I was warning him. He hardly seemed to notice. The zabaglione arrived and to my surprise I managed to limit myself to a couple of spoonfuls. My stomach was closed, and not just from the coke; my greed seemed to have deserted me. Alex dug into it with enthusiasm, the spoon sliding into the whipped yellow foam with the faintest of crackling sounds, a myriad tiny bubbles bursting.

'God, I love this stuff,' he was saying happily. 'I make it at home sometimes. It's easier than you'd think.'

'Just by yourself? I thought you had to make enough for two.'

'Oh yeah, I do it for dinner parties. It's my party piece. Sometimes I chop up strawberries and pour the zabaglione over them.'

'God, that must be delicious,' I said involuntarily. 'What is it – egg yolk, marsala and sugar?'

'Not very healthy,' he said cheerfully. 'But nourishing.'

'Hmmn.' I was thinking that maybe one could use artificial sweetener. That was the hell of always being on a diet; your instincts were to corrupt the good food you ate by messing it around with low-fat substitutes.

I was getting edgier. Alex had drunk a little less than me, which in practice meant considerably less, since he had a much bigger build. The coke was supposed to compensate. It usually made me brighter, driven to entertain, but tonight I was feeling almost sullen. Hostile, even. And yet the strange paradox was that I liked being with Alex; he made me feel comfortable, even secure. Maybe that was what I resented.

After dinner, the sensible thing to do, given my confusion, would have been to go home, lie down on my sofa and try to work out why I was feeling as if someone had tied ropes to my arms and legs and was pulling me in two different directions. So of course I didn't. It was barely eleven and we wanted to go on talking. I decided to invite him back to my flat. I would be on my own territory, and I wouldn't have to worry about getting home that evening.

I knew we wouldn't be spending the night together. The

very thought of kissing him made my stomach jump with terror.

'So finally I see inside your flat,' Alex said as I unlocked my front door. 'I was beginning to think I'd always be left at the entrance door.'

'Like wellington boots,' I said. 'All muddy. Mind you, they'd go with your corduroys.'

'What d'you think? A bit Young Farmer?' He stuck out one leg and contemplated it placidly. 'But they're so soft and velvety. They're the nearest thing men can wear to velvet without looking like they want to be rock stars. It's much harder for us, you know.'

'It's the shoes I feel sorriest about for men,' I said, going through into the kitchen and putting on the kettle.

How often had I done this with men I had brought back, I wondered, and realised that in fact the answer was 'hardly at all'. Usually we skipped the coffee and went straight to the alcohol. And drugs. I knew exactly the right place to cut the lines, both of us sitting on the sofa together, bending over in my carefully arranged golden lighting, candles flickering, trance music, hypnotic and slightly disorienting, playing on the stereo. What was I doing, boiling water? I hadn't lit the candles (which I had placed out earlier that evening) or switched on the stereo (I had my Guaranteed Seduction tape in there, ready to start turning on the spindles) or even turned off the main light. Nothing was going according to plan. I was too frightened of being with Alex in a half-lit room with soft music playing. If he touched me I thought I would scream out of sheer nervous tension.

I poured coffee into the cafetière and cast a glance at him. He was so calm; he had an inner confidence which didn't slip its boundaries and surge over into arrogance; he seemed happy in his own skin, despite its imperfections. It was why I had been driven to talk to him in the Spit and Whistle. I had seen his self-containment as a challenge. How I wished I had never thrown down my glove, or he had never picked it up. And then I thought that I was the only one here seeing this situation in terms of challenges and duels. Alex was just kicking back, enjoying hanging out with me, seeing what the evening might bring. The contrast between his well-balanced psyche and my neurotic one was too much for me. I propped my elbows on the bar and said flirtatiously:

'Want to do a line of coke?'

Alex refused at first. But I wouldn't listen. I heated a plate – it was a little damp – and cut up a chunk into two narrow lines. Not too much. And I insisted.

'Go on,' I said coaxingly. 'Keep up with me.'

He looked amused.

'I can keep up with you anyway.'

'OK, but go on anyway. Why not? It's Friday night. Keep me company.'

I didn't know why I was so keen for him to do a line. Maybe I wanted to corrupt him, do something to break down a little of that self-containment. I thought if he did a line he would be more on my level. If I couldn't be like him then I could make him be like me. And I wanted at least one thing this evening to follow some sort of pattern that I could recognise. So far everything was different, and I couldn't handle that. So I flirted and coaxed until he did.

'What do I do?' he said.

'Wow, a coke virgin!' I said.

I couldn't help being impressed that he would admit so easily that he'd never done it before; in his place I would have died rather than make that confession. But Alex seemed able to acknowledge his weaknesses so easily. (Maybe he didn't even see it as a weakness.) I thought I could never be like that, never learn that from him. Or I was frightened to try.

'Hold one nostril closed and just inhale up the other with the note. Here. Do you mind sharing it?'

He looked blank at the question. He'd never heard of people bleeding from their nostrils on to a rolled-up note and infecting others. Hepatitis and worse. He didn't have to worry about me; I had just asked as an automatic reflex. And maybe also to indicate how sophisticated I was, how streetwise. I despised myself.

Bending over the plate, he ducked his head and snorted the line. I felt triumphant.

'So!' I took the note from him and snorted the other. 'How does it feel?'

'OK.' He smiled at me. 'You lured me back here with the promise of coffee, remember?'

'You want coffee now?'

'Love some.'

I shrugged. Up to him if he didn't sleep. I poured us coffee and added some Cointreau to mine. He didn't want any. He didn't want any drink at all. The man was like a compendium of all the virtues.

And even though I had made him do drugs with me – popped his coke cherry – it didn't make the evening fall back into the familiar pattern. I realised how much I had been relying on that. Resenting him for my own unsettled state, my wit became sharper. I teased him hard, about anything I could think of. I disagreed with nearly everything he said on principle; I thought I was being funny, and maybe I was, but there was an edge to me that was getting sharper and sharper. The sensation of being pulled in different directions was growing stronger and, as it grew, I became more and more conscious of a space inside me, an emptiness that was being revealed. The more I was dragged apart, the bigger the void grew.

I chopped up another line on the table and snorted it, feeling like a character from one of those films intended to show how irredeemably sordid drugs are. Alex was perfectly at ease. He had propped a couple of pillows up behind his back and his big corduroy-clad legs with their unfashionably thick-soled shoes were stretched out under the coffee table. He looked as if he could sit there all night. I, on the other hand, was fidgeting around as if I had fleas, in a sort of parody of myself in seduction mode. I crossed my legs a lot and fiddled with my hair. It felt manic rather than alluring.

'I like the way you've done your flat,' he said. 'It's very cosy.'

'What's yours like?'

'Oh, standard bachelor decor, I expect.'

'Very expensive music system, TV, and video,' I guessed. 'Big sofas. Takeaway meals in the kitchen and dirty socks all over the floor.'

'You're half-right,' he said.

'The dirty socks?'

'The first part. I cook for myself, remember? And I'm very tidy.'

'In my experience,' I said airily, 'men are always very messy or anally tidy. Nothing in between.'

'And you had me pegged for a messy bastard. How does the anal tidiness fit into your view of me?'

'Doesn't fit with how you look,' I said rudely. 'You're a bit of a scruff.'

'But a clean scruff.'

He seemed unoffended. But what would I know? I felt my judgement slipping away from me.

He stuck his legs out.

'Look. The trousers may be corduroy but they just came back from the dry cleaners.'

I could hardly look at him.

'Do you make your cleaning lady go to the dry cleaners for you?' I said nastily.

'No, I go myself. Why do you ask?'

I shrugged. 'I don't know.'

I clapped my hand to my mouth, realising that I was yawning. It felt like sheer nervous tension rather than tiredness. But Alex took it as a signal to leave. I didn't want him to go. It was ridiculous. He made me feel like a cat on a hot tin roof, and I still didn't want him to go.

'It's three in the morning,' he said mildly, when I offered him another coffee.

That took even coked-up me by surprise.

'Is it really?'

'We've been talking for hours.'

He stood up and went to get his leather jacket from the hall. On me it would have been an overcoat, my hands lost in the sleeves. It was a little battered round the lapels and cuffs, the kind of jacket that's an old friend, one you love and wear forever till it literally begins to fall apart. I didn't have anything like that in my wardrobe. I had never worn a piece of clothing long enough to wear it down.

'I've enjoyed myself,' he said rather formally. 'It was a nice evening.'

'A long evening,' I said. I meant it as flirtatious – look how well we got on! – but it came out as rude.

'I'm sorry,' he said penitently. 'I've kept you up. I should have checked the time ages ago.'

'Oh no,' I flustered, 'that wasn't what I meant – I mean, I'm not even going to go to bed yet – it was just – oh, whatever.' A wave of tiredness big as a breaker hit me. 'Anything I say's going to come out wrong, I know it. Never mind.'

Alex smiled at me, and there was something so tender in his smile that I could hardly bear it. He buttoned up his jacket and pulled on a pair of woolly gloves.

'You're going to walk home?' I said idiotically.

'It's only ten minutes.'

'Oh yeah, right.'

There was a long pause. We were standing in the hallway now and it was so narrow that it was an effort to keep our bodies from touching. Pushing past him, brushing against his jacket, I unlocked the door. The cold night air made me dizzy. Or maybe it was the smell of his jacket, not the fresh tanned smell of brand-new leather, but the reassuring, familiar smell of leather softened by age and wear and love.

'Well, see you round,' I muttered, moving out into the walkway to give him room to exit the flat.

'Yes. Um, you too. We must do this again sometime.'

He smiled at me again. For a moment I thought he was going to say something else, and then he sketched that wave and turned to walk down the landing. I watched his wide back, broad from his wide shoulders right down to his solid buttocks, before I realised that if he didn't hear the front door close he would know I was still there. Nipping back inside I shut the door loudly, put it on the latch and then eased it open again, crawling out ducked over so that he wouldn't hear or see me. His footsteps were resounding in the stone stairwell. I reached the landing wall and eased my head over the waist-high stone parapet to catch sight of him coming out of the entrance door. It wasn't much of a sight; just a big, slightly overweight man walking away across the concrete car park in the direction of the station. And yet, propped up uncomfortably with just the top of my head sticking over the wall, I watched him until he faded into the shadows at the far end of the building.

I had made a complete fool of myself. I had been an argumentative, aggressive, drug-crazed psycho and he would never want to see me again as long as I lived and I couldn't blame him because I was so fucked up no man in his right mind would want to come near me – here I wanted to cry but couldn't – so actually it was a good thing that I had so thoroughly put him off that he would never get in touch with me again because if this was the effect he had on me it was a very bad sign. He hadn't even said he'd ring me. Which meant he wouldn't. I ached all over. And though more Cointreau helped, it wasn't enough. Not nearly enough.

Chapter Seventeen

'So! Tell me all the gossip!'

Jemima leant over the table and fixed me with beady eyes. We had spent the bare minimum on preliminaries: greeted each other, found our table, ordered straight away – Jemima knew exactly what she wanted, as always – and right now what she wanted was the dirt on Liam and Felicity.

It didn't faze me. I had invited her to lunch precisely for this reason, and she had accepted, precisely for this reason, though naturally I had invented a cover story. It was very important that I do some damage-limitation on the Liam/Felicity affair. The Sunday papers' gossip columns had been the last straw. I was having lunch almost every day this week with a series of influential people; I needed to circulate an acceptable version of the story as fast as possible, before the series launched to a chorus of derision from critics who wouldn't bother to watch it properly but would dismiss it as Felicity's BBC-sponsored campaign to get Liam into bed.

And of these, Jemima Thirkettle was one of the most important. Everyone respected her. She had been writing for the *Daily Standard* longer than most of us had been alive and she was the real thing, a committed foodie who knew everything about her subject of choice without pretensions to being more than a good amateur cook herself. Somehow the dowdiness of her appearance – the straggly bun, the beady eyes, their irises seeming magnified by her contact lenses, the *embonpoint* lovingly cultivated over decades of serious gourmandising –

worked in her favour. Her very unfashionability fixed her in the landscape, a solid figure around whom we all circulated; we came and went but Jemima, like some Old Testament prophet, carried on forever.

If I could get Jemima to look on Liam with favour, the battle was already half-won. It wouldn't be easy, though, after this recent bout of negative publicity. Thus, with devilish cunning, I had unleashed my secret weapon. He was sitting next to me, looking demurely as if he had no idea why he had been invited to lunch with us – apart from the cover story I had given Jemima.

'You don't mind if my assistant comes along as well?' I had said to her when fixing the date. 'He's a real up-and-comer – he's going on to very big things with the agency – and he'd love to have an opportunity of getting to know you a bit. He reads your column avidly and buys all your books.'

I crossed my fingers that she would take the bait. But she sounded a little disappointed.

'Oh, I was hoping for a nice little girlie tête-à-tête,' she crooned. 'You know, just you and me and lots of scurrilous stories.'

Decoded, this meant as clearly as if she had shouted it through a megaphone that Jemima wanted all the dirt on Liam and Felicity and felt that a man's presence would inhibit us from really dishing it. There was also a slight edge to her voice which indicated that she thought I was inviting Lewis precisely because I wanted an excuse not to have to tell her all. I hastened to correct this misassumption.

'Oh, Lewis loves a gossip with the best of them,' I said airily. 'He'll probably have loads of stuff to tell us! Surprising, really, for a straight man.'

There was a pause. I wondered whether I dared to risk my last try; I didn't want to be so obvious that Jemima would see right through my ploy. Dropping in that Lewis was straight had seemed to me clunky enough. But she said, 'Hmmn,' clearly unconvinced, and I decided to go for it.

'Do you remember meeting him at that Modern Gourmet dinner in May?' I said, still as casual as I could make it. 'I brought him up to introduce him to you. You were talking to—' I named an internationally famous chef. 'Lewis was so excited to meet you.'

'Oh!' Jemima said. 'My dear, you mean that young man who looks like a Greek god? Where on earth did you find him, you clever girl? I just assumed that he played for the other team, with looks like that!'

'Oh, I make them all state sexual preference and attach photos of themselves in swimming trunks to their CVs,' I said cheerfully. 'But anyway, let's leave it. Perhaps you're right – maybe it would be more fun just the two of us.'

Then I sat back and let Jemima fall over herself to reassure me that Lewis's presence would be more than welcome. God, I had my moments of brilliance.

Lewis knew exactly what his role was. Deferential, polite and of course blindingly handsome, he flirted with Jemima just enough to soften her up without provoking any suspicions. Jemima – like the rest of us – might have an eye for a startlingly good-looking young man, but she was no fool and it didn't do to underestimate her. Certainly she wasn't going to be content merely to stare into Lewis's melting dark eyes through lunch, forgetting the crucial information she had come here to obtain.

Hence her demand for juicy gossip.

'Oh, you mean the Liam thing?' I said casually, unfolding my napkin. My whole strategy involved treating this like the smallest of deals, so minuscule it was hardly worth mentioning.

'Of course I mean the Liam thing! Mmn, the bread's not bad.'

I pushed the basket to her side of the table.

'Keep it away from me, please. I'm having lunch out every day this week and if I don't exercise some self-control I won't fit into any of my clothes by the end of it.'

'Elasticated waists,' Jemima advised. 'They're a godsend. I order all my skirts from this wonderful catalogue I found at the back of the *Telegraph* magazine.'

It occurred to me that this must be where Felicity got her anti-fashion outfits. Another little mystery solved.

Jemima, meanwhile, was blushing at having confessed to this in front of Lewis. He smiled at her as roguishly as if she had just admitted to wearing thong knickers. Lewis, I had to admit, was a master player. He was wearing a skin-tight red V-neck sweater which showed off his sculpted pectorals to perfection. I could barely stop myself from drooling when I looked at him, and I was used to his charms.

'Come on, Juliet!' Jemima said, dragging her own gaze reluctantly from Lewis's naughty smile and thrusting pecs. Her high fluting voice made her sound like a coloratura in a tearing hurry. 'Spill the beans, girl!'

I didn't want to seem reluctant. Putting down my glass – of fizzy water, I was keeping a tight rein on myself this week – I said lightly: 'Oh, there's not that much in the beans department, sorry. Liam's shagging Felicity senseless, or vice versa, probably as we speak –' I couldn't help darting a glance around the restaurant to see if he had come in unbeknownst to me with Felicity, or an unidentified blonde, or the five members of the latest all-girl pop group, none of which possibilities would have surprised me for a moment – 'but that's just what Liam does, when he's not cooking. He has two main interests in life.'

'Two fixed poles,' Jemima cried, her voice carrying to the nearby tables.

'Well, one, certainly . . .' I said appreciatively. 'We should have had him combine the two on the series. Cooking and shagging.'

'Maybe he could do a show like that on cable,' Lewis added.

Jemima's magnified eyes bored into mine, so determined to get to the bottom of this that she even ignored the gorgeous Lewis.

'But did you know he was having sex with Felicity?' she persisted.

I avoided the question smoothly.

'The thing about Liam,' I explained, 'is that you assume he's having sex with absolutely everyone unless it's specifically proved otherwise.'

'But surely he must have his pick of pretty little girls?' Jemima persisted. 'I mean, why Felicity?'

'Oh, Liam's tastes are more catholic than the pope,' I said easily.

This was a slightly tricky area to negotiate; I didn't want Jemima coming away from our lunch and quoting me as having said, in effect, that Liam would fuck even stuff that was well past its expiry date. It would make Felicity look bad, which was definitely not my intention. The idea was simply to file their fling in the hundreds of other light-hearted frolics in which Liam was indulging on his helter-skelter career through life.

'This is all off the record, Jemima,' I said as our starters arrived.

I was having soup, on the theory that it would fill me up and make me less tempted to order dessert. Jemima, inevitably, given her taste for meat, had ordered pâté. It was a huge slice, practically a double portion – Jemima was well known at this restaurant – of brownish-pink meat beaded with great lumps of yellow fat and thickly sealed by a layer of clear aspic. She smeared a chunk of it with gusto on to a thick piece of sturdy bread, the fat melting slightly into the meat under the insistent pressure of the knife. My mouth watered. I reminded myself hard about floral skirts with elasticated waists.

Lewis, of course, could eat an entire fried horse at every meal and not put on a pound. Sometimes I found myself loathing him with every fibre of my being.

'Don't worry, I don't write this kind of thing anyway,' Jemima was saying through a bite of pâté. 'Gossip stuff. You know that.'

It was the perfect opportunity for some flattery even more unctuous than Jemima's starter.

'Of course I know that,' I said nonchalantly. 'But sometimes I don't think you realise how influential you are, Jemima. Everyone listens to you. You're the grande dame of British cookery.'

'And your writing is so sharp and funny,' Lewis contributed. 'Sometimes I save your columns for weeks.'

'You terrible people, you're trying to butter me up,' she said reprovingly, to conceal how much she was enjoying it.

I shrugged. 'It's just the truth, Jemima. Anyway, back to Liam.' I thought it best to move on; any more compliments and Jemima would become suspicious. If you flatter as if you take what you are saying for granted, it carries much more weight.

'Yes, back to Liam,' she prompted. She slugged down some red wine and smiled flirtatiously at Lewis, signalling that although she had repudiated his compliment she had appreciated it nonetheless.

'Liam's . . .' I began, searching for the right phrase, 'well, you know when girls are murdered, they're described as either

nice and quiet with no male friends or fun-loving with lots
of admirers?'

'Tabloid code for "boring virgin" or "raging tart",' Lewis
said succinctly.

'So you're saying that Liam's a raging tart?' she said, smiling
at Lewis in acknowledgement that she was using his phrase.

'Basically, yes,' I agreed.

'Have sex with anything with a pulse?'

Here Jemima was crucially underestimating Liam.

'Liam really likes the women he goes to bed with,' I said,
again squeezing my way around the question without actually answering it. 'And he's pretty honest. He's not a hit-and-
run merchant, he doesn't seduce anyone into thinking that
he's in love with them. He just wants to have lots of fun sex.'

I hoped all this was true. Perhaps I had rather overstated
Liam's sexual ethics.

'And, you know, he likes older women,' I added. I had no
particular reason for believing this but I scarcely thought it
would hurt. 'He's always had a big thing for them.'

'*Really*,' Jemima said, her beady eyes gleaming as she
polished off the last shiny forkful of pâté and picked up a
piece of bread to wipe her plate clean. She looked at Lewis.

'Isn't that very unusual?' she said. 'I mean, Felicity's my age!
Well, nearly.'

She was fishing outrageously, and Lewis knew just how to
take the bait.

'Oh, you'd be surprised, Jemima,' he said, filling her glass,
'it's much less unusual than you'd think.'

And he flashed her one of Lewis's patented knicker-melting-
at-twenty-paces smiles. Even I, who wasn't on the receiving
end, shifted in my chair. Jemima looked as if her lower body
were liquefying into a pool of heat.

The waiter came to clear our plates, which was a mercy, as

I wouldn't have known how to break the moment, and Jemima was definitely incapable of it.

'Hem!' she said, clearing her throat. She picked up her glass of water and finished it off in one go.

'And what about you, Juliet?' she said sharply, glancing at me.

'What *about* me?' I echoed blankly, nervously wondering whether she was asking me if I was representative of Lewis's tastes in older women. I was a little insulted. He was only eight years younger than me. I mean, it wasn't exactly granny-snatching.

'Yes, what about you?' Jemima persisted. 'Have you had a fling with him?'

Mercifully, the waiter was bringing our main course at that precise moment and I used this as an excuse not to speak until he had left. They were shooting our food out faster than bullets from an AK47. Obviously the restaurant was so keen to keep Jemima happy that they had put us on priority with the kitchen. I had realised by now that Jemima must be referring to Liam, not Lewis, which was a relief, but not much of one. I refilled my glass, knowing that Jemima was staring at me hard.

This was a difficult one. I couldn't plead the client/PR relationship as my excuse for not yet having sampled Liam's delights, because that would make Felicity, as his producer, look even worse.

'I mean, if he's as good as everyone says,' Jemima prodded. 'I would have thought you'd want to try him out.'

She winked at Lewis conspiratorially.

'He's not a gigolo, Jemima!' I protested. 'And besides, who says he's that good? I mean, who do you know who's shagged him?'

Attack was always the best form of defence.

'I heard their footsie scene at L'Orange was practically a live sex show,' Jemima said, snuffling with laughter as the waiter poured her some more claret.

'I'm not avoiding the question, Jemima,' I said, favouring her with my best limpid stare. 'I haven't slept with Liam. I'm not being holier-than-thou, he's very sexy. It's just that I'm – um, interested in someone else right now. And Liam's probably got a full roster of chicks. He has a big crush on a friend of mine, actually.'

'Well, I must admit that I heard that too,' she said coyly. 'That you were seeing someone.'

'You did?' I was baffled.

'I know who you were having lunch with during the footsie show,' she said. 'Rumour has it you were getting on very well indeed.'

I felt Lewis's inquisitive gaze on me. Jemima meant Johan. I couldn't help smiling, one of those smug little V-shaped smiles that indicate, clearer than if you were holding up a sign to that effect, that a person on whom you have something of a crush has just been mentioned. Things were looking good with Johan; despite my saying that I would ring him, I had had a call from him on Monday asking me to have dinner on Friday. All the lights were green and I was speeding through them.

'So you're his latest?' Jemima was saying inquisitively.

I bristled.

'Maybe he's *my* latest,' I said pointedly.

'Don't blame you. He's a very good-looking man.' Jemima's eyes were twinkling.

'You know him?' I said. 'I mean, you've met him?'

There was no reason Jemima shouldn't have met Johan. And yet I was beginning to have a bad feeling about the direction this conversation was taking.

'Oh yes,' she said, digging with gusto into her osso buco.

'He had an affair – fling – whatever you call it nowadays – with my assistant last year. She was very smitten. Naughty boy, though, he hadn't told her he was married. Poor girl was very upset when she found out.'

The bottom dropped out of my stomach. Not literally; or perhaps I was wrong. Certainly my intestines were churning like a cement mixer in overdrive.

And just then the manager came over, beaming, to ask if everything was all right. Having Jemima Thirkettle to lunch certainly ensured great service. Despite my guts clenching up at the mere idea of food, I was so grateful to him for providing a distraction that I could have cried. It was impossible for Jemima, no matter how much she wanted to find out all the juicy gossip about me and Johan, not to exchange a few words with the maitre d', whom of course was an old acquaintance, and by the time he slipped away, I had managed to collect myself.

'That's terrible,' I said automatically, hardly hearing my own voice.

Johan hadn't been wearing a wedding ring on any of the occasions we had met. I was definite about that. And I was damn sure that he wouldn't be planning to slip it on for our dinner date next week. Which I would be cancelling – via e-mail – the minute I got back to the office.

'But she was quite young, poor thing,' Jemima continued. 'Very naive. It wouldn't even have occurred to her to check him out.'

Every word was like another nail being driven into my ribcage.

'I'm sure you're much more sophisticated about this kind of thing, Juliet.'

Jemima wasn't aware that she was digging the knife in to more than her veal; she meant every word. She really did think I was too sharp to be caught out by that kind of behaviour. Fortunately her osso buco and its surrounding pool of steaming aromatic saffron rice proved so good that it engrossed her almost completely for the next ten minutes, which was enough time for me to get some sort of grip on my brain, if not my body. I pushed the components of my Caesar salad round my plate, hardly able to force a bite down. But I had already said I was on a diet. Jemima attributed this restraint to an enviable power of will.

It wasn't Johan, per se. It was the fall-out from Alex, who hadn't rung me and probably never would. Johan had been my treat to myself, a consolation prize for having fucked up, someone who would make me feel irresistible, who would wine and dine me and distract me from my comprehensive failure to manage one decent evening out with a man who actually saw me as a person. And no, I wasn't tempted for a moment to pretend I didn't know that Johan was married and have dinner with him anyway. I had never knowingly been involved with anyone who had a girlfriend, let alone a wife.

It wasn't principle. I was just much too proud to share.

On the short cab ride back to the office Lewis was, as always, the soul of tact. Not a word about Johan. Lewis was perfect, invaluable. (If I had been drinking wine at lunch I would have been grabbing his hand and telling him in maudlin tones that he was my best mate.) Instead, he occupied the time by speculating about Jemima and Liam in bed. It was horribly scurrilous and very funny. At least, I found it as amusing as I possibly could, given my fury at Johan. How dare he behave as if he were single? And clearly – given the way he had treated Jemima's assistant – this was his normal practice. Bastard. Still, I was hellbent on seeming as if Jemima's revelation hadn't affected me.

'Just because you wouldn't want to shag Jemima –' I finally protested, after Lewis had finished a vivid description of what he imagined her to look like naked.

'*Please* could we not mention me and her and that verb in the same sentence?'

'– doesn't mean that Liam might not be up for it,' I pointed out. 'I think it's a very good idea.'

'Unless she falls for him and turns nasty when he moves on.'

'The older ones don't,' I observed. 'They're much more pragmatic. It's the younger girls who make the scenes and sob all over your doorstep till four in the morning.'

Clearly this had struck home. Lewis looked more thoughtful than I had ever seen him, his expression almost comically serious. He was pondering this concept so hard that he didn't manage a snappy response, which was entirely out of character. I assumed that his latest batch of nubile young secretaries and account executives had been giving him even more trouble than usual.

'Yeah, mull that one over,' I said, feeling momentarily very old and wise. Which was exactly what I needed to feel like, given the idiocy of my failure to check out Johan. 'Maybe you should shift your target area to women my age and up. We know exactly what a quick roll in the hay with a firm young thing means. A happy couple of hours and no more strings than a post-transformation Pinocchio. Because most often, older women are married, or have steady boyfriends, and don't want any more trouble than you do.'

Lewis was relatively quiet until we got back to the office, doubtless mulling this over. I went straight into my office and put the kettle on to boil. I needed some mint tea before my stomach went into spasm.

There was a big Post-It note on my desk from Richard's

secretary, asking me to drop in to Richard's office when I got back. I left Lewis making a mental list of attractive women he knew in the thirty-three upwards age bracket, and went obediently to check in with my boss.

'Richard?'

I tapped on his door to observe the conventions, though it was already half-open. Richard was always talking about stripping out the interior of the office space and converting it all to open plan, a move I would resist with every bone in my body. I loved my little office. It had taken me years to earn it and I would have to be dragged from it bodily and held back, sobbing, as the wrecking ball ploughed through my dividing wall. What point was there being a partner if I had to sit in the same office with everyone else? I knew it was old-fashioned and reactionary of me, and I simply didn't care.

Richard's office, though larger than mine, looked like a cubbyhole because of the perpetual clutter. A bookcase on the left-hand wall was so full of samples of clients' products that it looked like a collection of raffle prizes. Many of the vodka bottles and biscuit boxes and vacuum-packed smoke-dried beef packets were ten years old and covered in dust. Magazines, equally dusty, were piled knee-high all around the walls like an amateurish attempt at sound insulation. It was an asthmatic's worst nightmare. Richard hated the cleaning staff coming into his sanctum, but equally he couldn't bear to throw anything away. It was a running joke at the agency that we could throw away a magazine only when Richard was out for the day or he would spot it in the wastepaper basket and stoop down to retrieve it, glancing reproachfully at the person who had callously discarded it, tenderly smoothing out the pages and bearing it back to his office.

'Come!' Richard yelled.

I never knew why he said that. It always sounded ridiculous. I pushed the door fully ajar and contemplated the scene in front of me. The magazines seemed to have been breeding since I had last been in here. They swayed in slanted piles on top of filing cabinets, covered the bottoms of the windowsills, teetered on top of Richard's sprawling desk, a beautiful antique which might as well have been a plastic folding table for all one could see of it. Stacks of periodicals twined themselves like ivy around its legs. With a sigh of relief, I realised that all Richard's threats to make the offices open-plan were so much hot air. He would never, ever be able to give up his clutter zone.

I cleared a chair and sat down.

'What's that?' Richard said, staring at my mug.

'Mint tea. I knew you wouldn't want any.'

'Bad tummy?'

'Heavy lunch schedule.'

'How did Jemima go?'

'Oh, great.' I gave him a brief summary.

After all, on the professional front, lunch had been a total success. Personally, too; it had stopped me just before I had been about to take the plunge with Johan, diving into what would have been very icy water. I should be very grateful to Jemima. The body rarely has logical reactions, though. My stomach had tied itself into a Gordian knot and I had developed an entirely irrational dislike for her. I managed not to indicate this, however. I sang Lewis's praises for a good few minutes – he had earned this – and shared with Richard Jemima's yen for the poor boy. Richard loved it. He hunched his head still further into his shoulders and rocked back and forth with mirth like a vulture who had just heard a really good rotting-corpse joke.

'You must make sure to introduce her to Liam at the

launch,' he said when the laughter had subsided. 'She probably fancies him too.'

'I'm sure she does.'

'How's all that going? The launch arrangements?'

'Pretty good. Hectic, but nearly there.'

Jesus, I needed to talk to Gill. She had worked out a list of appetisers all, naturally, made from recipes in Liam's book, and I had such faith in her that I had hardly bothered to mention the catering to her since. But now was about time to take her round the Jane's kitchen. And, though she and Liam had spoken on the phone, it was about time for me to introduce them to each other. From what he had told me, Liam was spending most of his time at Jane's anyway, on a busy dope-smoking and pool-playing schedule. I made a note to set up a meeting for them there – Liam, Gill and the Jane's staff who would be doing prep work in the kitchen for Gill.

'You're doing an excellent job, Juliet,' Richard said. 'I'm very pleased.'

'Thanks,' I said happily. Richard was good at positive reinforcement. 'Yeah, it's going pretty well.'

Acknowledge the commendation, don't try to be falsely modest, but give credit where credit is due.

'And Lewis really has been a tower of strength, too,' I added. Right now I couldn't praise him enough.

'Well.'

Richard pushed his chair back. It thudded softly into a deep pile of magazines. He stood up and started pacing around the room. Damn. This meant something was coming that I wouldn't want to hear.

'That's actually why I wanted to have a word with you,' he said, avoiding my eyes. 'I think Lewis is due a promotion, don't you? I want to give him a couple of accounts. I know he hasn't been here long, but he's ready, don't you think?'

What could I do but nod? He was absolutely right. I should have initiated this conversation with Richard myself, rather than waiting for him to think of it. I had been selfish. Lewis was more than ready. But I was going to lose him, and I would never have an assistant as good as Lewis again, let alone as pretty.

'Great,' Richard said. He must have seen that I looked reluctant, but he would understand why. Nobody liked to lose a great assistant; that was natural enough. 'I won't tell him till after the launch, though. We don't want to distract him just when all his energy should be going in to making this a raging success.'

I nodded again. I had Lewis's undivided attention for another ten days. It felt like a pathetic sop. I made myself drink some tea in an effort to calm down, but it didn't work. Suddenly it seemed that I was losing every man I had been so sure of just a short time ago: Lewis, Johan, Alex . . . a whole series of them slipping through my hands, one after the other. One would have been unfortunate; three was much more than carelessness.

I should have been happy for Lewis, but I wasn't. God, I was such a bitch. I felt miserable and doomed.

Chapter Eighteen

Expert fingers, wide and strong, sank deep into my body, probing, searching out its most sensitive areas, maintaining a steady, hypnotic rhythm. My head was spinning. The fingers reached an acutely susceptible point and burrowed into it, working it, pressing down deeper, bringing a pain that was indistinguishable from pleasure. The music, ambient trance, rose and fell in mesmerising waves, surrounding the bed, lulling me into semi-consciousness. I wanted to slip into sleep and yet to be awake, aware of everything that was being done to me, every press and twist of the hands working on my body, soothing, stimulating, sending me into a music-drugged haze.

I was swallowing back tears. It was all too much. The darkened room, the music swimming around me, the heat, the rich scent of oil rising from my skin, the warm fingers on me. I wanted to sink into it, releasing all my inhibitions, but I knew that if I did I would start bawling like a baby. I was lying on my stomach, so I could cry without being seen. But my arms were by my sides, I couldn't wipe away the tears, and as soon as I turned over they would be all too obvious.

The hands were kneading my buttocks now, working them hard, skirting the edges of the paper thong that was the only piece of clothing between me and nakedness. The sound of the paper rustling as the woman's fingers ruffled it briefly in passing recalled me – not to my senses, because I was all too aware of them, but back to some sort of self-control. I swallowed hard again. It was difficult swallowing, lying as I was, as if I were forcing a huge unmasticated lump of stale bread down my throat. The convulsive movement of my head alerted the masseuse.

'Everything all right, love?'

'Yes,' I said, my face muffled by the paper-covered pillow. 'Fine.'

'Good, good. Just relax, now.'

Her thumbs sank into the crease at the base of my buttocks, the muscles at the top of my thighs. It felt horribly poignant that the person touching me in this intimate, confident way was a professional I had paid, rather than someone who did so because they loved me.

I hadn't realised how exhausted I was till now. It wasn't the good tiredness that comes after you've been exercising hard and your muscles are pleasantly weary but fulfilled; this was the exhaustion of a week's frenetic activity, endless phone calls fuelled by coffee and cigarettes, a series of lunches with journalists at which I trotted out the same information, the same phrases, almost the same intonation, every single time, rushing back and forth from Jane's to the office, reassuring Liam constantly, crawling into bed every night with a sick headache, unable to sleep because of the lists that unscrolled before my eyes every time I closed them, reminding me of everything I had left undone that day that would roll over inexorably into tomorrow.

I had managed to talk to Gill, and set up a meeting at Jane's for her and Liam, but it had been strictly on a professional footing, and though I had timidly suggested afterwards that she and I go for a coffee she had said she was too busy and jumped immediately into a taxi. Liam, of course, had tried to flirt with her, but she had hardly seemed to notice. In fact she was very distant with everyone, not just me. I tried to take that as a consolation for feeling rejected by her. I assumed that she was having a terrible time with Jeremy. My heart went out to her. Still, I hadn't dared to ask anything beyond the most general of questions, to which she had muttered that she was OK and had promptly changed the subject. My one comfort was what Alex had said to me, that Gill might well eventually be grateful for my having let her affair with Philip slip to Jeremy, that I might in the end have done her a service. I sighed. It all seemed too much weight for me to carry right now.

This massage had seemed a perfect solution. Friday night, the end of the week: I would reward myself with an hour of complete pampering. Right now, however, I felt as if it were unwinding me too far. Soon there would be nothing keeping me in one piece.

'Turn over for me, will you, love?'

It was an effort even to move my toes. Stirring myself from my lethargy, I managed finally to heave myself over like a seal, my oiled back squelching against the paper covering. I stretched out, shivering a little as the front of my body was exposed to the air.

'Cover your eyes?'

'Please.'

She placed a pad over them. The red tinge faded. Gratefully, my eyes sank still further into darkness. Lying like this, I was more exposed. I welcomed it. Going too far into myself had been a mistake.

Alex still hadn't rung me. I doubted I would ever see him again, unless I dropped in to the Spit and Whistle every night, and what would that achieve? If he hadn't called me, he didn't want to see me. Forcing the issue would just prolong the process.

The masseuse's hands were working the soles of my feet, her thumbs sinking deep under the balls. She couldn't press hard enough for me. The more intense it was, the more I concentrated on that and only that, forgetting everything else for that single blissful moment of absolute release into acute sensation. I took a long slow breath and exhaled in what was almost a sigh.

I always asked for her when I booked. Most of the masseuses at the spa were younger, made-up, groomed. This one was much older, in her fifties, and looked after her clients with almost maternal care. Or maybe that was just my fantasy. Still, I liked it. Her plain, solid face, her big square hands, the chunky body under the uniform all reassured me in a way the younger girls did not.

'You were in another world,' she said cheerfully as she draped a towel across my front. 'You'll be wanting to get dressed now. I'll leave you to your privacy.'

Slowly I removed the towel. The room was warm, but I was shivering. I felt as if every last drop of energy had been drained from me.

I had been expecting to be greasy but my skin had absorbed the oil, leaving it as soft and slippery as expensive leather. I could put my clothes on without drying myself off first. My teeth were chattering as I sat down to pull on my tights. The room seemed very draughty, a chill breeze on the back of my neck. I fumbled myself dressed as fast as I could, my fingers stumbling over buttons and zips. Once I had my coat on I felt a little better. At least I was warm.

I found the masseuse waiting down the corridor, chatting to a colleague, and tipped her.

'Thank you, dear. You're bundled up well, aren't you?' she said. 'It's cold outside and you're all nice and relaxed now, which makes your body temperature go down. You don't want to catch a cold.'

'I felt a bit cold when I was putting my clothes on,' I said. 'Maybe you should turn the heat up in there a bit.'

She looked puzzled.

'Ooh, it's hot as an oven in there,' she said.

'Maybe it was a draught.'

The look of puzzlement didn't fade.

'Take care now,' she said, concerned. 'Have you got far to go?'

I nodded. I was going to my mother's for dinner.

This was another idea which had seemed inspired at the time. If I wasn't going to have dinner with Johan tonight, I would dedicate it first to a pampering session, and then to a quiet family evening. I would have to listen to Mum's latest theories about Chris, but I was so exhausted at the end of this long week that I was sure I could do that without expressing my own opinions. Or arguing, as she would put it. We would have a nice home-cooked meal and watch an hour or so of television before I caught the tube back home. Filial duty would have been performed with minimum stress to myself. I was so tired I would simply let Mum's flow of complaints flow over my head, nodding and agreeing with everything she said. It was perfect. I was very pleased with myself for having thought of it.

The only snag was the journey there. The spa was in Covent Garden; I had to change trains at Green Park to the Jubilee and then strap-hang till Finchley Road before I had a seat. By then I was so dazed I thought I would fall over if I let go of the overhead rail. I collapsed into the seat, my legs like jelly. The noise and motion and shovings of the tube, the tight proximity of the other bodies round me, the brightness of the stations had made me dizzy. My head was spinning. I must be even more tired than I had realised. I had to force myself out of the seat at Princebury station; I just wanted to sink into its saggy upholstery and fall asleep.

Mum's house was a quarter of an hour's walk from the station. I would have happily taken a taxi but this was suburbia, not Soho, and the streets were empty of anything but commuter cars on their way home. It was hard to believe that this was half an hour's tube ride from the higgledy-piggledy centre of London. All the streets were neat and kempt and as evenly spaced as they had been on the drawing-boards of the town planners who had designed them. From an aerial perspective this was one of those little towns made up of rows of perfectly parallel streets with perfectly parallel houses in Toytown configurations. Every time I took a flight and looked down on this kind of artificially constructed development, with its out-of-town supermarket and ruler-straight roads, I shivered, remembering how much I had hated living there, how I had sworn to get out as soon as possible and never look back. Mum could never understand why I hadn't bought a nice little house in Princebury instead of an ex-council flat in Chalk Farm.

I walked up the path to her front door, noticing how clipped and tidy the front patch of lawn was. It looked exactly the same as all the front patches of lawn I had passed, only even neater. That was Mum's cardinal value in a nutshell. Her idea of competition was not to own more valuable possessions than the neighbours; if you had precisely the same ones, it was easier to shame the rest of Princebury by how much better you kept yours in comparison.

Nothing had changed here. Nothing ever did. Mum opened the door in the same apron she had had ever since I could remember – or maybe it was a newer version, with the old one having been cut up for cleaning rags – and the entrance hall was filled with the same smells of air freshener and cleaning products, top scents of Fresh Pine and Ocean Breeze, the base notes aggressively chemical.

'Come in, come in,' Mum said. 'And wipe your feet. I've just hoovered.'

She bustled away into the kitchen. I hung up my coat and followed her through. This was the only room in which the cleaning odours were defeated by cooking smells. As a result it had always been my favourite room in the house. Passing the cupboard under the stairs, where Mum kept her arsenal of bleaches and cream cleansers and floor scrubs, I made sure the door was shut. The smell was so strong in there I had a sneezing fit whenever I so much as reached in to get something.

'I brought some wine,' I said, putting a bottle on the table. 'And I got you some Baileys.'

Mum loved Baileys. She wouldn't admit to it, though; she had the idea that it was lower class. When we were little and couldn't sleep we would sometimes catch her drinking it when she thought we were safely tucked away in bed. Her excuse was always that it soothed her stomach.

'Oh, right,' she said carelessly, as if the presence of Baileys in the house was completely irrelevant to her. 'Put it in the cupboard.'

'I'll open the wine, shall I?' I asked.

'Not for me.'

'Well, you'll have some with dinner, won't you? It's the same Rioja you liked last time.'

I sounded as if I were coaxing a child to eat its spinach.

'Maybe,' she said shortly. 'I'll see.'

I knew she would have a glass or two. But Mum had to refuse everything initially, on principle.

She bent down to open the oven. A delicious roasting smell poured out, wrapping itself round my nostrils like the animated clouds in TV advertisements for gravy granules. Which was ironic, as Mum would have cut off her own hand rather than use them.

'That smells wonderful,' I said, and my voice sounded almost pleading, as if I thought that this statement at least was one of which she would approve.

'It's a nice cut of meat,' Mum allowed.

She closed the oven door and swung round to face me. I could tell that she had recently been to the hairdresser; her hair, tinted an abnormally even mid-brown, was tightly curled to her head, making it seem as if she were wearing a wig. At least when the grey started to show it gave her hair more texture; it looked less artificial.

'So,' she said. 'Tell me about your brother.'

I sagged in my chair. I was so tired I felt as if I could lie down and go to sleep right there. I poured myself a glass of wine and took a drink before answering her.

'He seems fine.'

'Started this course?' she said with disdain.

'Next Monday. But they've given him some more info about it and he's been reading it all. He seems really enthusiastic, Mum.'

She sniffed.

'He's coming to lunch tomorrow,' she informed me. 'I'll talk to him then. I haven't given up hope, you know.'

'What's for dinner?' I said, hoping to change the subject.

'Roast beef, roast potatoes, peas and lettuce. I made the beef so Chris can have it cold tomorrow with horseradish. It's his favourite dish.'

Over dinner Mum told me about the varicose vein agony that she was suffering, her most recent squabbles with Laura Davis and Jean Withers, both of whom she discussed in terms that would have left a stranger with the impression they were recent acquaintances with clinically certifiable mental problems rather than her two oldest friends, and the latest outrage committed by the local council. All of this cheered her up so much that she was almost benevolent by the end of the meal.

'So!' Mum said, once dinner was over and we had washed up. 'There's a nice Agatha Christie on the telly. You've got plenty of time to stay and watch it with me, haven't you? It's not even nine yet.'

But ten minutes into the film I thought I was going to pass out. Sitting at dinner, having to keep upright and make conversation, or rather provide the right sympathetic responses to Mum's litany of woes, had at least given me something to concentrate on. As soon as I sank into the armchair I felt my head spinning as it had on the train.

'I'm feeling a bit exhausted,' I confessed at the first commercial break. 'I might just go and lie down upstairs for a while.'

'Lie down?' Mum looked at me.

'I feel a bit funny. If I can just have a rest for an hour I'm sure I'll pick up.'

'Well, it wasn't my cooking,' Mum said defensively.

'No, it's not that. I just had a very hard week. It's probably catching up with me.'

She sniffed. 'Suit yourself. Just take the top coverlet off the spare bed first. It's too good to lie on.'

I barely made it up the stairs. Each riser seemed two feet high. I shut the spare-room door and just managed to fold the coverlet before falling fully dressed on the spare bed. Dimly, some time later, I heard Mum's voice, a light coming on, a hand shaking my shoulder, but I was deep underwater and all those sensations were far above my head, faint ripples on the surface. I was ten feet under, so weighed down that I couldn't even move the tip of a finger.

It was thirst that woke me up. My throat was sore and dry and my head was pounding like a drum. For a moment I thought I was hungover, and assumed I had passed out at a party, in a stranger's bed. Then I realised where I was, and I knew that I was ill.

The bedside clock said that it was three in the morning. I had slept like the dead. As I turned my head to check the time I realised that my glands were swollen and throbbing; ever since I had had a glandular infection they popped up like pigeon's eggs at the first sign of illness. Fumbling on the light, I swung myself over the edge of the bed and got my feet on the floor. This made me so dizzy I had to sit for a moment, getting my balance. But I had to get up. I needed to drink about a pint of water. The simple act of moving my legs had made me run with sweat, and yet I was shivering as if it were cold in here. I knew it wasn't. Mum kept the house so overheated that even at night it was stiflingly warm.

Thank God for Mum's well-stocked medicine cabinet. I swallowed two paracetamol and kept filling and draining a toothmug which smelt so strongly of bleach it made me think of swimming-pool water. Nothing could satisfy my thirst. I felt as if I were pouring thimblefuls of water into a dried-up lake, watching them evaporate instantly into the hard muddy cracks of the lake bed. I only stopped when my stomach was too swollen and sore to manage another drop. But my thirst was still raging. Back in bed it was the same as before; when my head hit the pillow I passed out as if I had been suffocated. Four hours later I woke up again and went through the whole routine once more. Water, paracetamol, cold sweats. Daylight was filtering in and I closed the curtains, feeling like a vampire, craving the dark and unconsciousness, if only to escape from my aching muscles.

'Jules? Are you OK? What's going on?'

I prised open my eyes. My eyelids hurt. Everything hurt. I was as sore all over as if the massage had been administered by a pair of off-duty bouncers looking to relieve some excess tension.

'Chris?' I mumbled.

I was so disoriented I had forgotten again where I was. My surroundings didn't help. Mum had redecorated this room as soon as we moved out and it was unrecognisable; flouncy and lacy, the bedside tables carefully decked with vases of dried flowers, waiting for a mythical visitor. Mum would never invite anyone to stay. Apart from the fact that nobody would ever be considered worthy of such a high honour, a house guest would fatally mess up her cleaning routine.

'What are you doing here?' I managed.

'Came to lunch, didn't I?'

My eyes had fallen shut again, the effort of keeping them open too great to maintain. I heard Chris cross the room. He sat down next to me on the bed, the springs sagging under his weight, and put his hand on my forehead.

'God, you're burning up! Have you taken your temperature?'

'I can barely move,' I said pathetically.

Chris sounded shocked. 'Mum said you were just tired. I thought it was weird you were still in bed – fuck, I thought it was bloody weird that you even slept here! It's lucky I came up to check.'

'She tried to wake me up, I think,' I said, a faint memory coming back to me.

'Yeah, she said she'd ordered you a cab but she couldn't make you get up,' Chris said.

'She ordered me a cab?'

This was enough to open my eyes fully and even make me try to sit up. Chris helped me prop a couple of pillows behind my back.

'Typical Mum, eh?' he said. 'She wouldn't have wanted you staying here if she could help it.'

"'I'll have to wash all the sheets now and iron them after,'" I managed in Mum's voice.

"'You children have no idea how much work you make,'" Chris added. He always did Mum better than me.

'I hurt all over.'

'I can't believe she didn't notice how hot you were when she tried to wake you,' Chris said.

I wasn't even up to making a joke about my being the hottest thing in town. Which was lucky, since it wasn't true.

'Chris! Lunch is on the table!' Mum called up the stairs, sounding distinctly aggrieved.

'Hang on, Mum!' he shouted back. 'Jules isn't well!'

I winced at the noise. In my weakened state it sounded like he was screaming directly into my ear.

'I'll just go and get the thermometer,' he said, standing up.

'Can I have some more water? And some paracetamol?'

'No problem.'

I turned out to be running a temperature of 102.

'You've got flu,' Chris said.

It wasn't a surprise to me. But I still didn't want to hear it.

'I can't,' I said, panicking. 'I've got Liam's launch next week.'

'Well, you'd better stay in bed all weekend,' Chris said sensibly. 'Don't move. Try to sweat it out.'

I had stripped off all my clothes in the middle of the night, too hot and sweaty to bear them, and they lay in crumpled heaps beside the bed. Now I was cold. I pulled the sheets and blankets around my shoulders and stared at him pathetically.

'I've got to go home,' I said. 'I can't be ill here.'

'Well, I don't think you should move. It'd just make you worse. Here, drink some more water.'

'Chris! Lunch is ON THE TABLE!' Mum sounded furious. Our eyes met. Chris looked as nervous as I felt.

'Look,' he said, 'I'll go down and tell her you've got flu.

You just try to get as much sleep as possible, OK?'

'Can you bring me up some juice?'

'Sure. I'd better try to sweeten her up a bit first, though, or there'll be hell to pay.'

Chris closed the door behind him. I heard him running down the stairs, and didn't envy his having to break the news to Mum. She had always hated us being sick. Mum was supposed to have the monopoly on illness in the family; if Chris or I came down with something she would do her best to mimic the symptoms, taking them a few stages further to make the point that she was suffering more than we were. When Chris had had his appendix out Mum had been unbearable. She was so cross that Chris was unequivocally physically worse off than her that she had taken to her bed with a staged bout of food poisoning and I had run myself ragged trying to look after them both.

I managed to sleep, though fitfully. My brain was racing: all the things I still had to do for the launch, combined with dread of Mum's reaction to my temperature, prevented me relaxing enough to lose consciousness completely. When the door opened again I jumped nervously and felt myself breaking out in a sweat yet again. Mum would have to boil wash these sheets.

'Chris seems to think you have a temperature,' she said from the doorway.

'I don't feel good,' I said, hoping that wouldn't be too provocative a statement.

'You've probably caught it off me. I haven't been well for weeks.'

I couldn't think of anything to say.

'I haven't been able to give into it, of course. I've had too much to do. Chris said you wanted some juice.'

She came over to the bedside and put a glass down on the table.

Retreating back across the room, she said from the doorway: 'You should have a hot toddy. Lemon, honey and a little
whisky. It's good for a cold.'

Even through the pounding in my head I noticed how she
was downgrading my flu.

'I can't get up to make that, Mum,' I said between clenched
teeth. 'I couldn't get down the stairs.'

There was a pause. Then the door closed behind her. I waited
ten minutes, thinking that she had relented and gone to brew
me a toddy; but she didn't come back. I drank the juice. It was
wonderfully cool and soothing. Chris came up to see me again.
I heard him whispering my name at the door. But I couldn't
move, couldn't speak. My stomach was churning with hunger
but the idea of eating anything was abhorrent. My last thought
before passing out was that I might be ill, and in the house of
my nemesis to boot, but there was always a silver lining. I must
be losing pounds.

Chapter Nineteen

I slept for what felt like forever. The next time I woke up I found that Chris had left a carton of fruit juice and a packet of paracetamol on a tray by my bedside. At least I assumed it was Chris. I made frequent trips to the toilet but never once bumped into Mum. And in a way I was grateful. I was alone in my little world of flu. Time stretched out like over-masticated chewing gum. I had no sense of day or night; light filtering through the curtains was immaterial. I was fully occupied with the effort of keeping my head from pounding so hard it would explode. My back ached as if Mum had taken an iron bar to it while I slept.

It was Chris who finally woke me, a downmarket version of Prince Charming. He came into the bedroom with a steaming mug, his nose wrinkling up in repulsion.

'Pooh, sleepy smell,' he said. 'Stinks like a pig farm in here. OK if I open a window for a bit? Get some fresh air?'

'What's in the mug?' I sat up, aware that I was feeling slightly less as if I was about to die.

'Lemsip. Sissy had some at home, I brought it over.'

'You're the best brother in the world.'

I blew on the Lemsip to cool it down.

'How're you feeling?' Chris said, sitting down on the bed. 'You look like shit.'

'Gosh, thanks for the support.'

'But you're being snotty again! That's a good sign!'

'It is, isn't it?' I said hopefully. 'Oooh, this Lemsip's

wonderful.' I drank it down. 'What time is it?'

'Lunchtime.'

I had a terrible moment of panic.

'It's Sunday, isn't it, Chris? Please God tell me it's Sunday.'

'Yeah, of course it is.' He looked surprised.

I let out a long breath of relief.

'I was scared I'd slept right through till Monday.'

'Nah. You've been sleeping, though, right? Best thing for you.'

'I've just been passed out for twenty-four hours.'

'Perfect.' He paused. 'See Mum at all?'

'Not once.'

He pulled a face.

'She probably couldn't face the sight of you,' he said lightly. 'Looking so crap. Your hair's all sweaty and you've got pillow creases all over your face.'

'Don't make excuses for her,' I said sharply. I had finished the Lemsip by now and it had done wonders. There was nothing like a hot sweet drink to make you feel like something cared about you. 'She's been rubbish,' I said. 'It was you who left me that juice, right?'

He nodded.

'Well, then. All she's done is come in and tell me I need a hot toddy and then gone away again.'

Chris wriggled uncomfortably.

'Well, I mean, she made a good suggestion . . .'

'Chris, come on,' I said. 'I couldn't even have got down to the kitchen, let alone made myself anything. She's been a really bad mother.'

I couldn't believe that those words had just come out of my mouth. Chris stared at me, as horrified as I felt. We were both speechless. I opened my mouth to take them back, or at least to qualify them, but the words wouldn't come. I let the statement hang in the air between us, and I felt suddenly, despite my still-sore muscles, much better, as if I had just been given a huge vitamin injection. I was scared, too. It was such a huge taboo I had just broken. But no matter how much I wanted to put the pieces back together, I couldn't.

Chris was still silent.

'I'm going to have a bath,' I said. 'And then I'm going home. Will you wait with me and see me into the cab?'

He nodded mutely.

'And I think I should eat something,' I said, near delirious now with feverish excitement. 'Could you make me a bit of toast?'

My surge of energy lasted just long enough to get me into the minicab. Pride ensured that I hauled myself out of the bath and into my creased and sweaty clothes without asking Mum for help, but it had felt harder than wrestling elephants. The debility of flu was something the body forgot between bouts; it was impossible, when you were back to normal, to remember that it had taken you a whole five minutes merely to put on your trousers, and that you had had to sit down twice, overcome with exhaustion, during the process, your face flushed, so dizzy you thought you were going to faint.

Mum emerged from the kitchen as I came down the stairs, one hand on the banister and the other on Chris's shoulder for support. She looked down her nose at this proceeding as if it were the height of affectation. Clearly she could not have thought me more self-indulgent if I had been carried downstairs by Chris, wearing a flowing white nightie and coughing into a lace-edged handkerchief.

'You're better, then,' she said. It was an announcement rather than an enquiry.

'Not much,' I snapped. 'But I want to be ill in my own bed.'

Mum was wearing bright yellow rubber gloves and a kitchen apron. The hall smelt of bleach; over her shoulder I saw that the kitchen was in the process of undergoing a thorough clean, the chairs stacked on the table, the floor so shiny with cleaning products that it looked as dangerous as a skating rink. I had never understood why it was considered the utmost compliment for housewives to say that you could eat your dinner off their floors. Mum's must have absorbed enough industrial-strength detergent over the years to make any food that fell on it instantly toxic.

Mum, faced with the choice of taking to her own bed to demonstrate how much more sick she was than me, or cleaning the entire house from top to bottom to show how busy she was and therefore how little time she had to succumb (self-indulgently) to illness, had chosen Option B. It made more sense. I would have been far too ill myself to notice if she had stayed in bed; and what was the point of an act without an audience?

I had never analysed the workings of her mind quite so clearly before. Suddenly I understood for the first time the literal meaning of the phrase 'putting things in perspective'. It was as if Mum had been standing right next to me, suffocatingly close, and now she were abruptly receding down a long corridor smelling strongly of cream cleanser and air freshener, a small, faintly comic figure in her rubber gloves and laminated apron. I felt the hostility radiating from her but suddenly it was affecting me much less than before; with this new distance between us it seemed almost ineffectual.

'I'm just taking Jules out to the cab, Mum,' Chris said placatingly, sensing the atmosphere between us.

Mum didn't say anything, just clamped her jaw shut and

stared at us menacingly. I hadn't really been expecting a soft-ening of her position, a muttered 'Look after yourself', but this angry silence was too much for me.

'Thanks for the toddy, by the way,' I said, unable to resist.

I might have been poking a raw nerve in her tooth, she reacted so strongly.

'I've done everything for you!' she shouted. 'Brought you up all alone, fed and clothed you, put a roof over your head – the sacrifices I've made! And now I'm supposed to wait on you hand and foot because you've got a bit of a cold!'

There were so many possible retorts, and somehow it didn't seem worth giving voice to any of them. I felt exhausted even thinking about it. Instead I just shrugged and turned towards the door. Mum, infuriated by this refusal to engage with her, stepped up the insults. This was her pattern; she was deter-mined to get some kind of response. When I was younger she had kept it up, following me from room to room and screaming at me till I started crying; then she would be satis-fied because she had broken me down, but aggrieved because I was now officially more upset than she was. You could never win with her. The only solution was to refuse the challenge.

Through the open front door I heard her yelling at me as Chris helped me down the path and into the minicab.

'Selfish! Spoilt! Malingering!'

Mum was really getting into her stride. The words flew out like shotgun spray, peppering the side of the car. The driver looked extremely nervous. So did Chris. I didn't envy him having to go back in there and deal with her. Either he would have to listen to her abuse me for a good half-hour, in which case her wrath would abate somewhat, or he would try to defend me, which would be tantamount to suicide.

'Good luck,' I said, hugging him. 'And thanks for every-thing.'

'It wasn't much,' he said, looking embarrassed. 'Here.'

He handed me a couple more Lemsip sachets.

'You'll need those this evening. Every four hours.'

'Thanks, Chris. Love you.'

'Yeah, you too. I'll ring you later.'

I closed the car door, gave the driver the address, and slumped into the corner of the seat, feeling sick. As the car pulled away, I saw Chris walking back up the path, his shoulders slumped. He looked so like a whipped dog he might have been crawling on his belly, tail between his legs, in submission. Mum had retreated inside, and the open doorway was as dark and menacing as something from a horror film. It was no coincidence that all the worst crimes in Greek tragedy happened inside the family home: the chorus, standing outside, were the equivalent of the audience in the cinema yelling: 'Don't go in the house!'

But you always did. Where else was there to go?

There were a couple of messages on the machine when I got back. I hoped desperately that one of them was from Alex; but no, they were both from Mel. It was awful how, in specific circumstances, your heart could sink at the voice of one of your best friends. She sounded very odd, desperate to get hold of me without saying why. Obviously something wasn't right, but I hadn't had the strength to ring her back. I knew that talking to her would make me burst into tears. So I was a bad friend too. Something was up with Mel and I couldn't even ring her to see how she was. I slumped into the armchair, still in my coat and shoes, too exhausted by the climb up the stairs to move for the moment. My head was spinning yet again. I wanted another Lemsip but I didn't have the energy yet to get up and make it. Another few minutes of rest and then I'd put the kettle on.

It wasn't just lack of energy that was keeping me in the chair. I was so depressed that all I wanted to do was curl up in a ball and cry. I had never felt so lonely before. This must be the price of the perspective I had reached on Mum; for all the misery of having her inside my head, taking her insults and her phone hang-ups so seriously, at least it had been a sort of company, a defence against solitude. Now, no matter how I tried to hang on to it, it was fading, and I was all by myself. I thought of Chris, but he felt rather too fragile a reed for me to lean on. I loved Chris with all my heart, but we didn't have that much in common. We had the tight sibling bond that had been forged in our mutual struggle for survival against Mum, but our lives were very different. Different tastes, different friends, different values. We weren't friends, in the way that other brothers and sisters I knew were friends, hanging out, going to the cinema and out to dinner, an easy, happy part of each other's lives.

Tears pricked at my eyes. No matter how much I tried to tell myself that the flu was making me emotionally vulnerable, I was incapable of holding back the self-pity. It was at moments like this that I longed for Bart. But Bart was gone, and since him there had been lovers, not a boyfriend, no one I could ring up when I was depressed, whose job it was to comfort me. Reflecting on the current crop only made me feel even worse. Johan was married, and a slut to boot, while if I bumped into Alex on Chalk Farm Road he would probably throw himself across the street without even looking to see if a bus was coming rather than have to talk to me again. If this was the price of emancipation from Mum, it was almost too heavy to pay.

I must have sat there for at least half an hour, wallowing in a sump of unhappiness. Even Liam's launch – my biggest career triumph so far, the vindication of my promotion –

seemed yet another crushing burden, one more thing in my life that could go wrong. I was giving everything the most negative interpretation possible. The trouble with depression is that, when deep in its heart, you can see no way out, and that was exactly the case with me. It surrounded me, thick and heavy as a pall, and no matter how much I told myself that this was just the flu, and my fight with Mum, it wouldn't budge an inch.

I might have sat there for much longer if the doorbell hadn't rung, loud and startling to my over-sensitive ears. The thought raced through my head that maybe it was Alex, dropping by on a Sunday afternoon to say hello. That was just barely possible, wasn't it? Maybe I had been understimating the awkwardness of our evening together . . . maybe it really hadn't been the utter disaster that I had thought . . . As I struggled up to answer the buzzer I had a vivid fantasy of collapsing into his arms like Greta Garbo in *Camille* and being carried to bed to lie there docilely while he made me a nice comforting hot drink. God, I really was debilitated if I were fantasising about a strong man sweeping me off my feet. Still, I got up a good turn of speed crossing the room to the intercom.

'Who is it?' I said hopefully, wiping the traces of tears from my eyes and sniffing hard to clear my nose. Great. If he heard that he'd think I was up here having a drug binge.

'Jules?' Mel's voice fizzed through the speaker panel. 'It's me. Are you back yet? Can we come up? I've got Gill here.'

Even through the intercom, Mel sounded weird. I buzzed them in and managed to take off my coat while waiting for them to come up the stairs. I was deeply disappointed that they weren't Alex; but, look on the bright side, at least they would see how sick I was and possibly make me a hot toddy.

But, as Gill came through the door, all I could do was stare at her in horror. She looked as if she were suffering a particularly nasty allergic reaction. Her entire face was red and swollen and her big blue eyes were sunken into puffy slits.

'Gill,' I stammered. 'What is it?'

She fell into my arms, her sore, puffy face pressed against my shoulder, and started sobbing convulsively.

'That bastard Philip's dumped her, hasn't he?' said Mel, closing the door and kicking off her shoes with so much fury I imagined she were visualising Philip's face beneath each pointy heel in turn. 'Said he hadn't really been looking for a long-term relationship and things with Jeremy were getting too heavy for him. Fucking bastard.'

She took me in with one comprehensive glance.

'Jesus, look at you. What a pair. You look like death warmed up, Jules. That bloody mum of yours. Chris said she just left you in bed with a fever without even checking up to see if you were still alive. What a cow.'

'How do you know –' I said feebly. I was now supporting Gill's not inconsiderable weight and, in my debilitated condition, I could feel my knees beginning to buckle. Mel grasped the situation quickly.

'Come on, Gill, she knows you're sorry now. Sit down, why don't you, and I'll put the kettle on.'

I backed slowly towards the sofa, Gill following me, still attached to my neck like a limpet. I managed to manoeuvre round the coffee table, feeling my way, when at long last the sofa hit my calves. I sank backwards, guiding Gill sideways so she didn't land heavily in my lap.

'I rang you when she came round on Friday,' Mel said, getting out mugs from the cupboard. 'She was really upset, and she wanted to talk to you to say sorry about being funny with you before. Couldn't stop going on about it.'

She rolled her eyes for my benefit; Gill's head was still

buried in my armpit. Fortunately the tears she was crying would clog her nose and block her sense of smell. My armpit, never much fun at the best of times, must be like a swamp right now. I hadn't had a change of clothes at Mum's, and, though I had had a bath, I had broken out in a river of sweat just climbing my stairs.

'Anyway,' Mel was saying, 'Gill was mad keen to get hold of you, and finally I remembered you'd said you were going round to your mum's, so I thought it was odd you still weren't back yet, and I rang Chris's flat. He was round at your mum's, too, but I got Sissy – God, that girl's wetter than the sodding Atlantic – and she told me you were sick and Chris was having to look after you cos your mum wasn't lifting a finger. So I rang your mum's just now and gave her an earful – which, believe me, I've been wanting to do for years, and I thoroughly enjoyed it – and she said you'd just left, so we came round here straight away. All clear now?'

'Well . . .' I said, my poor brain struggling to take all this in.

'Oh, Jules,' Gill burst out. 'It wasn't your fault, about the message. It was *my* fault. I was so stupid.'

She raised her head. Despite my efforts to put on a sympathetic expression, I felt myself quailing at the sight of so much naked suffering. Her face was red and raw as pictures I had seen of the first stage of a chemical peel, where they strip off the top layers of skin with acid.

'I thought I could do it OK – just be lucky –' she was sobbing. 'I never left Jeremy because I was frightened of being on my own, and then when I met Philip I thought it was all going to be all right, that I wouldn't have to be alone, but I was wrong . . . and now I just don't know what to do – oh, I feel such a fool, I really thought I was the one lucky person who wouldn't have to go through this misery . . .'

'Is it definitely over?' I asked. I was realising that Philip, no matter how unsympathetic I might have found him, had shielded me and Mel from a great deal of the hard work that comes when a friend has a bad emotional crisis and leans heavily on you. Philip, keeping Gill happy and shagged, had absorbed it all, and now it was coming down on us instead. And, of course, on poor Gill. I didn't mean to minimise the pain she was going through. Still, it felt like almost more than I could cope with right now.

Gill sobbed harder.

'I don't know – I hope – I hope –'

'Pretty much,' said Mel, the voice of reason. 'He told her they needed to take a long break from each other cos he had too much on at work to be able to deal with her being upset as well.'

That sounded as clear as it could be.

'But he said he'd ring me,' Gill protested. 'He said he'd call to see how I was doing and if things got quieter at work he might have more time . . .'

Mel set down a couple of steaming mugs on the coffee table.

'Tea with whisky and honey,' she said. 'Just what you both need. Come on, get it down you.'

'Oh, Mel.' She had made me a hot toddy without even being asked. I started snivelling.

'I love my friends!' I said, hugging poor bruised-with-suffering Gill so hard that she squeaked in shock. 'I do, I love my friends –'

I caught hold of Mel's hand as she returned with her own mug, nearly spilling her toddy. I was imagining Mel giving Mum a piece of her mind, and her courage brought tears to my eyes.

'I love you, Mel,' I sobbed, clutching at her hand while

still grappling Gill to my bosom with my other arm. 'I love my friends, I'm so lucky to have you both, I don't need a man or my mum or anyone while I have you –'

This emotional outburst set Gill off again. She wailed hysterically into my right breast and armpit, both arms clamped around me, my sweater so soaked now with tears and sweat and snot that it was beginning to feel as clammy as a damp tea towel. The sound of each other crying was a huge release to both of us. We must have sounded like a pair of howling banshees. When one of us would start to wind down, the other would let out a great moan of misery that would set the first one off again, like a fit of the giggles which takes on a life of its own to the point that you can't remember what the joke was originally about. Gill, I'm sure, was all too aware what she was weeping for, poor thing; but for me my tears became an almost abstract lament for everything that was wrong in my life, every gaping hole that needed to be filled, a final grieving for Bart and the relationship with Mum I would never have because she simply wasn't capable of it, all the tears I had been wanting to cry on the massage table and hadn't been able to let out then.

It was a huge, cathartic letting go of control, and when I finally heard my sobs getting fainter and fainter, mainly because I was so exhausted I didn't have the strength to keep going, I realised how tired I was, but also, in a strange way, how satisfied. I had completely lost it, in the company of my two closest friends, and they still loved me. Mel might be looking at me and Gill as if we were a pair of lunatics, but that was just her way.

And she had thoughtfully covered over our mugs of toddy so that they would still be hot when we finished our crying jag. That was what I called true friendship.

Chapter Twenty

I was well aware that the main reason Mel had been so keen to get Gill round to my flat – Gill's urgent wish to apologise to me notwithstanding – was that she wanted to offload the burden of looking after Gill on to my shoulders. I didn't resent this. You have different friends for different needs. Mel was the person to go to when you needed someone to cut through all your bullshit and spell out, in words of one syllable, how things really stood. Mel had been the one – despite her affection for Bart – to tell me flat out that he had a gambling problem that would never change, and that I needed to leave him before he pulled me under. When it came to tough talking, Mel was the most courageous person I had ever met. She just didn't do sympathy well for any length of time; over half an hour and she began to get impatient.

Helping Gill feel better, however, was going to take a lot longer than that. It was sadly ironic that Gill, out of the three of us, was the one whose well of sympathy never ran dry. She was brimming with pent-up maternal impulses. I wasn't as naturally caring as Gill, but I did well for her by remembering all the little things she had once done for me, during my breakup with Bart. I wiped her poor tearstained face with a damp facetowel to cool it down, put on gentle music, and sat beside her, holding her hand, as she went round and round on the same track of thoughts, nodding and making soothing comments as she sobbed out her misery.

Having delivered Gill into my care, Mel stayed on. She

wasn't disturbed by unhappiness or emotional upset; she just wasn't good at being the primary person to deal with it. Less responsibility, and some practical tasks, suited her perfectly. She kept the toddies – and later, the wine for her and Gill – flowing, and sorted out some buttered toast. Gill couldn't eat it, but she was still grateful for the thought.

'I just feel so *complicated*, and so *torn*,' Gill said, clutching my hand as tightly as a woman in labour. 'I miss Jeremy so much! I mean, I always missed him, but I didn't think of it so much. Well, I did, but not when –'

'When you were shagging Philip,' Mel contributed.

I shot her a reproving look.

'It was all the little things,' Gill went on, ignoring this. 'I know you'll understand, Jules. Like, oh, everything, like Jeremy and me knowing whether we take sugar in our coffee, or who gets the bathroom first, or – oh, you know, when you're in a relationship, you get to know all the little bits and pieces that make up someone, all their habits, and though it can be really annoying, you think that you'll die with boredom if you see them folding the newspaper that way one more time, actually when you don't have it you miss it a lot. I thought it would be really exciting getting to know someone else, and it was, but I found myself longing for Jeremy – the old routine, not having to spell things out. I felt much too old to be going through all this again. Getting to know a new person, all the work it takes. I felt much too burnt-out to put the effort in.'

'You're only thirty-five, Gill,' I pointed out firmly. This was partly to reassure her, but also myself. If Gill, a mere couple of years older than I was, was over the hill, then I was coming up to the summit pretty fast, and I didn't like that picture one little bit. Mel rolled her eyes at me. She knew exactly what I was thinking.

Gill hardly heard me, anyway. She was in full flow.

'I kept forgetting that Philip took milk, so I'd never remember to buy it for his flat –' both Gill and Jeremy took their coffee black – 'and that would annoy him, he'd say I hadn't got over Jeremy and wasn't concentrating on him – Philip – as a person, and I'd feel awful. But at the same time it would really make me miss Jeremy, I'd remember our lovely breakfasts together at the kitchen table before he'd go off to work . . .'

Gill sniffled.

'What did he mean?' I said indignantly, bridling at Philip's treatment of her. 'How on earth did he expect you to have got over Jeremy! You were married to him for nearly ten years and you only left him a couple of weeks ago! He sounds really insensitive.'

But Gill wasn't ready to hear criticism of Philip yet.

'Oh no,' she protested. 'He wasn't like that. He was just a bit jealous, that's all, and I understood that – I was doing my best to reassure him. I just couldn't help getting upset some-times, and that would make him really insecure, he'd accuse me of missing Jeremy and storm out for hours. I used to cry and cry. But then, when he came back, it was so wonderful and passionate – the sex was fantastic.' She started crying. 'I just didn't manage to reassure him enough,' she wailed. 'I tried so hard! I did everything I could! I just asked him to give me a little time, and he kept nagging me about sorting out the divorce. But I wasn't ready to talk to lawyers, or think about splitting up our stuff, or the house – Oh God, I don't want to leave our lovely house, I can't bear even to think about it . . .'

She dissolved again. I understood just how she felt. Gill and Jeremy's house was a haven, something they had built up painstakingly together over the years, as Jeremy began to make serious money and Gill's career took off. Having to sell it would be a terrible loss to both of them. God, the thought of that house going on the market, all Gill and Jeremy's beautiful

furniture and paint finishes and carefully-thought-out decorating touches being dismantled and torn out was upsetting
enough to me. I looked around my living room. It was a great
flat, and I would hate to lose it, but it was a swinging single
pad, not a much-loved family home created by two people
who had debated most of the decorating decisions together, as
a couple, making something that was uniquely their own. The
house was the symbol of Gill and Jeremy's marriage, and it
seemed that to lose it would be, for them, to lose everything,
in total failure, to wash away the last ten years as if they hadn't
achieved anything at all. My heart bled for Gill.

'And, Jules,' she said, grasping my hand, 'I'm so sorry. I
wanted to tell you how sorry I was.'

'Oh, Gill, that's fine.' I squeezed her hand affectionately.
'I shouldn't have left that stupid message. I wasn't thinking.
I'm sorry I got you into so much trouble.'

She stared at me. 'The message? Oh, that. That was terrible. It was awful for Jeremy finding out that way.'

'I said sorry,' I muttered sullenly.

'I was really angry at you. But now it just doesn't matter.'
She started sobbing again.

'So what did you want to say sorry to Jules about?' Mel
interrupted. 'I thought it was that bloody message too! She
kept going on about saying sorry!' she said to me, perplexed.

'Oh – I wanted to say sorry for not being supportive enough
when you broke up with Bart,' Gill said through floods of tears.
'I wasn't supportive, really, I just kept telling you it was for the
best. But I didn't know how awful it is to break up with someone you love – even if it's for the best – and I do love Jeremy,
I really do – but I love Philip too – and I just wasn't there for
you enough, Jules. But I didn't know. I'd never really been
through a bad breakup before, apart from in college, and I was
so young then I'd forgotten it . . . I'm so, so sorry . . .'

'Water under the bridge,' I said, still squeezing her hand. I was very touched. I had felt at the time that Gill was a bit too brisk with me, a little Well-it's-painful-but-it-was-the-right-thing-after-all-he-was-spending-all-your-money-at-the-casino-and-now-you-can-settle-down-with-some-nice-reliable-man-like-my-Jeremy. It was great, even after all these years, to hear her say she had been wrong, to realise she cared enough about me to look back and re-analyse her behaviour towards me.

Still, her thoughts had veered off on quite another track by now.

'Do you think if I tried to tell Philip –' she was suggesting anxiously. 'I thought maybe I could write to him, explaining how difficult it is for me, and telling him how much I care about him and want to be with him, it's not that I haven't left Jeremy properly, it's just hard to break up a marriage – but telling him that I want to be with him a hundred per cent – Philip always said I wasn't with him a hundred per cent . . .'

Her voice trailed off. Mel and I exchanged glances.

'But, Gill,' I began slowly, 'Mel said that Philip told you he wasn't looking for a long-term relationship . . .'

'But that's not true! He was begging me to move in with him when I was still with Jeremy!'

'You said he told you it was too stressful having to nurse you through your breakup when he was really busy at work,' Mel said, with no inflection at all. Somehow this was more telling than if she had sounded utterly indignant.

'I know . . .' Gill looked deflated. 'But he really has been busy at work, the agency's restructuring and he's under a lot of pressure . . .'

People have to get there in their own time; you can lead a woman to water but you can't make her drink in the unpalatable truth about her ex-boyfriend, not until she's ready.

Water. Concentrating on the one thing I could actually do something about, I stood up and went to dampen the hand towel for Gill's face. Sitting down beside her once again, I patted her cheeks and eyes gently with it, cooling her down. She submitted as docilely as a just-fed baby. Her usual eye makeup washed away, probably hours ago, her face was bare, as I had seen it only in the mornings a few times when I had stayed over at her and Jeremy's. With her swollen face and blue eyes swimming in twin seas of red, she looked like a little pink pig, snuffling and tired. It was incredibly endearing. I gave her a big hug.

'I'm so exhausted,' she sighed into my shoulder. 'I'm so tired, Jules, I just want to sleep and sleep.'

'No problem,' I said. 'You can take my bed. I'll stay up and talk to Mel for a bit and then I can kip on the sofa bed. Let me just get the sheets out.'

Of course, Gill being very well brought-up, it took ten minutes to persuade her to agree to take my bed, and I only succeeded finally by standing up, pulling her to her feet and frogmarching her into the bedroom to pull out a nightie of mine that would fit her. I tucked her up, gave her some homeopathic sleeping pills and left her to pass out. She was asleep almost before I turned out the light.

'So what d'you think?' I said to Mel, coming back into the living room. I was exhausted too; Gill had consumed more energy than I knew I had available. Still, it would have been inconceivable not to talk this over.

''Bout what?' Mel had lit up a cigarette, and though I usually enjoyed second-hand smoke, in my fluey state it made me cough. She ignored this completely.

'Philip? D'you think it's a temporary thing, just a fight, or is it over?'

'Oh, over. One hundred per cent, as he'd say,' Mel added

ironically. 'You don't have an affair with a married woman and encourage her to leave her husband and then tell her after a couple of weeks that it's all a bit much and you're not looking for anything long term. I mean, who the fuck does that? I reckon he was just messing her around. Got a kick out of being able to break up a marriage but had no intention of dealing with the consequences. Bastard.'

Though I hadn't warmed to Philip, I was willing to give him the benefit of the doubt.

'He *did* seem very keen on her,' I pointed out. 'You didn't see them together. I think maybe he did really like her but got very jealous that she couldn't just leave Jeremy cold turkey and start up with him all fresh and new. Anyway, it might be that. Jealousy, I mean, rather than just fucking with her mind for the sake of it.'

'Comes to the same thing in the end,' Mel said, shrugging. 'I mean, I can understand the jealousy thing, but he should have got over it. Should've been so excited to have Gill to himself that he didn't have time to think about anything else. She's well out of that.'

I sighed. 'Do you want to tell her that?'

'He's a wanker any way you slice it,' Mel said stubbornly. 'And he needs it slicing. Off. Bastard.'

'Gill'd kill you if you cut it off,' I said sadly. 'Considering it actually sprang to attention every time she wanted it to.'

'Could Jeremy not get it up, then?' Mel asked curiously. 'I didn't know that was the problem.'

'I dunno. Couldn't, wouldn't . . . no, actually, from what Gill's said it was more that he wouldn't than that he couldn't.'

'That's always baffled me,' Mel said in wonderment. 'People not wanting to have sex when they've got the chance. That's got to be the biggest perversion of all time.'

She looked at me pointedly. I knew what she meant. It was

exactly what I'd been doing recently. I wasn't up to talking about that right now, however.

'And you'd be the biggest perversion expert,' I said, sipping a little more toddy. I had declined the wine, much though I wanted it, on health grounds. I was feeling less achy – having taken some paracetamol – and very virtuous.

She sniggered.

'What about you?' she said. 'Let's talk about something more cheerful, eh? You shagged your Dutchman or your scruffy architect yet? Please tell me you got your leg over without any big emotional traumas. I've had enough of those to last me the rest of the year.'

Her voice had risen slightly. I frowned at her, holding one finger to my lips. I was sure Gill was asleep, and we did have music on, but there was no point waking her up to hear us tearing her ex-boyfriend apart.

Actually, in truth, I was just playing for time. The last week had been so busy that I hadn't had time to update Mel on the woeful state of my love – or sex – life. No, that actually wasn't quite true. I hadn't rung her because it would have depressed me too much to relate my failures to a close friend. Now there was no escaping it. I couldn't decide whether Gill's disastrous romance had made me feel better or worse about my own. On the plus side, it indicated that no one was immune from tragedy, that, as Gill herself had said, no one had the kind of luck that enabled them to sail through life without some heartbreaks and abandonments. So that should have cheered me up to some degree: we were all subject to the same fate, and I had been foolish to secretly envy Gill for what had seemed like a miraculous stepping from one stone to another without getting her feet wet.

However, there was the minus that we all – Mel perhaps excepted – hoped to find the perfect romance, one that wouldn't break up or have hidden affairs or grow stale with time. And Gill and Jeremy had seemed – maybe – an example of the kind of real-life relationship, flawed but happy, that was actually possible. If they had failed to sustain it, and Gill had failed, too, at finding someone else to help her escape it, then the future looked bleak for me and everyone else. There were no happy endings. And yet we'd all kill ourselves if we didn't keep dreaming of them.

I filled Mel in on my current state of play. That was something of a misnomer, since there wasn't very much play involved at all. I hadn't been hungry up till then, but I found myself reaching gloomily, in a primitive reflex, for a slice of buttered toast. Cold though it now was, it was still comfort food.

'Why don't you just shag him?' Mel said rather impatiently. 'Johan, I mean? He sounds horny.'

'Which part of "he's married" did you miss?' I enquired caustically through a bite of soggy toast.

She shrugged and threw herself back in her chair, playing with her amethyst rings. The low lighting caught her face half in shadow, half touched with gold, and her sharp features and heavy frame of hair looked more than usually witch-like.

'I just don't see why you're making such a big deal about this,' she said. 'I mean, it's just a shag, isn't it? You didn't want to marry him, did you?'

I thought of the way I had reacted to Johan – all my public persona on display – and, by contrast, the ease I had found when I was talking to Alex, just being myself.

'God, no. But that's the point,' I said sadly. 'I don't think I can do the just-a-shag thing any longer. And having an affair with a married man – all that sneaking around and making complicated assignations – it sounds so exhausting. My life's busy enough as it is. Besides, I don't like to share.'

'Well, don't think of it as sharing. Tell yourself you're just playing with wifey's toy for a while, before you give him back,' Mel suggested.

'Nah.' This didn't convince me. Though I liked the way Mel put it.

'Filthy sex in hotel rooms –' she went on. 'Weekends away in Paris – lots of expensive presents – no responsibility, no picking up his dirty laundry, no relationship –'

Mel's eyes were gleaming.

'That does sound fun,' I admitted reluctantly.

'Married men are really generous,' she observed. 'I should know. They're practically my whole clientele. It's safer, you see. They've got the wife and kids already, so they know they're "normal".' Besides putting the last word in big inverted commas with a couple of flicks of her fingers, she laced this whole sentence with heavy sarcasm. 'So they can tell themselves they're just indulging in a bit of harmless stress release, instead of admitting that they're actually raving pervos who get their kicks being tied up, hung from a beam and having the shit whaled out of them. Sometimes literally,' she added.

'Mel, *please*,' I said feebly, not feeling remotely strong enough for this. 'I just hope you sterilise that dungeon after every session.'

'I should get your mum round to clean it, shouldn't I?' Mel said evilly. 'She'd do a lovely job. Very thorough, your mum is. I can just see her wiping up a bit of come and tut-tutting about its germ content.'

Mel might not be the most sympathetic person in the world but she did know how to cheer me up. I laughed so hard I started coughing.

'But don't you ever want something more?' I asked, when finally I was more or less recovered. I finished my hot toddy, the honey deliciously soothing to my sore throat.

'What d'you mean?' She looked blank.

'Well, you know! A relationship. Or, you know, something like that,' I added hastily at Mel's stare of naked incredulity.

'You must be joking. No way. I wouldn't trust a man as far as I could throw him. Not after my dad.'

Mel hated talking about her family, and, by extension, her private life. But I knew that bad things had happened when she was growing up, though she alluded to them only in the most elliptical of terms.

'And then I had some really dodgy boyfriends in my teens. Ugh, no way. I don't trust 'em. And I don't trust myself to pick 'em. I kept going for guys who'd do me over. So I gave up. It just wasn't worth it.'

This was the most Mel had ever confided in me. My first impulse was to feel incredibly flattered that she had told me something so personal; then that faded, and I wanted to give her a hug. Mel wasn't Gill, however. If I put a hand out to her now she'd bite it off. I confined myself to an empathetic 'Mmn,' and even that was probably too much.

'I wouldn't mind having kids,' she added, completely unexpectedly. 'I'd just be worried about –'

'Finding a dad?'

She sneered at me.

'Don't be ridiculous. Getting pregnant's not the problem. And the dad'd never know, either. I wouldn't dream of telling him. Nah, it's that I don't trust myself not to fuck it up. I mean, I didn't exactly have the best family in the world, you know? And they say you repeat their mistakes. I'd hate to think I was just fucking up the poor little sods the way my parents did with me.'

She looked suddenly sadder than I had ever seen her.

'Mel, you are not fucked up,' I said, sounding firm to hide my nervousness at saying the wrong thing. 'Well, no more than any of us are.'

She gave me a sketchy smile.

'What, that's supposed to reassure me?'

'Bloody right it is!'

'Ah, I don't know.' She lit another cigarette. She had been chainsmoking all the way through this conversation, I had noticed, a sign of how hard it was for her. 'I always say my clients are my kids, really. Load of big babies. Least I don't get the ones who want to dress up in romper suits and wet their giant nappies. Maybe that's enough kids to be going on with. Real ones might be pushing it a bit.'

'You never know,' I said, treading on eggshells in my effort to stay cool. I instinctively knew that if I pressed Mel on anything she would close up tighter than a clam. I had to sound light and neutral for her to feel comfortable enough to talk about this.

She blew some smoke rings.

'Well, we'll see. Just something I've been thinking about a bit recently. But it's not a big deal.'

I shook my head dutifully.

'Though I tell you what, if I did get pregnant, it'd be good for my costumes, actually, having some tits for a change,' she said thoughtfully. 'I'd just have to be careful with the corsets.'

This was classic Mel: half-provocation, half-serious. I grinned at her.

'It'd be a laugh, seeing you with bosoms.'

'Think what it'd be like for me! I'd probably be honking myself all the time!'

She looked down at her near-flat chest.

'God, no wonder men get obsessed with tits. If I had big ones I bet I wouldn't be able to stop playing with them. So.' She gave me a wicked grin, signalling a change in conversation. 'Tell me how my new boyfriend's doing. Is he still being naughty with old bags in public places?'

I had filled Mel in on Liam's antics with Felicity, which had amused her tremendously.

'He's your biggest fan, actually,' I said. 'Every time I see him he asks me for your number.'

'You know better than to give it to him.'

'Of course.'

Mel ran her hand through her hair, momentarily disturbing her black bob before it resettled, as smooth as ever, the fringe a thick line above the arches of her eyebrows.

'But he's really been pestering me,' I said, which was perfectly true. Liam had a huge crush on Mel, which was only being exacerbated by my refusal to put him in touch with her.

Mel tutted.

'He needs putting in his place,' she said nonchalantly. But her eyes were glinting. I could tell that, despite her cool pose, Mel actually found Liam pretty cute. And she was the one friend of mine who I wouldn't have any worries about if they got off with each other. Mel could handle Liam with both arms tied behind her back. Actually, it would be Liam with the arms tied behind his back, but the principle remained the same.

'Well, I expect I'll see him at the launch,' she said, with a glittering smile. 'See if he still needs a good spanking.'

'No question there,' I assured her. 'Liam always needs a good spanking.'

Chapter Twenty-one

I had barely been able to admit it to myself, let alone to Mel, for fear that saying it might actually make it true. But ever since I had tucked Gill into bed the night before, I had been increasingly terrified that she might very well, in her state of total emotional turmoil, completely fall to pieces under the challenge of catering for an enormous and very high-profile launch party in a mere four days. I had envisaged her holed up in my flat, sobbing her way through industrial-sized boxes of tissues, while I ran around in circles like a frantic chicken with its head cut off and arterial blood squirting from the stump, trying desperately to find someone to take over the job on such short notice. Hiring Gill for the job hadn't been favouritism; she was a well-respected professional, and though Richard knew she was my friend he hadn't blinked when I had suggested using her. Still, if she collapsed on me, I would carry the blame more because of the personal connection.

I spent a very nasty night tossing and turning on my sofa bed, imagining hideous scenarios. The worst one involved Liam upending one tray of canapés after another in the middle of his own launch party, yelling to all and sundry how rubbish the replacement chef was and how badly his, Liam's, world-class recipes had been executed. It was all too plausible: Liam was perfectly capable of behaving like that. The flu still had me in its grip, but I sweated extra buckets that night out of nervous tension. The mattress was practically a waterbed when I awoke the next morning.

To find Gill standing over me with a steaming cup of coffee. She had managed to locate the milk steamer I had bought but never used, and the mug was topped with a frothy puff of milk dusted with a little cinnamon.

'I'm making French toast,' she announced. 'I thought we could both do with a nice breakfast to start the week.'

I squinted at her through the gunk that had accumulated in the corners of my eyes.

'French toast?' I said incredulously.

'Yes, I popped out to the corner shop and got some maple syrup. It's not great quality, but it'll do. I thought we could have a bit of a talk over breakfast about the schedule for this week. The good news is that I don't have to hire as much equipment as I thought. The kitchen at Jane's is actually quite well-equipped, I just had to go rooting round and dig out a lot of the stuff because they hardly use it. I think they should serve more food there. I know it's more a drinking club than a proper restaurant, but still, the demand would be there. I was actually wondering about suggesting that to the manager and seeing if she wanted me to work out some sample menus, what do you think? Some simple things that the chef could put together on his own, that people would want to nibble on? Sort of late-night snacks?'

This was way too much information for me to absorb at eight thirty in the morning. Clearly I had got Gill completely wrong. Instead of going into crisis, she was reacting quite the other way; cramming in so much work that she didn't have much time left to think about anything else. From a professional point of view, at least, I was hugely grateful.

'Why don't you get the launch over and done with first,' I suggested carefully. 'But I think it's a great idea in principle.'

Wiping my eyes clean, I sat up and surveyed Gill. She

looked a little rough, as was only to be expected. Her eyes, in particular, were still puffy from the crying jag of the night before. Still, she had showered and washed her hair and made an attempt to cover the worst ravages with makeup, all of which were hugely positive signs. Depressed people didn't pat concealer into their under-eye circles and make French toast; they slumped around all day in a bathrobe with greasy hair, watching daytime TV. A great sense of relief flooded through me.

'Thanks so much for last night, Jules,' she said. 'I really needed someone to cry over.'

'Any time.'

We hugged, awkwardly, because of the mug still in my hand, the way the sofa-bed mattress, being not of the best quality, sagged ominously as Gill tried to lean on it, and me turning my head away, not wanting to subject her to my nasty toxic morning breath. Still, the goodwill was there, which was the important thing.

And I didn't have to worry about the party food. That in itself was cause to celebrate. The week was starting well. I just had to dose myself with enough Lemsip to get me through till after the launch and then – if the party had been a success – I could pass out for days. I could hardly wait.

'If you can't face the cocktail, do you want me to get you some Day Nurse?' Lewis suggested. 'There's a chemist just round the corner.'

We were at Jane's, doing our daily drop-in to ensure that everything was going smoothly. Lewis was sampling the cocktail the bar manager had created especially for the launch; usually this was one of the perks of my job, but I had had to pass today. Fortunately I could trust Lewis's judgement. If anyone was sophisticated-man-about-town enough to give the thumbs-up to a new cocktail recipe, it was Lewis. He was more cutting edge than a razor blade on a pile of coke.

'Thanks,' I said, reluctantly shaking my head, 'but I think I'm already over my paracetamol limit. The local chemist has got me on their blacklist already. Me and the people coming in with forged prescriptions for designer painkillers. They practically threatened to set the dogs on me if I showed my face in there again this week.'

'Are you OK?'

There was enough concern in Lewis's voice for me to interpret this badly.

'Oh dear, do I look dodgy?'

I tried to glance at myself in one of the mirrors behind the bar, but they were deliberately silvered and frosted so that Jane's celebrity clientele wouldn't catch sight of themselves at three in the morning, bleary and drug-smeared, and throw drunken maudlin hissy fits.

'You do look a little delicate round the edges,' Lewis said tactfully.

'Oh God.'

I coughed. I didn't know if the flu was wearing off, or just releasing its grip temporarily so that it could pounce more thoroughly when I had time for it, or if, simply, the cocktail of pills and gel capsules and hot drinks I was pouring down myself every four hours was suspending me on a paracetamol/codeine cloud of unreality. And frankly, I didn't care. I was fully functional for work, which was the only thing that mattered to me right now.

Everything here was proceeding to schedule. The video screens on which we would be showing highlights from Liam's series were set up and working. We were using a giant flat-screen TV in the main living room, but there would be screens all through the warren of rooms in the rest of the club – even in the toilets, which I prided myself was a nice touch. The fake tattoos that the serving staff were going to wear, exact copies of Liam's own body art, had arrived and looked great, especially when worn with the rest of their outfits – big combat trousers and the tight little Liam At Large t-shirt, featuring a photo of our cheeky chappie star on the front, winking outrageously while peeling a banana. Those t-shirts had been my idea, and they looked wonderful. I bet I'd see them walking down the trendiest streets in Soho by the end of next week.

Also, Lewis had just assured me that the cocktail was delicious. I took his word for it. With the amount of drugs I already had racing through my veins, a Liam At Large Hot Shot (cinnamon schnapps and vodka, topped with tabasco) would probably stop my heart dead.

'I might sit down,' I said, sinking into one of the battered leather armchairs. It was mid-morning, and Jane's didn't open till noon, so we had our choice of the best chairs. These ones by the bay window, and the sofas on either side of the big fireplace, were the most prized seats in the whole club – well, that and the red velvet chaise longue in the upstairs bar. Dissolute young actors and conceptual artists would pile in here at lunchtime, claim a sofa and barely stir from it till Jane's closed at two thirty next morning. Apart from trips to the loo to refill their nostrils with Bolivian marching powder, of course.

'You're taking it slow, aren't you?' Lewis said, sitting on the arm of the chair facing mine and observing me with a slightly worried expression.

I held out my hand and waggled it back and forth, to indicate that I was doing my best, considering.

'I mean, there's no point killing yourself,' he said.

I treated this with the contempt it deserved.

'Come on, Lewis,' I said impatiently, 'you know as well as I do that this is the most important week of my life to date. Workwise, anyway. Even if someone severed both my arms I'd have to get them cauterised and shoot back to work. After Thursday night I can crash. Until then it's panic stations. Still, I'm going to bed nice and early, so I'm getting plenty of rest.'

'Good.'

He brushed his hair back from his face and I noticed how well groomed his hands were, the nails neat and gleaming. Lewis really was like a male model come to life. And I was about to lose him. I sighed.

'Feel free to lean on me, Juliet,' he said seriously. 'I mean it. I've got loads of energy and I can take on more than I'm doing. You know how much I love this job. It's pretty much my life right now. I can work as long as it takes to get everything done. And you don't have that much to prove, you know. Everyone at the agency thinks you're a star. You've done so much prep work that this launch is going to go really well anyway. You don't have to kill yourself rushing round after every little detail when you're struggling with the flu.'

I was hugely touched. And I knew that Lewis really meant it, too. It wasn't just a brown-nosing of the boss. I came to a sudden decision. I had been mulling this over ever since Richard had spoken to me about Lewis's imminent promotion, and this was the perfect time.

'Lewis, there's something I want to tell you,' I said. 'But you can't let anyone else know for the time being. I know that's not going to be a problem for you.'

I had already tested Lewis's powers of discretion when he first started working for me, and been more than pleased by the results.

'Yeah! Sure!' he said excitedly. 'What?'

He leant forward eagerly, sharp enough to perceive by the

tone of my voice that something good was coming.

'It won't be official till next week,' I said. 'Richard wanted to wait till after the launch to tell you.'

It was mean of me to string him along like this. He reminded me of a little boy about to open his Christmas stocking, eyes popping out of his head with anticipation.

'You're going to be leaving me,' I said. 'Which I'm not very happy about, I can tell you. Because ...' I paused evilly – 'because you're going to be getting your own accounts!'

All Lewis's Christmases had come at once. He looked ecstatic. That was one of the things I had always liked about Lewis, that I had noticed even when I was first interviewing him: poised though he was, smartly though he was dressed, if he was happy about something he showed it. He didn't feel the need to prove his cool by rigidly resisting any show of emotion.

'Wow! Wow! That's so great!' he blurted out. 'I wasn't expecting this for another six months, at least! Oh wow, that's brilliant!'

The sight of him so happy cheered me up tremendously. And it helped me come to terms with my sulk about losing him as an assistant.

'You've done really well,' I said. 'And everyone's noticed it, not just me.'

Lewis was momentarily speechless, as it all sank in.

'You deserve it,' I said simply.

'Oh, *wow* ...' he said, his already handsome face so lit up that he looked positively radiant.

He leant over and grabbed my hands.

'Juliet, I know I've got you to thank for this. Thank you so much. I've learnt so much working with you, you've been the best boss I could ever have imagined, I feel so lucky to have been able to work for you, it's been a total pleasure and

I'll really miss you – not that I'm going far, but you know what I mean . . .'

I basked modestly in this acclaim. I saw no need to dis-illusion Lewis about the origins of his promotion. I was build-ing my power base at the agency, and he would be one of my cornerstones. Lewis would always be loyal to me. I wouldn't have gone so far as to lie to him about having pushed for his promotion, but if he wanted to assume it was due to me, I wasn't going to correct him.

'It's not quite over yet,' I warned him. 'You're going to have to keep covering my assistant's job till I get someone else in. It shouldn't take long, though.'

'No problem! Whatever you say!'

He looked as shiny with happiness as a freshly minted coin.

'And when Richard swoops down and takes you to lunch next week, you behave as if this is all a total shock to you,' I said sternly. 'No dropping me in it.'

He gave a mock-salute, clicking his heels together.

'Don't worry, ma'am. Our secret goes no further than these four walls.'

I saluted back.

'Good, soldier,' I barked. 'At ease.'

Lewis gave me the widest, most gorgeous grin. His teeth flashed white against his pale olive skin. Accustomed as I was to his beauty, it still took me by surprise now and again.

'Request permission to kiss commanding officer, ma'am,' he said.

I grinned back.

'Permission granted.'

I thought Lewis was going to kiss me on the cheek. But instead he picked up my hand, brought it to his lips, and kissed my knuckles, gazing all the while into my eyes. It was like something from a silent film: corny, but incredibly effective. I felt my insides melting like soft brown sugar. Lewis didn't release my hand immediately afterwards, either; he held on to it, keeping a firm, even pressure on my fingers, caressing my palm gently with his thumb. God, he was good at this.

Suddenly I realised that Lewis was pulling one of his moves on me. He had never done this before; we had joked and teased each other, but always, clearly, as boss to assistant. I remembered my advice to him, about dating older women. Had he put it into action already? Or did he want me to be his test case?

I found myself jerking my hand clumsily out of his. Well, it was that or snog him passionately. That little bastard had really turned me on. And from the smirk he was giving me, I bet he knew it, too.

'Hey!' Liam bounded over to us, waving excitedly. 'Thought I'd find you guys here!'

Liam was always hyperactive, but in the last week he had become like a parody of himself. He couldn't just walk; he bounced, as if his trainers had giant springs in the heels.

'All right! My favourite lady!' He planted a huge smacker on my cheek. 'And Lewis! All right, mate!'

He and Lewis exchanged some long, complicated, gangsta handshake, with much twisting of wrists and flexing of forearms. I was momentarily distracted by wondering where on earth Lewis had learnt to do that. Or maybe you didn't learn at all; maybe you simply grabbed hold of another bloke's hands and pushed and pulled for a while till mutual heterosexuality had been fully demonstrated.

'I've just come from my other favourite lady's!' Liam announced. Unable to stand still, he shifted from one foot to the other while talking, keeping his knees slightly bent, as if ready to burst into a sprint at any second.

'Who's that now, Liam?' I said. 'I can't keep up with you.'

It was literally true. Just watching him was making me exhausted. I did a quick mental calculation as to the next time I could take some codeine, which always seemed to perk me up. Another two hours. Damn.

'Gill, of course!' he said, gesticulating. 'That was one of the best things you've done, Jules, hooking me up with Gill. She's a wonder. I was testing some of the party food. I won't say she does 'em better than me – cos that would be stupid, I mean, they're my recipes – but, y'know, I don't think I could do any better myself! And that's really saying something, know what I mean?'

This was a huge relief. I exchanged glances with Lewis, who grinned at me.

'She's had some great ideas,' Liam was continuing. 'Really. Can't thank you enough, Jules.'

He looked almost abashed.

'Actually, I was thinking – if I do another book – they were talking about me doing another book, y'know, if this one does well . . . Anyway, Gill'd be a really great person to work with me on it. Not like I need help or anything, I've got loads of steaming ideas. But, well, just talking to her about food really helps me get my head together. She's really sussed, but she doesn't talk down to me. I wouldn't mind at all just, y'know, tossing round some ideas with her.'

'That's great,' I said enthusiastically. I had no idea whether Gill would want to work with Liam on a putative sequel, but maybe if it were uncredited and she got a large consulting fee . . . who knew? It was irrelevant in any case. The point was to keep Liam happy now, and I would say pretty much anything to achieve that goal.

He fingered the giant chain he was wearing round his neck, which was large and heavy enough to be used as an offensive weapon. Mind you, Liam himself was something of an offensive weapon, so perhaps that was all too appropriate. He was wearing a Playboy t-shirt with a couple of bunny girls in the kind of position I was sure that bunny girls were strictly prohibited from assuming while still in costume.

'And Gill's pretty bloody horny, too, isn't she?' he leered. Liam always had to over-compensate for his moments of vulnerability. 'Whooah! I like 'em with a bit of meat on them! She's got a really sexy older-woman vibe going on, doesn't she?'

I noticed with amusement that Lewis was nodding sagely in response, as if he had always appreciated the unique attraction of older women.

'Wouldn't mind giving her one over that kitchen table!' Liam continued.

Jesus. That was probably the last thing Gill needed. Or maybe – I reflected – maybe it wasn't a bad idea at all. Certainly it would be the Band Aid shagging theory in action – slap another man over the gaping wound left by the first as quickly as possible.

'That's a really nice kitchen she's got, though,' Liam said, suddenly serious. 'Wouldn't mind one like that myself.'

Lewis couldn't repress a snigger at the abrupt change of tone. Liam misunderstood it.

'No, really, mate,' he said earnestly. 'It's really well laid out, lots of light; it's got a really nice vibe, I'm telling you.'

Someone was going to have to sit on Liam's new tendency to spit out half-digested words of American slang. They didn't work at all with his cheeky Cockney chappie persona.

'I would have thought you'd have wanted something more modern, Liam,' I said. 'I imagine you all chrome fittings and granite countertops. Gill's place is very country kitchen,' I explained to Lewis. 'Yellow – pine-fitted cupboards and lots of painted tiles.'

'Nah, I like Gill's,' Liam insisted. 'It's really homey. That chrome stuff is for those wankers who fantasise about being chefs, y'know. I tell you, if you really do that for a living you don't want to come home to it as well. You want something nice and cosy with lots of space, like Gill's.'

He stroked his balls reflectively.

'That hubby of hers is a lucky bloke,' he said. 'Just hope he appreciates her, that's all. He looks really down in the mouth. I tell you, if I had a bird like Gill to come home to I'd be bouncing through that door with a stiffie in my trousers every night, not crawling in like a whipped dog. He isn't much in the looks department, is he?'

I tried not to jump in my seat.

'You saw Jeremy?' I said, keeping my voice even.

'Yeah, he popped in just as we were finishing up. Stuck his head in the kitchen and went straight upstairs. Maybe he didn't like wifey hanging out with a hot young stud while he's out at work, eh?' Liam nudged Lewis familiarly in the side. 'We know how dangerous that is, don't we, mate?' he said.

Lewis actually flushed. He must have confided some exploits to Liam; he wouldn't have coloured up if there hadn't been some substance behind Liam's suggestion. I was glad that Liam had embarrassed Lewis in front of me. Somehow I felt that it paid me back for my reaction to his kiss of my hand.

'Not that we were doing anything,' Liam continued. 'Though I don't mind telling you I was thinking about whipping up some cream and—'

'Liam,' I said reprovingly. 'Spare me. She *is* a friend of mine.'

'Ooh, yeah, talking about friends of yours –' Liam bounced eagerly over to the arm of my chair – 'how's your mate Mel? Does she ask about me? She's a really tough chick, that one,' he added admiringly to Lewis. 'She got me thrown out of this fetish club. Encouraged me to go over the top and then got me thrown out. No messing with that one, eh?'

This was for me. I shook my head.

'And if you do mess with her,' he said enthusiastically, 'she makes you pay for it, I bet. Big time. God, I can't wait to see her again. She coming to the launch?'

'She might.'

'Make her come, Jules, make her come!' he pleaded winsomely, rocking back and forth on the arm of my chair till it creaked. 'Tell her I'm going to be a very naughty boy and I need her to keep me in order!'

God, Liam and Mel were so much on the same wavelength it was terrifying.

'We'll see,' I said.

'Do it, Jules, do it . . . Oh, Howie! All right, mate!'

The club must have opened, and in strolled one of its population of dissolute actors, a young heartthrob soap star who had left the tyranny of three episodes a week and was now knocking around London looking for starring vehicles in hot British films that would be his passport to Hollywood. If the legions of adoring fans who had fallen in love with him – as the clean-cut young market-stall holder struggling nobly to bring up two children as a single parent – could see him now, they would be shocked beyond belief. He looked rougher than sandpaper.

Liam fell on his neck. They did that handshake twiddle, but briefly. Howie was not to be distracted from hitting the bar. Hair of the dog, no doubt. He looked still drunk from the night – or morning – before.

'You know that actress I was talking to at the Eis Shots launch?' Lewis said in my ear. 'Susanne Saunders? She says he's gay.'

'Does that mean he turned her down?'

Lewis grinned. 'No, really gay. But that's not the real dirt. Apparently he's only got a three-inch willy.'

'Poor bloke.' I looked over at Howie with new compassion. No wonder he needed to hit the bottle.

'Do you think Liam's all right?' Lewis said.

'No,' I said simply. 'I've been worried for the last week. He's completely manic.'

'Do you think it's drugs?'

I shrugged. 'No more than usual. I think the bottom line is that he's terrified. He's been ringing me up all the time – well, you know that, you've taken enough messages. But he rings me constantly at home as well. Talking about everything and nothing. He just needs a lot of reassurance.'

'It's not surprising, really,' Lewis observed. 'It's all happened so quickly. And he's so young.'

'Yeah, classic recipe for disaster.'

I looked over at Liam, who was having a heated argument about football with Howie and the bartender. The trouble was that as long as Liam didn't actually implode, everything he did would be excellent copy. I could see him in a year's time in the gossip mags, marrying some supermodel, breaking up with her months later because he was shagging an entire catwalk of her best friends, dating minor royalty, getting busted for drugs, in and out of rehab – but as long as he managed to keep making the TV programmes and putting the books together, no one would discourage his worst behaviour, because he was a gift to the tabloids. And, of course, to a PR. Representing Liam was like having a tiger by the tail. Oh well. At least it made a change from having to embellish stories about our more boring clients.

'I think it's a lot to do with him being bored,' I said. 'Liam's always worked really hard. He's been working in restaurants since he left school at sixteen, and when Felicity took him away from all that he was busy getting all his recipes together and doing all the work for the series. It's only since they wrapped that he's had any time to himself at all, and it's just not good for him. He needs an occupation.'

'He should open a restaurant,' Lewis suggested.

'Something like that.'

I watched Liam for a little while, his hectic gestures, his barely controlled, leaping energy.

'You know what chefs are like,' I said to Lewis. 'Most of them are really busy, snapping, energetic people. They have to be, their job is so demanding. I should have thought of this before. We need to get Liam involved in something. Even if another series gets commissioned –'

Lewis and I held up crossed fingers in unison.

'– it'll be a while before they start filming. And I don't want him self-destructing. There's a real danger that could happen without work to keep him on the rails. That's the great thing about Liam,' I added. 'He's one hundred per cent dedicated to his work. He wouldn't let any amount of temptation get in the way of that.'

Lewis was nodding.

'I think you're completely right,' he said.

I grinned at him.

'That's my favourite sentence in the world.'

A wave of exhaustion hit me. I sighed.

'Lewis, I'm shattered, and I've got a couple of hours' phone calls to make yet. Can I leave you here to see the manager about the brackets for those last three TV screens? And have a bit of a chat to Liam, man to man? Someone needs to check in on him properly and I just haven't got the energy to do it right now.'

'No problem, boss.'

Lewis gave me a distinctly flirtatious smile.

'I do enjoy saying that,' he said. 'I'm definitely going to miss it.'

I had never had the full beam of Lewis in seduction mode turned on me before. I had simply watched its devastating effect on a series of young women who had gone down like dominoes. I bet he had shagged Susanne Saunders; he had been unable to resist putting a spin on the phrase 'talking to at the launch', which indicated clearly that it was by no means the only verb available to describe his activities with her. I could see why Lewis was so effective. It wasn't just his world-class good looks, it was the concentration he brought to his gaze, his attentions, as if you were the only person in the world who could possibly interest him. It was hard not to feel like a rabbit in the headlights.

He was standing up, holding out his hands to me.

'Come on, sicknick. Up you come.'

I let him pull me out of the chair, his hands lingering slightly longer than the effort dictated, and leaving mine with a gentle, significant press. Had Lewis simply not been coming on to me all this time because I was his boss?

This speculation dissolved as I thought over what Liam had said about Jeremy coming round to Gill's. God, how quickly I was calling the house 'Gill's', when poor Jeremy hadn't even been gone for a fortnight. If he could still let himself in, that meant that she hadn't changed the locks. But everything was altered now, of course, since the departure of Philip the Real-Estate Love Rat. I had spoken to Gill that morning and she hadn't mentioned Philip, which meant that he still hadn't been in touch. If he had, she would have wanted to analyse every nuance of the conversation.

Maybe she had asked Jeremy round to talk about the divorce? I made a mental note to ring Gill that evening. Oh, and I needed to call Chris too, to confirm that he was coming to the launch, and see how the first day of his course had gone. And then there was Liam, naturally. Though he would probably ring me. I had had three calls from him yesterday evening, in various states of drunkenness. Right now I felt like I was providing moral support to the universe, with not much of it coming back my way. I just hoped that the big karma wheel would swing round sooner rather than later.

Even Lewis, who I had always been able to count on before for buckets of moral support, was now compromised. I glanced at him. He caught my eye and ran his hand through his hair, smiling at me. It was a mating call. If he had been a girl it would have been the pout and the hair flick from one shoulder to the another. In one sense, it was depressing. I hadn't realised that I would lose Lewis so completely with his promotion; it was hard to keep someone as a rock-solid ally when they were busy trying to impress you with a rock-solid part of their anatomy. Still, I couldn't help being flattered. Who wouldn't have been? Lewis was much younger than me, besides being a complete and utter stud puppy. It put a spring in my step for the rest of the day. Even if I didn't have Liam's special trainers with the built-in bounce.

Chapter Twenty-two

I rang Gill twice when I got home, but her machine picked up both times. I left the most cautious of messages, paranoid after my recent *faux pas*. Actually, I had to admit that I was quite glad not to speak to her right then. The emotional upset of people you care about is always very draining; and I was exhausted, and not really up to an hour-long conversation in which she rehashed everything Philip had ever said to her, finishing with the bit where he asked for his spare keys back.

I was even tempted to unplug the phone, something I never do. What stopped me, sad to relate, was not the awareness that my top client might ring me, wanting to hear for the fifteenth time that day that his launch would go fine, his TV series would be a hit and that he deserved his success because he had worked very hard for it. Gill and Liam were both going round and round on their own obsessive little loops right now. No, I was still, stupidly, hoping for a phone call from Alex – even though it had been a week and a half since our dinner and I knew perfectly well that if he had been intending to ring me he would have done so already. If he rang this late, it would be almost an insult, requiring some long complicated excuse about a work or family emergency, and then we would be into messy half-lie territory and whatever was between us would be doomed anyway. I was a firm believer that if things got convoluted in the early stages of dating, they would never right themselves afterwards.

I was still at the stage of setting the answering machine

when I had a bath, in case the phone rang while I was running water and I missed a call from him. It was pathetic, I knew. Hopefully in a couple of weeks the spell would start to dissolve and I could pick up the phone without hoping to hear his voice. Why he was having this effect on me was still a mystery. What the hell did he have that would make him so fascinating to me, while I never lost a heartbeat imagining Johan ringing me, say, or Pieter, or that guy I had nearly shagged at the conference – what was his name? Oh yes, Tom. Alex was scruffy and a little overweight – well, maybe that was an exaggeration, but he did have love handles – and he didn't flatter me, or take me out to super-smart restaurants, or kiss superbly. I didn't even know how he kissed. This was ridiculous. I was beating myself up over a man I hadn't even kissed, for God's sake. Mel was right. I *had* changed. In my glory days I would have at least kissed him on one of the nights he had walked me back and jumped his bones after we had been out to dinner.

The doorbell rang, startling me so much that the towel wrapped round my head detached itself and slumped over my face, blinding me momentarily. Fumbling it off and cursing, I scurried across to the intercom. I was sure it was Alex, too nervous to ring in case he got the machine and had to leave a message, dropping round faux-casually to see if I wanted to go to the Spit and Whistle with him. I had promised myself an early night, but already I was planning what I would wear – my pulling jeans, the ones that hoiked up my bottom pertly but weren't so tight they left unattractive red marks from waist to thigh . . . and my new dark green stripy sweater that didn't look too smart, but still gave a nice hint of cleavage . . .

'Hello?' I said excitedly into the intercom.

'Ju? It's me. Can I come up?'

It was like a flashback to four years ago. I froze with my finger reaching out to the intercom button.

'Ju?' said the voice patiently. 'It's Bart, idiot. Go on, press the button.'

I did it automatically. Then I looked down at myself. I wasn't opening the door to Bart dressed only in a towel (though I had been contemplating doing exactly that for Alex – give him a quick-flash of a near-naked me and then head off to change, thus tantalising him for the rest of the evening). I shot into the bedroom and emerged as the buzzer went on my front door, in my most restrained and figure-covering pyjamas, towelling my hair dry.

Bart looked exactly the same as ever. No, that wasn't quite true. He was slightly better dressed, and around his neck was a narrow leather thong with some sort of silver talisman hanging from it. I couldn't make out the exact shape. But his hair was as ruffled and sunbleached and resistant to any specific style as it had always been, his chin perpetually stubbled, and his big happy smile at seeing me was like a light bulb going on. That smile had always melted my heart. No matter what latest atrocity Bart had committed, that smile always made me feel warm and completely loved and ready to forgive him.

'Hey, Squashy Bum!' he exclaimed, folding me in a big hug. 'How's it all going?'

'Uh, good,' I muttered into his shoulder.

It was so weird for me to be in Bart's arms again. His body felt almost as familiar to me as my own. It wasn't an instant sexual charge, more a coming-home. His pectorals, his hard flat stomach – Bart had one of those Irish bodies that stay lean and taut no matter how much abuse, in the way of all-night drinking sessions and endless bags of chips, is thrown into them – I could have shut my eyes and traced his body from memory just from the way it felt against mine.

He held me by my shoulders and looked narrowly into my face.

'You look a bit tired,' he said. 'Been overdoing the late nights?'

'I'm just getting over the flu. And working really hard.'

'Oh, poor Squashy Bum.' He tutted. 'You've got to look after yourself, my girl. Now that I'm not around to do it for you.'

Huh, I thought. It was Bart's fantasy that he was great when I was sick. In fact he was pretty hopeless. He never knew what to do. His idea of looking after me was to go to the deli and bring home weird and wonderful foods to tempt my appetite – sushi, mint chocolate fingers, cold duck rolls – when all I really wanted was some hot soup and endless cups of tea.

'How's work going?' he said cheerfully.

'Good. I've been made partner. I'm really happy about it.'

'Wow, that's great!' He picked me up and swung me around, making me dizzy. 'I always said you'd do really well! Remember I said you were my best investment, Ju?'

When I had left my crappy temping job to try to get into PR, Bart had been there to support me, emotionally and financially; he had ended up bearing most of our living expenses for six months or so while I went through a whole series of near-misses at jobs. He was wonderful. Never once did he complain. He wiped away my tears when I didn't get the jobs I really wanted and wouldn't have dreamed of reproaching me about not bringing in much money. It had been his finest hour.

'You did,' I said, kissing him on the cheek. 'You were just an idiot. You made the investment and didn't manage to stick around for when it got to be partner.'

'I'm a fuck-up!' he admitted, throwing his arms wide. 'What can I say! So, what have you got to drink round here?'

I gestured to the drink stand in the kitchen.

'You know where everything is. Help yourself.'

Bart didn't need telling twice.

'What do you want?' he said, getting busy making his favourite whisky and soda.

I rolled my eyes.

'Bart, I just said I'm getting over the flu.'

'Doesn't mean you can't have a quick drink with me, does it?'

I caved in.

'Oh, all right. Give me a Cointreau. A small one,' I said hastily, remembering Bart's way of pouring drinks.

'So!' he said, clinking glasses. 'To promotion!'

Bart's happiness for my success was evident and unfeigned. It was always one of the best things about him – that, and thinking I didn't have cellulite. While women I knew were complaining that their boyfriends were competitive and jealous of any career triumphs they had, I basked in the knowledge that Bart would never be anything but supportive. Of course, he partly wanted me to do well so that he could work less – ideally, not at all – and be able to borrow off me whenever he lost heavily at the roulette table, but still, at least he wasn't threatened by my ambition.

'You look very nice,' I said, noticing his ribbed sweater in a shade of blue that brought out the colour of his eyes. And that thong at his neck looked great. I loved men who wore jewellery.

'Oh, thanks. Lucy buys my clothes.' He pulled at the neck of his sweater to show me the label. 'Paul Smith, very posh. She threw out loads of my stuff when we got together.'

'Lucy?' I said cautiously.

'My girlfriend! I told you I was seeing someone.'

'No you didn't.'

'Yes I did.'

We glared momentarily at each other. Then Bart burst out laughing.

'God, we never change, do we? Yeah, I've been seeing her for a few months now.'

'What is she, older and rich?' I said nastily.

I felt incredibly proprietorial about Bart. The way I saw it was that if we hadn't managed to make our relationship work, given his gambling problem, then he would never be able to do better with any other girl, since he and I had been so happy together apart from that. Bart had plunged into a fling with someone when I had kicked him out, but it had been disastrous and shortlived – she had tried to convert him to Buddhism – so I had been able to be smug about that, in between breaking down in floods of tears every time I thought about him. But this was the first time I had heard about someone described as an actual girlfriend. It was an awful feeling, as if someone were removing my stomach with a rusty, jagged spoon. My one recourse was to jeer at Lucy.

'What do you mean?' Bart said crossly.

'Well, buying you a new wardrobe. She sounds like a sugar mummy.'

I was bitterly jealous. I had always wanted Bart to dress better: he had a great body which he tended to hide under droopy old t-shirts and saggy jeans. Lucy, by flexing her credit card, had turned him into the sleek, sophisticated version of himself I had dreamt of. But I hadn't wanted to resort to buying him clothes. That was pathetic and shallow. Besides, I hadn't had the money.

'I like the stuff she's bought me,' he said defensively. 'You said yourself you thought this sweater was really nice.'

I bit back a response along the lines of: That was before I knew that sad old bitch bought it for you. Instead, I shrugged.

'Yeah, it is,' I said. 'What did you have to do for her in return? Dress in a silver G-string and give her wizened old body a full massage?'

Bart's eyes narrowed.

'Don't be more of a bitch than you can help, Ju. Lucy's my age, OK? She isn't some sad old slapper, and I'm not a fucking gigolo.'

'She must have a really good trust fund, then.'

This was just as mean of me. And sexist. For all I knew, Lucy might be a high-flyer at a City bank who made hundreds of thousands a year and could easily afford to buy Bart cupboards-full of cashmere sweaters without even noticing it. But clearly I had hit home.

'She's got a job! She works!' he said defensively. 'It's not her fault her family's loaded.'

'I see you've fallen on your feet,' I said nastily.

I didn't like the way I was behaving. It didn't take Bart's angry reaction to bring that home to me.

'What the fuck's wrong with you, Ju?' he said furiously. 'Are you jealous?'

'No, of course not,' I said quickly, wondering if Lucy's trust fund was large enough for her to cover Bart's gambling debts without breaking sweat.

I wanted very much to ask Bart if he was still gambling. It was really important to me. I had always maintained that he wouldn't be able to stop without serious help from people like Gamblers Anonymous, which he had categorically refused to accept. The thought that everything might be fine in his life now – that Little Miss Trust Fund Lucy had sorted him out by giving him unlimited access to her bank account – was very hard for me to digest. And it nagged at me, even though I knew that – if it were true – it was incredibly unlikely to last.

I managed not to ask him. It wouldn't do any good, anyway. He wouldn't admit it if he was, and I wouldn't believe any denial he made. This was how we had spent our last year together, caught in a vicious circle. And ever since then, on meeting up, we lurched along from moment to moment. Our happiness at seeing each other, our effortless familiarity, always snagged on this problem. We were like a beautiful white yacht with furled sails getting caught and dragged along a reef, which proceeded to tear the bottom right out of the boat.

Feeling that I owed him some sort of apology for my remarks about Lucy, I struggled to think of something nice to say and came up with a feeble: 'So, everything's going well, is it?'

'Yeah, it's good.'

He grinned at me. It hadn't been such a feeble question after all. Bart preferred the wide-focused kind of conversation; specifics about anything to do with work or finances made him very nervous.

'And how did you meet Lucy?'

'Oh, I was doing a shift for one of the doormen at Source, and she came out for a breather and we got chatting,' he said easily. 'You know, helping out Dave. He does Friday nights there. He asked me for a bit of a favour and I said Sure.'

This was classic Bart. Translation: Bart owed Dave money and was paying it off that way.

'And what does she do?'

I was trying to sound relaxed and casually interested, but I could tell from the wary glance Bart shot me that I was not altogether succeeding.

'She's a teacher, actually,' he said.

'Oh yeah? Inner-city deprivation or posh public-school kids in uniform?'

God, I was being a bitch.

'Neither,' Bart snapped. 'She teaches kindergarten. And yeah, it's a private school, but they have assisted places.'

Oh, pre-posh public-school kids in uniform, I thought, but didn't say. I could just imagine Lucy: blonde, Sloaney, slender and trim, her hair streaked by the best colourist in

Kensington, tending to her privileged little charges like some lesser version of Princess Diana. She would love Bart – a toy she could dress up and flaunt at her posh family to prove that she had a rebellious streak. Perhaps I was being utterly unfair, but I couldn't help myself.

'That's perfect!' I said. 'If she's used to little kids all day, coping with you should be a breeze.'

This could have been taken either way, and Bart chose the better interpretation. He burst out laughing.

'That's exactly what she says!' he exclaimed. 'You two should meet up some day, you'd have a lot in common!'

Yeah, why not bring the Kensington princess round to what she would doubtless consider my squalid ex-council flat in Chalk Farm for a nice cup of tea? Or maybe she could take me shopping and smarten me up with some well-chosen cashmere sweaters . . .

'So, to what do I owe the honour of this visit?' I asked. 'Is it still about your record player?'

'Yeah, mainly,' he said, finishing his whisky and soda. 'I've been meaning to pick that up for ages.'

'Bart, it doesn't even work. It never did, even seven years ago when you moved it in.'

'Yeah, well, I thought I'd give it a try. I've got all these old records I want to play.'

'I know,' I said patiently. 'They're here too.'

'Are they?' He brightened up. 'Brilliant! I was wondering where I'd left those!'

'I would have chucked them out,' I said pointedly, 'only they weigh too much for me to carry downstairs.'

'Oh, Ju, you wouldn't have done that!' he protested, eyes widening in shock. 'Those records are priceless!'

'I expect that's why you remembered where you left them,' I observed caustically.

Instead of bridling at this, Bart laughed.

'That's my Ju,' he said affectionately. 'Sharp as a whip.'

He had an extraordinary capacity for defusing my snottiness.

'I think that record player – and the records – are the last thing you've got left here,' I found myself saying.

Bart had brought very little when he had moved in, and taken even less when he left. Things we had bought together, or been given as joint presents, had all been left for me. He wasn't grown up enough to accumulate possessions; he moved through life too lightly, or too childishly, expecting the women he lived with to provide them for him. I imagined Lucy was doing a fine job in this area.

He was looking sad.

'I expect it is,' he said. 'I had some old clothes here, but you can throw 'em all out now.'

'I did that years ago!' I snapped. 'And why should I have had to throw them out? You should have sorted that out for me!'

'You changed the locks, remember? After throwing me out on the streets!'

I snorted.

'Oh, Bart, please. The *streets*? Like you dossed down in doorways for a couple of months! I thought you moved straight in with that Buddhist nutcase!'

Bart started to giggle.

'Oh God,' he said unforgivably, 'I completely forgot about Eileen.'

I was giggling too.

'You were awful to her,' I said reprovingly. 'You broke her heart.'

'She was awful to me!' he retorted indignantly. 'She made me eat tofu and boiled greens three times a day! I wouldn't have gone near her if you hadn't broken my heart so badly! It was any port in a storm.'

I giggled still harder at the idea of Bart on a tofu and cabbage diet.

'Well,' Bart said, looking at his watch, 'I suppose I'd better load up my stuff and hit the road. I said I'd be back by eleven.'

'Back to where?'

Why did I ask questions I really didn't want to know the answer to?

'Lucy's, of course,' he said, as if it were the most obvious thing in the world.

'What, she's got you on a curfew?'

'What is wrong with you, Ju?' Bart said crossly, coming late to the theory of attack as the best form of defence. 'You're in such a bad mood this evening!'

He said it as if he had seen me just the day before. It was that familiarity that weakened me so much. I looked at him. His face was all creased up in bewilderment. Men were extra-ordinary. He truly did have no idea why I was being so nasty whenever Lucy was mentioned. It would have taken a woman a mere ten seconds to diagnose me as a jealous dog – or rather bitch – in the manger.

'Is the record player still over there?' He crossed the room to my stereo system. 'Great! Just where it always used to be!' he said nostalgically, before he reached round the back and started pulling out handfuls of wires.

'Just make sure you leave everything else connected up,' I said sadly, curling up in a tight little ball. I never used that record player; for years I had complained about it as a nuisance, cluttering up space I could have used for storing magazines; and yet the sight of it being removed, together with the equally annoying cube of records, nearly broke my heart all over again. Bart was gone for good, and in a couple of minutes there wouldn't even be a trace in my flat to show where he had once been. I knew it was right that he had gone. We couldn't have stayed together. Bart couldn't stay with anyone; I was the longest relationship he had had in his life. But I had loved him so much, and it hurt like hell to watch him blithely sliding his record player out from the shelf, where it had stood unused for so long it must have its own perfect dust outline to mark where it had been.

Bart's almost perpetual good spirits had been a source of great pleasure to me when we were a couple, but now they felt like a weapon that had been turned against me. They meant that he could happily sail through this significant moment, hardly affected by it at all, seeing only the positive: Hey, Ju and I are still friends! I have a cool new girlfriend waiting for me! And look, I have my record player back! Plus all my priceless records!

'You can't carry those down the stairs together,' I said, as Bart stacked the record player precariously on top of the cube. Wires hung down each side and the rubber feet of the player didn't quite fit on the cube.

He looked at the construction dubiously.

'Maybe I'll take the cube down first, then,' he said. 'I've got the car parked outside.'

'Oh, you've got a car?'

'Yeah, a Jeep, actually. It's pretty cool. Borrowed it off Lucy's brother.'

He opened the front door and heaved out the cube.

'Back in a sec!' he called. 'I'll put the downstairs door on the latch, so you don't have to buzz me in again.'

Listening to his heavy, cube-burdened footsteps proceeding along the walkway, I felt bereft. Never had it been so clearly indicated to me that I needed to move on. It wasn't that I had spent the last four years in a haze of nostalgia for Bart, secretly fantasising that we would get back together again, and this time it would work forever; I had done exactly what I needed to do. Worked my way through a large section of the cuter males in London, got my wild oats comprehensively out of my system. It had been hard at first to leave memories of Bart behind, but I had managed it in the end. I had had enough fun for myself and a couple of others as well; I had certainly had Gill's fun as well as my own. But I had thought that would be enough. I didn't know the time would come when I would need to make another big step into the dark.

I didn't have any choice. There was no home to go back to. Bart was as feckless as ever. The day he came around with his own Jeep and his own cashmere sweaters, I would know he had changed: but that was obviously as far away as it had ever been. So what was my tally? No Bart, a mother who would probably stone me on sight, and a brother – well, actually, Chris seemed to be doing OK. He was apparently really enjoying his course. But Chris becoming more mature just made me realise that it was time for me to do the same. I was thirty-three. I didn't want to be chasing blokes in fetish clubs in ten years' time. Well, I did want to, but I probably wouldn't be able to. Alex's face floated for an instant before me, the fan of lines around his eyes crinkling as he smiled, and the image was hugely endearing. I sighed. He's just a symbol, I told myself. You're never going to see him again. He's only a symbol of the new, boring grown-up life you're going to have to lead when blokes in fetish clubs don't want to shag you any longer.

The buzzer went on the downstairs door. Was it Bart? But surely he'd have unlatched the door as he'd said; he'd done it a million times, he knew the trick perfectly well. Someone else, then, who didn't realise that the door was open . . . And I was in my flannel pyjamas! I rushed over to the intercom and stuttered frantic 'Hello?'s at it, with no answer. Oh God.

Quickly I twisted my hair on top of my head and fastened it with a clip and then dashed into the bathroom to get at least some basic makeup on my face. I couldn't change, because then Bart would comment on it as soon as he came back up for the record player, and I would look like an idiot. And anyway, I didn't have time . . .

'Hello?' came a male voice at the door. 'Juliet?'

Definitely not Bart. He'd be banging on it, yelling, 'Oi, Ju, let me in!' impatiently.

I patted some perfumed talc over my exposed areas – putting on perfume would be too obvious – and, trailing a cloud of white dust attractively behind me, shot out of the bathroom and to the door. I stood there for a second, gathering my courage. This time I would be calm and relaxed: no drugs, no drinking, just happy, ready-for-a-mature-relationship me. Oh fuck, who was I kidding? I unlocked the door and threw it wide, hoping the talc had settled. I didn't want Alex to think I was opening the door to him with a flurry of cocaine trailing behind me.

The figure on the doorstep had his hand raised. Clearly he had been about to ring the bell. He looked incredibly happy to see me.

He'd have to be happy enough for both of us. My heart sank.

'Liam,' I said wearily.

'Jules!' he said. He stumbled across the doorstep and fell heavily into my arms. I reeled backwards under his weight. 'Jules! Oh, Jules, I'm so fucked up!' he sobbed into my bosom.

He raised his head briefly. His eyes were totally rimmed with red. I had never seen anything like it outside of a horror film.

'I'm so fucking scared!' he wailed.

Chapter Twenty-three

Poor Liam. As I had predicted, the tension of anticipating his launch had caught up with him. He was a nervous wreck. Clearly he had been dosing himself with enough drink and drugs throughout the day so that he could finally break down and sob without disgracing himself; tomorrow he would doubtless pretend to have forgotten the entire incident and blame it on some dodgy speed. Tonight, however, I had to deal with him as he lay sobbing on my sofa, wailing disjointed sentences about knowing the series was going to fail, the book wasn't going to sell a single copy, and how there would be nothing left for him to do but shoot himself.

Bart, returning to pick up his record player, paused on the threshold, aghast.

'God,' he said, 'I can't leave you alone for a second without men coming in and throwing themselves – um –'

'On my sofa,' I finished.

'Well, yeah. I was going to say "at your feet", but it wouldn't exactly have been accurate.'

'This is Liam,' I said, feeling utterly overwhelmed both by the situation and my disappointment with both Liam and Bart for not being Alex. 'He's a client of mine. He's about to be really famous.'

'I didn't know you represented musicians,' Bart commented, leaping to a not unusual conclusion, considering the way Liam was dressed.

'He's a chef. A trendy chef. His TV series starts in a couple of days. He's going to be the next big thing.'

I said this partly for Liam's benefit, to demonstrate my faith in him, and partly to show off to Bart how cutting edge and trendy I was too by association. Behind me I heard Liam sit up, obviously embarrassed about being caught in a moment of severe emotional distress by a bloke he didn't know.

'You're sure he's not a muso?' Bart said to me. 'Cos I didn't know chefs did that kind of thing. Doesn't it interfere with the tastebuds?'

I swivelled round. Liam was cutting up some coke on my coffee table. I clicked my tongue in frustration.

'Liam!' I said. 'Don't be an idiot!'

He looked up, horrified. 'But Jules – I just want to do a quick line –'

'Well, get the tray from the kitchen! That coffee table's much too rough a surface to do drugs on! There's a black lacquer-looking tray on top of the fridge – yeah, that one –'

I turned back to Bart, nearly bumping into him. He was making purposefully for Liam.

'All right, mate? I'm Bart, a friend of Juliet's. How're you doing?'

'Bart, Liam is not doing any drugs with you,' I said firmly, blocking Bart's attempt to reach the coffee table.

'I don't mind,' Liam said. 'I've got lots.'

'NO. No, no, no,' I said loudly, raising my hands. 'Stop right there.'

I knew that both of them were capable of pulling an all-nighter on coke, and I certainly wasn't hosting that in my flat. A nasty little thought popped into my head; what a revenge that would be on Lucy if Bart missed his curfew coming back from his ex-girlfriend's flat, didn't return till dawn, in fact, because he was busy doing coke . . . Serve her right for her trust fund and her rich brother with a Jeep and

how smart she had made Bart look and her streaked blond
Sloaney hair. It was an awful temptation, and I couldn't help
yielding to it in fantasy. I let myself imagine with great relish
the scene between Lucy and Bart: the reproaches, the screaming, the jealousy.

The trouble was that the more I imagined it, the closer it
got to the many, many scenes I had thrown myself when Bart
had staggered in at dawn. Not that he had been with an ex,
or any other girl. The casino was his mistress, or the late-night
poker games, or the dog track. The thought of Lucy – or
anyone – going through what I remembered – the waiting up,
the worry, the imagining that he would never come back,
beaten up by someone he owed money to and left to bleed to
death somewhere . . . exaggerated, maybe, but at four in the
morning, with your boyfriend missing and uncontactable, your
brain raced down all kinds of crazy tracks. I couldn't let Lucy
go through that.

It wasn't purely selfless. I would have sent Bart away anyway.
I knew that he would just encourage Liam to get even further
off his face and stay there, and that was the last thing Liam
needed right now.

'You,' I said to Bart, 'are going home. You have a curfew,
remember?'

I couldn't resist this little dig. I wasn't a saint, after all.

His face fell.

'Just one little line?' he wheedled. 'Come on, Ju, he says
he's got plenty!'

'No. If you have one you'll want more.'

'She's right, y'know,' Liam said unexpectedly. He had been
busy with the tray; thick white lines, like marks on a prison
wall showing how many days had elapsed, were spread neatly
along its surface. 'That's how it works. Have some, want
more.'

Bart caught sight of the tray and looked like a little boy being told he couldn't have any sweeties.

'Oh, come on,' he said, eternally hopefully. 'Just a quick one for the road.'

'Bart,' I said crossly under my breath, 'Liam's all worked up and needs to calm down. The last thing he needs is a drug buddy.'

Bart ignored this completely.

'Oh, it'd probably do him good to do a few lines, chat about what's bothering him—'

'OUT,' I said. 'O-U-T OUT.' I frogmarched him to the door. He was so fixated on Liam, now bending over the tray and hoovering up a thumb-sized line, that he completely forgot about his record player. I grabbed it and shoved it into his arms.

'It's what you came for, remember? Now go on back home to Little Miss Kindergarten. I bet she's already ringing the end-of-playtime bell.'

I slammed the door in Bart's pleading face, furious with him. He hadn't listened to a word I said. All he had thought about was free drugs. For the umpteenth time I told myself that I was well out of my relationship with Bart, and, more than ever, I meant it. I felt angry, but very liberated. No regrets.

Well, not about Bart. I found my thoughts slipping to Alex, who would – I imagined – have been great with Liam. I remembered his sympathetic words about Liam the night we had dinner, how well he had analysed his problems without even having met him. Alex wouldn't have exploited Liam's unhappiness by helping him to snarf up his coke. He would have sat down and talked to him, and Liam, impressed in any case by Alex's manner, and even more so by the fact that Alex wasn't doing any drugs with him, would definitely have listened.

Liam had found the alcohol, and was pouring himself some wine.

'Who was that bloke?' he asked from the kitchen, his tone incurious.

No further indication was needed of how far Liam had come from his normal happy-go-lucky self. In any other circumstances he would be pestering me with questions about Bart; when had we broken up, and why; did we still shag; had we been shagging now; what was Bart like as a shag; who was Little Miss Kindergarten, was Bart shagging her, and what was she like as a shag? Etc., etc. ad nauseam. But when I said: 'My ex. He was just dropping round to pick some stuff up,' Liam responded: 'Oh, right,' almost vaguely, and wandered back into the living room with his glass in his hand, as listlessly as a man could who had just ingested enough cocaine to kill a lab rat.

'So look,' I said. 'Sit down and tell me everything that's bothering you.'

'You have some too,' Liam said, indicating the tray.

'All right.' I shouldn't, I knew I shouldn't, but it was so tempting . . . And I was tired, I would need some to keep up with Liam . . . 'But just the one. And then we're going to have a nice long talk and get all this sorted out.'

Two hours and more wine than I cared to think about later, I had somehow failed to bring about the perfect nice-and-quiet scene I had envisaged: Liam either sent home or tucked up on the sofa bed, all troubles dissolved; me snug in my own bed, getting a good night's rest. Liam had passed through anger: 'Why the fuck did Felicity pick me? She must've known I couldn't hack it!'; to panic: 'I'm going to be crap and everyone will see it, I'm going to get trashed in the papers!'; to desperation: 'I'm just going to do a bunk. Run away for a year to Goa or somewhere no one knows me, get a job cooking fish on the beach, stay the fuck away till this is all over and everyone's forgotten all about me!'

Finally, aided by more than one bottle of wine, he had settled into self-pity. He was curled up on the sofa, holding my hand – he was in one of those states where he really needed to touch someone – and pouring out a version of his life story in which everything had always gone wrong for him, and he had always been unlucky. Told this way, the TV show became the culminating strike of a malevolent universe against him, the ultimate gesture of destruction, deliberately setting him high up on a pedestal just to knock him off and watch him smash into pieces.

At first I let him talk without pointing out all the absurdities of what he was saying. If someone is really worked up, being rational with them doesn't help at all. Men often try to do this – argue you out of feeling bad by listing all the reasons you should have to feel cheerful – and it's always a towering mistake. It actually makes things worse. What's needed, instead, is for someone simply to sit there and say soothing, meaningless things, until you gradually pull yourself out of your depression. And that was what worked for Liam.

It was lucky I'd had some coke. I wouldn't have been able to stay awake otherwise. Liam maudlin was pretty damn boring. Fortunately, after a couple of hours I was able to introduce some levity into the proceedings.

'And now I think Felicity got me the show only because she wanted to get into my pants,' he was saying in pitiful tones, like a starlet who had just been horribly taken advantage of by a producer who had made her all kinds of glittering promises.

'Oh, poor Liam,' I teased. 'Seduced and abandoned. Cast

aside like a worn-out glove once Felicity's had her wicked way.'

It was at least the fourth time he had said something like this: I felt I was justified in making a joke of it now.

'Oh no, wait,' I said, pretending that an idea had just popped into my head. 'Hang on a minute, you're not actually abandoned, are you – don't you have your own TV series?'

Liam managed a watery smile.

'But I still think she got me the series only because she wanted to shag me,' he whined.

'Yeah, that's right, Felicity's so unprofessional she'd risk her entire career just for one cute bum and some nice tattoos,' I agreed.

Another watery smile.

'World-class tattoos,' he corrected.

'World-class tattoos,' I agreed docilely.

'I'm so *scared*, Jules,' he said suddenly. He had been saying this for hours, but in tones of high drama. Hearing him say it so simply made it much more effective. And what could I do to talk him out of it? It was true that he faced a terrifying prospect the day after tomorrow. I didn't think that Liam was going to fall on his face. Everyone who had seen previews of the series had loved it. But still, there was no such thing as a stone-cold certainty. It might be a critical success but not find an audience, for instance.

'You're right to be scared,' I said soberly. 'It is scary. You'd be a lunatic if you weren't.'

This turned out to be exactly the right thing to say. Liam grabbed hold of me and hugged me convulsively. He smelt of aftershave and his own body, which was sweet, almost like cinnamon. It was one of the major sources of his attraction. Liam *au naturel* smelt really good. And his arms about me were very strong. I could feel his muscle definition right through the flannel of my pyjamas.

'I don't know what I'd do without you, Jules,' he said into my hair. 'I really don't. Mmn, you smell good.'

'You too,' I said without thinking.

'Really?' He tightened his arms.

I cleared my throat.

'Well, I just washed my hair,' I muttered. 'It's probably that.'

He pulled away and looked at me appealingly, his big blue eyes wide.

'Jules, you've been so great to me. Look at me, just turning up on your doorstep all wrecked and unhappy, and you've just taken me in and looked after me and joked me out of feeling crap –'

I didn't want Liam thinking of me as a latter-day saint.

'Liam,' I said gently, 'I represent you. Anyone who represented you would have taken you in and tried to get you to feel better.'

'Yeah, but you're special.'

'I'm really not.'

'No, you are,' he insisted. 'You care about me. Don't you?'

What was I supposed to say? No, Liam, I just see you as my promotion and my meal ticket? Besides, I did care about him. He might pull the little-boy-lost thing for effect, but it had more than a grain of truth in it, like most poses people adopt.

'Of course I do,' I said gently, taking his hand. 'I want you to be happy and successful and know how talented you are. I mean, everyone's going to be saying that in a couple of days, but I want you to know it for yourself as well.'

'Oh, fuck . . .' Liam looked freshly overwhelmed by the thought of his series actually airing. 'I'm going to be a wreck, I know I am.'

'That's normal too,' I reassured him. 'Everyone gets in a

panic before a new project comes out. You're not the only one, believe me.'

I named some famous chefs I had seen flapping around like chickens with their heads cut off before big events I had helped organise for them. Liam deluged me with questions: 'No, he didn't! In the bathroom for two hours refusing to come out! You're bloody joking!', and cheered up again to some extent.

'I'll never leave you, Jules,' he said earnestly. 'I know I got loads of people after me, wanting to represent me, but I'll never leave you. I owe you big time.'

I took this for what it was worth – not that much. Clients always say this, and often they mean it at the time. But no one is immune to temptation, and you learn not to be resentful when people do leave you, lured away by big promises from a rival PR who says they can get them the cover of a gossip magazine and a full-page splash in every single newspaper simultaneously. It rarely happens. And sometimes they even come back.

Liam leant over the tray, pulling his card along the pile of coke to cut out a line.

'Come on, Liam,' I said, trying not to sound impatient. 'You've had loads already. And it's just working you up into more of a state. I thought you wanted to calm down.'

'I do,' he said childishly.

'All right then, no more coke.'

'Last one. If you do a little with me.'

I sighed, and bent over the tray myself. It was all too true: once you'd had one, you wanted more. Then I stood up and picked up the tray.

'That's it,' I said firmly. 'No more drugs. You can have wine if you want,' I added quickly, seeing the expression of panic that flitted across his face.

He poured himself some more. I went through into the

kitchen and under cover of messing with the kitchen cupboards, I opened the oven door and slid in the tray, slamming a cupboard door at the same time to cover the all-too-distinctive sound. It wasn't the most sophisticated hiding-place in the world. If he really went looking, it wouldn't hold him for long. But there weren't many places to hide a tray. I just wanted to remove it from his vision, and hopefully thus from his mind, as quickly as possible.

'Now,' I said, settling myself back on the sofa. 'Are you tired?'

He nodded. 'A little.'

'Well, maybe you should try to get some sleep. Me too. I've got a long day ahead of me organising a launch for my most troublesome client.'

I was hoping at least for a feeble grin, but instead Liam looked panicked.

'What?' I said nervously.

'Don't send me home!' he pleaded. 'I don't want to go back to mine!'

'Why? What's wrong with it?' I said, baffled. Liam had rented a nice flat on the borders of Notting Hill a few months ago. I knew his accountant had suggested he buy somewhere, but he had been nervous about taking on that kind of commitment, not quite trusting that the TV series or book would really happen, or that they would produce any kind of income for him beyond the advance. Liam was the kind of person who in the old days would have kept his money under a mattress.

He ducked his head, looking incredibly embarrassed.

'It's all bare,' he muttered finally.

'What d'you mean, all bare?'

'No furniture. I didn't get anything in.'

'Why not?'

'I dunno – I didn't know what I wanted –'

I stared at him incredulously.

'Really?' I said. 'I thought you always knew what you wanted!'

Liam coloured. 'Actually, I was scared of spending the money,' he confessed. 'I just thought I'd hold on to as much as I could. For a rainy day, y'know.'

I refrained from pointing out that Liam had no problem buying munificent rounds of drinks for everyone at Jane's on a regular basis, or spending a fortune on drugs. And his new neck chain must have cost a lot. It was designer made and solid silver; he'd been boasting about it to everyone. Still, even though I saw myself as Liam's older sister, there were limits. I didn't want to cross the border into mumsy territory.

'It's not completely bare, is it, Liam?' I asked.

He waggled his hand to and fro, indicating: more or less.

'I got a mattress – a nice one – and a TV and DVD player, obviously, and a stereo.'

He tailed off. I looked at him expectantly.

'No,' he said, seeing I was waiting for more. 'That's about it.'

'Liam.'

'I got my kitchen stuff!' he said hastily, as if that makes it better. 'I brought all that over! Oh, and an answering machine.'

'Which no one ever uses because you don't listen to the messages.'

'Well, yeah,' he admitted. He drank some more wine. 'I did keep thinking about getting stuff,' he said suddenly, 'but I couldn't decide what. I mean, I couldn't decide what to get first. There's so much stuff you need, and I didn't really know how to start.'

'Didn't you have some bits and pieces already?'

He laughed. 'Nah, not really. I was living in this shared

house with me old mates and it was like a bomb hit it, y'know. And when I got the new place, it was too posh to move anything over, it wouldn't've looked right. It was cool at first. It's got wooden floors and me mates would come over and we'd rollerblade round it. But then it stopped being so much fun. I didn't even want to go back there till it was really late, and I was off my face, or it'd bring me down, y'know?'

'You need a girlfriend,' I commented.

'What,' Liam said with some of his old bravado, 'to spend all me money on posh furniture? No way!' Then he sighed. 'I know what you mean, though. I've got all me clothes on the floor 'cause I haven't got any cupboards. I went to buy cupboards and I got so freaked I had to leave the shop. I mean, there's so many kinds! I just wanted, y'know, A CUPBOARD. I didn't realise it was going to be so complicated.'

He looked at me pleadingly.

'Would you come with me, Jules? To look at furniture?'

I was completely taken aback.

'I'm not an interior designer, Liam. I don't know anything about, um, cupboards. Mine were all built-in when I got this place.'

'Yeah, but you've got a good eye. You've made this place really cosy. That's what I'd like, somewhere really nice and cosy, with nice warm colours.'

'Well, we'll see,' I said rather hopelessly. The last thing I wanted to do was trudge around shops picking out stuff for Liam's flat. But he was looking at me like a lost soul. And besides, if I didn't, another agent might latch on to him, spot his vulnerability and take him under her wing. Liam was ripe for that.

'So can I sleep here tonight?' he said, perking up.

'Sure.' I patted the sofa. 'This makes up into a bed.'

'Lovely. Thanks, Jules,' he said, almost humbly.

No crappy chat-up lines, no lubricious speculation about sharing my bed with me. Liam was, for tonight anyway, a different man. I relaxed. If he had started leering I would have had to send him home. I wasn't going to risk having Liam sneaking into my bed at four in the morning and having to wrestle him off. But there wasn't a trace of suggestiveness on his face.

'We should try to get some sleep,' I said. 'I've got to be up for work tomorrow at the crack of dawn.'

'Fine by me,' Liam said, docilely. He finished off his wine.

'Here,' he said, reaching for my feet. I was sitting sideways on the sofa, with my feet curled out under me, and Liam pulled them towards him, into his lap. 'I'll give you a foot rub to help you sleep. You'll need a bit of relaxing after that coke.'

I looked at him narrowly, but all I could detect was innocent helpfulness.

'That'd be really nice,' I admitted, stretching out my legs.

Liam was really, really good at footrubs. His hands were very strong and deft, as a cook's probably have to be, and he hit every single pressure point, one after the other, sinking his fingers deep into the pads of my feet, finding the sensitive areas and massaging them gently till they released their tension. I couldn't help remembering the massage I had had last week, and how sad it had seemed to me that I had to pay someone to do this for me. Admittedly, I had been suffering the onset of flu, and was hypersensitive; but still, to have this done by someone who cared about me, who wanted to make me feel better, gave it an extra significance.

Liam pulled each one of my toes in turn and wiggled them between his fingers. It felt wonderful. I sighed in ecstasy, then winced as he caught a painful spot under my big toe.

'Oops, a sore bit. Let's be having you, then,' Liam said, expertly working it till it yielded up under his fingers.

'Aaah,' I murmured. 'That feels so good.'

'Yeah?'

'Mmmn.' My eyelids were sinking in sheer relaxation.

Liam's large hands were closing around each one of my feet in turn, making them feel very small and gracious, sweeping down the top of the foot in long, tension-releasing strokes, working the little ankle bones to find points I hadn't even known were aching until he dealt with them, one by one.

'Flip over and I can do your calves,' he said matter of factly.

The sofa was long enough so that I could lie down on it. I turned over and propped my face between two pillows so that I wouldn't suffocate. Liam was kneading my calves now, sinking his fists into the knot of muscle at the back of each one and working it like bread dough.

'God, that's good,' I said again. 'I didn't know you were a massage supremo.'

'Did a course once.'

'Really?'

'Yeah. I was thinking about getting into sports massage. Long time ago. Then I got into cooking and never looked back. Funny how your life turns out.'

'Your hands are really strong,' I said, as he reduced my calf muscles to pliant rubber.

'That's cooking,' he explained. 'Using your hands all day, chopping, kneading, lugging big pans on and off the burners – even the fatties are pretty strong. You just have to work your lower body a bit, go running or something. I've got into blading recently. Love it.'

Liam was working the same magic on the backs of my thighs. No one had ever done this to me before. The occasional massages I went for were supposed to be relaxing, emphasising aromatherapy and ambient music rather than digging into the biggest muscles in the body and pounding away all their tension and stress. I closed my eyes and gave up any effort to talk. Liam didn't seem to mind. In fact he seemed positively happy to be doing this. Maybe after a bad bout of depression and self-doubt, doing something he knew he was good at was the perfect way to let him regain some self-esteem. Afterwards I could get him to do my shoulders. They twitched in anticipation.

Though this might have been an all-too-obvious set-up for seduction – massage on the couch at two in the morning after a heavy drink-and-drug session – the thought had entered my mind only for a moment, to be dispelled as soon as Liam started work on me. Usually when men offer to massage your feet or your shoulders in these kind of circumstances, their actual attempts at massage are brutally perfunctory; once having been allowed to put their hands on you, their only interest is getting to your vital parts as quickly as possible. Liam's obvious skill and competence, by contrast, had completely reassured me. He had spent ages on my feet, which no one who was using massage merely as a ploy did. Nor had he asked me to take off my flannel pyjama bottoms so he could see what he was doing, or some other weak excuse like that.

So even when he reached the top of my legs and started digging his fingers into the twin creases between my thighs and buttocks, I thought nothing of it. I would have tensed if he had touched my bottom, but he didn't; he just sank his knuckles gently into the crease, and started easing along it, finding the muscles there and easing them out. I felt my lower body relax still more into the sofa cushions. Liam kept finding places I didn't even know needed massaging till he touched them. It was wonderful. I turned my face to one side and closed my eyes, feeling sleepy but pleasantly stimulated at the same time. Faint sounds of pleasure issued involuntarily from my parted lips, the primitive half-grunts, half-moans you make during a good massage.

Liam's fingers were reaching round my thighs now, the thumbs pulling deep along the creases, smoothing them out, the pads of his fingers beginning to massage the front of my thighs at the top of the quadriceps. Just below my hipbones, perilously close to my groin. I noticed that I was beginning to get a little turned on, but ignored it. After all, how could I not be? Liam was a man, and a very attractive one, touching me very close to the most sensitive area on my entire body. And, despite all my fooling around, it had been a few months since I had actually had sex, in the full meaning of the word. No wonder I was finding this exciting. I moved a fraction, sinking my groin into the sofa cushions. Though I thought at the time that it was my body just relaxing a shade more, a second later I realised that what I had actually done was grind my crotch into the sofa. How embarrassing. I hoped Liam hadn't noticed. I was definitely getting, um, stimulated by this. Thank goodness I had bought new batteries for my vibrator yesterday.

Then I tried to remember whether the batteries were still in my bag – which would mean I would have to take it through into the bedroom when I went to bed – or if I had dumped them in my bedside table drawer. So I didn't immediately notice that Liam's hands had stopped moving. They were clamped around my legs, under the thighs, his thumbs reaching round to the base of my bottom. It was really frustrating, like someone stopping dead in the middle of sex. I wiggled experimentally to try to jog him into movement again. Big mistake. The hands came to life, but one of them slid up on to my bottom, open-palmed and unmistakably caressing, while the other shot round my leg to the surface again, paused momentarily to stroke between my buttocks and then dived between them, grabbing my crotch.

'Liam!' I said into the sofa cushions. I put as much outraged dignity into it as I could, but it's hard to sound righteously indignant when you're lying on your face on your own sofa with a man practically sitting on top of you. 'What are you doing?'

Moronic question number 107. It was all too obvious what Liam was doing. In reflex I jumped, or rather my crotch did, giving him even more room to manoeuvre. He had been doing pretty well even without it, though. Those fingers weren't just talented at massage. In fact, as well as they had been doing before, now I had to admit that they had really come into their own.

'Aah. Oh God,' I mumbled involuntarily in pleasure.

'Yeah?' Liam said. 'You like that?'

'Well, yes, of course . . .' I was really trying to recover my senses. 'Anyone would, I mean, anyone who still had a pulse . . . mind you, that would bring a girl back from the dead if anything would . . . aaah . . .'

The amount of stimulation Liam was managing to provide through a layer of flannel and my more unattractive winter knickers was tremendously impressive. I was barely touching the sofa with my lower body at all now.

'God,' I mumbled, clutching the sofa arm for better leverage.

'Hang on,' Liam said, still working his fingers. I thought he meant the sofa arm, and was about to point out that this was exactly what I was doing, when I heard him move. The fingers withdrew. I moaned in protest. Then there was a sort of eruption of movement behind me on the sofa, and I felt my hips being raised even higher. Liam had flipped himself on to his back and was wriggling underneath me. Or rather Liam's head was wriggling underneath me. He grabbed my bottom in both hands and pulled me hard against his mouth.

'No,' I said feebly, deeply annoyed with myself for sounding like some wretched romantic heroine refusing to yield to the hero's advances before she had a ring on her finger. 'Liam – no – this really isn't a good idea –'

'I'll just do it through your pyjamas –' he mumbled, sinking his mouth into my crotch.

'I don't think that'll work – Oh God – no, OK, it *does* work – Oh God – Jesus – God – but – oh . . .'

If Liam had been able to work wonders with his fingers through the multiple layers separating my crotch from the outside world, what he did with his mouth was nothing short of miraculous. What it would feel like on my naked flesh was too overwhelming to contemplate.

'God, you feel so good –' he mumbled into me, his fingers now beginning to slide under the waistband of my pyjamas and on to my bare bottom. I writhed, half in protest, half in pleasure. Liam, understandably, chose the second interpretation and took it as encouragement. He ripped down my pyjamas – having a little more trouble with my knickers, which were ancient – and sank his fingers into my naked buttocks.

'I really want to taste you,' he groaned, 'let me taste you . . . please . . .'

He grabbed the elastic waist of the pyjamas at the front and started to move them down, licking my stomach as he went. For a brief second the novelty of having a man actually plead to go down on me was so erotic that I simply lay there and relished it. Well, to say I lay there was euphemistic. My forehead was shoved between the cushions and the arm of the sofa, my hips were high in the air and my feet were trailing somewhere in space, bumping against Liam's upraised knees. Liam had got my pyjamas off my bottom by now and dragged me back down on to him, sinking his mouth right into me. It felt incredible. I bucked like a bronco. How Liam was managing to breathe at all was a complete mystery to me. He grazed me with his teeth and I practically screamed in pleasure. I could feel one of his thumbs tracing down the cleft of my buttocks and I knew exactly what he was planning to do with it. Liam really was a filthy bastard.

'Oh – Oh God, oh yes –' I yelled as he sank it inexorably in. As I came I whacked my head against the arm of the sofa, having loosened my grip on it in the throes of passion. It hurt quite a bit.

'Ow!' I yelled, still coming.

Liam thought his thumb was hurting me and withdrew it, much to my disappointment. I slumped back on to the sofa.

'No,' I said, 'put it back in – put it back in right now – Oh God, what am I saying?'

For some reason I had suddenly had a flash of Liam and Felicity having sex – him on top, Felicity telling him to put it back in – and though this picture was fairly repulsive, it wasn't that which had caused me to reconsider what I was doing. It was the imaginary flash I had had of Liam's face. It had reminded me exactly what was going on. Somehow, with my face buried in the sofa, his hands and mouth working on me, Liam had been anonymous. I could pretend that it wasn't my sex-addicted, psycho-Casanova of a client giving me an incredible orgasm. But as soon as I had pictured him, it all fell apart. I simply couldn't have sex with Liam. I turned my head under and squinted down along the sofa at the top of Liam's dark curly head. I could just about see his nose as well, though not the tip – that was buried in me. Aaagh!

'Let go of me!' I said urgently. 'Liam! Let go!'

I clambered off him in what had to be the most ungainly sex manoeuvre of all time, only barely managing not to kick him in the face by accident. He sat up and licked his lips.

'You taste fantastic,' he said eagerly, reaching for me.

'No – stop –'

I had my pyjama bottoms tangled round my shins, which was hampering my attempt to get off the sofa. As Liam tried to grab me I lunged away, tripped and rolled heavily on to the floor, legs in the air, arse bare, flannel pyjama trousers waving from my ankles like a perverted flag. Even Liam couldn't take this as encouragement. He cracked up instead.

Still lying on the floor, I grabbed my bottoms and pulled them up firmly, touching my crotch in passing. The brief contact gave me a near-electric shock. I was still really turned on. I got to my feet, steadying myself on the coffee table for support.

'Liam,' I said firmly. 'We are not having sex.'

'Could have fooled me!' he said, still laughing.

'We're not having sex any more. Ever.'

He looked wounded.

'But, Jules! What about my blue balls?'

I sneered at him.

'Does that usually work?'

'Yeah,' he said, quite unembarrassed. 'Look, you've got me really hard.'

He thrust his crotch out at me. Thank God he was wearing baggy trousers. A straining erection through a nice tight pair of jeans would have been much harder – no, make that more difficult – to resist.

He put his hand on his crotch and stared at me.

'It's all for you, Jules. This is how hard you get me.'

Liam was undeniably sexy. His dark curls, dampened now by a light sweat, his wide blue eyes, his filthy mouth, all presented a picture that was nearly irresistible. But this was Liam, my client, whose launch I was organising, who I wanted to work with for years and years, as his career hit the stratosphere. I didn't intend to lose that. I called up an array of images of Liam: flashing his newest tattoo in hip London restaurants; getting a foot-job from Felicity under the table at L'Orange; pictured in the *Sunday Times* magazine, reclining naked on a sofa with a naughty grin, wearing only a trail of whipped cream leading down his bare chest to a heap of strawberries covering his crotch with a minimum of discretion. This all had the twin-barrelled effect of reminding me (a) that Liam was a CLIENT and (b) that he was a MERE CHILD. I took a deep breath.

'Things just got completely out of hand,' I said, in tones of declaration.

'I thought they were in hand,' Liam leered. 'Well in hand.'

'Shut up. We had too much to drink and too much coke.'

'Speak for yourself.'

'Shut up. I'm going to bed now and so should you. On the sofa bed. By yourself. Not with me. Is that clear?'

Liam nodded sulkily. He put up much less of a fight that I had anticipated. In fact he snapped very fast into naughty-little-brother mode, making sarky remarks about my spare sheets, which were admittedly rather old. (Actually, they dated back to the late seventies. I had nicked them out of my mum's linen cupboard when I went to college. They were in beige, piped with brown, and had a signature swirly seventies print in rust and brown on the matching pillowcases, which were probably an historical document by now. I should try to sell them to the V&A.) The only allusions Liam made to our recent romp on the sofa were one quick grab at my bum, which I repulsed severely, and a request for porn mags to work off his blue balls. I told him to use his imagination and avoid staining the sheets. Even if they were old. Damned if I was showing him where I kept the porn videos. It would only encourage him.

I put his unexpected compliance down to a realisation that sex between him and me would be a bad move. Hence his instinct to treat me like an older sister. It was hard to rely on unbiased career advice from someone you were shagging. And Liam had loads of girls to shag; he didn't need me for that. I assumed that his experiences with Felicity had taught him not to mix work and sex. Well, sex with the higher-ups at work. He was doubtless still trying to nail every other attractive female on the set. I knew he and the *Elle* photographer's assistant, for instance, had shagged in his studio after the photo session. And I suspected him of making the beast with two backs with the journalist too.

I retreated to bed, propping a chair under the door handle in case Liam's good resolve weakened in the night, having checked that yes, I had put my new batteries in the bedside-table drawer. Excellent. You couldn't help but laugh at the picture; me on one side of the door, Liam on the other, both of us busily concentrated on very much the same thing. At least he was probably shaking the sofa so much he didn't hear the buzz of my vibrator and shout rude comments at me through the door. Worries about how we would handle tomorrow morning, and indeed the rest of our working relationship, did run through my mind, but fortunately I had had much more wine than coke, which meant that I was exhausted and – once thoroughly sexually satisfied – desperate to fall asleep.

I thanked God yet again for the invention of sex toys. It was my way of praying.

My dreams that night – or what remained of it – were incredibly vivid and highly detailed. I didn't remember much of them afterwards, but I knew that I had had sex with a lot of men in even more positions. It was all very complicated and mostly unsatisfying, as sex dreams often are; I don't think I ever came. I just ran around from one sexual scenario to another – oh, look, now I'm on a train and here's the cute conductor wanting to, um, punch my ticket. But we would inevitably be interrupted before the ticket was, um, thoroughly punched, and I would be off out the train window and falling into a male harem faster than you could say 'Supersaver Return'. Then I was trying to have sex with someone in a kitchen, but every time we got going a piece of bread would get stuck in the toaster and burn, and the smoke alarm would go off, and we would have to uncouple and fish out the burnt piece of bread, and disable the alarm before we could get going again, which got more and more frustrating, and the smoke alarm got louder and louder and the smell of burnt toast got stronger and stronger and suddenly I was awake, with my alarm ringing madly in my ear and a very nasty burning smell in my nostrils.

I smashed my hand down on the alarm and jumped out of bed, stumbling to the door, still half-asleep and forgetting about the chair I had wedged there last night. I cracked my shins on it and screamed. I could hear an answering yell from the other side of the door. Maybe Liam had got his hand stuck in the toaster and was shouting for help. I managed to drag the chair aside and heaved open the door. The kitchen wasn't enveloped in the cloud of smoke I had expected, but there was some, and the stink of burning was overpowering. It definitely wasn't toast, or even burnt flesh – it smelt inorganic, and very nasty indeed.

Liam, in the middle of the kitchen, looked at me with an expression of utter guilt and despair.

'What the fuck is that awful smell?' I said, clawing the sleep out of my eyes and giving myself a nasty scratch on the side of my nose which I would have to cover up with concealer for the next three days. 'What have you done to my kitchen?'

'Uhhhhhh –'

He stepped back from the scene of the crime. The oven door was open, and from it was issuing a toxic-looking stream of smoke. Inside I could see a mauled, contorted, black and red shape which had once been my plastic faux-lacquer tray from the cheap Chinese shop round the corner. And on top – fused into it beyond hope of recovery, by now – would be the remains of Liam's coke.

'My God,' I said, slowly processing what had happened.

'I wanted to make you a really nice breakfast, to say thanks, and sorry about last night, and everything,' Liam wailed. 'So I made scones. I was going to make muffins,' he added, eyeing me severely, 'but you don't have a sodding muffin tray. Outrageous. And I preheated the oven while I was making the batter and it really started to stink but I couldn't think what it was – I did see something in there but I thought it was just a baking tray – and now all my coke's gone and melted into that sodding thing!'

I started laughing. I couldn't help it. And, after a pregnant moment where he glared at me evilly, Liam followed suit. We staggered around the kitchen, clutching our sides, roaring with laughter, and in the process any tension from the night before evaporated forever.

Chapter Twenty-four

'Juliet! Darling! Raving success, absolutely raving! You must be very pleased with yourself!'

I was, actually. Still, it was never politic to admit it.

'Well, it's really Liam's night,' I said diplomatically, as Henry Ridgely enfolded me in an embrace. There was something different about Henry tonight, and it wasn't one of those subtle changes it took you ages to identify. He looked – for Henry – positively dapper. Spruce. His shirt was white and its front was unstained. He was sporting a red silk waistcoat, equally spotless, and though his jacket was the colour of mustard that seemed the closest it, too, had come to any food product.

'Henry!' I said. 'You look so . . .' I tried to find another word for 'clean', and settled on '. . . great! Very smart,' I added.

Henry preened complacently and fiddled with his blue spotted tie (the spots, I hasten to add, were part of the print).

'I'm on the prowl,' he said mysteriously.

'Really?' I looked around the room, which was packed to the gills with young sexy women in backless tops and low-waisted jeans. 'Some cute chick caught your eye?'

He smiled. 'That would be telling, now, wouldn't it?'

A waiter slipped a tray in front of us, his wrist carefully turned, just as I had instructed all the staff, to show off the specially made fake tattoo on his forearm. The tattoo was based on Liam's own body art and looked fantastic. As I had predicted. People were already fighting for the fake tattoos and t-shirts. I smirked in satisfaction.

'Very striking,' Henry said approvingly.

'I know. Doesn't it look great?' the waiter said.

Henry looked baffled.

'I meant the tarts,' he said to me, taking one. They were tiny pastry confections, filled with cream cheese and dill, topped with two miniature balls of golden sautéed courgette and a baby carrot arranged suggestively on top of them. Liam had wanted the entire menu to be rude food, but I had nixed that idea; I wanted him to be taken seriously as a chef, not just a flash-in-the-pan gimmick merchant. Still, I had agreed to the occasional saucy canapé. It was undeniably great copy.

'Mmn,' Henry said, 'delicious.'

I beamed.

'Gill's done an amazing job,' I said.

'She certainly has,' Henry agreed. 'I—'

'Jules!'

Two thin but strong arms enfolded me from behind, and a cloud of Poison perfumed the air. I didn't need the nip on the side of my neck to tell me who it was.

'Mel!' I said happily. 'When did you get here? You missed the first episode!'

It was looping round on the video screens, but the whole of Jane's had gone more or less quiet during the actual transmission. The reaction had been all I had hoped. Most of the assembled media had seen it already on preview tapes, but, despite that, everyone had whooped and applauded with such enthusiasm I had thought they were going to sweep Liam up on to their shoulders and carry him in triumph through the streets of Soho. And they had laughed at all the funny bits. It had been an unmitigated success.

'Nah, I didn't,' she reassured me. 'I was downstairs watching it in the bar. I saw you before but you're always talking to someone and I didn't want to interrupt. Then finally I thought, ah, bugger it.'

Mel looked amazing. She was wearing her new gunmetal corset over jeans, which shouldn't have worked, but did. Around her neck was a silver choker made from hundreds of loops of tiny chain. Her hair was tipped with silver and her lipstick was as red as a postbox.

'Henry,' I said, squeezing Mel's bottom affectionately, 'this is Mel, a really good friend of mine and Gill's.'

Henry was frankly goggling at the spectacle Mel presented. I could tell he didn't know where to look first.

'And a vision of loveliness to boot,' he said, taking her hand and kissing it. Mel actually looked flattered; she wasn't usually big on compliments from men, but Henry's genuine old-fashioned charm seemed to have made a hit.

'Thank you kindly,' she said pertly. 'I stuck my head into the kitchen to see how Gill was doing, but she looked manic, so I left her to it.'

I checked my watch.

'Another hour and she should be done,' I said. 'We're not serving food all night.'

'I must make sure to compliment her too,' Henry said gallantly. 'Later, when the rush is over. Jolly good. I particularly liked those penis tarts.'

'You *what?*'

I let Henry explain them to Mel while I surveyed the room. Everything seemed to be going fine. More than fine. The food was great, the cocktails were flowing, practically every single journalist we had invited had shown up – there was a big buzz about this launch and no one wanted to miss it – and everyone had been fulsome in their reaction to Liam's show. And to Liam. He was basking in glory. It had a good effect on him; he actually wasn't half as wound-up, or strung-out, as I had expected him to be. I had been worried he would be coked-up to the eyeballs, but he seemed fairly in control of himself.

'Juliet! What a success, my dear! You must be terribly pleased!'

No mistaking those high, fluting tones. I looked down. I was in three-inch heels and Jemima, as always, was in the sensible flat shoes that I should be wearing. Well, they could bury me in them if they wanted. The only time I didn't wear heels was in bed. And even then there were exceptions.

'Jemima!' I said, planting the requisite two air kisses on her powdered cheeks. 'I'm so glad you could make it.'

'Oh, I wouldn't have missed it for the world!' She giggled girlishly. 'I just had one of those naughty little cream cheese tarts with the little willies on them. What fun! Liam really is a very naughty boy.'

Her beady eyes gleamed. They matched her sweater, which was one of those Christmas novelty embroidered numbers with green beaded and sequinned snowflakes on a red woolly background. We weren't even in December yet; God knew why Jemima had dug this out of the wardrobe. Particularly as Jane's was packed with people, and had the fires going to boot. In the heat Jemima's cheeks were nearly as red as her sweater.

'I was actually looking for your charming assistant,' she said confidingly. 'I was terribly interested in what he had to say during our lunch.'

'Oh really?' I said evilly. 'How interesting! What in particular?'

But Jemima was too old and canny to fall into this obvious trap.

'Oh, everything!' she declared with aplomb. 'He has such a fresh perspective, doesn't he?'

'Absolutely,' I agreed politely. Fresh perspective, my arse. Fresh flesh was more like it.

I swivelled around, surveying the room, and by a lucky chance caught sight of Lewis in conversation with a very attractive waitress on whom the tight Liam At Large t-shirt was particularly fetching. She had to be wearing a Wonderbra. It wasn't physically possible to have tits the size of grapefruit on a ribcage no bigger than a twelve-year-old's. I took malicious pleasure in signalling to Lewis that his presence was needed. Jemima being already short, and in her flats, he didn't see who I was talking to till he was right on top of us. And then it was too late. His face fell as if it had been pushed off a ten-storey building. Fortunately he caught it before it hit the ground.

'Miss Thirkettle!' he said charmingly. 'How lovely that you could come!'

'Jemima, please,' said the lady in question, bridling up in pleasure. 'Now, why aren't you wearing one of this evening's t-shirts, you naughty boy? What's this?'

She poked his chest, her finger lingering a little too long on his silk t-shirt.

'Mmn, what lovely material,' she said coyly. 'What is that? Silk? And the colour does look very nice on you. I'm sure we forgive you for not wearing Liam's face all over your chest, don't we, Juliet?'

'Oh, absolutely,' I said demurely.

Jemima wasn't even listening to me anyway. Her attention was entirely concentrated on Lewis's pectorals. Well, they were at her eye level. Lewis shot me a look over her head that said: 'Rescue me!' as clearly as if he had sent up a distress flare. I grinned. After all, cosying up to journalists was a big part of the job. He should be grateful that he now had such a great media contact.

'He's lovely, isn't he?' Mel said, winding her arms around my waist.

'Who?' I said. 'Lewis?'

Jemima was practically pressed up against his chest by now. It was crowded, but not quite sardine-tin level yet; but still, every time someone passed her, she would nudge closer and closer to Lewis, to 'give them room to get by'. I couldn't help admiring her technique.

'Nah,' Mel said. 'Henry. He's really sweet.'

Mel never reacted this well to men. I looked at her suspiciously.

'You aren't thinking of him as a possible client, are you, Mel? Because I really, really don't want to know what Henry gets up to in bed. Or in your basement.'

Mel looked genuinely shocked.

'No way!' she exclaimed. 'No, I didn't mean that!' She giggled.

'Well, good. And behave yourself. Henry's one of the most important food critics in this country and I don't want anything upsetting him. God, I sound pompous, don't I? Sorry,' I apologised. 'I'm a bit worked up. I just want everything to go well.'

'Don't you worry about Henry,' Mel said wisely. 'It won't be me that'll upset him, if anything does – Ooops!'

Something barrelled into her and swung her off her feet. It was Liam, targeting her like a heat-seeking missile.

'I've been looking all over for you!' he shouted enthusiastically. 'Where have you been? Jules said you were coming! Did you see my programme?'

'Put me down,' Mel commanded.

Liam was holding her by her hips in mid-air, swinging her back and forth. Mel clearly considered this position much too undignified. She glared down at him furiously, which he blithely ignored.

'Not till you ask me nicely,' he said, winking at her.

Oh my God. I had the sudden impulse to cover my eyes. He had no idea what he was messing with. That kind of challenge was a red rag to a bull.

Mel didn't waste time arguing. Instead she reached down, grabbed both his ears and twisted them violently in opposite directions. Liam screamed and dropped her, his hands coming up to clap over the sides of his head. Mel hit the ground, adjusted her corset and surveyed her work with a small, pleased smile.

'That really hurt!' Liam said, wounded, still rubbing his ears.

'Should have done what I told you, shouldn't you?' Mel said, not giving an inch.

A group had formed around the two of them, watching this little scene with avid enjoyment. It had even distracted Jemima from her pursuit of Lewis. I saw him making his escape: he was backing away slowly through the crowd, checking to make sure Jemima didn't turn her head and spot him leaving. I tutted. I would have to have a word with him later.

Liam and Mel were facing off. He took his hands away from his ears, which were reddened, though it was hard to tell whether from Mel's assault or his subsequent rubbing of them. His blue eyes were shining.

'So,' he said, shoving back the curls from his forehead, 'if I grab you again and you don't like it you'll do something even worse?'

'You got it,' Mel said calmly. Her eyes were sparkling too. I was dying to see what would happen.

'Ooooh-er! I can hardly wait!'

Liam ducked his head and ran at her, scooping her up over his shoulder in a fireman's lift. I knew Mel well enough to be aware that she wouldn't for a moment have let him do that if she hadn't wanted him to. Liam kept running in the direction of the stairs, and the two of them disappeared from sight as he crashed down the staircase with Mel's arse hanging over his shoulder. I heard him yelp in pain.

'What happened?' I yelled.

'She's grabbed his balls!' someone called back from the staircase.

The spectators burst into a round of applause. Whether this was for Mel's self-defence techniques, Liam's recklessness or simply the general entertainment factor, I didn't know. But I joined in too. I was madly curious to know what would come out of their encounter.

'Oh, I seem to have lost Lewis,' Jemima fluted, looking distressed. 'Did you see where he went?'

'I think he might have gone to check that Liam didn't break his neck falling downstairs,' I said glibly. 'We don't want our new client dead the night of his series launch.'

'That would be very rock star, wouldn't it?' Jemima commented. 'Oh, look who's here!' She stared at me pointedly. 'It's your – um – lunching partner, Juliet!'

I looked over. Sure enough, it was Johan, advancing purposefully towards me through the mass of people, tall enough to be instantly recognisable. Clearly there was no avoiding this encounter. I willed Jemima to vanish, but she was far too keen on this piece of gossip to budge an inch.

Johan looked very straight compared to most of the guests here tonight. We had a large complement of Beautiful People, all of whom were frantically competing to carry off the latest unwearable fashions. They clashed with the food and TV critics, most of whom were a scruffy, eccentric bunch. Johan's smart suit and tie didn't really fit in with either group, but they looked so good on him that I could scarcely complain.

'The lovely Juliet!' Johan said, shouldering his way past a complement of fashionistas in gold lamé butterfly tops and jeans so low cut I didn't know how they managed to sit down without their bottoms popping out. He gave them only the most cursory of glances, which I noted approvingly. 'You look even more beautiful than usual tonight. It is your triumph, no? That's what Richard is saying.'

Despite myself, I blushed as he looked me up and down. The stress of the last couple of weeks, combined with my bout of flu, had helped me lose the extra few pounds required to get me comfortably into my new frock. I would never be thin: I would always need a back to my tops and a bottom to my jeans. The dress represented my personal best. It was a halterneck, of green silk suspended from a gold loop round my neck, and it had certainly been a triumph – if not the kind Richard had meant – to get into it without having to wedge myself first into the hip-slimming underpants I had gloomily been anticipating having to wear. I swished my uncorseted hips smugly.

'Thank you,' I said demurely. I had been expecting Johan to show up tonight; I knew that Richard had invited him, along with most of our clients. Still, I hadn't known whether he would come to find me, after the snub I had given him in cancelling our dinner date.

'Hello, Johan,' Jemima piped up. 'Long time no see, eh?'

Johan was visibly taken aback. Clearly he hadn't noticed her standing next to me. I chose to attribute this to the blinding fabulousness of my dress, rather than her lack of height.

'Oh. Hello, Jemima,' he said stiffly. The look he gave her indicated that however much time had passed since their last encounter, it hadn't been long enough for him.

'I brought you a glass of champagne, Juliet,' he said pointedly, handing it to me. 'I thought we could toast the success of your new client.'

I took it and chinked glasses with him. He had turned his

shoulder on Jemima to exclude her, which was a mistake. He should have known better. Jemima was perfectly capable of making her presence felt.

'Well, I can see you two want to be left alone!' she piped. 'I'll stop playing gooseberry! Oh, and Johan, you should give Eve a ring sometime. I know she'd love to hear from you. We were talking about you just the other day.'

And with a bright smile, she disappeared into the crowd, probably to hunt Lewis down like the dog that he was.

Johan was frowning very crossly. Eve must be Jemima's assistant, the one who had had an affair with Johan and been devastated to find out that he was married. No wonder Johan hadn't been happy to see Jemima.

I drank some champagne and waited to see what he would say. He decided to ignore the whole Jemima contretemps.

'I like your flower,' Johan commented. He reached out and touched the side of my head, where I had pinned a silk flower into my chignon.

'Thank you.'

'Now, when are we going to have dinner?' He leant towards me. I could feel his breath on my face. 'I got a message that you couldn't make the time we had fixed, but you never rang me to let me know when you were free.'

He really was attractive. The firm mouth, the grey eyes, the wide shoulders . . . and the more I saw him, the more suggestively flirtatious he became.

'That's because I don't know when I will be free,' I said firmly.

Understanding flickered in Johan's grey eyes. He picked up my free hand. I was more grateful than I could say that I had got a manicure that afternoon. I had really needed it. My nails had been so ragged I had been surprised the manicurist hadn't had to use a sander.

'This is because of Jemima, isn't it?' he said acutely. 'She has told you things, and now you do not want to have dinner with me.'

I admired him for confronting the issue head-on. Now I was the one floundering. I didn't see why I should be the one to say the word 'marriage' or 'wife' first, though. He had them: he could say them.

'More or less,' I admitted, without removing my hand from his. It looked very nice there in his large palm. God, I loved my nails when they'd just been French manicured. They made me feel so woman-of-the-world. I had got the new silver tips, and they shone so prettily I had been twiddling my fingers ever since to watch them flash in the light.

'Jemima has told you about her silly little assistant who got a crush on me and behaved very stupidly,' Johan suggested.

I wasn't sure how to react to this. Maybe this Eve had been silly; Jemima had said that she was young. Still, there was the issue of female solidarity, not to mention that a man who would so casually dismiss a woman he had slept with was probably not the best bet in the world for an affair. Oh yes, and his wife. I broke down and said it.

'Well, she told me you were married,' I said rather coldly.

'Ah, yes.' Johan was quite unfazed. 'It is true that I am married. But we lead very separate lives. My wife lives in the country, she is very quiet, she is not sophisticated and glamorous like you.'

He gave me a very seductive smile. How awful that merely those words could have me melting.

'Oh, she's in Holland?' I said, thinking that this was what he meant.

He looked embarrassed.

'No,' he said, involuntarily letting go of my hand, 'she is in our house in Suffolk. But I have an apartment in London where I spend most of my time.' He smiled at me meaningfully. 'It is very nice. I would love to show it to you.'

I bet you would, you cheating Dutch hound, I thought. But still, I had a flash of myself and Johan going back to his bachelor pad that evening. How lovely it would be, instead of going home alone after a roaring party signifying the culmination of months of hard work, to be starting an affair with a gorgeous foreigner dying to sweep me off my feet. What a perfect end to the evening that would be. I imagined Johan's flat as having lots of black leather sofas and an enormous, cunningly lit bed with a white fur throw and a huge Jacuzzi in the bathroom and nothing but champagne and caviar in the fridge. And it could all be mine, for the night. I just had to stretch out my hand, give him one little hint, and he would be all over me, even keener to please because of my resistance. And I wasn't even wearing my ghastly hip-huggers, which I would have had to slip off in the toilet if I were planning to have sex but which always left tell-tale red marks where they had compressed the excess fat on my bottom; I had on a sexy little black lace thong instead, in celebration of my temporary slimness, which Johan would doubtless appreciate tremendously.

I imagined removing it in front of him, before lying back seductively on his white fur throw, and sighed.

'I really don't think so,' I said, my regret sounding clearly in my voice.

Johan looked at me long and hard. He could see that my decision had been made, no matter how hard it had been, and he was too smooth an operator to persist right now. It would only mean failure. And the more I refused, the more I would be likely to go on refusing. His best bet would be to catch me off guard. In fact, if he waited till the end of the night, when I was feeling depressed about going home alone, and suggested a nightcap, he could probably have me. I wondered if he realised that.

'I must respect your wishes, of course,' he said. 'But it makes me very sad.'

Capturing my hand once more, he raised it to his lips.

'You know how to find me,' he said. 'Let me give you my mobile phone number also.' He produced a card from a little silver case and handed it to me. 'I will wait and hope that you do ring me one of these days, Juliet.'

It was a nice last line. But as I watched him turn and walk away, I couldn't help noticing that he hadn't given me the number of his flat; the card simply bore his name and his mobile phone number. I bet he had had it printed specially for prospective girlfriends. He wouldn't want to risk them ringing the flat and having his wife, there on a visit to London, pick up the phone.

I revolved the card in my silver-tipped fingers. Johan really was too smooth to be true. He was perfect for meaningless sex, or the kind of affair Mel had suggested, weekend trips to Paris, nights in expensive hotels, completely unconnected with any sort of reality and all the more fun for that. I sighed again. Maybe I would ring him. I just had the strong instinct that ringing Johan for what would be, frankly, a booty call, would be a step back for me. I was supposed to be moving forward into a new life, free of encumbrances like unreliable boyfriends and control-freak mothers. Well, maybe I could just celebrate my new-found liberation with a roll on a white fur throw with a Viking-shouldered Dutchman? Put like that, it didn't sound so retrogressive . . .

'Ju! Hey, great party!'

'Chris!'

I fell into his arms and gave him an enormous hug.

'I'm so happy you came,' I said. 'I was worried you wouldn't show up.'

'You must be joking. Free drink, all the movers and shakers in London to take the piss out of . . . how could I not come?'

He smiled at me shyly.

'I saw Mel just now,' he said. 'She was wrestling on the pavement with this mad bloke.'

'Nobody was getting hurt, were they?' I said anxiously. Mel was my friend, and Liam was my talent. Right then I didn't know who to worry about first.

'Nah. They were having a great time. I've never seen Mel like that. With a bloke, I mean. She was roaring with laughter.'

'Good!' I said happily.

'I didn't really get to talk to her, cos she had her hands full,' Chris said with considerable understatement. 'But she made a thumbs-up at me.'

'Nice.' I wondered if we would see Mel and Liam back inside or if they would take off for somewhere where they could abuse each other's bodies in more privacy.

'I'm really glad you asked me, Ju,' he added. 'I mean, it's not exactly my world, but it's fun to hang out in it every now and then. And it looks great.' He gestured around him. 'You've done a brilliant job.'

I actually felt tears prick at my eyes. Not a word about me being a jammy cow, or having a dossy job where all I had to do was hang around at parties. If I had changed, then so had Chris; it hadn't happened in a vacuum. Now that he was finally training for a job, he was treating mine with much more respect. It felt wonderful. I hadn't realised how much I had wanted it till it happened.

'Oh, thanks,' I muttered, brushing away a tear, unable to say any more. I was choking up.

'Yeah.' Chris looked embarrassed. 'I just wanted to say – I've been doing some thinking – well, I know why you didn't invite me to this kind of thing before. I was a bit funny with you, and I'm sorry. I was always really proud of you, Ju. It just came out all wrong. Anyway, I'm sorry.'

I still couldn't speak. I gave him another huge hug instead, and sniffed back my tears on his shoulder.

'So how's the training course?' I managed at last.

'Great!' His whole face lit up. 'I'm really enjoying it! I've got a real knack for it, they're letting me do all this advanced stuff as well. I never, never thought I'd have so much fun doing something, you know, work-y. And they've already set me up some interviews. I could make a lot of money, you know. A good programmer can write his own ticket, apparently. And just –' he beamed – 'thinking about actually having some money, it's amazing. Even Sis's coming round when I tell her how much I could make.'

Damn. I'd been hoping that Sissy would walk out when she realised how serious Chris was about this course. Still, you couldn't have everything. As Bette Davis said in *Now, Voyager*: 'We already have the moon, darling – let's not hope for the stars as well!'

'And Mum?'

As soon as I said it, I wished I hadn't. I should learn not to mention her name when everything was going well. It always brought us down.

Chris grimaced.

'No change there. But, you know, I can't live my life the way she wants. I'm going to be thirty next year. I've got to stop pissing around. And all this not inviting Sissy to dinner. Sis's been on at me about that for years, and she's right. If Mum wants me to dinner she can have my girlfriend too. I mean, we've been living together for ages.'

One dinner at Mum's and Sissy would never pester Chris to be taken back there; Mum would make sure of that. Still,

I almost felt sorry for Mum. Chris was slipping out of her grasp. It was the worst punishment anyone could have devised for her.

'She rung you?' Chris said. This was a big indication of how far he had come in recent weeks; before, he would have asked me if I had rung her, and ticked me off if I hadn't.

I shook my head. Chris looked violently embarrassed.

'Oh well, I'm sure she will, sooner or later,' he muttered.

Just then someone tapped me on the shoulder. It was a TV critic from a weekly listings magazine.

'Juliet, hi, sorry to bother you,' she said. Her eyes were glazed and her words were running into each other like a multiple pile-up. 'It's about those fantastic t-shirts – I was wondering if I could have some more for, um, the guys at the office . . .'

We had brought a large amount of goodies tonight, and they must have all gone. This was great. The saddest thing at launches was when people disdained even to take the freebies. That was when you knew your product really was in trouble. But I had deliberately not kept a backup here. I knew from bitter experience that if I started going into the back office and handing out extras, the word would get around faster than a speeding bullet and everyone would be pestering me for more. And when I really did run out, they wouldn't believe me and would be insulted, thinking I didn't consider them important enough.

'We've got lots more back in the office,' I said. 'I'll get my assistant to send you some tomorrow.'

'Oh, thanks, Juliet,' she slurred. 'You're cool.'

'Do you want them to your home address or the office?'

A look of feral cunning swept over her face.

'Um, maybe home,' she said. 'Cos, um, if they go to the office everyone'll want one.'

'Fine.' I didn't bother to point out that she had just contradicted herself.

'And could I get some tattoos as well?'

'Look,' Chris said, as the critic stumbled away, her four-inch stack heels rocking precariously on the creaky floorboards, 'I can see you're really busy. I should let you go and deal with – um –'

'Drunken liggers,' I finished cheerfully. I thought quickly. Chris didn't know many people here, and I didn't want to leave him on his own.

'I wanted to go and have a word with Gill,' I said. 'Why don't you come with me? She should be cleaning up by now.'

And maybe if we saw Lewis on the way I could introduce Chris to him. Lewis would look after Chris for me. He was very good that way.

'How's Gill doing?'

I had kept Chris more or less up to date with the developing Gill saga, but I hadn't told him about Philip's abrupt termination of the relationship. I filled him in now.

'God,' Chris said. 'So what's she going to do now?'

'I don't know. I know she's been talking to Jeremy, but . . .' I exhaled. 'She knows she shouldn't go back to him, but she's finding the whole idea of divorce really hard. The house, the marriage, the security . . . I think Jeremy's desperate enough to promise that everything will change, and she's tempted to believe him, even though she knows it's unlikely.'

Downstairs was still as packed as ever, despite the precipitate exit of the star turn with Mel over his shoulder. I looked for them, but they seemed to have vanished permanently. The kitchen was tucked away behind the bar, a couple of small, rickety rooms knocked together and, as usual in the cramped conditions of Soho restaurant kitchens, looking as if they violated every single health and safety law going. Several trays of miniature dessert nibbles were laid out on the table as we entered, waiting for the next waiter to come and collect them. I swiped a cherry mousse tart.

'Mmn,' I said, handing one to Chris. 'Finger-licking good.'

Then I stopped dead. Chris, just behind me, ran into me. I just hoped he had put the tart in his mouth already, or I would have it all over my hair. Gill was at the sink, swathed in a big white apron, her hair tightly pinned back. And standing next to her was the last person I had expected to see here, his round, amiable face as hangdog as a bloodhound's. Even his jowls drooped in misery. Wearing a dark business suit, he couldn't have looked more out of place in Jane's than if he had been dressed in a full Mickey Mouse costume, tail and all.

It was Jeremy.

Chapter Twenty-five

Chris and I had made enough noise stumbling into each other, even over the sound of running water, that Gill and Jeremy looked round to see who it was. I was worried that Jeremy would sneer on seeing me, but his expression didn't alter much. He still looked sad.

'Hi, Juliet,' he said wearily. 'Hi, Chris.'

We mumbled hellos.

'I was just going, actually,' he said. 'I just dropped in to say hello to Gill.'

'Oh no,' I said idiotically, 'do stay if you want to – I mean, don't feel that, um, you're not welcome – can I get you a drink?'

Gill shot me a furious look over Jeremy's shoulder. Fortunately for me, Jeremy was not to be persuaded.

'No, I really should be going. Early hours and all that,' he said. 'I just had a business dinner nearby, and Gill told me she'd be here . . .'

His voice tailed off. I stared at the ground. It was awful to hear Jeremy making excuses to me for having dropped in to see his own wife. I didn't know what to say.

He gathered up his raincoat from where he had draped it tidily on a chair, and pulled it on, slowly, as if giving Gill time to say something. She didn't. She just waited at the sink till he was ready to go.

'Well, I'll be seeing you,' he said to her. They hugged awkwardly, Gill's big yellow washing-up gloves fluttering over his shoulders, not wanting to get his coat too wet. I didn't think he would have minded.

'Um, goodbye,' he said to me and Chris.

Jeremy and I would always have hugged before, but now it didn't feel right. I settled for an awkward pat of sympathy on his upper arm, which looked as clumsy as it felt. He wended his way through the crowd towards the door, his head bent, and I saw him pull his umbrella out of the stand. That was so Jeremy. No one at Jane's ever put an umbrella in the stand; people were always nicking them. But it wouldn't have occurred to Jeremy that anyone might take his umbrella. Then again, it hadn't occurred to him that someone might take his wife.

'Has he gone?' Gill said urgently.

I watched the door close behind Jeremy. It was unbearably poignant. I realised that I might never see him again; his good-bye had sounded sadly valedictory.

'Yes,' I confirmed.

Gill clapped her hands to her face and burst into tears, without even taking off her washing-up gloves.

'Aaaah, aaaah,' she wailed. Blindly she walked backwards till she collided with the chair, and sat down, still sobbing.

'Oh, Gill –' I rushed over and knelt down in front of her, stroking her knees. 'Here.'

I prised one hand after the other away from her face and pulled off the gloves.

'There,' I said, chucking the gloves on the side of the sink.

Gill's crying burst subsided as abruptly as it had started. She choked out a little laugh instead, and took a deep breath.

'Oh, I'm so tired of crying,' she said, wiping away the tears with the back of her hand. 'I can't help it, it's like a reflex action when I see Jeremy – like you, Jules, when anyone used to mention Bart.'

'I'm over that now.' I grinned at her. 'Don't worry, it only took about four years.'

'Oh, great,' she said ruefully.

Chris had crossed the kitchen and was busy putting the kettle on one of the hobs.

'I thought I'd make Gill a cup of tea,' he said gently. 'Ju, want one?'

'No thanks,' I said. I didn't think it would sit that well with the alcohol. I had avoided the schnapps-and-tabasco shots, not wanting to void my guts all over the pavement at the end of the evening, and had stuck entirely to champagne. What a nice ring that had to it.

'Oh, Chris, you're an angel,' Gill said in gratitude. 'I'd love a cup, I really would.'

'A toast to the chef!' shouted a voice from the kitchen door. It was Henry. He thundered in bearing a bottle of champagne and two glasses, looking positively blithe. On seeing me and Chris, however, his face fell a little.

'Oh,' he said. 'I, um, I suppose I should get some more glasses.'

He sounded about as enthused at this prospect as Liam had at the idea of having to get some more coke for the launch.

'Yup, a couple more would be great,' I said. 'Just grab them off the bar.'

But Henry ignored me. He had caught sight of Gill. Though she had stopped crying, the traces of the tears were very evident.

'Gill!' he said in tones of great concern. 'What's wrong? What happened?'

Gill sniffled. Seeing that she was incapable of answering, I said: 'Jeremy just came by to see her.'

Henry bristled. This was odder and odder. I stared at him, wondering what on earth was going on.

'I told him I'd be here,' Gill explained. 'He wanted to see

me and I thought if I was working it'd be easier, I wouldn't get too upset because I'd be distracted, and there'd be people all around. It's just – oh, thanks, Chris, that's lovely –'

She took the mug of tea Chris was handing to her. Somehow he had managed to find teabags, milk, sugar and a mug without asking anyone or even distracting us by banging cupboards in his search. He was being a tower of strength.

'But it was still upsetting,' Henry suggested.

Gill nodded, still sniffing.

Henry looked as if he was taking a deep breath. Then he made his way across the kitchen, squeezing his bulk clumsily between the table and the counter, and stood next to her. Gently, tentatively, he reached out a hand and patted her shoulder comfortingly.

Gill looked up in surprise. Then she managed a small, grateful smile. He reached into his breast pocket and produced a handkerchief as large as a napkin, handing it to her with a courtly gesture. Gill took it silently and started to wipe her eyes. The blue mascara and eyeliner had run, and was leaving traces all over the handkerchief, but I doubted Henry would care.

It was an unexpectedly tender little moment, into which I was hesitant to break. Finally I went over to hug Gill, feeling as clumsy as a third wheel.

'You get back to the launch,' Gill said, hugging me back. 'I know you've got things to do.'

'Really?'

'Yes. I'll just stay here for a bit and get myself back to normal.'

She looked at the handkerchief in horror.

'Henry, I'm sorry –' she said.

'Not to worry,' Henry said, pulling up a chair and sitting next to her. 'Stacks more at home.'

'I must look such a fright –'

'Not at all. Lovely as ever.'

Henry was definitely infatuated. Gill looked like a nasty accident in a mascara-testing factory.

'I'll look after her, Juliet. Don't you worry,' he said to me. 'You've got a full party out there.'

'Really, Jules,' Gill chimed in bravely. 'It was my own stupid fault for telling Jeremy to come here. I'd feel terrible if you stayed.'

'Well, OK,' I said reluctantly.

Chris had opened the champagne but Henry didn't even seem to care about the drink; he was completely concentrated on Gill. It was the first time ever I had seen Henry not perk up when someone put a glass in his hand. This was definitely an evening of surprises. Gill sipped her tea, head bowed. Henry bent over her protectively. Chris and I had been dismissed; there was nothing left for us to do but slip away.

'*Well,*' I said once we were safely back in the bar. 'I never saw that coming.'

'Who's that guy?' Chris asked.

'He's a famous food critic,' I said. 'Who's obviously mad keen to be Mr Gill, if she'll let him.'

'God yeah, he couldn't take his eyes off her!' Chris said. 'D'you think they're, you know, doing it?'

I shook my head.

'From what Henry said earlier, no. I got the impression he was still chasing her. I didn't realise it was Gill, of course,' I added. 'I had no idea.'

'He's not exactly a male model, is he?' Chris observed. 'But then again, neither is Jeremy.'

'So Jeremy's definitely out of the picture,' I observed sadly. 'Poor Jeremy. I liked him so much.'

'But you said it really wasn't working out,' Chris said.

I hadn't actually told him about Gill and Jeremy's sex life

problems. It wasn't the kind of thing you shared with your brother.

'No,' I confirmed. 'I mean, it's probably for the best. I don't think the kind of problems they have get resolved, really. It's just . . . sad for Jeremy, that's all.'

I remembered Jeremy fishing his umbrella out of the stand and leaving the club, his shoulders slumped, to head back to his empty flat and, probably, cry himself to sleep. I wished so much that there was something I could do for him. But there was nothing. Even my getting in touch with him would give him false hope that I was bearing news from Gill.

'Juliet! Where have you been! I've been looking all over for you!'

Richard, trailing a cloud of cigar smoke, descended on me, his head poking forward from his bony shoulders, his entire expression that of a bird of prey that has just killed and eaten three small furry animals in succession and is glutted with satisfaction.

'Isn't this going well?' he said happily.

I introduced Chris. Richard pumped his hand up and down and offered him a cigar. Chris, to my surprise, actually took it. Richard lit it for him cordially and turned back to me.

'Darling,' he said, 'I was wondering if we have any spare tattoos kicking around? Samantha Fortune –' this was an up-and-coming pop star I had seen earlier flirting with Liam – 'was wondering if we have any and I'd hate to disappoint her.'

I bit my lip.

'There might be some in the office,' I said thoughtfully. 'Let me just go and check.'

'I should be getting off, Ju,' Chris said through the cigar, which he had clamped between his teeth like a Hollywood actor. 'Got to get up for my course in the morning. Thanks for inviting me, I had a blast.'

We hugged.

'I'm so glad you came,' I said. 'I really am. Call me soon, OK?'

'Next couple of days. Maybe we could go out for a drink or something?'

A warm rush of happiness swept over me.

'I'd love that.'

'Cool.'

We shuffled our feet. Though we had said our goodbyes, it was hard to leave. I was so happy at this new, more equal, brother-and-sister relationship Chris and I were building that I just wanted to stand there for a little while and bask in it.

Chris saved me.

'Off you go and get those tattoos, Jules,' he said. 'Can't keep Samantha Fortune waiting.' Despite himself, he blushed as he pronounced her name. 'Is she really here?' he said shyly to Richard. 'Where is she? I'd just like to get a peek.'

'Over there on the sofa,' Richard said cheerfully. 'A bit the worse for wear, but who of us isn't at this stage?'

'I'll bring the tattoos over,' I said.

'Great. Good girl.'

Only Richard could say 'Good girl' without it sounding horribly patronising. He had a gift.

'Oh, and by the way,' he added, 'if you see young Lewis – I've told him about the promotion. I thought he deserved to know tonight. I've seen how hard he's been working and I wanted him to know so he could celebrate at the weekend.'

'Very thoughtful of you,' I said approvingly.

Waving goodbye to Chris, I headed upstairs to the manager's office in which we had stored most of our stuff. I was rifling through one of the boxes, in which I had the feeling I might have spotted a spare envelope of tattoos, when the door opened. It was Lewis.

'Oh, hi,' I said. 'Give me a hand, will you? I need some more tattoos for Samantha Fortune.'

'All sorted,' he said cheerfully. 'Richard just told me where you'd gone and I had some on me. Gave them to him already.'

'Great!' I relaxed, pushing back the box into the corner. I stood up and stretched, yawning briefly. 'Panic over. God, I just feel like putting my feet up for a few seconds.'

I plopped myself down in the manager's swivel chair.

'Here,' Lewis said, proffering me a glass of champagne. 'I thought we could toast my . . .' he paused for effect . . . 'PROMOTION!'

'Congratulations!'

We chinked glasses. People kept bringing me champagne this evening. It was more welcome.

'Richard was so great,' Lewis said. 'He did this whole big welcome-to-the-agency spiel – you know, now-that-you're-a-grown-up. He said some really nice things about the work I've been doing. In detail.' He flushed. 'I had no idea that he knew about all that kind of thing. I mean, he mentioned some really small pieces of work I'd done – well, I mean things that would seem small to him.'

'I keep him updated,' I said. 'But you remember what I said to you when I took you on? About never assuming that Richard doesn't know everything important that goes on at the agency?'

'I thought you were exaggerating,' he admitted, sitting down on the corner of the desk.

'Everyone does at first. But the clever ones behave as if they know it's true.'

He grinned.

'I'm so happy, Juliet,' he said. 'I really am. I feel over the moon.'

I got a real kick out of seeing Lewis this ecstatic.

'Good,' I said, feeling my face break into a big smile that mirrored his own. 'Well, you deserve it.'

'And tonight's been such a success. I mean, hearing about my promotion – well, you know, officially – on a night like this, that we've worked so hard for – it's the icing on the cake.'

'The cream on the coffee.'

'The fizz on the champagne!' Lewis said, draining his glass and reaching for the bottle he had put on the desk.

'More?' he said.

'Oh, go on then.'

He filled my glass.

'I was thinking,' he started. 'I was thinking maybe I could take you out to dinner one of these nights to say thank you for everything. I couldn't have done it without you.' He gave me a very sweet look. 'You're the best boss in the world.' He paused for a moment. 'And the sexiest. With the best legs.'

What was I hearing? I played for time while I tried to decode this.

'Uh, thank you,' I said. 'But that's not that much of a compliment. I mean, who are you comparing me too in the sexy boss stakes? Richard?'

'Anyone,' Lewis said firmly. 'You're still the sexiest.'

I smiled and sipped some more champagne, my brain spinning through possibilities. What I was most worried about was that I was misreading Lewis, and he was just being flattering. I didn't want to be one of those awful women who automatically assumed that every man in the world was after their body.

'So?' he persisted, when I didn't answer him. 'What about it?'

'What about what?'

'Dinner! On me! Anywhere you want.'

I decided that I had drunk enough that nothing but clear speaking would help. The last thing I wanted was for Lewis and I to get tangled up in a misunderstanding that would mess up our entire working relationship.

'Lewis,' I said. 'Do you want me to mentor you, or are you trying to shag me?'

He burst out laughing. His black hair tumbled forward over his smooth forehead, falling into his eyes, and he pushed it back, still laughing as he leant forward till his handsome face was very close to mine. I could smell the champagne on his breath as he said: 'Both,' his mouth only a few inches away.

I had had a lot of champagne. I hadn't got laid in longer than I cared to think about. The other night with Liam had only served to wind me up still further. And Lewis was, frankly, sex on a stick. It needed all my willpower to gently take hold of his shoulders and push him back to his original sitting position.

'Look,' I said, trying valiantly not to notice how sexy his aftershave was, not to mention the well-defined muscles at the caps of his shoulders. 'I might mentor you, if I'm not too lazy. But I'm certainly not going to shag you.'

Lewis looked at me. He was a very, very smart boy. He could see that I was decided.

'I really do fancy you, Juliet,' he said seriously. 'I mean, you're not just a number on my list.' He cleared his throat. 'What if I make partner? Then we'd be on an equal basis. Would you have dinner with me then?'

He grinned at me.

'Go on, say yes. What have you got to lose?'

I cracked up.

'OK,' I said. 'It's a deal.'

We shook hands on it.

'It'll give me something to work for,' Lewis said, assuming

such a pious expression that I burst out laughing again.

'You bullshitter,' I said fondly.

'We can still have lunch, though,' he said. 'In the meantime. I can pick your brains and give you lots of hot gossip in return.'

'Perfect. Why break up a beautiful friendship? Now.' I pointed out the door. 'Go out there, find Samantha Fortune and offer to apply her tattoos personally. I know you want to.'

'Ma'am, yes ma'am!' Lewis saluted me. Before I realised what he was doing, he leant forward and planted a quick, soft kiss on my lips.

'Sexiest boss in the world,' he murmured. Then he stood up, did a very military spin on his heels, and marched out the door.

The conversation with Lewis had put me in an even better mood than before. I was, naturally, really flattered that Lewis had made a pass at me, and equally happy that it had gone so well. There was no way I was sleeping with him, for all sorts of reasons. But in a few years – well, who knew? I would probably still be available. No, make that definitely. I was clearly utterly unable to sustain anything resembling a long-term relationship with a man who didn't have serious personal issues. I would be single for the rest of my life. At least I had a sexy young thing to look forward to. Once he made partner.

I was giggling to myself as I rounded the corner of the bar and bumped straight into a large, unyielding body.

'Whoops! God, I'm sorry,' I said, tripping on my heels. Luckily my glass had been nearly empty, so there had been nothing to spill. I steadied myself.

'No problem,' said a voice I thought I recognised. But I must be hallucinating. A fortnight of waiting to hear that voice on the phone, and being disappointed, was clearly messing with my mind. I looked up cautiously.

'Hi, Juliet,' said Alex.

I was so taken aback I did everything wrong. My mouth dropped open like a guppy fish. My glass slipped in my fingers, trailing the last drops of champagne on my shoes. And when I finally managed to speak, the words that came out of my mouth could not have been more ungracious.

'What are you doing here?' I blurted out.

Alex looked very taken aback. His nice craggy face fell, and the bright light that had been in his eyes on seeing me faded as if I had turned a dimmer switch in his back.

'Uh, Henry brought me. Well, invited me,' he stammered, sounding as embarrassed as I was. 'Well, he said to drop in. On my way back from work. So I did. But if it's not a good time –'

'No, no,' I said quickly. 'It's fine. I mean, it's winding down now, anyway.'

Oh God. What I had meant to imply was that now the party was on its last legs, I had more time to spend with people; but obviously it had sounded much more as if I were telling Alex that he would not have been welcome when the launch was in its full, fashionable swing. I felt like smashing the glass over my head.

'I mean –' I started, and then dismissed any attempt to explain as a lost cause. My instincts with Lewis had been sound. Direct communication was the only way.

'It's really nice to see you,' I said bravely. 'You never rang me.'

He looked abashed. I noticed suddenly how nice he looked. He had tamed his hair, which looked considerably less unruly, and he wore a simple black sweater over grey trousers. He fit into this atmosphere a lot more easily than I would have imagined. Of course, Alex wasn't a hick; he was an architect, and presumably not unused to media parties. But it still took me by surprise that he seemed very much at home in Jane's. As Mel would have told me, I did have a way of compartmentalising my life.

'I know,' he said. He took a deep breath. 'Shall we sit down for a moment? Are you rushing off somewhere?'

'No,' I said. 'I'm pretty much as free as I can be at a thing like this. Like I said, we're winding down.'

'So my timing wasn't too bad,' he said, looking relieved. 'I was worried I'd come too late. I was just on site most of the day and I needed to pop home and change into something that wasn't covered in dust.'

So much for dropping in on the way back from work. He had made the trip into Soho specially to see me. Hah! But then, why hadn't he rung me? Lurid imaginings of his telling me about being married, or having a girlfriend, rushed through my head. All more than possible. I was so nervous that when he started to walk away from me I thought he was going, only to realise a few seconds later that he was in fact heading for a sofa in a quiet corner.

I followed and sat down carefully, smoothing my dress under my bottom. I really wished I had a drink in my hand.

'You look gorgeous, by the way,' he said appreciatively.

'Thanks. It's a new dress.'

'Well, it was worth whatever you paid for it.'

'I hope so!' I said. I hadn't worn the shoes I bought at the fetish shop with Mel; they hadn't gone with the dress. Ah well, another time.

'Juliet, another glass of champagne? And one for your friend? We're running out of the cases you ordered, and I wanted to make sure you had some before we finish.'

It was Gwen, the manager of Jane's, popping over solicitously. I greeted her offer of drink with as much relief as if I'd been buried alive in a snowstorm and heard the padding paws of a St Bernard digging its way towards me with that keg of brandy round its neck.

'Gwen, you're an angel,' I said happily. 'This is Alex, by the way. Alex, this is Gwen, who manages this dive.'

'For my sins,' Gwen said. 'I tell you what, why don't I get someone to bring over a bottle?'

I nodded my head vigorously. Gwen had great social antennae. She would have stayed to chat, but could tell immediately that it was a tête-à-tête.

'Well, I've got things to do. Great launch, Juliet. Any time you need to use the place just let me know. This is just the kind of party I want to be having at Jane's.'

Blowing me a kiss, she slipped away. I was happy that Alex had seen me in successful, party-throwing, on-first-name-terms-with-trendy-club-manager mode. Still, it was always a source of distress to meet Gwen when you were with a man you fancied.

'Yes, she used to be a model, before you ask,' I said to him resignedly.

'I thought so,' he said placidly. 'She's very skinny.'

'Wow,' I said. 'You couldn't have said anything better if you'd tried for a week. Now I don't have to tell you that those are hair extensions.'

'Why? Do you want to put me off her?'

He gave me that lovely smile of his, when his whole face creased up. Even the lines round his eyes were smiling.

'Maybe,' I muttered.

A waiter arrived and opened our champagne, but we hardly noticed him.

'So why didn't you ring me?' I said, to the hands I was

clasping in my lap. I couldn't believe I was harping on this. I was utterly failing to be cool. Had I learnt nothing from all the dating I had done?

'I was nervous,' he said. The waiter handed us two glasses. Alex actually reached for his enthusiastically and drank half of its contents in one gulp. Most unlike him. He really must be nervous.

'Nervous?' I said. 'You?'

'Yes, me. Why shouldn't I be?' He looked me directly in the eye.

'Oh, I dunno,' I mumbled, retreating.

'Well, I was,' he said firmly, his voice gaining resolution, as if he were nerving himself up to say something that he had been practising in advance. 'I find you – I find you very attractive. I was really pleased that you agreed to go out to dinner with me.'

He caught himself, laughing.

'God, I sound ridiculously formal, don't I? You can tell I'm not used to this sort of thing. Um, where was I? Oh yes, dinner. I really enjoyed it. And then, um, you asked me to come up, and that was great. I had a really nice time. But, you know –'

He put down his glass on the table and stared at it for a moment. I finished my own, terrified of what was coming. He wasn't ready for a relationship. He thought I was too psychotic and drug-addicted. He was engaged to someone else.

'I'm just a boring architect,' he said finally. 'And I can see the sort of life you lead.' He gestured around him. 'I mean, look at tonight. Even I recognise some of the people here, and I never read the glossy mags, or keep up with pop stars.'

He glanced across at the bar, where the dissolute young actor – Howie, of the small willy and, I had thought, gay status – was snogging a very famous TV presenter twice his age, who had just split from her husband. After she had caught him in a threesome in their Jacuzzi. With two barely legal boys. But that part hadn't made it into the papers.

'I mean,' he said, 'that's –'

'Yup.'

'And isn't she kissing the guy who just played Henry V at the Barbican?'

'I think so,' I said, ashamed of my low-culture side. 'He's just wrapped the new Levi's commercial, that I do know.'

'You see what I mean?' Alex looked back at me. 'This is normal for you.'

'Well, it's more work, really . . .' I murmured.

'That's why I didn't ring,' he said simply. 'I thought you were out of my league.'

His openness, his frankness, filled me with such admiration that I could barely speak. He made me feel like an immature, game-playing moron by contrast.

'No!' I blurted. 'God, that's ridiculous! I mean, you know about Henry V at the Barbican and stuff like that, and all I have to contribute is the latest stupid jeans ad. You're out of *my* league.'

I drank some more champagne.

'This is about me doing coke, isn't it?' I said courageously.

'I don't mind about that,' he hurried to say, sounding very earnest. 'In itself. I mean, you're obviously not a drug addict or anything. But, yes, in a way. It's just – the coke seemed to symbolise something – and then you got very tired and I thought I'd kept you up so late, boring on – I thought you wouldn't want to hear from me again –'

'So what happened?' I said, looking not at his eyes – that was too scary – but at his collarbone.

'Every time I bumped into Henry at the Spit and Whistle, I couldn't help talking about you. I was hoping you'd drop in, but you didn't. I thought you were avoiding me.'

'Well, you said you were going to ring me,' I mumbled. 'And when you didn't, I thought you didn't want to.' This was like having the words ripped directly out of my stomach; but I felt I owed him honesty, after his breathtaking display of it. 'So I didn't think I ought to go in there. I mean, it's your local, not mine. If you didn't want to see me, I shouldn't be in there.'

He laughed.

'How ironic. Meanwhile, I was wandering up and down Chalk Farm Road in the hopes I'd bump into you, and driving poor Henry mad, going on about you when all he wanted was to sink his cognac,' he said. 'Though actually, Henry's been different recently. He was surprisingly sympathetic. He insisted I come along tonight and see you.' He looked thoughtful. 'I wonder what's got into him.'

'He's keen on a friend of mine,' I said. 'He came in tonight all smartened up and shot over to her side with a bottle of champagne.'

Alex snapped his fingers.

'Of course,' he said, 'I remember now. She's called Gill, right? He's mentioned her a few times. I thought it was just a hopeless crush, though. Apparently she was with someone who didn't deserve her, or something like that.'

I didn't know whether Henry had meant Jeremy or Philip; but it didn't matter. I nodded.

'Well, she isn't any more.'

'Good! I mean, for Henry. I got the impression he'd had a thing about her for years.'

'Really,' I said curiously. 'He never showed it.'

'Well, that's why I came along tonight,' Alex said, putting down his glass. 'Faint heart never won fair lady, and all the rest of it.'

My head was spinning. This was all such a sudden change it was hard for me to adjust to it. I had been completely convinced that someone not ringing me for two weeks meant, clearly, that he wasn't interested. It seemed like a fantasy to find out that in fact it meant that he was very interested, but intimidated by my so-called trendy lifestyle. God, what a joke.

'I'm glad you came,' I mumbled, still unable to look him in the eye. I felt as shy as a fourteen-year-old being asked to go behind the bike sheds by a bloke in the Lower Sixth.

'Me too,' said Alex.

We sat, frozen in place, for what felt like a lifetime of cramp and embarrassment, neither of us getting up the nerve to say anything else. It seemed that we had only two options – to go with the moment, turn to each other and start kissing, or to slide over it and start asking if we had seen any good films lately. I was much too terrified to touch him, let alone kiss him, and tongue-tied to boot. It took Richard, bounding up the stairs, to break our stalemate.

'Juliet! My sweet! I'm off into the night, just wanted to say thank you again for a job more than well done . . . No, don't get up, you look very cosy there. Good!' He winked at us. 'Young Lewis is having a very nice chat with Ms Fortune. I wish him the best of luck. Not that he'll need it. Anyway, see you tomorrow. Not too early, eh?'

'Who was that?' Alex said as Richard disappeared down the stairs again.

'My boss.'

'What an extraordinary-looking man.'

'Yup.'

I did a brief Richard imitation – shoulders hunched, head jutting forward and constantly on the move, swivelling to take in everything in the room. Alex laughed.

There was another pause.

'So,' he said, leaning towards me.

'I have about twenty minutes clearing-up work to do,' I said gruffly.

'Why don't I wait for you? Or is there anything I can do to help?'

I shook my head. Then I realised that this was capable of misinterpretation.

'I mean, there isn't anything you can do,' I said over-quickly. 'Not, you know, whatever.'

'Well, do you want to get a drink somewhere else?' Alex suggested. 'Or share a cab back to our neck of the woods? We could stop in at the Spit.'

'That sounds like a nice way to round off the evening,' I said, trying to sound as casual as I could, my heart leaping with excitement and nerves.

There's nothing like being interested in someone who lives round the corner from you. Of course the downside is that if it goes pear shaped, you spend the next few years dodging round corners to avoid bumping into them. But who thinks of that in the first heady flush of enthusiasm, where, instead of organising elaborate pretexts to end the evening close to one or the other's houses – 'Oh, you know what, we're actually so close to mine you might as well come back there for a drink now the pubs are closed' – you can simply take a minicab together to familiar territory, knowing at least that if things don't work out you won't be stranded on the mean streets of East Dulwich or Mill Hill at one in the morning.

It was definitely embarrassing getting into the car with Alex. After all we had said that evening, the atmosphere was charged with significance. Somehow we had simultaneously gone slowly and run far ahead of ourselves. We had both signalled our interest in a relationship, without even having kissed. That was definitely looming in the next hours, and I was, for some reason, petrified of it. No, I knew exactly why I was scared. What if he wasn't a good kisser? How was I going to get out of that one? Make an excuse and leave, and then have to get rid of him in a series of excruciating phone calls? And what if, God forbid, we had sex, and it was no good? If someone can kiss well, they're pretty much bound to be good in bed – unless their proportions are disappointing. You can't be mistaken about whether or not a man has his tongue in your mouth. But penis size, alas, is not so reliable. I was so busy frantically worrying about what I would do if Alex had a small penis that when he broke the silence with a 'Penny for them,' I jumped in my seat so far I nearly hit the roof of the car with the top of my head.

'Uh,' I said at random. 'I was, um, wondering how Liam's getting on.'

'Oh yeah, your boy wonder. Was he there? I didn't see anyone like you'd described to me. It sounds like he'd pretty much stand out, even in a crowd.'

'Especially when he's charging through it carrying a friend of mine on his shoulder,' I said.

The cab was just rounding Soho Square. I heard a war whoop from inside the fence, and the voice was strangely familiar. Liam? It couldn't be. I turned to look through the window and saw what looked like a naked man, half obscured by the trees and the encircling fence, hanging from a tree by his hands, swinging back and forth.

'Oh my *God*,' I muttered.

'Is that –' Alex said.

I had seen Liam's bottom enough to recognise it, even without the tattoos. A witchy cackle responded to the war whoop and a slim dark shadow flitted across my field of vision. Liam dropped from the tree and beat his chest like Tarzan. Then he yelled: 'Wait! Wait for me!' and started struggling into his trousers, hopping along in the direction Mel had taken. 'Mel!' he shouted! 'Come back!'

Then he went flying. Mel had sneaked back and tripped him up. It looked as if she were straddling him triumphantly, but I couldn't be sure, because the cab was turning on to Tottenham Court Road. I squinted through the back window but could make out nothing else.

'Do you want to stop the cab?' Alex said, watching my appalled expression with great amusement.

'*God* no,' I said fervently. 'I'd need a missile thrower to break that one up.'

'Looks like they're made for each other,' he commented.

'Goodness knows. I have no idea what either of them wants in anything remotely resembling the long term. But it does seem a match made in – well, hell.'

Alex laughed. We were performing the classic manoeuvre of a couple, or at least a nascent one; discussing the relationships of everyone we knew, with an undercurrent of we-can-do-better-than-that.

'I said good night to Henry while you were rushing round tying up your loose ends,' he observed. 'He was tucked away in a quiet corner having what looked like a serious conversation with a very attractive blonde. I take it that's your other friend.'

'Yup,' I said, stifling a pang of jealousy at hearing Alex describe Gill as attractive. 'My friends are in full swing tonight. I didn't see her with Henry – she came over to say good night to me. She seemed very happy.'

'Yes. It was a nice conversation. Serious, like I said, but in a good way. Some surreptitious hand-holding, which always bodes well.'

I couldn't help looking down at Alex's hands, where they

lay in his lap, and being incredibly self-conscious about mine. Suddenly I didn't know what to do with them; I fiddled with my nails, then, reminding myself that I would start to chip my manicure, tried to relax them. To no avail.

We were heading up Camden High Street, towards the pub. I had a rush of impatience, or maybe it was nerves. If we stopped at the Spit and Whistle we would have to sit with a drink for at least half an hour, then negotiate about Alex's walking me home, then an awkward moment when I invited him up. I decided in an instant just to cut to the chase. The suspense was bad enough as it was. If he was a bad kisser, I wanted to know as soon as possible.

'You'd just be having coffee in the Spit, wouldn't you?' I said.

He nodded, his black leather jacket creasing at the movement, making a faint creaking noise.

'Me too,' I said. 'I've had more than enough champagne tonight. Why don't we go back to mine and I'll make us some coffee instead? It'll be better than Neil's.'

'You forget,' Alex said gravely, 'I take my own coffee to Neil's.'

'Still,' I said. 'He doesn't have a cafetière.'

'He would rather die than own one.'

'Well, there you go.'

We considered this for a moment. Then Alex leant forward and gave the driver directions to my block of flats.

'This is very nice of you,' he said rather awkwardly.

'I *am* very nice,' I said firmly. This was a much better response than simply muttering 'Oh no, not at all, no problem, blah blah blah', and I was pleased with it. I wasn't expecting an answer.

'Yes, you are,' he said simply, and turned to smile at me. I was lost. He had such a lovely smile, I could drown in it. I found myself leaning towards him, knowing that he was leaning towards me. The moment was brief but seemed interminable. We paused, looking at each other, orange flashes from the streetlights flickering over our faces, and then the car did a sharp left into my side street and swung us both off-balance. Alex caught my arm to steady me, his hand feeling very strong. I found myself leaning into it, and we didn't even realise for a few seconds that the car had come to a stop. Alex paid, brushing away my bleatings about it being on account. I expected that would be too much for his pride.

We clambered out, me already fishing for my keys. I couldn't have borne another repeat of standing in front of the block door, making awkward conversation. I just wanted to get into my flat and get on with it. My teeth were set, my jaw hard. This was ridiculous. I was behaving like I had a nasty task to perform that I wanted to get over and done with as soon as possible. Charging up the stairs, along my walkway, I went as fast as I could in high heels and a tightish skirt, feeling a bit like a drag queen in a hurry. I was about to open my flat door when Alex said gently: 'Juliet.'

I turned, expecting to find him right behind me, about to pull me into his arms. But instead he was leaning on the concrete balcony of the walkway, his back to me, broad and solid in his leather jacket.

'Come here,' he said.

My heels tap-tapped on the concrete floor. He turned his head and pointed, with the arm closer to me, up into the dark night sky. Through the oak trees surrounding our local church I could see the moon, clear and full, its light bright and clear and creamy white.

Without a word I leant on the balcony too. The arm that had been pointing fell, cautiously at first, around my shoulders, and then settled, pulling me against his side. He smelt of new leather and faintly of aftershave, but mostly of himself. It was very heady. I stared up at the moon, feeling his eyes on the side of my face, too nervous to turn and look at him. I shivered.

'You're cold. Maybe we should go inside,' he said reluctantly.

'Not just yet. It's so beautiful.'

He reached out with his other hand and pushed a lock of hair very delicately back from my cheek.

'It's an awful cliché to say, "Yes, you are",' he observed. 'But I want to say it anyway.'

The hand movement had brought him round, so now he was facing me, and his arms were almost around me. I admired his technique. And that sparked off something in me. I had technique too, goddamnit. I reached up and stroked his cheek. He took my hand and brought it to his lips. Suddenly, I was reminded of Johan, and as nothing else could have done so well at that moment, it underlined the differences between them. Johan had kissed my hand in the most seductive way possible; turning it to kiss the palm, his eyes looking significantly into mine. It had been very sexy. But Alex grazed the knuckles with soft lips, his eyelids closing momentarily, and then drew my hand up to his cheek, holding it there. When he did look at me, his eyes were very dark and serious.

I can't do this, I thought. You're a nice man. I can't be what you want me to be. I'm just not up to it. But, thank God, I managed to bite my tongue before I could say any of those things. Instead, before I could change my mind, I leant towards him, my coat brushing against his jacket, and kissed him on the mouth.

Time sped, slowed down to stasis, rushed past again. A minute could have passed, or half an hour. So, yes, my doubts were put to rest. Alex was a great kisser. And, pressed against him as tightly as I was, that wasn't the only doubt that had been resolved. That wasn't a Palm Pilot in his trouser pocket. He was more than adequately pleased to see me.

We drew apart finally, our mouths moist with each other, and smiled.

'You look incredibly smug,' I said reprovingly.

'Can you blame me?'

God, he had the loveliest smile. He wasn't handsome, but his smile made him so. Or made me forget that he wasn't handsome.

In one movement, he picked me up and sat me on the balcony. I caught on to the wide stone ridge for support.

'Don't worry,' he said, winding his arms around my waist. 'I've got you.'

I took his face in my hands and kissed him again. He could pick me up without staggering, even faintly. This was very good. He buried his face in my throat, and I moaned. Better and better. As I shifted to tilt my head back I felt something in my coat pocket bend. It was Johan's card, getting increasingly mangled. I had a flash of guilt. Well, it was nice to know it was there, as an escape clause, even if I might never use it.

'Do you want to go inside?' I said, my voice hoarse.

Alex lifted his face from my neck and looked up at me. His arms tightened around my waist.

'Mmmn. In a while,' he said. 'There's no rush, is there?'

I smiled back at him, feeling my whole body relax, wrapping itself even tighter around his.

'No,' I said, sliding my hands through his thick, coarse-cut hair. In the moonlight I could see where it was silvering faintly at his temples. It filled me with tenderness. 'No rush at all.'